A MARRIAGE OF ATTACHMENT

a sequel to
A Contrary Wind

Book cover design by Dissect Designs
www.dissectdesigns.com

Also by Lona Manning

THE MANSFIELD TRILOGY

A CONTRARY WIND
A MARRIAGE OF ATTACHMENT
A DIFFERENT KIND OF WOMAN

QUILL INK COLLECTIVE SHORT STORY ANTHOLOGIES

Available in e-book, paperback and audio
Edited by Christina Boyd

"The Address of a Frenchwoman"
A short story about Tom Bertram of Mansfield Park, in
DANGEROUS TO KNOW: JANE AUSTEN'S RAKES &
GENTLEMEN ROGUES

"The Art of Pleasing"
A short story about Mrs. Clay of Jane Austen's
Persuasion, in
RATIONAL CREATURES

"By a Lady"
A short story about Anne de Bourgh in
YULETIDE: AUSTEN-INSPIRED SHORT STORIES
E-book and paperback proceeds to Chawton House
and the Centre for Women's Early Writing

Praise for *A Contrary Wind*

Winner, Wishing Shelf Book Awards, Silver Medal, 2018
Golden Squirrel Book Awards, Silver, 2018

Jane Austen Centre, Bath: ...Excellent.. it's a novel which certainly deserves a place on the bookshelves of a Jane Austen fan.

Austenesque Reviews: Brava to Lona Manning for her thoughtful twists and skilful execution in this variation. This story was in no way predictable and it kept me guessing almost until the end!

Historical Novel Society: A Contrary Wind is well-written, keeping close to the style of Austen. I thoroughly enjoyed it and highly recommend it.

First Impressions podcast: Her writing is not Austen, of course, but it is so good that she manages to blend it seamlessly with actual passages from *Mansfield Park*. Her grasp of the vernacular of the Regency era is incredibly well-researched and accurate.

Lost Opinions.com: This is an excellent read. Rich storylines, authentic characters (old and new), and writing I found hard to discern from the original (truly that good).

BlueInk Reviews starred review: A Contrary Wind is an impressive feat... Many try to emulate Austen; not all succeed. Here, Manning triumphs. She has retained Austen's spirit, while providing a stronger Fanny who will surely win today's readers.

PRAISE FOR "The Address of a Frenchwoman" AND *DANGEROUS TO KNOW*

Diary of an Eccentric: What surprised me is the ability of these authors to make me feel some compassion for the characters I love to hate, like the heartache experienced by George Wickham and Tom Bertram in their stories, which emphasized the complexity of Austen's characters.

JustJane1813: As a fan of Jane Austen Fan Fiction, I can't imagine a lover of Austenesque fiction not wanting to devour each and every one of these stories. Simply stated, these stories are, from start to finish, insightful, brilliantly plotted, and layered with that terrific combination of emotive tension and dry humour that Austenesque readers find so entertaining.

PRAISE FOR "The Art of Pleasing" in RATIONAL CREATURES

Elizabeth Adams, author: of This story is nothing short of brilliant and I LOVED every line of it. It is wildly entertaining, perfectly written, and disturbingly plausible.

"...whose views of happiness were all fixed on
a marriage of attachment..."

Jane Austen, *Mansfield Park*

Author's note: *A Contrary Wind* concluded in the fall of 1809. *A Marriage of Attachment* commences in April 1811. A few Jane Austen phrases and references, from *Mansfield Park* and other writings, are included in this book. Devoted Janeites should have fun spotting them.

This novel ends at page 293 of this volume. There are more than 40 pages of bonus material.

TABLE OF CONTENTS

CHAPTER ONE

April 1811
Thornton Lacey, Northamptonshire

"I AM NOT ANGRY."

"Forgive me if I dispute that assertion, my dear. After twenty-seven years of marriage, I recognize this frosty silence."

"This is merely resignation, sir. The resignation of a much-tried woman whose husband believes what he is told by any random stranger while refusing to give credence to the same information offered by his wife."

"I simply enquired of the man mending the hedge if this was the road to Thornton Lacey."

"And I told *you*, not a moment ago, 'this is the road to Thornton Lacey,' and then you talked to the man mending the hedge, and asked *him* if this was the road to Thornton Lacey, then you graciously informed *me*, 'this is the road to Thornton Lacey' —I, who went to great pains to obtain—"

"And there, I think, is the parsonage."

"A parsonage-house? Surely not. Not for a village of such limited extent as this. It must be the country home of some independent gentleman. Edmund Bertram would have to wring a guinea from every parishioner for marrying and burying to maintain so handsome an establishment."

"I think you do him an injustice there, my dear. I think, left to his own devices, Mr. Bertram would not have attempted half so much. Mary and her brother commissioned a great many improvements, she told me so herself."

"That accords more with the character of Mr. Bertram as I knew him in London," Lady Delingpole acknowledged. "And in the end, Mary did leave him to his own devices. He deserves better! But, I

1

can never scold Mary as she deserves, not when I remember her dear mother."

"I believe I see our host stepping out to greet us, Imogen. So, now that you see his house, are you content to stay here for the night, in preference to an inn? I think we shall be tolerably comfortable, though it is a bachelor establishment."

"Yes, Miss Bertram is in town, so we shall have no hostess tonight. But I believe we may do very well."

The carriage pulled up to the handsome front portico of the dwelling of the young clergyman, where every servant of his modest establishment was assembled.

Edmund swiftly glanced over his shoulder to see how his housekeeper, Mrs. Peckover, was bearing up. She had spent the last week in a quiet frenzy of preparation; the prospect of a visit from an Earl and his lady had alarmed her into near-insensibility. Thankfully, and unexpectedly, Baddeley had appeared that morning with a basket of apricot preserves and his usual imperturbable air. The old butler from Edmund's boyhood home 'had learned from Mrs. Grant, that exalted guests were expected at Thornton Lacey, and he ventured to presume he might be of some assistance.'

Mrs. Grant was not the only old friend to come to Edmund's aid on this momentous occasion. His parishioners, viewing the noble visit as something that reflected upon the credit of the entire village, came forward with their contributions—one family sent a brace of hare, another a fine large trout, another some early wisps of salad from their greenhouse, all to uphold the proud name of Thornton Lacey and to burnish this new and illustrious chapter in the annals of the town.

However, were it not for Baddeley's timely arrival, Edmund suspected Mrs. Peckover might now be lying prostrate in the pantry instead of waiting on the stairs, wearing a fresh apron and cap. He could see the details of the evening to come chasing themselves across her forehead, even as he greeted his guests.

"Lady Delingpole, Lord Delingpole, you do me great honour. I trust your journey was pleasant."

Firstcourse-calves'headsoup-mashedturnips-dressedsalad-pottedhare-troutwithonionsauce —

2

"Not at all, Bertram. What cursed weather we are having for April, hey? Where is that charming sister of yours?"

"Julia is visiting our cousins in Bedford Square, sir. She will greatly regret not being here to welcome you both."

"A great pity. Imogen, my dear, it seems Miss Julia will not be here to keep you company tonight. She is in London."

Secondcourse-bakedcelerywithraisins-carrotswithhoney-roast beef with pepper sauce-creamed potato—

"Is she indeed? I had no idea. Mr. Bertram, thank you for inviting us to break our journey here. I never saw such a charming country parsonage—very elegant, indeed!"

Lastcourse-cheeseboard-applesinmadeira-apricottart- orangebrandy-ladyfingers.

"Well, therein lies a tale. My home is yours, Lady Delingpole. Baddeley and I will look after your husband and Mrs. Peckover will escort you to your room."

"This way, oh, this way, your ladyfingers—oh no! *Your ladyship!*"

In due course, Baddeley took his station by the sideboard, and Edmund's housekeeper and several other able women from the village, all at the highest pitch of excitement and anxiety, toiled in the kitchen.

Edmund escorted Lady Delingpole to her seat, and surveyed with some complacency the elegant table Baddeley had laid out for his guests. Even in the absence of a wife to direct the proceedings, he thought his household had done tolerably well, consistent with his desire to demonstrate his respect and affection for the noble couple, but without that ostentatious show which would betray an overly-servile disposition, a too-eager wish to please. This was why he had not brought his aunt from Mansfield to serve as his hostess. Aunt Norris had met the Delingpoles in London and it would not be impertinent to invite her, but she would have destroyed whatever of tranquillity his home offered in her zeal to demonstrate her deference and gratitude.

Instead, the host and his guests sat down together with every evidence of satisfaction, ease, and enjoyment. They were all of superior understanding and information. The youngest of them, Edmund Bertram, was in fact the most subdued in manner, and tended to formality in his address. He was tall, well-made and handsome, and in his dark blue eyes there gleamed a subtle, understated wit.

His Lordship, spare of frame and angular of feature, was clearly accustomed to having the full attention of his audience. His countenance was mobile and alert, and his address forceful and decided. Lady Delingpole's quickness of speech and sometimes of temper tended to disguise her essentially kind-hearted nature. She was fashionably and richly attired; but anyone who made the mistake of thinking her a mere London fashion plate, was soon set to rights. She was shrewd, well-informed, and as deeply engaged in the public matters of the day as was her husband.

"You must be well pleased, your ladyship, to enjoy your husband's company away from the unceasing demands of Parliament," Edmund offered.

Lady Delingpole almost replied "evidently, you have not been married for very long, Mr. Bertram," but just in time she recollected, and she only smiled and nodded.

"It is in fact politics which calls us to Northamptonshire. We make for Castle Ashby in the morning," said her husband. "Do you know it, Bertram?"

"Not I, sir. My father attended there frequently when he was the member for Northampton. He often remarked on the elegant grounds."

"I am looking for some little home-stall in this area myself, you know, since our family seat in Wales is so remote. I want some place where I can leave public affairs behind for a few days, while the House is in session."

"Leave public affairs behind! Life would be an arid desert for both of us, without politics. What my husband means, Mr. Bertram, is that he is excessively fond of fox-hunting. He is determined to risk his neck, even at his age."

"Well, and here I am, and my tailor hasn't altered the waist to my breeches for these twenty years. Still as fit and hearty as I was in my youth, and how many can say the same?"

"If you are looking for something in this county, sir, would your Lordship care to examine Mansfield Park? The house is well situated on rising ground and is not more than forty years old. I can personally attest to the excellence of the supply of game in my father's woods, and we are but five miles from the kennels at Brixtol."

His Lordship's formidable eyebrows shot up. "The Pytchley hunt? So, your family home is for let, sir?"

Lady Delingpole gave her host a compassionate look, to let him know she, at least, remembered how the Bertram family's fortunes miscarried two years ago.

But Edmund said only, "Yes, my father and mother moved to Norfolk to live with my widowed sister Maria."

"Ah, yes of course, and how is dear Sir Thomas and—I do not recall ever having the pleasure of meeting your mother—but I trust she is well? And content, residing in a place so remote from her native home? I believe she was not inclined to travel so far as London before."

"They are both tolerably well, I thank you, ma'am, and tolerably content, especially since Maria gave them a grandson."

"Yes—yes," interjected his lordship. "And your estate stands empty, does it?"

"Yes, sir. Mansfield Park is nothing like the size of Castle Ashby, of course, but I fancy your Lordship is not looking for anything so grand by way of a hunting-lodge."

"Are the roads at Mansfield any better than those hereabouts, Bertram?"

"Somewhat superior, sir, for the coaching inn is there. The neighbourhood is a pleasant one. Dr. Grant, the vicar, is a learned man, he takes all the papers, and his very agreeable wife is half-sister to—to my wife."

A number of questions swiftly followed—from his Lordship, concerning the land, the deputation, the stables, and the kennels, and from her Ladyship, wanting a description of the offices, the drawing rooms, and the surrounding society, and Edmund's answers inspired in both husband and wife a strong inclination to examine Mansfield Park with a view to taking it for their country retreat.

The war against Napoleon, the public debt in consequence of that war, and the rumoured insanity of the King, all formed the balance of the dinner conversation until Lady Delingpole retired, leaving the gentlemen to themselves.

Baddeley was dismissed, and that worthy man bore away the platters with a silent dignity which gave no hint of the ideas now teeming in his imagination—Mansfield Park alive and alight once again, quietly humming from garret to cellar with servants, the housemaids chasing away every speck of dust, the blindingly white table linens fluttering in the sun where the laundry maids toiled, the gardeners pouncing upon every weed, the kitchen filled with steam and good smells, and himself presiding over it all, serving an Earl and his lady.

*   *   *   *   *   *   *

Same Day
Stoke Newington to Camden Town

Fanny Price could count on the fingers of one hand the number of times she had been given the best seat in the carriage, facing forward, in the direction of travel. When she lived at Mansfield Park, she always sat with her back to the horses because her cousins took precedence, or, as her Aunt Norris would say, she was "the lowest and the last."

She wondered if only being able to see what she had left behind—not what she was moving toward—had left its mark on her character. She was feeling extremely anxious about her future on this particular day, but then, hadn't that been true of all the important journeys of her life?

The first time she rode in a carriage was the day she left her family to go live with her wealthy cousins. Her father had picked her up like a rag doll and stuffed her into the crowded mail coach, calling: "well, goodbye then, Fan my girl, and be a good girl and obey your aunt and uncle, for if they send you back to us I shall give you a proper hiding! Do not move and do not make a sound—not a sound, mind you—and don't get out 'til you reach Northampton." Years later, she learned that her uncle, Sir Thomas, had supplied sufficient funds for a companion to escort her, but her father had pocketed the difference and sent her on the journey by herself.

She had watched silently while Portsmouth and everything she knew disappeared from view. Her father's warnings kept her frozen in her seat, but the trip was lengthy, and her bladder was nearly bursting well before they reached Newbury. A kindly merchant's wife, also making the journey, observed her distress, guessed its cause, and came to her aid at the next stop of the coach.

The parents who sent her away, and the aunt who met her at the end of her journey, admonished Fanny to be always good, and always grateful. If she failed to show sufficient goodness and gratitude, she would be a very wicked girl indeed, and would be packed back home to Portsmouth in disgrace. These warnings, working on a sensitive, docile temperament, left so indelible an impression upon Fanny's character, that she was still, at the age of one-and-twenty, afraid of disobliging anyone and anxious not to give offense.

And today she was in the carriage of her friend and benefactress, Mrs. Harriet Butters. The brusque but kindly widow had been a constant friend and advisor ever since Fanny had escaped her unhappy home situation at Mansfield Park. Mrs. Butters had introduced Fanny to a large circle of intelligent, benevolent people who fought slavery abroad and the miseries of the poor at home. More significantly for Fanny, Mrs. Butters had lovingly teased and scolded her into overcoming her timidity.

Fanny and Mrs. Butters' lady's maid were both in their usual places, travelling backwards as the carriage jolted and bumped along the muddy lane for the four-mile journey from Stoke Newington to Camden Town. Another phase of her life was ending, and she could not see, could not fully imagine, what awaited. For, after months of discussion, preparation and delay, the long-awaited sewing academy, the project so dear to Mrs. Butters' heart, would finally open.

"Oh! Fanny! Did we remember to bring the application papers?"

"Indeed, ma'am, they are here in my portmanteau. And quills and ink bottles."

"And the instructions for the parents? Not that half of them will be able to read it."

"Yes ma'am. We collected everything from the printer yesterday."

Mrs. Butters leaned back and sighed. "Of course you did, my dear. How silly of me. It must come of spending so much time with

Laetitia—she is so inclined to mistrust everyone's competence but her own."

Fanny smiled in response, but out of politeness, she refrained from heartily agreeing with the assessment of Laetitia Blodgett, Mrs. Butters' sister-in-law. Laetitia Blodgett was of an age with Mrs. Butters, and both were outspoken, active, managing sorts of women, but there, Fanny reflected, the similarity ended.

Before her marriage forty years ago, Mrs. Butters had been Miss Harriet Blodgett, of the prosperous and well-known family of linen-drapers in Bristol, a busy sea-port that had profited from the African slave trade. The Blodgetts foresaw that the government's edict outlawing the slave trade would mean the wives of ship captains and the wives of merchants would have to curtail their spending on silk, satin, muslin, and lace. And they were correct: the factories and the dockyards of the city were quiet, and the shopkeepers of Bristol waited in vain for customers.

The Blodgetts resolved to expand their business into London while at the same time establishing a school for instructing impoverished girls of good character in the needle trade. This was to be both a charitable and a commercial enterprise, the profits from the latter providing the funds for the former. The school was under the supervision of a committee of lady patrons, all members of that reputable organization, the Society for Bettering the Condition and Increasing the Comforts of the Poor.

Mrs. Butters attended many lengthy meetings of the ladies' committee, and Fanny acted as their secretary, taking excellent notes in her neat handwriting, while the charitable ladies debated and discussed every detail of the enterprise. They examined and rejected possible locations, eventually selecting a spacious brick warehouse in Camden Town, but it was found to need many more alterations and fittings-up than first anticipated, and all in all, it was such a complex and drawn-out business, requiring so much in the way of talkings-over, second and third thoughts, and polite disagreement and irritated feelings, that Fanny could only wonder how other, truly ambitious operations were ever successfully conducted. How did ordinary mortals put aside their petty vanities and uneven tempers to construct canals, or build cathedrals or invade countries?

Even the most appropriate name for the enterprise had been debated at length. One lady had proposed "The Academy for the Needle Arts," others protested that "Academy" was too... well, verging on being pretentious, and another suggested the "Camden Town Needlework School and Emporium operated by the Society for Bettering the Condition and Increasing the Comforts of the Poor."

A polite silence followed, and eventually Laetitia Blodgett observed that, of the half-a-dozen names put forward, none of them included the name of "Blodgett," that is, the name of the family sponsoring the scheme, and perhaps it was not too presumptuous to expect, etc., so in the end it was agreed, or rather, some ladies resigned themselves to the fact, that the school would be called "Blodgett's Charitable Academy."

Thereafter everyone called it, simply "the Academy," including the Blodgetts.

Fanny wholeheartedly supported the benevolence of the scheme; her strong sense of gratitude to Mrs. Butters alone assured her participation. Thanks in large measure to Mrs. Butters, Fanny believed she acquired confidence and wisdom. She could recall the past, and her difficult childhood, with forbearance. Her stern uncle, Sir Thomas Bertram, used to frighten her, and her cousins Tom, Maria, and Julia alternately bullied or neglected her as they grew up together. Her aunt, Lady Bertram, was too indolent to take an interest in raising her children. Fanny remembered them all, and Mansfield Park, with fondness. She could even feel pity for her Aunt Norris when she imagined that lady living all alone in Mansfield village, no longer able to direct and advise, to scold and warn, to bustle about the great house engaged in the important little nothings which had given purpose to her existence.

As for the fourth cousin, Edmund....

Her wish to avoid thinking about Edmund helped, just a little, in quelling the doubts that assailed her, for she realised that plunging her mind, heart and hands into this new enterprise was the best way to put the past behind her.

"So, here we are at last, ladies," exclaimed Mrs. Butters as the coachman drew up to the three-storied brick warehouse which was to be Fanny's new place of employment. A scaffolding was erected across the front of the building, and a man was perched up high, painting "Blodgett's Charitable Academy" and "Blodgett & Son, Linen-Drapers" in large gold letters above the door. "What a busy day is in front of us! And we breakfasted so early—I am already feeling famished. I hope Matron has got some tea ready."

"I shall examine the shop, Madame, if you please," announced her lady's maid Madame Orly.

The ground floor shop was presided over by Mr. Blodgett and his son Horace, who were brother and nephew to Mrs. Butters. They would display and sell the fabrics which the students would learn to ornament with embroidery in the upstairs classroom, and on the top floor, the dressmakers would assemble the finished garments. Madame Orly was to assist in the shop, while Laetitia Blodgett supervised the dressmakers.

The excitement and bustle of the day would inevitably draw forth Mrs. Blodgett's most querulous reactions and anxious imaginings. Fanny was arguably too young, gentle, and yielding to make a creditable instructress; the asperity of Mrs. Blodgett more than made up the balance.

As Fanny descended from the carriage, she saw a long line of fidgeting, hopeful girls standing in the lane, waiting to be called in and interviewed, some with their mothers or grandmothers, others with a sister or dear friend to hold their hand and whisper encouragement. Some clutched small pieces of cloth which Fanny knew to be samples of their skill with a needle.

Fanny gave the applicants a brief, self-conscious smile before she hurried inside, passed through the shop, greeted Mr. Blodgett, and climbed the wooden steps to the classroom.

The upstairs room was cold, bare and musty-smelling. Fanny walked to one of the tall windows which overlooked the street, the broad wooden planks of the floor creaking beneath her feet, and counted the waiting girls below. At least sixty girls waited to apply for four-and-twenty vacancies in the school.

Looking down the street to her right, Fanny saw the veterinary hospital—not a very likely source for customers—and beyond, thankfully out of sight, was the large and formidable St. Pancras workhouse, where the destitute of the parish were consigned, where young and old toiled at picking oakum and breaking up rocks, in exchange for a vermin-ridden bed and a hot meal.

To the north, Fanny could see a street of newly-built town homes, looking strangely out of place in the midst of the surrounding fields and pastures. There were very few gentlemen's families living here. She wondered who would patronize the new shop. Would fashionable gentlewomen journey to the farthest outskirts of London to buy fabric and gowns?

The matter had been much debated by the charitable committee, who chose the Camden Town location because they had obtained the lease on highly advantageous terms.

"It is no farther to go to Camden Town than to go to Cheapside," Mrs. Wakefield had argued.

"That is so," Mrs. Blodgett had agreed. "And we will be offering our garments at an advantageous price, so the ladies will come flocking to our door."

"I often travel to town to shop or visit," said Mrs. Butters, "but in my experience, when I ask someone from London to come out to Stoke Newington for dinner, they react as though I had invited them to Botany Bay. Any place beyond Moorfields is a howling wilderness to a Londoner."

"Harriet, I come from London every day," argued Mrs. Blodgett. "The journey is a trifle—I should even call it a pleasant one."

"Very true, Laetitia. I do not dispute the point. But you are a transplant from Bristol, not a true Londoner. I am speaking of habit and custom, not of logic and reason, and you may be assured of it— we would draw more business if we were in Cheapside or near Covent Garden. However, this is not to say for a certainty that Camden Town will fail to draw adequate trade..."

Time would tell, Fanny thought.

Mrs. Renfrew, the school's new matron, appeared at her elbow. "Miss Price, when should we call in the applicants?"

Fanny was startled at being applied to for her opinion. "Yes — or, no—I think, ma'am, we should wait for word from Mrs. Blodgett. And there is Mr. Edifice coming up the street." Fanny pointed to a tall, slender man, dressed all in black, walking in their direction. The broad brim of his round black hat shielded his face from view, but she and Matron recognized him as Mr. Frederick Edifice, the local curate.

Fanny turned from the window and began setting out papers, ink, and quills on one of the large, broad tables. She was to interview each of the applicants for the academy, assisted by Mrs. Renfrew and Mr. Edifice. Fanny was to concentrate on their sewing skills, Matron was to evaluate them for deportment, cleanliness and neatness, and Mr. Edifice was to question them upon their knowledge of the catechism.

Fanny had feared that Mr. Edifice, Mrs. Renfrew, and even the young applicants, would sense she was at least as nervous as they. But as soon as all was in readiness, and the first slender little urchin came in and executed her awkward curtsey, Fanny's own innate kindness and sympathy came to her aid, and she soon forgot herself when enquiring into the backgrounds and needs of the girls before her.

The prospective students were between nine and twelve years of age. Only a few of the girls were lucky enough to have an active, healthy, employed father at home; some fathers were disabled for work, others so long away in the army that it was not known if they were alive or dead, some families were one misfortune away from being sent to debtors' prison or disappearing into the workhouse.

These girls knew they lived near "Lunnon," and that there was a King and a Queen, but beyond that, they knew almost nothing that could be learnt from books. In vain did Mr. Edifice ask each applicant, "what then is your duty towards God?" or "how shall we overcome temptation and sin?" The poor girls would goggle at him, eyes wide and mouths hanging open helplessly, and a few burst into tears. By the time the last two dozen girls were ushered upstairs, one at a time, they had obviously profited from some hints from the ones who had gone before, so they could tell Miss Price they knew how to do cross stitch and chain stitch, they could show their clean hands and their smallpox inoculation scar to Matron, and they could loudly declaim a mangled version of the Lord's Prayer, whenever Mr. Edifice asked them anything.

If Fanny had been free to follow her own inclinations, she would have engaged everyone. In fact, she had timidly suggested to Mrs. Blodgett: "Should we not enlist two or three superfluous students, ma'am? I should fancy that on any given day, some students will be absent, owing to illness, or family responsibilities, and we could—"

"Miss Price, there are four and twenty places in the school."

"Yes ma'am, but we should expect some degree of—"

"The committee assigned us to select four-and-twenty students, Miss Price."

And Fanny had to turn away more than half of the applicants, to her regret.

*   *   *   *   *   *   *

"NO PROSPECT, THEN, of a reconciliation?'

Edmund looked down at his wine glass, slowly turning it in his hands. He was acquainted with Lord Delingpole's directness of manner, and in fact, welcomed an opportunity to speak candidly on a subject that he could not, out of discretion, discuss with most of his acquaintance.

"She is still my wife, my Lord. And will be until death us do part. I have made no enquiries about Mary's doings because I do not wish to know—I believe I may call myself very reluctant to know—what I may be required to forgive. Were she genuinely desirous of returning to me, it would be my duty to try to forgive her. But my parishioners, the good people of Thornton Lacey—they would tie her to a cart's tail and flog her through the village. She could never return here."

"Humph. No doubt their disapproval of her is in proportion to their affection and esteem for you."

A silence followed, broken only by the crackling of the fire in the grate and the distant sound of servants washing up in the kitchen. At length, Edmund sighed and continued.

"The situation is a complicated one. To effect a reconciliation, I would have to give up this living—the one thing I told her I would never do. Furthermore, I provide a home for my sister Julia. My father feels that the notorious circumstances surrounding Maria's marriage preclude the possibility of Julia residing with her in Norfolk. Our family name has been injured by Maria's indiscretion, and my father thinks it best for Julia to stay apart from her sister."

"What about leaving England entirely? Your wife would welcome a sojourn abroad, no doubt. And you could leave the past behind you."

13

"Yes, should the war on the continent ever be successfully concluded, Mary and I might go to live in Italy or Switzerland. The idea is not unattractive to me, either. But were I to do so, I would abandon every duty and family tie that keeps me here. My parents are growing older, my oldest brother has left England, never to return—what am I to do?

"Does Mary know you would not put an absolute negative on a reconciliation? Do I understand you correctly?"

"Yes, but as for her—I have not received one word from Mary since she left me. Her actions conveyed the message that the separation was to be a permanent one. I do not say this to lessen her in your opinion, only to explain—she emptied this house of its contents, as well as my stables. I was left with my own clothes and the horse I was riding on when I came back from visiting my parents. The furnishings you see with me today are all from Mansfield Park. This table used to sit in the breakfast room there."

"And I was informed you gave Mary very generous marriage articles—she retained entire control of her fortune. I knew Mary had a mercurial temper, but I did not imagine she could be so ungenerous."

"One suspects the influence of her uncle, there. He holds me in utter detestation. At any rate, knowing of your long-standing kindness to my wife, I do not ask you to render judgement on Mary or me. Nor have I resorted to the courts, for that matter. I have not asked for a legal separation nor brought suit against anyone for criminal conversation with her—"

Edmund coughed awkwardly, at the acknowledgement that his wife was rumoured to be the lover of Lord Elsham. Lord Delingpole picked up the decanter and refilled his own glass, then Edmund's, and waited for the young man to continue.

"While I do not hold myself blameless for the rift in our marriage, I think in the eyes of the world, sir, I am the injured party. Yet, if I reunite with her and leave my position here, she gains everything she desired, while I lose everything I built my life upon. She didn't want to be a clergyman's wife and she didn't want to live in the country. Everything and everyone else would have to give way to her inclinations. Would my forgiveness be truly answered by her repentance, in such a case?

"Mary knows she is still my wife, and I am still her husband. I remain frozen in place, sir. I cannot move backward or forward. She knows I am here. Of *her* whereabouts and her current sentiments, I know nothing."

And perhaps, I never knew her, he added to himself.

Lord Delingpole leaned back in his chair, and sighed. "Well sir, *my* wife may be able to shed some light on this question. She has a letter for you from your wife, but it was given to Imogen on the condition you not even be told of its existence unless you demonstrated yourself to be amenable to talk of a reconciliation. I fancy Mary rather expected you to be implacably opposed. She must acknowledge that she abandoned you in the most unfeeling manner."

"Lady Delingpole has a letter for me—?"

"I believe she has retired early, though. As should I. Good night, Bertram."

* * * * * * *

The following morning, Lady Delingpole was extremely vexed to discover she had been defrauded of the opportunity to reveal the existence of Mary's letter, a matter she deemed much better left in her own hands rather than her husband's. But upon Edmund's applying to her at they sat at breakfast, she parted with it, with the whispered words, "Mary will not own to it, but I have known her for years, Mr. Bertram, and it is my belief she loves you still. You may not be aware, she has not been living for pleasure in London; she has spent much of her time in the countryside in Wales, shunning all company and, I think, eating her heart out."

Edmund tucked the letter into his waistcoat and resolved not to look at it until his guests were gone, even though the anticipation of reading it had cost him a sleepless night. And even after his guests' horses, driver, grooms, valet, and maid had all been assembled in front of the parsonage, and after his lordship and ladyship had been bowed out to the road, and waved along to the next stage of their journey, Edmund called all his servants together and congratulated and thanked them, and he poured glasses of wine for Baddeley and Mrs. Peckover, and left them to toast each other.

Only then did he retreat to his study and break open the seal to see the familiar handwriting of his wife.

Dear Edmund, the note began:

Since the day I left you without a single word, I have begun with a fresh sheet of paper over a hundred times, and tossed it into the fire, and on more occasions than I can give number to, I have written to you in my head, or my heart. Now, finally, this letter may reach your hands, and I know you will read it, because I rely upon your goodness.

It may not be necessary for me to describe the feelings and motives which impelled me to leave Thornton Lacey eighteen months ago, but I never explained my thoughts at the time, nor have since, and you are certainly entitled to hear them.

After my poor brother's death, my uncle importuned me repeatedly to return to London. He blamed you entirely for Henry's accident and could not endure to see me reconciled with you. Henry was my other self, my chief consoler in the loss of our parents, my source of joy, pride, and delight. He was the most vividly alive person I ever knew. It is still exceedingly difficult to accept that he is dead, that he walks the earth no more, that I shall not see him again. I told myself I could mourn Henry in private without burdening you. Edmund, you cannot know what it is to lose someone so dear to you, so abruptly, so unexpectedly, so unjustly.

My uncle sent me frequent, lengthy letters which I cried over, all alone in my chamber. He said I was disloyal to my family, that my brother's spirit would curse me for living with his murderer—and oh! I do know Henry's recklessness was the foremost cause of his death. Had he not been racing to the duelling grounds, he would not have come to grief! Also, had my uncle not taken him home when he was too weak to be moved, perhaps Henry might have survived and lived to hold his son in his arms.

But knowing that Henry and my uncle were not blameless in this matter has not spared me a moment's torment from the fact your challenge for the duel should never have been issued.

At any rate, my uncle's unrelenting pressure upon me to be revenged upon you was a secret canker upon our marriage.

Then came the catastrophe that befell your father, followed by his decision to leave Mansfield Park. You knew my sentiments, you knew my wishes, you knew I was able to endure living at Thornton

Lacey only so long as I could believe we would one day end our dreary exile. But, without consulting me, without even acknowledging my feelings, you told me you thought we should never live at Mansfield Park, and that you intended to live, work, and die at Thornton Lacey!

Was I not justified in thinking I had been imposed upon? We have every reason to believe the baronetcy would revert to you and your—may I say, 'our'—descendants, yet you were determined to live like an anchorite in the desert and force me to do the same!

I have since learned, to my sorrow, that having Thornton Lacey for a home is in every way preferable to having no home at all! I cannot live with my sister at Mansfield Parsonage, as her husband would never permit it, I cannot live with my uncle, not so long as his mistress is in residence there, and there is no tranquillity to be found with Janet Fraser or Lady Stornoway. I know you always disapproved of them.

At least dear Lord and Lady Delingpole have been extremely kind; they put a cottage on their estate at my disposal. I have come to be a little envious of the Delingpoles' capacity for finding fresh matters to quarrel about every day. It is the opposite of indifference, you must allow, when a long-married couple can still contrive to aggravate each other as they do. It is something very like love, and perhaps it is love. Lady Delingpole is one of the few people who encourages me in my wish for—

But I can hardly bring myself to hint. Why? Chiefly pride, I fear. Pride and a refusal to be the kind of wife who has no will or thought of her own apart from her husband's. But you, Edmund, you gave me to believe you did not want that sort of a wife. Do you recollect?

Thus far, you have made no recourse to the law, which tells me you are too merciful to ruin my reputation with a bill of divorce. But everything is in your power, not mine. Do you wish to continue as we have done—living apart and estranged? Or do you, my dear Edmund—can you propose some solution to this impasse?

I shudder at the thought of entrusting our correspondence to the public post. A line directed to Lady Delingpole will reach me.

Your sorrowful wife,
Mary

CHAPTER TWO

JULIA BERTRAM AROSE early to work in her garden on the morning after her return to Thornton Lacey from town.

Her mother used to sit in the shade, playing with her pug dog, as the gardeners at Mansfield Park dug and trimmed, and her Aunt Norris flitted about, directing and admonishing. But as there was no army of servants at her command at Edmund's house, Julia taught herself to weed and plant, and found she rather enjoyed it, for the activity soothed her restless spirit.

Her flower garden was on a sunny slope behind the house, her own private retreat. She was exceedingly proud of her new hedge. At present her yew trees barely reached her waist, but with the mind and eye of a gardener, she saw the day when an imposing green avenue would trace the path of a gravel walkway, leading to the winding stream at the foot of the garden.

As she examined the promising new growth on her rose trellis, Julia indulged in recollections of a warm autumn day two years ago when her cousins William and Susan Price were visiting at Mansfield Park. The three of them went to pick rose hips in the hedgerows. It was the day she knew she was in love with William Price.

Julia closed her eyes and lifted her face to the sun, summoning up the moment when young Susan, enjoying the freedom of the outdoors, went running on ahead, looking for a better patch of rose bushes, and she was left alone with William. She saw William's face; the look in his eyes when he took her hand and asked her if she could wait for him. She had whispered 'yes,' and his face lit up with joy, and he embraced her. His radiant smile, the feel of his strong arms around her—this was her most precious memory, the most exciting and wonderful moment of her young life.

His pledge of love, and her acceptance, was a promise jointly given and taken with a sweet, lingering kiss. Neither one said another word. There was no need to. They stepped apart before William's sister Susan returned, and if she suspected, she gave no sign. A few days later, William was gone to resume his duties as a lieutenant with His Majesty's navy. Julia gave him all the dried rose hips to take with him to Africa.

19

As far as good intentions spoke for her future conduct, Julia believed she would only marry with her parents' consent. In the meantime, she lived on the memory of one moment, one kiss. While her father respected William for his talents and industry, she feared he would not be pleased to welcome his nephew as a son-in-law. The Prices were poor and undistinguished.

During her visits to London, Julia had met many highly born, prosperous, eligible young men, and perhaps with a little more enterprise on her part, a greater willingness to please and be pleased, she might have attached one of them. But the lieutenant had conquered her heart.

Julia waited at Thornton Lacey while William sought promotion, prizes, and distinction in the West African Squadron. The lovers agreed to keep their understanding a secret until the day he could step forward as an eligible claimant for Julia's hand. William would not even correspond with her directly. Instead, he wrote long letters to her brother Edmund, recounting the success of his crew in apprehending slave ships along the African coast. With every ship captured and every slave freed, he was promised his share of prize monies. And the subject of rose hip tea often figured in his correspondence.

"Julia, are you out here?" Her brother's voice pulled Julia out of her reverie.

"Yes, here I am, Edmund. I was just going to water my peonies."

Edmund strolled down the path and picked up his sister's heavy clay garden pot for her. "How well your daffodil cuttings are growing, Julia!"

"Bulbs are grown by division, not cuttings, Edmund." Julia corrected him, proud of her acquired gardening knowledge.

"Well, at any rate, I remember these daffodils from our old garden. Could you accompany me to Mansfield this Wednesday? Lord Delingpole has sent us a note from Castle Ashby. He asks if we are at leisure to show him around Mansfield Park. I suppose he would rather talk to me than the steward. Could you attend on Lady Delingpole, or would you find it too painful?"

"I'm afraid I might weep, just a little, when I see our familiar old rooms silent and empty. But after all, I am a woman, we sometimes cry for pleasure. Otherwise, we would not speak of 'having a good cry.' I will go with you on Wednesday, Edmund."

If so amiable a young lady as Julia Bertram might be said to have a fault, it was that she tended to think only of herself and her own concerns. But, as she watched her brother absently-mindedly drowning a peony bush with the full contents of the watering jug, she thought to ask: "Edmund? Will you give Lady Delingpole a reply for Mary?"

"Yes, of course, but... I cannot help wondering, Julia, why is Mary writing to me now? Why now? What does she want?"

"What else but to come back to you, Edmund dear?"

"But, shall I take this purely as a compliment to me," Edmund said drily, "or is there something else? What has occurred, or what has changed, to impel her to break her silence? Mary always has a motive for her actions."

*　*　*　*　*　*　*

At sea, off the African coast
March, 1811
Lt. William Price to William Gibson

DEAR FRIEND:

We shall put in at Freetown in a few days, and I rely upon finding a letter or two from you waiting for me there. I hope to read news of your book—perhaps it is published by now. Captain Columbine desires to be remembered to you and he, too, is looking forward to reading your narrative.

I am not with the Captain at present, for I am currently in command of a captured slaver, the Volcano, *which we boarded about a fortnight ago, with 300 Negroes packed aboard, in the usual miserable conditions, and a Spanish captain and crew.*

Captain Columbine put me in charge of the prize crew—you will remember how envious I was of the other lieutenants who were given this distinction—and we set out for Sierra Leone and the Admiralty Court.

As the brig was very heavy laden with its human cargo, we set about jettisoning surplus supplies (for, of course, the ship was no longer going to make the Atlantic crossing), spare sails, and everything we thought we could do without, to speed the journey. All of the cursed manacles and branding irons were tossed overboard, with the greatest satisfaction and cheers from the crew!

I wanted to keep a few of the manacles to lock up the slave-ship captain and his crew, so they could feel all the torments they subject the Africans to, but it is not permitted. We stowed the captives in the wardroom under the guard of a few Marines—but this proved to be an error.

A few days out from Freetown, I was in my cabin, updating the log book, when the door slammed open and there stood Midshipman Castle, very agitated, telling me that when the cabin boy had brought victuals to the prisoners, they overpowered their guards and seized their weapons—the lad had barely time to form a single intelligible sentence when, to my horror, I saw a bayonet emerge through his chest—blood spurted from his mouth— he slid to the ground, and there stood one of the escaped Spaniards pulling out the blade and preparing to come at me.

I jumped to my feet—I picked up my little round table and used it as a shield, as he came at me with the bayonet, and in the small quarters of the cabin, he was unable to get at me, as the table effectually blocked his way, but I was equally unable to draw my sword. We struggled, on top of poor Castle's body; until I managed to pin the Spaniard against the wall, pressing with all my strength, wrest the bayonet from him, and turn that same weapon on him.

I then ran out to the deck with my sword in hand. I saw two of our sailors hanging dead in the rigging, killed, as I later learned, by musket balls, while the rest of my prize crew, recovering from the initial surprise, were mounting a spirited counter-attack. I joined in the fight, but we were outnumbered three to one and the outcome might have been in some doubt, had not our cook, an African of the Kru tribe, flung open the grate and allowed the captive Africans to come swarming up on the deck. More than one of the Spaniards jumped overboard rather than face the vengeance of the persons whom they had recently abducted from their native country.

Thankfully, this decisively turned the tide in our favour, without further loss of life to my remaining crew. As it is, I lost half of what I had—the two marines, the midshipman (only fourteen years of age), and two sailors. Their loss grieves me. When I close my eyes,

I can see poor Castle's face and the surprise in his eyes when the killing thrust pierced his body. So, Gibson, I don't close my eyes! We are all working double shifts at any rate. Writing to you has provided some relief to my feelings.

I thought this incident would be of interest to you, but have refrained from sending the same particulars in my letter to Fanny, as I don't want to alarm her, or anyone else who is anxious about me. If you see my sister when you return to London, please don't mention this note from,

Your friend,
William Price

* * * * * * *

Mrs. Butters' carriage, driven by her laconic coachman, Donald McIntosh, conveyed Fanny and Madame Orly to the academy every morning by nine o'clock. Madame Orly enlivened the store on the ground floor—the voluble Frenchwoman darted swiftly around the more stolid Blodgett clan, expressing her delight or her abhorrence for the various fabrics and ribbons and laces under consideration by the customers. Spending half of her time as a lady's maid to Mrs. Butters and half in the shop was very agreeable to her, for Mrs. Butters wanted very little in the way of fashionable primping, and, while at the shop, Madame Orly could enjoy sugar in her tea—for sugar, made as it was by slaves, was forbidden at Mrs. Butters' house.

Fanny's realm was upstairs in the classroom, where her students practised their skills; acquiring the discipline to make perfectly regular and minute straight stitches, or learning how to decorate fabric with ribbon and beads, while a few senior girls worked at the embroidery frames, making simple designs with silver thread upon white muslin bands, which would be sewn on to hems and bodices. In time, the girls would be allowed to try their hands at birds, and leaves and vines and more elaborate needlework.

Fanny found her new charges to be both exasperating and endearing. Her pupils were cynical and sentimental and superstitious by turns, easily moved to the wildest effusions of happiness and sorrow. She did not suppose the scantiness of their

23

education meant they were lacking in native cleverness—or indeed, as she was to discover—native cunning. Many of them knew more about the world and its vices than she. Of education, of reason, of security, they knew little; of privation, they knew too much.

Fanny quickly won their affection and loyalty, but she had to temper her natural gentleness to earn their respect as well. In fact, Fanny's greatest shortcoming as a teacher was that she had been an extraordinarily docile child herself, for whom obedience and submission were second nature. It never had occurred to her that a girl might bring someone else's needlework and present it as her own, or another might plead ill-health and a need to visit the outhouse as an excuse to shirk.

Within a fortnight, Fanny was able to rank the girls in order of ability and diligence. She wanted to rearrange the seating in the classroom, so they sat together in small work teams, with the most experienced girls presiding over four or five younger ones. But Mrs. Blodgett would not agree—the ladies' committee had decided the students would be seated in alphabetical order, the better to call the roll in the morning, and that, accordingly, was that.

The charitable ladies of the Society for Bettering the Condition and Increasing the Comforts of the Poor understood that securing the future welfare of the girls comprised more than teaching embroidery, which would merely improve their material well-being. They were obliged to attend to the students' moral improvement and religious knowledge.

"It would be much better to omit much of the Old Testament," declared Mrs. Wakefield at one of their regular committee meetings. "Except for the Psalms—but not of course those referring to the situation of David. It would be best to confine the children chiefly to the New Testament, I think. And some other improving works intended for young persons."

"Oh, indeed, my dear Priscilla," answered Mrs. Blodgett. "We have agreed to engage Mr. Edifice to read aloud, every morning. A most respectable and worthy young man."

Therefore they engaged Mr. Edifice to commence each day of instruction with a prayer, to be followed by the reading aloud of improving literature. Mrs. Blodgett urged him to keep the prayer as "short as may be, for the girls cannot be at their sewing while you pray, but they will sit and sew while you read."

Thereafter, every morning, the students stood next to their work stools with bowed heads while Mr. Edifice prayed over them, enjoining the Almighty to instil their hearts with gratitude and obedience.

Then there was a general clamour and bustle as the girls settled down with their needles and thread. Once order was restored, Mr. Edifice would open his book, stand with his back to the tall windows which filled the room with natural light, and read aloud to them for an hour with the utmost gravity.

"...We are next enjoined, girls, to submit ourselves to all our governors, teachers, spiritual pastors and masters. By our 'teachers, spiritual pastors and masters,' are meant all those who have the care of our education and of our instruction in religion; whom we are to obey, and listen to, with humility and attention, as the means of our advancement in knowledge and religion.

"The lower orders of men have their attention much engrossed by those employments in which the necessities of life engage them; and it is happy that they have. Labour stands in the room of education, and fills up those vacancies of mind, which, in a state of idleness, would be engrossed by vice. It is an undoubted truth that one vice indulged, introduces others; and that each succeeding vice becomes more depraved."

It was more entertaining than not to have Mr. Edifice's voice filling the high-ceilinged room, even if some girls didn't listen and some didn't understand. They were otherwise commanded to keep strict silence during working hours, enforced with the slap of a ruler on their back from Mrs. Blodgett or Matron, but no admonitions could entirely suppress the collective urge to communicate of four and twenty young persons.

Despite his clerical garb Mr. Edifice was, self-evidently, a man, and he could not appear in the classroom, that place so dominated by the feminine, without setting off waves of whispers and giggles. Most of the students would not pronounce him to be handsome; his face was too cadaverous, and his lips were too thin, but his sallow complexion was thought by many to be pale and interesting.

Before long, the active imaginations of the girls contrived a match between the curate and Miss Price. She seemed born to be a clergyman's wife, and Mr. Edifice must be in need of one. Further, they observed he would often find some excuse for lingering in the schoolroom after Fanny's arrival every morning. Whenever she and Mr. Edifice chanced to speak together, there was much grinning and nudging of elbows and suppressed laughter amongst her pupils.

Mr. Edifice's manner was excessively formal, and he was so alarmed at the thought of saying something indelicate or overfamiliar, that his manners, while privately amusing to Fanny, could not give offence.

"Well, Miss Price, I fear the air has been exceptionally smoky these past few days—I trust you are well? You look very well—that is, you do not look ill—no, that is—but I was alarmed to hear you cough yesterday," he ventured on one grey morning.

"I am tolerably well, Mr. Edifice, I thank you. Mrs. Butters threatens to send me to the countryside for a few weeks, but I could not imagine deserting my responsibilities here."

"Your devotion is admirable, Miss Price, but please, do not neglect your health—your friends would agree you must not injure your health, and if I may be so bold as to count myself among your well-wishers—that is, as curate of the parish, your well-being is—that is, a spiritual leader is also..."

"You are all consideration, Mr. Edifice. Perhaps in a while, matters will be in such a train that I could pay a short visit to my cousins in Northamptonshire. But I should not like to leave Mrs. Butters."

"Oh, certainly, you could be in no doubt you would be very much missed—very much—and if I may venture to add, your absence would be felt, not only by the worthy lady you have named, but also by your other friends—that is, by these young sempstresses, whose devotion I believe you have secured—and it is not to be wondered at, not at all. And it is not merely as an instructress of the needle arts that you have benefited them. You are, if I may quote the poet, the pattern of a gentlewoman. 'Unobtrusive, serious and meek, the first to listen and the last to speak.'"

A half-smile and a nod was her best response here, for if Mr. Edifice approved of her tendency to be 'the last to speak,' she could easily oblige him.

Alas for Mr. Edifice's hopes! He could not know that Fanny had loved another clergyman before she ever met him, and further, he stood no comparison with Edmund Bertram, her cousin—not in understanding, nor in address, nor in true benevolence and integrity.

Fanny's love for Edmund was a carefully guarded secret. When she was a child, he had opened the world to her through reading and conversation. His good principles were her guide. But, convinced of her own lowliness and unworthiness, she never presumed to hint of her attachment. She had watched helplessly when he fell in love with the beautiful and fascinating Mary Crawford. Even though he and Mary were estranged, he was still a married man. Fanny harshly reproved herself for entertaining any thoughts of Edmund which were not entirely cousin-like. She knew it was wrong to think of the touch of his hand, or his embrace when they last parted, or the feel of his lips brushing her cheek.

She missed him, every day, his friendship, and his company. She longed for him even as she recognized it was best to stay far away from him. He filled a place in her heart, that no-one else ever could.

* * * * * * *

Edmund dipped his quill in his ink, and paused, looking up from his blank sheet of paper to gaze out of the window. He recalled when Mary's brother Henry suggested they build a garden "*at what is now the back of the house; which will be giving it the best aspect in the world, sloping to the south-east. The ground seems precisely formed for it.*" Henry used to pique himself on his abilities as a landscape designer, and the Crawfords and Bertrams once travelled together to the country home of his sister's fiancé Mr. Rushworth, so Henry could advise on improvements to his grounds. The visit to the gardens of Sotherton turned out to be anything but innocent for all of the young people hovering on the brink of love or desire. Henry had flirted with Julia all the way there, and, once arrived, had transferred his attentions to Maria. And Mary had discovered that Edmund intended to be a clergyman. Her reaction to this news, ought to have taught Edmund to guard his heart from her. Instead, she had bewitched him.

Edmund recalled, with painful clarity, how delightful Mary had been, when he and she and Fanny strolled through the patch of forest known as the Wilderness. When Fanny, pleading fatigue, had asked to rest for a while, he immediately found a bench; he warmly urged the ladies to sit down, and his heart beat faster when Mary declined, saying, in her delightfully contrary way, that 'resting fatigues me.'

The opportunity was so fair and so was she. They left Fanny behind and walked along the secluded footpaths, which curved and wound about until they found themselves at a side gate which led to a broad oak avenue, one of the approaches to the manor itself. Mary was still playfully arguing with him about how long they had been walking in the Wilderness, and how far they had come.

"You may put your watch away, Mr. Bertram. I have now walked long enough to want some rest—so, since I am never tired, it does follow that we have covered a prodigious distance," she said.

"If my watch does not refute you, perhaps the poet will." Edmund recalled some lines from Cowper:

> *We tread the wilderness, whose well-roll'd walks,*
> *With curvature of slow and easy sweep—*
> *Deception innocent—give ample space*
> *To narrow bounds.*

"'Ample space to narrow bounds,'" Mary repeated. "One is reminded of Hamlet: 'I could be bounded in a nutshell, and count myself a king of infinite space.' Not I. I should hate to be confined. Even these noble trees crowd in upon me."

Mary spread her shawl on the grass under one of broadest oaks, and they sat down together in its welcome shade.

"You are correct in what you said, Mr. Bertram," said she, pointing down the avenue. "The house is ill-placed. If only it had been situated at the crest of the valley, instead of the bottom! How much more could be done to improve the setting! Sotherton must have a decidedly gloomy aspect in winter."

"It is highly pleasing to *me*, just at present."

A sideways smile awarded his attempt at gallantry.

"I think you *have* almost blundered upon some repartee, Mr. Bertram, and I will own myself flattered."

"You are generous to admit the sentiment while overlooking the lack of eloquence which clothed it. Well then, Miss Crawford, do you think your brother will recommend that this avenue be taken down?"

"I think he would sweep everything away—the gates, the walls, the hedges, to open up the view as much as possible. He would return it to a state of untouched nature—-which is an exacting business, as you know, for these so-called natural landscapes are the product of artifice."

"And how about you, Miss Crawford?" Edmund could not resist asking. "Would a scene of rustic simplicity please you? Could *you* be satisfied to contemplate such a view every morning, or would you prefer to look out at a busy London street, thronged with carriages, wagons, bawling costermongers, pushing throngs? I think I see your eyes brighten at the thought."

"You must allow there is more variety to be found in the city, Mr. Bertram—more variety of company, more diversions of all sorts—plays, concerts, lectures—and more opportunities to distinguish oneself—more avenues for happiness, in short. Here I see only one avenue—this heavy and respectable line of oaks marching sedately along. The quiet and the peace is enchanting at present, and will do very well, just for the moment that is—not for a lifetime, certainly!"

"Cowper disagrees with you there," said Edmund, taking a mock-heroic pose and declaiming:

He is the happy man whose life e'en now
Shows somewhat of that happier life to come
Who, doomed to an obscure but tranquil state
Would make his fate his choice—"

"Fiddlesticks! If the poet really believed that obscurity breeds felicity, he would not have sought fame by publishing his poem! It is in our natures to seek immortality, Mr. Bertram."

Edmund smiled. "I will concede, the notion that the greatest happiness is to be found in rural simplicity, is a too-common poetic conceit amongst our men of letters."

"And amongst educated men who ought to—" Mary stopped herself and laughed. "The day is too lovely for quarrelling, Mr. Bertram. Although disputing with you has brought me more pleasure than I've known while exchanging compliments with many another gentleman. Why should this be?"

Edmund wondered if she knew how ardently he wished to fold her in his arms there and then, how he wanted to kiss her with passionate intensity. And no wonder cousin Fanny was completely forgotten on her park bench, for quite some time longer!

Ah, well. They had talked and quarrelled and quarrelled and talked for the better part of a year, and then she married him. And then she left him.

In an upswelling of bitterness, Edmund briefly contemplated letting a long silence elapse before he sent his answer, another year perhaps, as long as *her* silence had been, for it would be no more than she deserved, but of course he had been prompt in composing a reply in his head. He knew his tone was forbiddingly formal, that his letter might almost have come from his father's pen, but, being himself, he could not write in a cavalier manner on such a topic.

Dear Mary, (he wrote)

Lady Delingpole will be calling on us in a few days, which gives me the opportunity to send my answer through her hands, as you requested. Your recent letter invites me to suggest any means by which we may be reconciled.

A reconciliation would comprise many things—that we would once more be in charity with one another, the errors of the past repented, forgiven and forgotten. We would live together under one roof. We would be of one accord as to how and where to live out the rest of our days. I could desire nothing more—if such a thing were possible.

I can change nothing about my former actions, Mary. Misunderstanding and not malice led to my challenging Henry to a duel, if you could only choose to believe it. My regrets will not restore your brother to you and you have already heard me apologize many times for my part in the tragedy.

As for Mansfield Park—my father feels, as every good man must feel, how discreditable it would be, to place a lesser estate into the hands of his heirs, than the one he received from his father. It is for this reason he and I agreed to make Mansfield available for lease, and for my parents to live with my sister in Norfolk. In my opinion, this economical resolution lends more honour and dignity to the name of "Bertram," than living in a style that his income no longer justified, could ever do.

However strongly felt my own inclinations are, they must be subordinate to my duties. Julia has no other home, but with me. We have determined it is not appropriate for her to live at Everingham with Maria. And the same considerations which preclude her going to live with my sister, apply to her sharing a home with you.

Edmund threw down his pen.

My g-d! How does a man say to his wife, *you have been in another man's bed, and I know it*, as casually as though he were making arrangements for a weekend party in the country, he thought. Mary, what have you brought me to!

He would have paced about his study, but it was too small for the exercise. Already cramped in dimension, owing to Mary's desire for a larger sitting-room, it had become even more confined when Edmund installed bookcases on three walls, to accommodate his father's library from Mansfield. Now there was barely room for his desk and two chairs. He instead bounded up the staircase, went to his dressing-room, tore off the Geneva bands which chafed at his neck, and put off the rest of his clergyman's attire. He splashed cold water on his head, ran his fingers through his curling hair, and pulled on a loose lawn shirt and doeskin breeches before returning to his study and his letter.

...Until Julia is respectably settled in her own establishment, she is my responsibility.

You have upbraided me for choosing a life in the country, contrary to your wishes. I had persuaded myself that when you accepted me, you also accepted the limits my circumstances imposed upon me. Did I surprise or disappoint you so much, Mary, after we had lived together for a fortnight, a month, six months? Was I not the person you thought you had married? And, what do you suppose I might say, were the same question to be posed to me?

I need not explain why you cannot return and resume your role here at Thornton Lacey. To be re-united with you elsewhere, I would be compelled to hire a curate to take my place, something I vowed I would never do. To accept the income from this parish and be an absentee clergyman is as abhorrent to my feelings, as it is scandalous to my principles.

What alternatives do we have which would be consistent with my profession and my duty to my family? Under such constraints as have been imposed by past events, there appear to be no simple solutions. If you have any ideas, Mary, I would be—

(I would be what? Pleased? Eager? Curious? He scratched it out and started again.)

However, you must understand me, Mary. I will not consent to resume living as husband and wife as though nothing had occurred, as though there was nothing to discuss, nothing to repent, nothing to atone for.

Your husband,
Edmund

CHAPTER THREE

THE MONTH OF MAY brought Fanny's friend William Gibson to London for the publication of his book, over which he had laboured in self-imposed exile in the countryside. His writing had appeared in print before, of course, in the pages of the *Gentlemen's Magazine* and in the abolitionist newsletter, but nothing compared to the pride and wonder of visiting his publisher in the Strand and holding his first book in his hands. Even better was to read his name on the title page. Indeed, he would not have wanted his closest friends to know how frequently he opened the volume to admire those few words: *Amongst the Slavers, being a narrative of a voyage with the West African Squadron, with additional remarks upon the customs, governments, and political economies of the African tribes, by William Gibson.*

Mrs. Butters, already a warm advocate for the young writer, was eager to assume the rôle of literary patroness, and to help spread his fame. She held a reception at her home and bestowed invitations to her considerable acquaintance amongst London's abolitionist set, including her friend and neighbour James Stephen. The fiery old man was a particular favourite of Fanny's. Mr. and Mrs. Wakefield also promised to attend, Mr. Wilbraham Bootle and many other directors of the African Society accepted with pleasure; and a half-dozen clergyman from the Society for the Propagation of the Gospel in Foreign Parts were also expected.

Fanny felt the most delightful sensations of pride and nervous anticipation as she sat in Mrs. Butters' parlour, surrounded by so many eminent persons, as Mr. Gibson stood in the middle of the room and began to read aloud from his account of the adventures of the West African Squadron.

Mr. Gibson's prose was direct and forceful, without excessive ornamentation or discursion, for he had the happy ability to invoke a scene with a few well-chosen words. Moreover, he read aloud exceedingly well, and although Fanny always kept a piece of fancy work in her hands, she was glad to have the excuse of *listening* as an excuse for *looking* at her friend without interruption. His figure was tall and slender, and his hands expressive and graceful. As an impecunious poet, he had not the means or the inclination to attend to dress or finery, but his posture, his movements, and his air, were all perfectly gentleman-like. For that matter, gaudy dress and an affected air of fashion was no recommendation to the people of this particular gathering. James Stephen's wife, a sister of the saintly Wilberforce himself, refused to wear anything better than washer-woman's rags; and gave all her monies to the poor, instead.

There was something peculiarly charming about Mr. Gibson's countenance. His long face with its high forehead announced intelligence, but without pomposity or severity. His features were individually good. There was sometimes a tinge of sadness about his dark blue eyes, but his mouth, in repose, was always curved in a gentle smile. As he read his own words to the assembled party, his expression was one of diffidence mingled with quiet pride.

Mrs. Stephen, and all of Mrs. Butters' guests, along with Fanny, were captivated by the power of Mr. Gibson's recital. There were no fidgettings, no throat-clearings, no whisperings—a most profound silence was observed by all. When Mr. Gibson came to describe the interception of a heavily-laden slave ship, and the rescue of hundreds of shackled men, women and children from the miserable mid-Atlantic crossing and a lifetime of bondage, his hearers, including Fanny of course, were moved to tears by the power of his narrative.

Sometimes the doings of her own brother William were described and at such times, Mr. Gibson would glance over to the far corner where Fanny sat—his eyes, peering over his spectacles, met hers for a moment of silent acknowledgement of their shared affection for her brother. "Lieutenant Price" never appeared in the tale but to great advantage, and Fanny, in a glow of high spirits, imagined Mr. Gibson's book being read with fascination by all of the Lords of the Admiralty, resulting in a resolution, taken at the highest levels, to promote that exemplary young officer to the rank of captain to command of his own ship. She was also privately delighted that, in a room filled with so many eminent, accomplished, and powerful people—politicians, abolitionists, captains of industry—her friend had made especial note of where she was, of where *she* sat, so that his eyes could seek her out.

At the end of the reading, the servants pulled open the doors to the dining room where a bountiful collation was laid out, and Fanny hurried to her station by the tea and coffee trays, barely ahead of

Mr. Stephen, who demanded, with an impish smile, to be served first, in honour of his grey hairs.

"When I think back, Mrs. Butters, to when I first met Miss Price, I must say that she has *grown* considerably," William Gibson chanced to remark a little later, and after he had modestly received the thanks and praise of Mrs. Butters' guests, who, after contemplating the rigours of an African sea voyage, found themselves to be extraordinarily inclined to eat heartily of ham and chicken and bread and butter and puddings and trifles. The writer and his hostess stood a little apart, observing the success of the evening with some complacency.

"Grown? I should be pleased if she grew a little taller. A more commanding height might help her overcome her timidity. She has put on some flesh, after she was so ill two years ago. That is not to be wondered at, since she has had my example before her! I have been her dining companion this past twelvemonth."

"But you know that I am referring to her *character*. She was excessively shy upon first acquaintance, and could hardly meet one's eye when speaking, and appeared to think so lowly of herself. You have done a great deal for her, ma'am."

Mrs. Butters smiled proudly. "It was mostly my doing, I cannot deny. Of course, when you met her, she was employed as a governess, so she was naturally speaking with the diffidence of a servant. As my guest, she can meet you as an equal. Still, she never expects to be singled out in any way, and it always seems to take her by surprise. Therefore she can be overmodest, tiresomely so. That is what I have set about correcting and bless her, she has borne with my chiding very patiently."

"But only look at her now, conversing so composedly with Mrs. Stephen, and Mrs. Wakefield and Mr. Bootle as well!"

"Believe me, she would have crawled under the table or fainted dead away had I placed her with such eminent persons a year ago!"

Mr. Gibson nodded and smiled, and once again, that urge to protect Fanny Price rose strongly within him, a wish to take care of her and keep her from harm, and see her always as happy and well-respected as she was tonight.

"Fanny still thinks herself unequal to anything and everything. She will give an immediate negative to any proposal which catches her unawares," Mrs. Butters added, laying particular emphasis on the word *proposal*. "For example, when I suggested she become a sewing instructress, her first reaction was to decline it absolutely, and I was at some pains to persuade her she *could* do it, and do it very well, and of course I was proven correct."

Her friend nodded thoughtfully. "She needs time to adjust her thoughts, when presented with something new. We can always expect her first answer to be 'no.'"

"But, we are not to be discouraged upon that account!" His hostess exclaimed, for it had long been her belief that Mr. Gibson and Miss Price would make an excellent match, if they only had enough income between them to enter on married life. "And now I think she sees us, my dear Mr. Gibson, and suspects we are speaking of her. See how she blushes."

At the close of the evening, Mrs. Butters held on to Mr. Gibson, making sure he was the last of her guests to leave, so that he and Fanny had a few moments' opportunity for private conversation. The kindly widow's manoeuvrings were apparent to both of her young guests, and brought more self-conscious blushes to Fanny's cheeks, but she loved Mrs. Butters too well to resent it, and their final parting exchange, with Fanny's warm and intelligent praise of his work, did nothing to lessen Mr. Gibson's good opinion of her.

* * * * * * *

Edmund recalled discussing the vagaries of memory with his cousin Fanny—how retentive memory could be, how faulty at other times. He had taught her that memories can be deceptive, even about things one feels certain of—the dimensions of the family drawing room, for example. It ought to look larger with half the furniture gone—Maria's pianoforte, his mother's sofa, both gone to Norfolk, yet the room seemed smaller than he remembered. All the windows were boarded over now. It was at *this* window he had stood and star-gazed with Fanny, then turned and been enchanted by the sight of Mary Crawford, who had walked up that evening from the parsonage with her brother Henry, and she had joined in singing a glee with the other young people. He had watched the singers, their faces aglow in the candlelight, and hoped she would stay in his life forever.

That night, Mary's presence had filled the room with life and spirit—she was more dazzling to him than the constellations. But now—could things inanimate be called sad? A light film of dust lay over the once spotless floors, and the abandoned side tables and wing chairs, covered with sheets, looked like an assembly of ungainly and unambitious ghosts. Surely this room was melancholy and reproachful. The family was gone— *she* was gone.

"The prospect from these windows must be quite pleasant, Mr. Bertram," he heard Lady Delingpole say, and he was brought again to the present.

"Indeed it is ma'am, our family always gathered here in the evening. Through here, of course, is the main dining room. With the communicating doors opened, there is adequate room for dancing. We have had a dozen couples stand up here in the past. And if you would care to follow me..."

He led the Delingpoles from the east to the west wing of the house, through the breakfast room, the billiard room, his father's study, and the library. "You must visit my home to sample the actual volumes, your lordship, as I inherited most of my father's books, those he did not take with him," Edmund explained.

"It appears you also purloined half the furniture for your own house, Mr. Bertram!" Lady Delingpole observed. "No matter. This lovely home *should* be all new furnished, should it not, Lord Delingpole?"

"My dear, if undertaking such a project will keep you happily occupied, I give my joyful consent to the expenditure."

"You speak as though *you* would be happy to dine sitting upon a packing crate, and sleep on a bale of straw. Mr. Bertram will form false notions of the simplicity of your tastes."

"Here we see demonstrated the logic of the female mind, Mr. Bertram. I generously give her *carte blanche* and she finds something to be aggrieved about."

"Your lordship," Edmund said blandly, "would you care to look over the stables and the kennels next?" He looked over at Julia, who nodded almost imperceptibly.

"And, your ladyship, it would be my pleasure to show you the rose garden and the shrubbery," Julia added. "I fear the rain will return shortly—shall we walk out first and go over the upstairs rooms later?"

Their noble visitors decided with one accord to go outside, with Edmund ready to lead his lordship in one direction while the ladies went the other. "And I think I spy our steward, Mr. Rivers, walking up to meet us," Edmund said, pointing out a portly gentleman with a tidy sheaf of papers under his arm, making his way slowly up the hill.

"Mr. *Rivers*, eh?" enquired Lord Delingpole. "Does he *bank* a lot of money from this place? Will he *brook* no interference from us? Is he *currently* attending to only the farmlands or does he manage everything in your father's absence?"

"As a matter of *course*, your Lordship, Mr. Rivers will be at your *beck*. And your call."

"Lord, give me strength," murmured Lady Delingpole.

*　*　*　*　*　*　*

Aboard the Crocodile
Sierra Leone, May 1811
Dear Fanny,
Thank you for the several long, excellent letters I have received from you. Your latest arrived less than two months after it was written, which is quite astonishing! I wish you could see the delight with which every letter from home is greeted here.

We are at anchor outside of Freetown, which is built on a low peninsula with forested mountains beyond. I was surprised when I first saw the extent of the colony, as I expected it to be little more than a collection of mud huts.

William Price paused, frowning, over his blank page and wiped the sweat from his face so it would not drip on his letter. He had barely begun, but he was struggling over how much of his situation, or his sentiments, he ought to share with his sister.

The heat—

He scratched it out again irritably. She knew about the heat. He always mentioned the heat. It was stifling, smothering, and humid. One had to constantly struggle against an inclination to complete lassitude. Every movement, every breath, was an effort at times.

And what to say of Freetown? The dismal, dirty, disease-ridden outpost which was supposed to be a beacon of hope to the enslaved Africans?

Freetown has grown tremendously since I first saw it eighteen months ago. It makes one's chest swell with pride, Fanny, to consider that wherever we English go, we bring so much with us, in the way of education and improvements. We are making roads and opening waterways, building harbours, and erecting permanent barracks, hospitals, churches, and schools, all built with red bricks made from the local soil or stone quarried from the nearby hills.

But of course the most interesting thing about Freetown is the wide variety of peoples living here—we have soldiers and missionaries, and shopkeepers and there are thousands of negroes who have been returned to Africa from as far north as Nova Scotia and as far south as Brazil, all different shades of brown and black, and all with different manners, language, and customs.

He didn't want his sister to know that after several years' service with the West African Squadron, he was fighting a sense of futility. Many slave ships escaped their patrols, and those Africans who *were* rescued, faced an uncertain future, so far as his observation could reach.

I am extremely fortunate in my current assignment. The Crocodile *has seized two more slavers—the* Marianne *and the* Esperanza. *We brought several hundred freed negroes onto the beach before the town and there was the usual misery and to-do of finding a place for them all, and half of them being too sick to help themselves at first. We cannot send them back to wherever they came from, of course, because they would just be captured again and sold back into slavery. The missionaries do what they can with feeding and clothing them, and there is a little school established for the children.*

Wherever possible, the freed Negroes are apprenticed to some local tradesman or merchant to learn to support themselves. At first, I thought it a little queer that one black man may purchase another black man for twenty dollars—but it is not so different for poor people here, than for poor folk in England, really. If they were not indentured, then how else might they feed themselves?

"Mr. Price?" came a soft and plaintive female voice.

William jumped up and opened the door of his cabin.

"Yes, Mrs. Columbine? May I be of assistance, ma'am?"

His commander's wife tucked a stray lock of limp hair back under her cap with a shaking hand. "Oh, Mr. Price, please come and mend the punkah! The boy would not leave off trying to climb up the rope. I scolded him and told him he was only to pull on it gently, but he pulled down the entire contraption! And after you were so clever and obliging as to make it for us! My poor Charlotte cannot sleep without someone fanning her constantly!"

"I shall be there on the instant, ma'am," William promised.

William grabbed his jacket from his chair and hurried to the captain's cabin, where he found a frightened black child cowering in the corner, and on the floor was the punkah—a small carpet which William had earlier attached to the ceiling beams with rings and pulleys, so it waved back and forth when the little boy—a freed slave—pulled the rope.

He needed only a few moments to repair and set everything going again, while Mrs. Columbine murmured unhappily over her baby daughter, smoothing back the damp curls from her head.

"Now, Petey," she said crossly to the little boy, "If you break my punkah again, I shall have you beaten, do you understand?"

She handed him the rope, and his eyes filled with tears.

"Oh no, Petey, don't cry." Mrs. Columbine turned away and sighed. "It is the heat, lieutenant, and having to stay in the cabin all day."

"I know the captain very much wished you to avoid exposing yourself to the dangerous vapours in town, Mrs. Columbine."

"Of course. And I know that his every word is law to you, Lieutenant!" She mustered a weak smile. "That is, I know you respect my husband very much, and he thinks well of you. But cannot you take my side, and help me persuade him to let me out of prison? Here I am, threatening a poor orphan child who has lost his parents and his home and doesn't understand a word I say. How terrifying everything must be to him, the poor little savage! And I nearly struck him when he broke the punkah! I am not myself in this heat."

Lieutenant Price crouched down and patted the little boy on the back, murmuring a few words of the local pidgin dialect in his ear.

The child nodded, brushed his tears, and resumed his rhythmic pulling on the rope.

"Is there anything else, ma'am?"

"No. No. Thank you, Mr. Price. I am quite obliged to you."

William returned to his cabin and his letter. What else to say?

You will be pleased to hear that I hold to my resolution of avoiding all games of chance, and I cannot resist calculating, almost daily, how many monies I shall have acquired in just a few years' time—apart of course, from what I send to our mother.

Money, Julia, the future... everything and everyone seemed so impossibly far away in this alien country.

I received a long letter from our friend Mr. Gibson, and he sends me a good account of you and your sewing academy. I wish all of the members of the family were as faithful correspondents as you and Mr. Gibson. I don't mean to say that Mr. Gibson is one of the family, but see there how I coupled your names together?

Delicacy and consideration prevented him from revealing his low spirits to Fanny, the sister who had always been his closest confidante. He could not share the secrets of his heart, but he imagined she must have some idea of the truth.

I'm sure Miss Julia's garden is doing very well by now. I should greatly like to visit Northamptonshire when I return.

You are all always in my thoughts.

Yours most affectionately, your brother

William

The letter from William provided Fanny with an excellent excuse to call upon her younger brother John. Four years ago, their uncle Sir Thomas, through his influence in Parliament, had obtained a clerkship for John with the Thames River Police Office. This public office was unique in London, for it had the charge of patrolling the docks and wharves and surveying the busy port, and overlooking the loading and unloading of the cargoes that poured in from all over the world, to suppress theft and vice in that teeming and disreputable part of the city.

John was two years younger than Fanny, and he lived in Wapping, which also made him the closest relative in point of distance. These circumstances might suggest the two young Prices, making their own way in the busy metropolis, had only each other to supply that sympathy, interest, and affection which attaches those who have known each other since infancy. John retained a faint memory of the way Fanny tucked him into bed at night with a song or a story before she was sent away, but he was entirely unused to having anyone enquire after his well-being or his pursuits. Growing up in a large family led by a distracted mother, John was used to taking care of himself, and he valued solitude and silence above all, and the freedom to indulge in his own meditations. The construction of a new crane at the docks, or an article in a scientific journal would arouse more animation and interest in him, than any type of social intercourse. When Fanny visited him, he never enquired about the details of her life, nor expressed regret when she wound up her visit.

Fanny persisted however, and went to see him at least twice a month; she believed that a boy of barely nineteen years of age, living alone in the wicked metropolis, could only benefit from her affectionate attentions. She would take him out to dine on a roast chicken or beef pie, and take his shirts and stockings away to mend them, and kiss his cheek when she said goodbye.

John's experience of life, Fanny reasoned, consisted of a constant exposure—ten to twelve hours, six days in the week—to thieves and vagrants; persons who would not hesitate to falsely accuse their sworn comrades or their nearest relations, to save themselves from prison or the gibbet.

Fanny feared such a prolonged, unremitting acquaintance with so much that was disgraceful to humanity, might put her brother in danger of becoming cynical about his fellow creatures, even to the point of corroding the most tender ties of filial affection.

"I think you might write to our mother more frequently, John," Fanny remonstrated with him gently on this latest reunion of brother and sister. "It is true *she* is no regular correspondent, but she desires to hear from you more often."

"If you had a pen in your hand sixty hours in the week, Fan," was his reply, "you would not be so anxious to write letters in your spare time, neither."

"True! I do not even hold a needle so much as you must use your pen. Very well, I shall talk with you and ask you questions, and I shall undertake to write to our mother for both of us. I may tell her you are well?"

"Tolerably, I thank you."

"And that you abstain from vice?"

"Do you mean, do I stay away from cards, tobacco, women and excessive drink? I cannot afford any of those vices. But I do not smoke by choice, because even if I had the money, I loathe the habit. The air in our house, you may recall, always stank of father's pipe. I used to lay on the floor to read my schoolwork, to stay beneath the cloud of it."

"So..." said Fanny, overlooking the disrespectful words about their father, for they could not be contradicted, "how do you pass your leisure hours?"

"I am taking wrestling lessons, twice a week, to build up my strength. William and Sam, they are broad shouldered, burly fellows, but I cannot seem to put on any flesh. I look like what I am—a clerk, capable of lifting nothing heavier than a ream of paper."

"Are you attending divine services regularly?"

"Oh yes, I am quite regular." The young man laughed and sipped his ale, confident that his innocent sister would not understand 'regular' to mean 'regularly, twice a year.'

"How about your lodgings, John, are they adequate? Comfortable?"

"Do not scold me for being extravagant, but I rented a private room, so that I might be alone at the end of the day—it is in the cheapest boarding house I could find."

"I know what you mean, John, a little solitude is necessary to refresh the spirit. And do you associate with good company?"

"Oh, certainly. Mostly clerks like myself. Earls and Duchesses, unaccountably, are not returning my morning calls, though I leave them my card most assiduously."

"You are laughing at me, brother. I want only to draw a portrait of you. Working in a public office—I fear that such employment has a tendency to coarsen those who are engaged in it."

This drew a broad grin from John, for his sweet, sheltered sister had no conception of exactly how coarse a young man, especially one living in Wapping, could be. However, John was being truthful about his lack of vices—the common pursuits of most young men

43

held no interest for him. Gaming he held in contempt; he disliked excessive drink because it clouded the mind. The fair sex was something of a *terra incognita* for him. He called very few by the appellation 'friend.' He and some of his fellow clerks would spend their Sunday afternoons at a coffeehouse, purchasing one dish of coffee and leaving it untasted on the table between them, so they might play a game of chess or peruse and discuss the journals and newspapers—that is, until the proprietor demanded they leave. Or they would stroll along the river to the Tower of London, to commune with the shades of the prisoners once consigned to its dungeons, and debate the likelihood that there ever really had been a dragon for St. George to slay.

"My work is simply tedious, Fanny. I am an automaton. I am a collecting clerk. I note down all the imports that are unloaded—quantities of sugar and tea and so forth—in long columns and add them all up, and get it all signed and counter-signed."

"But, as you explained to me, the officers oversee the loading and unloading of the ships, and therefore, what you do prevents crime. So you can take pride in that, can you not?"

John nodded. "Yes, Mr. Harriott says that our office is unique, a *preventative* police office. He says that our office saves the merchants of London thousands of pounds. But all of that prevention does not prevent my work from being tedious. I *want* to witness more vice and depravity, Fanny. It would be interesting. I want to be a judicial clerk; they are the ones who record the criminal cases brought to the magistrates—but there are only two judicial clerks in our office. Of course, Mr. Laing, the head clerk, is quite ancient—he must be nearly fifty years old—so, perhaps I will get my chance in a few years."

"Well, I can't deny that crime would be more interesting than sugar," Fanny conceded. The subject of sugar reminded her of slavery, and she rummaged in her small portmanteau.

"Oh John! Here is my copy of *Amongst the Slavers*. You may borrow it."

When she held out the volume, Fanny had the gratification of seeing her brother's eyes light up with interest.

"Thank you, Fan! This is the book that mentions our brother, does it not?"

"Yes, you can read all about William's exploits in it. John, I want to introduce you to my—to the author, Mr. Gibson. He and our brother William are quite good friends, you know. And I fancy you should find Mr. Gibson a very interesting fellow."

"And he will find me likewise, no doubt. Perhaps he will put *me* in his next book."

The thought of increasing Mr. Gibson's ties to the Price family was singularly pleasing to Fanny, and served to give her cheerful reflections for her journey back to Stoke Newington.

CHAPTER FOUR

THE CRISIS BROUGHT about by the King's descent into insanity kept both Houses of Parliament at their duties well into the summer months. The Crown Prince was appointed as Regent until it pleased God to restore His Majesty to health. Lord Delingpole and his fellow Tories continued the war against Napoleon in an uneasy partnership with a prince they could neither trust nor respect, as his political sympathies were with the Whigs, and his private vices were notorious. Unable to make the longer journey to his estate in Wales, Lord Delingpole retreated to Northamptonshire whenever possible.

The people of Mansfield rejoiced in the reanimation of the principal estate in the vicinity. Once more, their sons and daughters were employed as scullery maids and laundresses, gardeners, and stable boys. The butcher and the greengrocer sent hampers of beef and cheese, onion and marrow, up the hill. His lordship's handsome hunters, walked through the village by their grooms, drew the admiration of the men, while whispers of Lady Delingpole's extensive wardrobe—in particular, her vast collection of bonnets, turbans, and caps—aroused the interest of the females.

The Delingpoles declared themselves tolerably pleased with their new home, although there were some trifling discontents—a draughty window, and primitive water closets.

"Imogen! What am I supposed to do with these?" Lord Delingpole called out one morning from the billiard room.

"Since I am in another room, David, and do not possess the ability to see through walls, I am unable to answer your question."

Lord Delingpole opened the door connecting the billiard room with the study, where his wife sat looking over the household accounts.

"These—what are these—the pockets of the billiard table are filled with them."

"They appear to be curtain rings, dear."

"What were they doing in the billiard table?"

"Now you flatter me, dear, by assuming I am in possession of information denied to lesser mortals. But, having only just moved into this dwelling, at the same time as you, I do not know why someone was hiding curtain rings in the billiard table. Perhaps Baddeley can enlighten you. How is the table otherwise?"

"Vile. Wretched. I do not know what Bertram could have been thinking."

"A great pity, indeed, my dear. But, you know, grouse season begins shortly, and you will not care for billiards at all, soon enough."

Lord Delingpole was not to be placated. "I intended to play a game with Bertram after dinner."

"Oh—I should imagine Mr. Bertram will want to ride home before nightfall. I am keeping country hours on purpose for him."

"Can he be persuaded to spend the night?"

"If he did, then I would be under the necessity of inviting his aunt to join us for dinner as well. It would only be fitting."

"His aunt? The lady who called upon us the day we moved in and gave us her opinions concerning which servants we ought to engage and which merchants we should patronize?"

"Yes, dear. That lady. Mrs. Norris. You did meet her in London, you may recall, when she chaperoned her nieces."

"I think we shall wave Mr. Bertram off directly after dinner, then."

Edmund Bertram rode the long way around to Mansfield, so as to avoid passing by the parsonage-house on the outskirts of the village. He did not want to be under the necessity of stopping and exchanging greetings with Mrs. Grant, Mary's half-sister, until he had learned if Mary had sent a reply to his letter. Even though Dr. Grant *would* not say anything about Mary, and Mrs. Grant *could* not say anything, on account of her husband, her eyes spoke for her—she lamented the tragic circumstances of the separation, she missed her sister exceedingly, and she longed for a reconciliation to take place.

It had been somewhat trying to his feelings to observe his boyhood home when it was dark, boarded up and empty; and yet, Edmund discovered, it also pained him somewhat to see the house brought to life again, with many familiar faces amongst the servants, now serving another family! A family that would not know of the memories which clung to certain rooms, certain places.

The path between the estate and the parsonage, which he and Mary had walked so many times, arm in arm. Fanny's little refuge in the East Room, where she and he would read poetry together. When he was a little boy, it was a cause of great apprehension to hear the words, "your father wishes to speak to you in his study," but now, how good it would be to see his father at his usual place, behind his desk!

Edmund tried to dismiss his emotions as ungenerous, unreasonable. As an invited guest of the Delingpoles, he would not appear before them with a long face or a distant air, and as he strolled from the stables, he commanded himself to greet them cheerfully, to enter into their conversation and their interests, as a welcome distraction from his own cares.

And Lady Delingpole supplied him with another distraction, rather more startling than Edmund could wish for. As soon as their cordial greetings were exchanged, and enquiries as to horses, health, and weather were all given and received, she handed him a letter from his wife. She intended, in her good nature, to spare him any suspense as to whether there was such a letter in existence, but her disinterest did not extend so far as to give him leave to read it immediately. Civility dictated that Edmund give all his attention to his host and hostess, and none to the letter which he took and placed in his waistcoat pocket.

The presence of James, Viscount Lynnon, the Delingpoles' only son, ensured that there would be no talk of Bertram family matters at the dinner table. Viscount Lynnon had recently returned from Oxford to bestow some of his summer holidays upon his parents. He had arrived at Mansfield the day before, with a large hamper full of dirty linen and two dozen books he meant to have read.

In appearance, Viscount Lynnon resembled his father, being slight of build, with a mobile and engaging countenance. He inherited his mother's Irish loquaciousness and no small degree of her charm. His views, however, differed pointedly from theirs, and, fired with the ardour and certainty of youth, he made no pretence of hiding them.

He surveyed the fare laid on the dining table with suspicion, enquired into the freshness of the fish, refused all the meat, and finally ventured upon only vegetables with bread and butter. "One of my friends at Oxford has persuaded me that eating meat is both unhealthy and immoral," he explained between mouthfuls of asparagus.

"An all-vegetable diet has much to recommend it," said Lady Delingpole, "especially against gout, or *avoirdupois*, but you, my boy, suffer from neither. Reverend Bertram, what does the Church say about the *morality* of eating meat?"

"Well, your ladyship, from Genesis of course we are taught that man was given dominion over the animals. The Bible is quite explicit on that point. However, there is on the other hand no positive commandment in *favour* of eating meat, so the Church can have—on general principles and without reference to individual cases—no objection to an all-vegetable diet."

"The Almighty preferred Abel's sacrifice to Cain's, and from Leviticus we know the Lord likes his mutton. At least his priests did." Lord Delingpole reached for a toothpick.

"If you believe there *is* such a creature as God," laughed his son. "'Every reflecting mind must allow that there is no proof of the existence of a Deity.'"

"I had hoped, sir, that the presence of Reverend Bertram at our table might induce you to refrain from some of your more outrageous remarks, but I see you are as dead to courtesy as you are to common sense."

"I was quoting my friend's excellent pamphlet on the subject, father. He says—"

"Your friend? What is the name of this philosopher-sage?"

"Shelley, sir. Percy Shelley," the son answered with evident pride and affection.

"And he is a student, I gather, and not one of your masters?"

"He *was,* sir, but he was expelled for publishing the pamphlet."

"No wonder! We want no heathens at Oxford!" Lady Delingpole exclaimed.

"I think Shelley is very courageous and principled!" Viscount Lynnon cried.

"Rather, he is both imprudent and impudent, with the egoism of youth," his father averred. "What does anyone care what this Mr. Shelley thinks or believes, so long as the fool refrains from publishing it? He knew, everyone knows, you cannot obtain your degree without being a member of the Church of England. He entered into a contract, so to speak, and has, in the most insulting terms, failed to honour it. Further, no right-thinking gentleman would promulgate such a pernicious dogma, so damaging to the fabric of society, and particularly harmful in its effects upon the lower orders."

"The lower orders!" Viscount Lynnon replied, unable to contain himself. "They groan under the restraints of pseudo-morality on the one hand, and taxes and tithes on the other, under a system calculated to keep them poor, and to maintain the rich and mighty in their place, while the clergyman tells the poor cottager that his miserable lot is divinely ordained, and it is sinful to resent it. But the day of awakening is at hand! All wealth must be equally distributed, and we will do away with greed and oppression forever."

Edmund ventured a glance at Baddeley, keeping his usual place by the sideboard, but that worthy man's composure did not waver in the slightest. If their butler was moved by the fervent speeches of the young viscount, if radical notions stirred in his breast, he betrayed no sign.

"I do apologize, my dear Mr. Bertram," her Ladyship said. "James, apologize to Reverend Bertram, immediately."

"Pray, do not concern yourself, ma'am," Edmund laughed. "These sentiments are neither modern, nor unique. They are discussed in the Scriptures themselves. '*The fool hath said there is no God.*'"

"This puppy, this Shelley—still under-age, I presume—must think very well of himself," said Lord Delingpole with some asperity, "if he believes all of mankind has been waiting, since the dawn of coherent thought, for an Oxford undergraduate to survey the cosmos, examine and sift the debates which have preoccupied the wisest scholars and our most eminent divines, and to publish his final pronouncement on the matter."

"The idea of the perfectibility of mankind *is* a beguiling one," added Edmund composedly, "and Mr. Shelley is undoubtedly one of those confident young men who can clearly see what eludes his elders. I for one, do not understand why eliminating God is a necessary first step to the work of creating paradise on earth, but most radicals do insist upon it."

"But my friend Shelley truly is the herald of a new age!" cried the Viscount, as Baddeley re-filled his water glass.

"This is my fate, my inevitable fate," Lord Delingpole sighed. "I sired a son, and we saw to it that he received the best education in England—the best in the world, in fact. Before he was out of skirts, we taught him his letters and his sums. Naturally, he went to Eton. In the summer months, he had music and dancing masters and his own tutor. Then we sent him up to Oxford, where—when he has not been applying to us for more spending monies—he has been cramming his head full of the most errant nonsense, seditious poison, and immoral folly. So my reward—my reward, Mr. Bertram, for all my anxious cares and my costly expenditure—is that my son is a confirmed radical, and now, I gather, an atheist."

Lord Delingpole raised his glass in salute.

"To me, this is another proof of the existence of God, and that he possesses a good sense of humour."

* * * * * * *

Edmund rewarded himself for his unstinting patience through the dinner, by ripping open the letter from his wife as soon as he had ridden out of sight of his boyhood home. His horse knew the way home, and his wife Mary's handwriting was bold and clear, and he could make it out even in the gathering dusk.

Dear Edmund,

I thank you for the receipt of your letter, despite the fresh pain it has occasioned me. My hopes, it seems, hang upon the slenderest thread. Shall I further diminish myself in your regard if I point out that once again, my wishes, what I want and desire, come last with you in your calculations? Everyone else—your sister —your family, anything and everything—are to be placed ahead of your wife.

Do you not begin to understand how it is you broke my heart?

I envy the devotion you express for your parents, and I envy your sister and your cousin. You still have a family— my own was shattered when I lost my brother. They have your love, and they have each other regardless of the errors and follies they committed and the falsehoods they perpetrated. I alone stand outside your family circle, waiting, petitioning, hoping, for re-admittance.

My unhappiness makes me unwise—I should not upbraid you thus—I can only hope that time, absence, distance will soften your severity and reanimate your love for

Your lonely wife,

Mary

The note was so brief that he read the whole, twice over, before he passed Mansfield Parsonage. He had intended to stop and pay his respects, but he could not sufficiently master his emotions so as to meet the Grants with composure, after reading such a letter. A letter that once again blamed *him,* for *her* betrayal.

* * * * * * *

After losing her husband, Harriet Butters was left with an ample jointure. She chose to leave Bristol and settle in Stoke Newington, to be near her only son and his family. However, Fanny observed, while Mrs. Butters sometimes called upon her son George in his law offices, she seldom met with her daughter-in-law or the family all together. There appeared to be some estrangement.

Mrs. Butters' daughter-in-law Cecilia Butters was an active, clever woman; discontented with her lot in life, but blessed with sufficient discernment to understand the source of her difficulties—her unhappiness was owing to the faults of her husband and his mother.

Those qualities which once attracted her, not fifteen years ago, to Mr. George Butters—namely, his gentle wit and his placid temperament—were precisely those which now aroused her contempt. Her husband was a solicitor, but his ambition and his income did not answer her wishes.

The younger Mrs. Butters was a devoted horsewoman and her three daughters were in the saddle not long after they were able to walk. Unfortunately the expense of maintaining a stable of horses was such as could not be easily borne by her husband.

In addition to her horses, Cecilia Butters kept an ill-disciplined menagerie of dogs and cats, which Mrs. Butters was unable to tolerate. After only five minutes in her daughter-in-law's shabby parlour, her eyes began to water excessively, and she started to gasp for breath. Nor could Mrs. Butters observe the disorder around her with any composure, or refrain from inwardly lamenting that the income earned by her son was spent by his wife on the acquisition of animals who seemed bent on the destruction of every item of furniture in the house, including those pieces she had bestowed upon them. The veneer on the pianoforte was reduced to shreds, the wainscoting and doors were all scratched and marred, and the carpets were stained.

A coolness had arisen between the mother and daughter-in-law, for the younger Mrs. Butters could not always conceal her expectation that the older lady ought to do more for her son, and her disappointment when she did not. The fact that Mrs. Butters had given away much of her fortune to philanthropic causes, such as fighting the slave trade, was particularly galling to Cecilia Butters, who subscribed to the maxim that charity begins at home. Nor did Cecilia Butters scruple to teach her daughters to think as she did. Instead of duty and courtesy, forbearance and respect, the three girls were tutored in resentment and envy.

Mrs. Butters, for her part, contended that she had done as *much and more* than most would do.

This difference of opinion between the two principals was seldom carried out openly, save in the form of veiled barbs and dropped hints. With the censure of selfishness and folly reposing in one female breast, and accusations of ingratitude and ill-breeding in the other, the meetings between the two households were few and marked by frosty politeness.

Mrs. Butters' solicitations to her family to come and spend a day, an afternoon, or an evening at her home, were declined more often than not, on the pretext of some ailment of one of the children or even a mishap to one of her horses, who came a close second to her children in Cecilia Butters' affections.

More recently, a new cause of contention had arisen between the ladies: Mrs. Butters' dining room table. The younger Mrs. Butters refused to dine with her mother-in-law until the table was replaced, for she declared she absolutely would not eat off a table on which a dying man had once been laid. (Without having been apprised of any other of the particulars, she knew Mrs. Butters once offered assistance to a man terribly injured in a carriage accident.)

The demand to discard the table was vigorously resisted by Mrs. Butters. She liked her dining room table very well; it had been a gift from her husband on their tenth wedding anniversary.

Both ladies were implacable, and the *impasse* continued for several months. For the sake of seeing her granddaughters again, Mrs. Butters finally relented, most grudgingly.

"I suppose many women would feel the same, Fanny, but you know we placed a mattress and many blankets on the table before we laid poor Mr. Crawford upon it, so it makes no earthly difference whatsoever. Cecilia is not in the least squeamish or sentimental, and no-one who spends most of their waking hours in a stable or paddock can claim to be superfine or fastidious, in my opinion. But if I was ever to see my own granddaughters again, I needs must do as she commands!"

The family was accordingly re-united—although the longed-for granddaughters, the eldest of whom was ten years old, were banished to the breakfast room, at the desire of their mother, so the adults were free to gather for dinner in elegance around the new dining table.

"I declare, this tired old gown of mine creases so abominably!" complained Cecilia Butters, brushing at her skirt as she took her place opposite her mother-in-law. "I was forced to take little Isabella on my lap, to squeeze into your carriage to come here, and she wrinkled my skirt so frightfully I am not fit to be seen! But it cannot be helped—we have not the means to set up our own carriage, even though a used barouche can be had at a quite reasonable price."

"You look very well, as always, Cecilia," Mrs. Butters replied composedly.

"Speaking of gowns, is your new project prospering well, Mother?" George Butters asked.

"You refer to our needlework academy? Tolerably well, I thank you, dear. We have had many more applicants than we can engage—"

"I should think so, considering the easy hours you promised!" cried Cecilia Butters.

"Yes, we have established a workday of only ten hours for the children, because we think it inhumane to operate from dawn until midnight. We shall not sacrifice the health or eyesight of the students at the altar of fashion. Our customers will pay less for our garments, but they may have to wait a little longer for them to be delivered. And in that regard, my dear Cecilia, I hope you will patronize us when you need new garments for yourself or the girls, and encourage your friends to do likewise."

"What, ma'am, shall *we* pay for these clothes as though we were merely members of the public, and not your own *family*?"

"Oh. By all means, Cecilia, I am sure my brother and sister-in-law would be happy to dress you and all your daughters. I should think they would be delighted. But, perhaps you had not understood when I explained that the profits of the enterprise support the charitable academy for the poor?"

"It can hardly make any difference to the Blodgetts, for it requires very little fabric to run up a dress for *me*, or my daughters. *We* are all quite *petite*. I am still only twenty inches round my waist, even after three children."

"Will you have some creamed potato, Cecilia?"

"Potato? I think not. It is most unhealthy, is it not? You are not serving this to the children, are you?" Their guest turned to Fanny. "Miss Price, please tell the servants not to let the girls have any potato. Quickly."

Fanny was out of her seat and almost to the door when she caught sight of Mrs. Butter's glowering face, but she judged it better to do as she was asked, and she hurried to the breakfast room with the message, and lingered there a few moments to confirm that the grandchildren would be brought into the parlour after dinner, while unbeknownst to her, she became the topic of discussion around the new dining table.

"Miss Price is most obliging, my dear Cecilia, but allow me to remind you she is not my servant."

"Indeed? You have kept her by your side for so long, and I have seen her fetch and carry for you, and assist in the running of your household, so I naturally fell into the error of assuming she was your paid companion. You say she receives no remuneration for everything she does?"

"She is employed by the Society to teach fine needlework at the academy. Her parents are in Portsmouth and her uncle and aunt reside in Norfolk. So I keep her with me. Indeed, there is no-where else she could live, while in London."

"So, she is your tenant, then?"

"No, she is my guest."

"How convenient for Miss Price! No expenses to bear."

"Forgive me, Cecilia, but a moment ago *I* was the fortunate one, in having a companion who performed her duties without recompense. Then, in your next breath, you insinuate that I am the dupe of Miss Price. Is she eating me out of house and home and I all unawares? Why, pray, do you tend to see all relationships in mercenary terms?"

The younger Mrs. Butters sighed and rolled her eyes at her husband, who was quietly spooning up his soup.

"I meant no disrespect, ma'am. You and Miss Price are quite fortunate if the acquaintance makes both of you happy. You manage so well together, do you not? She is of a very yielding temper, I think."

The imputation that she could only tolerate young ladies with yielding tempers was not lost on Mrs. Butters, but she had regained her composure and did not wish to quarrel any further with her daughter-in-law. The rest of the evening passed harmoniously enough, with only a few more trials of Mrs. Butter's patience when they all gathered in the parlour, where Fanny made the tea and cut the cake and the others absorbed themselves in various activities. Mr. Butters read the newspaper, the girls played with paper dolls that Fanny had prepared for them and the other ladies brought out their needlework.

"Are *you* a horsewoman, Miss Price?"

"I should not describe myself as one, ma'am. When I lived in the country, I used to ride a very gentle little mare for my health. But I never went above a trot. My cousin Thomas Bertram is the real expert on horseflesh. He emigrated to Virginia two years ago, and has established a breeding stables there."

"Is that so?" And Cecilia Butters began to speak knowledgeably of studs and bloodlines and covering mares, while her little daughters played at her feet.

The youngest girl finished several slices of cake with milky tea, then joined her grandmother on the sofa and stroked her arm entreatingly. "Grandmama, do you know that I need a new saddle?"

"Do you indeed, Isabella? I have purchased several new saddles for you girls. Have you not the use of Ethelinda's first saddle? Has it not passed down to you?"

"But I want a new one—I never have anything new—Ethelinda always has new things, and I never do, because I am the youngest.

Mama said I should ask you, because Grandmamas often buy nice things for their granddaughters. Don't you want to, Grandmama?"

"You can tell your mother from me, that Grandmamas buy nice things for granddaughters who have been taught to write thank-you letters."

Isabella was confused by this answer, but understood it to mean 'no,' and she desisted in her efforts, and pouted and glowered until Fanny led her away and tried to distract her with examining a collection of beetles under glass, left over from her father's school days.

"You see how your mother *has* contrived to acquire a companion without the expense of paying for one," the younger Mrs. Butters whispered to her husband after they took their leave for the evening.

Had Fanny actually been paid for those services which she provided out of affection, the circumstance would have been as equally useful to Cecilia Butters. Whether Mrs. Butters had extra money to spare, or whether she had been spending funds that could be better spent elsewhere, her daughter-in-law could draw the appropriate moral lesson.

* * * * * * *

Lieutenant William Price, red-eyed and weary, stumbled into his cabin at the end of his watch, tore off his hat and jacket and collapsed at full length in his bunk, too tired to remove his boots. He closed his eyes and fell into a dreamless sleep, all-consuming and all too brief. The cabin boy came banging through the door with his kettle, jolting him awake.

"Four bells, Mr. Price, sir. Here's for your tea, sir."

William groaned, swung around, and sat up. In the cramped confines of his berth he only had to reach out his hand to pull open the biscuit box that held the last of his supply of dried rose hips. Starting every day with a cup of rose hip tea had become almost a superstition with him. He drank it even when there was no sugar or honey to be had—he ignored the bitter taste and the friendly jibes of his brother officers.

After eighteen months patrolling the shores of Western Africa, the HMS *Crocodile* was returning home. The crew laboured day and night to catch the feeble winds of the horse latitudes to fill her sails as she tacked her way north; everyone was anxious to feel the cold, freshening breezes of the Channel. Only then, the sailors said, would they escape the miasma of the fevers that clung to the unlucky ship, that had killed two dozen members of the company. More were lying on the brink of death—including, most lamentably, their captain, Edward Columbine.

Thinking of the captain, William resolved to look in on him before resuming his duties. He threw some rose hips into the kettle, grabbed two enamel mugs from the wardroom, and made his way to the captain's quarters, thanking his good fortune that unlike Lieutenant Lumley, he did not need to shave every morning to make a creditable appearance. William had a handsome head of thick golden hair, bleached almost white by the African sun, but his cheeks and chin seldom needed to meet with a razor.

His captain lay, grey, weak and drawn, in his cabin; the unmistakable mask of approaching death on his face. William took care to compose his features carefully to greet him with his usual good cheer.

"The wind's picking up sir, veering to the west. We'll be home soon."

Columbine answered him with a slight smile, then closed his eyes, as though even that effort exhausted him. "Lieutenant Lumley is most impatient to be home. He is to be married. A vice-admiral's daughter—a good catch for a lieutenant!"

"Yes, sir."

"I wish him a better fate than mine."

"I am sorry, sir, extremely sorry for your loss."

Captain Columbine's wife and baby daughter had died of fever in Sierra Leone.

"Listen to me, Price," Columbine spoke with an effort. "I would not say this to Lumley, but so far as I know, you are a bachelor and have not engaged yourself to any young person. If I am wrong, pray stop me."

"Please go on, sir."

"Did you know I was married once before? Jane is—was—my second wife."

"No, sir."

"Of course, you were just a youngster at the time, otherwise you would have known of the matter," said the captain with a sigh, "for it was in all the papers." He drew a breath and continued: "I married in '97, after I made lieutenant, but almost immediately I received a posting to the West Indies aboard the *Sybille*. Anna Maria was young and beautiful, and I was gone for nearly three years. Another man seduced her, and she ran away with him."

William did not interrupt the Captain, but dipped a cloth into the washbasin, wrung it out, and gently dampened his captain's forehead as he spoke.

"A few years later, I wished to re-marry. But to obtain my divorce, our sorry history had to be paraded before the House of Lords. The vultures of the press reprinted all the sordid details. My first wife's shame was made notorious across the country! The experience was in every way horrible."

William tenderly lifted the captain up from his pillow and placed a cup to his lips. Captain Columbine rested against William's arm, silently for a time, then resumed:

"I determined that I should never expose Jane to the temptations and regrets that destroyed my first marriage. I would not leave her at home for years at a time, so upon my appointment to Sierra Leone, I urged her to come with me. My fears for her fidelity became her death sentence! Africa killed her, and killed our daughter."

Columbine took a long, slow, rattling breath. The effort to speak was tremendous, but so was his need to share his burden of grief and remorse.

"My first wife is now infamous and cast out of all good society. Jane, in devotion to me, went to her grave, thousands of miles from her home and family. What man—who calls himself a man—would want to visit either of these fates on a woman he sincerely loved? While I do not entirely blame myself for the first outcome, it would not have happened but for my selfish wish of pursuing both domestic life and a naval career. And as for Jane and our baby daughter, my soul tells me they are dead by my agency as surely as if I had laid a knife to their throats."

"Oh—sir—you cannot think that—"

Columbine finally opened his eyes and looked at William, who felt the full force of his captain's anguish and regret. Between laboured breaths, he continued: "Had I to do it all over—but it is all too late. Reflect, Price—ask yourself—whether you are conferring any benefit worth having—upon a woman—when you offer her marriage. What loneliness, what worry—will you inflict upon the woman you love—by your lengthy absence—or worse, what dangers—will you expose her to if you bring your wife with you?"

The exertion of speaking had exhausted the dying man. A tear streamed down his shrunken cheek, and he fell back into unconsciousness.

CHAPTER FIVE

THE SUMMER HEAT often rendered the upstairs classroom very disagreeable, even with the windows open to admit every faint breeze. By the afternoon, the girls were all drooping and yawning at their places, after having been kept at their tasks, with little intermission, since seven o'clock in the morning. Yet, when Matron ran the bell for dismissal, it was as though a bolt of lightning passed around the room. Those who were but half-awake instantly regained their vivacity. Whispers grew to excited chatters and trills of laughter, aprons were quickly doffed, and the girls scampered happily away.

On one particular Wednesday afternoon, the girls forgot their eagerness to escape the classroom, for they awaited the appearance of their instructress in her new gown. It was white, with blue trimming and had been designed by herself and Madame Orly, and she was to wear it to an afternoon reception given by Lady Delingpole. The young sempstresses would not be satisfied until Fanny promised to call in at the academy on their way into town, to show herself to them.

When Fanny appeared, the girls squealed and exclaimed in pleasure and pride, examining their own handiwork in the stitchery which decorated the hem and fashionably low neckline. Madame Orly had arranged Fanny's hair; she was accoutred with gloves, fan, ear-bobs, shawl, and new slippers, and she looked very well indeed.

Fanny smiled as her pupils congratulated themselves; for indeed, their new-found skills had transformed their sewing instructress—who ordinarily wore the plain garb of a governess—into a vision from a fashion plate.

"Her hair looks so pretty! I wish my hair would curl like hers," cried Martha.

"And her cheeks are so rosy, and her lips so pink," said Tansy. "Like a picture."

"I am sure someone will fall in love with her."

"I should not like for her to get married, because then she would leave us."

"Perhaps. Mrs. Blodgett is married, ain't she? And at any rate, Miss Price should get married soon. She is already twenty."

"She should go to St. Pancras at midnight, and take a brick from the church-yard," said Sarah knowingly, "and place it under her pillow, then she will dream of her husband."

"St. Pancras—Mr. *Edifice* is the curate, at St. Pancras!"

And the girls dissolved into giggles.

And upon examining her own feelings, Fanny discovered she was not unhappy to know she was in good looks, and further, to know that William Gibson would also be in attendance at the reception. His book, *Amongst the Slavers,* was a prodigious success and had sold out three editions. In fact, Gibson was the literary lion of the hour in London and received many invitations from London's political hostesses.

These thoughts, pleasant as they were, contended in Fanny's mind with the fear of walking into a London drawing room filled with titled and powerful persons. Fanny depended upon finding some obscure corner from which to observe the gathering without drawing attention to herself. She was also very conscious of her exposed bosom, and kept her light muslin shawl clutched firmly around her shoulders as she descended from the carriage.

"Come now, Fanny, take a deep breath and plunge in," Mrs. Butters whispered to her, with some asperity, as they waited in the entrance hall to be received by their host and hostess, "you do not often have such a fine opportunity of meeting with so many interesting people, so try not to look so timid. You are the niece of a baronet and you are involved in a commendable charitable project. Hold your head up high and know your own worth."

And Fanny began well enough. Lady Delingpole received her kindly; Lord Delingpole, once he understood who she was, gallantly hailed her as "another beauteous bloom from the Bertram bouquet," and she heard herself responding politely.

Mrs. Butters' attention was instantly claimed by some of her many acquaintance, and Fanny was left for a moment to look about herself. Past the lobby, still busy with recent arrivals, a large archway led to a gilded reception room, which appeared to be so crowded that Fanny wondered how the great mansion could admit any more guests. What was at first, to her bewildered senses, a blur of noise and bustle, began to sort itself out—she saw many elegant persons, all strangers, all conversing, all ignoring the efforts of the string trio playing from an upstairs balcony. There was much laughter, much heat, much candlelight. But finally, just inside the entrance, she discerned the tall slender form of William Gibson.

He was newly and neatly attired, his unruly brown hair trimmed and pulled into a queue. His snowy white cravat had been wrapped and arranged by some expert hand. He even wore new spectacles. He looked—Fanny could think of no better word—*beautiful.* She then saw that she was not his only admirer, for a cluster of young women surrounded him, all gazing up at him with rapt attention. Fanny could not have supposed that even two or three young ladies of high birth could be so passionately curious about the West African slave trade, and here were half-a-dozen. Mr. Gibson leaned over slightly, to better hear a question posed by one of his fair interlocutors; his countenance, as usual, enhanced by his twinkling eyes and his lips, as always, curved into a gentle but knowing smile.

Fanny watched from a distance as Mr. Gibson, without raising his voice or indeed, with a posture and air the most mild and unassuming, captivated one fair admirer after another. She and Mrs. Butters had been used to thinking and speaking of him as their own particular friend, but as Fanny saw, Mr. Gibson possessed the happy knack of looking at the person with whom he was conversing as though she was the only one in the room, and this gave her some uncomfortable sensations.

He was, as far as Fanny could judge in all candour, not flirtatious. His address was not insinuating, not flattering, not to be compared to the late Henry Crawford, but his manners were such as must please.

What was this dismay, this unwelcome feeling, which took possession of her and made her want to drop through the floor into oblivion? As she watched, another young lady fearlessly approached and joined in the conversation. Fanny could not conceive of having the audacity to do the same in this glittering company.

Inevitably, her inner voice—that familiar and dolorous companion from her childhood—awoke and plunged her into self-reproach. *Who was she to resent?* What right had *she* to be jealous of any of the ethereal creatures now swarming around her friend? Who was she to begrudge the flattering attentions he received? Of course Mr. Gibson, once penniless and unknown, now prosperous and famous, should move in more exalted spheres. She was merely an ex-governess, insignificant and awkward. She felt herself to be an impostor in borrowed clothes, as she beheld the easy way the other young women wore their beauty and their privilege.

One of the ladies attending on Gibson, who stood with her back to Fanny, now turned slightly, affording a view of her profile. Her form was slender and elegant. She wore a turban, out of which a few dark curls escaped to adorn her forehead, and her gown was a bold shade of cerise. She was the image of self-possession, beauty and fashion.

Fanny startled, she gasped. The lovely vision was none other than Mary Crawford—that is, Mary Bertram, the estranged wife of her cousin Edmund.

Quickly Fanny snapped open her fan to cover her face, as she squeezed through the crowd to hide herself behind one of the lobby's marble pillars, thickly wrapped with artificial ivy. She stood on tiptoe, craning to peer through as the crowds between them moved and separated, but there could be no mistaking—it *was* Mary. Her face was perhaps a little thinner, her nose and chin a little more pointed, but it was the same confident and witty beauty who won Edmund's heart three years ago and, having won it, had broken it.

At the same moment that Fanny found a hiding place, William Gibson turned all his attention to Mary, laughing and nodding in response to one of her witty remarks, and Mary—how did she possess such skill?—managed somehow to separate him from the other women clustered round him, to claim and secure him for her own, to pull his arm within hers, and to walk away. Fanny watched as Mary leaned confidingly toward him, the feathers dancing above her head; she saw Mary tap him playfully with her fan, and Gibson did not appear in the least anxious to escape her company.

"Fanny! What on earth are you doing—why are you tangled up in the ivy? This is an absurd beginning. Come with me, you silly girl."

"Oh, dear Mrs. Butters," Fanny whispered in stricken tones. "Pray, allow me to wait for you in your carriage. Please, I cannot go in there. I cannot."

Mrs. Butters frowned.

"Fanny, this will not do. You must get the better of yourself. You must show more confidence."

"Dear Mrs. Butters," Fanny repeated, "I will explain later, but there is a person in there whom I *cannot* encounter—I could not endure it—"

"What? Cannot endure a social meeting?"

"Please, ma'am. I am very sorry, but I cannot, I cannot."

"Oh, very well. I am no less sorry than you, and we are giving a grave insult to our hosts as well. What shall it be—a headache? A sudden indisposition?"

"Ma'am, please do not say anything to Lord and Lady Delingpole. Nobody will miss me, or know that I am gone."

"Ah, so now the truth will out. You are feeling most particularly creep mouse and insignificant. Well, we will discuss this later, Fanny Price. I shall send word to McIntosh to bring the carriage round."

Terrified that Mary Bertram might appear in the lobby, Fanny brushed past the persons entering at the front door, and watched anxiously from the portico for Donald McIntosh and the carriage. She urged Mrs. Butters not to sacrifice her own pleasure for her sake, and begged to be allowed to wait in the carriage until her benefactress was ready to leave the reception.

"I will tell McIntosh to drive you around the park and then come back for me in an hour. I hope you shall be warm enough. Up you go, Fanny—I begin to fear that perhaps you *are* falling ill. You are quite pale."

The horses slowly made several circuits of Hyde Park. No doubt anyone seeing the carriage would assume that it sheltered a loving couple enjoying a romantic *tête-à-tête*, not an unhappy, humiliated young woman sitting all alone. Fanny continued tormenting herself by re-visiting in her mind the scene she had witnessed at the Delingpoles and wondering what had come after, when Mary and William Gibson had walked out of sight. She feared Mr. Gibson would fall as completely under Mary's spell as Edmund had once done.

* * * * * * *

"Mr. Gibson, I must not continue to engross you. I promised to take you to Lord Mulgrave. He is exceedingly well-informed about the doings at the Admiralty. Thanks to my uncle, I am well acquainted with the highest ranks of the Navy, and I would be pleased to introduce you to anyone able to give you the particulars you seek."

"I am vastly obliged to you, ma'am. But will you not first do me the honour of introducing yourself, before I meet Lord Mulgrave?"

"Oh! In my vanity, I thought you knew who I am. I am such a particular friend of Lady Delingpole, that I supposed she had already drawn my portrait for you. I am Mary Bertram."

"I am your servant, ma'am. May I ask, are you related to the Northamptonshire Bertrams? Of Mansfield Park?"

"Indeed, sir. By marriage."

Mr. Gibson tried to maintain his friendly composure, but for him, the name "Bertram," meant the family who he suspected of bullying and mistreating his friend Miss Price, when she was a child. He realized his arm, which was supporting the lady's hand, grew rigid beneath her fingers. She gracefully withdrew it, and snapped open her fan.

"Indeed." Mr. Gibson said after a moment's silence. "Well. Indeed. And I trust that they are all—that is—I have the honour of being acquainted with some relations of yours. Miss Price and her brother, the lieutenant."

"Do you indeed?"

"Yes," answered William. "Indeed. Yes."

He waited for the lady to speak again.

"Pray, Mr. Gibson, how long have you known little Miss Price? Did you meet her while you were in Portsmouth? Her family resides there. Her mother made a most imprudent marriage, you know."

"An unfortunate marriage, you say, ma'am? A lesson for the rest of us, perhaps."

"I should caution you, Mr. Gibson, that Miss Price's true character is not soon understood. Fortunately for her, she possesses the ability of appearing to be the embodiment of wounded innocence. I have come to deeply regret my acquaintance with her. Were you aware of her involvement in an episode involving my late brother, almost two years ago?"

"Yes, I was ma'am, and may I say, I am very sorry for your tragic loss."

Mr. Gibson wondered if his fair companion intended to lay all the blame for Henry Crawford's misdeeds—his seduction of a girl of respectable family, his refusal to marry her, and his reckless driving—on Fanny! He was curious to hear Mary Bertram's version of the tragedy, but he also expected to see Mrs. Butters and Fanny appear at the gathering at every moment. He added, "I happen to know that Miss Price is highly remorseful, and blames herself for circumstances which, in all candour, cannot with justice be laid at her feet."

"You have your version of events from Miss Price directly, I suppose?"

"As well, I am a writer, ma'am, and as such, have a hunger for accurate information."

"There *is* more to the story, Mr. Gibson, and were it not for my own pride and my sense of what I owe to my family, I would confide in you."

"Indeed, ma'am, you are quite right in not unfolding so much to a scribbler, and *that* on such short acquaintance. I honour your discretion. Perhaps we will have the pleasure of speaking again in the future. How long will you be residing in London, ma'am? Do you divide your time between town and Mansfield?"

"I *will* take you into my confidence on that head, Mr. Gibson, as it is no secret amongst my friends. I am an exile. I am forbidden to return to my home in Northamptonshire." Mary looked about her, then moved closer, standing on tiptoe and almost whispering into the writer's ear.

"My husband has written to tell me that so long as his sister Julia remains unmarried, he forbids me his roof."

"How eccentric of him! Are you to be looking out for a husband for her, then?"

Mary laughed. "I should be pleased to interview any applicants for the post. Miss Julia Bertram is a handsome, accomplished young lady, and will make someone a very good wife, to be sure."

"Splendid, there should be no difficulty there. With you to champion her cause and with her own attractions, she is certain to make some fortunate gentleman happy before long."

"Attractions or no, depend upon it, her father will insist she make an advantageous match. The family must repair their fortunes, after the unfortunate incident—oh, but of course you know all about it. *Your* ship intercepted Sir Thomas' slave ship, did it not?"

"That is to say, the ship on which I served. Although I understand that Sir Thomas Bertram had been deceived by his business partners, for he was told the *Clementine* was transporting palm oil. We may at least acquit him of attempting to flout the ban on trading slaves."

"True, true. But the result is, Miss Julia Bertram is now for sale to the highest bidder. If you knew Sir Thomas, you would understand he would not recognize the irony in selling his *daughter* now that he has been debarred from selling *Negroes*."

Mr. Gibson was a particular confidant of Lieutenant William Price, and he knew the private hopes his friend cherished in regard to Julia Bertram. He could not help asking, "So, an alliance with a navy lieutenant of unblemished courage, enterprise and character, for example, would not satisfy Miss Bertram's family?"

"Fortune, Mr. Gibson, more than rank or title or even character, is what is wanted here."

Her companion nodded his head in acknowledgement of the ways of the world. "Well, perhaps the disposal of Miss Bertram's hand is best left with her parents, who are older and wiser. No doubt Sir Thomas feels that young people do not always choose so well for themselves. Now, ma'am, if we have exhausted this topic, may I request that introduction to the First Lord?"

Fanny shrank down into one corner of the carriage as Donald McIntosh returned from the park to retrieve Mrs. Butters. She greatly feared being noticed by anyone. But to her chagrin, Mr. Gibson himself opened the carriage door and exclaimed, "There you are, Miss Price! I had been watching for you! Mrs. Butters informs me you are feeling unwell. I am sorry to hear it."

"I am—-I am not—-I am quite recovered, thank you, Mr. Gibson," she managed, and then turned her head to look out of the opposite window. She still lacked the self-command to greet him with her usual warmth, and the realization that she must have sounded unfriendly, threw her into even greater confusion and embarrassment.

Mr. Gibson stepped back to assist Mrs. Butters into her coach (a manoeuvre which called for both muscular strength and discretion), and Fanny was preparing to bid him 'good-bye,' when she became aware that he was climbing in himself!

"We are going to first take Mr. Gibson to his lodgings," Mrs. Butters explained. "I trust this will not inconvenience you, Fanny?"

"Oh! Oh! Madam....by no means," Fanny stammered, huddling into her shawl so that it covered her bosom, acutely aware of Mr. Gibson's presence beside her on the seat. Her mind was a blank— she could think of no innocent topic to bring forward. If she asked if he had enjoyed the reception, she might receive information she would rather not hear.

An awkward silence, punctuated by the clip-clop of the horses' hoofs, continued for what seemed to Fanny to be an eternity as she continued to resolutely stare out of the window. Finally, Mr. Gibson asked Mrs. Butters "if she had passed a pleasant time?"

"Oh yes! And dear Mrs. Wakefield introduced me to some new acquaintance. You remember Mrs. Wakefield, Mr. Gibson. A very good woman, I wish I had her industry and zeal. Or, her industry at any rate—I should just as soon not have her piety! I would not want to disapprove of half of the things she disapproves of! It is too tiring altogether! But the crush of people was, perhaps, excessive. So many in attendance! It is a fine thing for *you*, is it not, Mr. Gibson? I made sure of telling everyone they had better purchase your book."

Mr. Gibson laughed. "You are my fiercest advocate, ma'am."

Fanny listened as the two chatted amicably, until the carriage reached Covent Garden, and Mr. Gibson asked to be let out at the corner, so that he might find some supper before returning to his lodgings.

"Good bye, then, Mrs. Butters. Thank you. Good-bye... Miss Price."

"Good-bye, Mr. Gibson."

And he was gone.

Mrs. Butters frowned. "I may as well tell you Fanny, that Mrs. Wakefield was particularly disappointed when I told her you were not attending after all, because she intended for her acquaintance to see your new gown, so that we might find more customers for the academy."

Fanny gasped, conscience-stricken. "Oh, no! I had not thought of that. I am so very sorry, so...."

"'Sorry' butters no parsnips, Fanny. What afflicted you so suddenly? You were in excellent spirits before we arrived."

And Fanny explained about Mary Bertram, and to her great consolation, Mrs. Butters immediately softened her severe expression, and took her hand, and exclaimed: "Ah! Of course! I had forgotten Mary Crawford's mother was Lady Delingpole's first and dearest friend, when she came from Ireland. For the sake of Elena Crawford's memory, she will never throw off the daughter."

"At any rate, the sudden surprise of seeing her, seeing her there" —Fanny was about to say, "with Mr. Gibson," but checked herself, while blushing furiously— "I was quite unprepared, I did not have the presence of mind to encounter her. And I should add, I know she bears the greatest resentment toward me, for the death of her brother."

Mrs. Butters sniffed. "Mr. Crawford drove like a reckless fool and overturned his carriage. How are you to be blamed for his folly?"

"Ah, ma'am, you know the dreadful misunderstanding which occurred! I can never stop reproaching myself on that account. And it is no wonder that Mary seeks to excuse her brother, and throw the blame elsewhere. How partial we can all be, and ill-judging, when it comes to defending the persons we love. Mary Bertram and I will never be friends, I fear."

"Well, child, I am sorry I was so vexed with you. I do understand how awkward it would have been. Let us forget the entire business."

Fanny thanked her profusely, they reached Stoke Newington, and the beautiful gown was packed away for another, and hopefully more successful, trial of its powers to enchant admiring gentlemen. Fanny requested a hot bath in her room, and then went to bed without supper.

Images of Mary Bertram, gazing up at Mr. Gibson, haunted her dreams. And what was even more disturbing, the sight of the sister stirred up long-buried images of Henry Crawford.

Fanny dreamt she was back at Everingham in Norfolk, and she and Henry were sitting by the fireplace. That much *had* occurred in real life, but in her dream, unlike in reality, Henry was sitting next to her, looking at her in a most insinuating fashion, with his familiar insolent smile. He was not handsome—she had never thought him handsome—but he was graceful and well made and the intensity of his gaze was unsettling. He reached out and traced the outline of her jaw, then slid his hand around the back of her neck. Fanny tried to move away, but her limbs were as lead—she was unable to move or resist as he drew her to him.

"Your skin is so soft, Fanny," he murmured. "The blush rises to your cheek at my slightest touch. Did you know, you are very pretty, indeed?" His finger traced her delicate collarbone, then trailed down to the gentle rise of her bosom. "So soft. Here. And here."

"Mr. Crawford, pray, stop." Fanny whispered, her breath catching in her throat.

He laid his hand on one breast.

"What's this? What do I feel? A wildly fluttering little heart? Afraid?" Crawford's lips brushed her ear as he whispered, "Come, my timid little girl. You long to know, do you not? Allow me to show you."

She turned her head away from him, and tried to will her arms and legs to move. He kissed her cheek, her jaw, and intimately nuzzled her neck. She could hear his ragged breath as his warm hands slowly slid her gown off one shoulder, then the other.

"Ah, Fanny. You are truly lovely."

With a painful, desperate effort, Fanny pushed him away, and awoke with a gasp, with the most peculiar sensations flooding through her, so that she could hardly meet the eyes of the housemaid who came in soon after to help her dress.

CHAPTER SIX

DEAR COUSIN EDMUND,

The Crocodile *is making for Portsmouth. We stop over in Gibraltar, so this note may reach you by packet before I return to England. In any case, I shall write again to confirm my safe arrival, and to repeat the message I am sending in this letter.*

As you know, many of our crewmen have died, owing to the fevers and plagues of Africa. To this list I must add, with the greatest sorrow, our well-respected commander, Capt. Columbine. He always treated me in a most kind and fatherly fashion, and I feel his loss exceedingly.

When our poor Captain became so ill he was unable to carry out his duties in Sierra Leone, he resigned the governorship and we took ship for England, but he passed away last night, and we have just sent his body to the deep. His wife and little daughter died in Africa.

My heart is full as I write, and the deepest sorrow overpowers me. Cousin Edmund, whatever were once my wishes, and my hopes, the example of Captain Columbine and his family has brought home to me the conviction that the risks and dangers facing any lady who marries a naval officer are so considerable, that her friends ought to caution her against it. Furthermore, no man of sense or humanity would want to visit such miseries on the head of the woman he loved and esteemed.

This was my late Captain's advice to me, cousin Edmund, almost his last words, and I intend to take them to heart.

How would it be an act of love to ask a lady to wait, in anxiety and loneliness, while her husband engages in war? For her to be a wife only in name, for perhaps years at a time? Nor could I imagine placing any woman, least of all one I loved, in the path of danger.

You will therefore understand my reasons for continuing in bachelorhood and denying myself the happiness of matrimony. Believe me most sincerely, it is not so I may avoid pain and unhappiness, but so that I do not inflict either on someone I most tenderly love and treasure.

I send you all my sincere prayers for your continued health and happiness.

I have the honour to remain, Sir,

Your obedient servant and friend,
Cousin William

Edmund sat at the breakfast table, with William's letter in his hands, thankful that Julia had slept late that morning, as it gave him time to harden himself to the necessity of telling her that her lieutenant—the man she dreamt of and waited for—would not be coming to claim her.

He decided it would be better to give her William's note to read for herself. Solitude would be her best friend in her first effusions of sorrow; his sympathy would be her surest comfort in the days to come, but, when the news first broke upon her, he did not wish to force her into restraint. Accordingly, later that day, he pressed the note into her hand, kissed her forehead, and assured her that he was nearby in the event she wished to speak with him.

Hours passed. Julia did not come downstairs for dinner, and a tray left outside her room remained untouched. The household did not see her until night had fallen, and Edmund was sitting by the fire, with just a few candles to keep the darkness at bay, when Julia entered the drawing room, quiet and composed, but with reddened eyes.

"This letter, Edmund, this letter, it is in William's hand, but these are not his words. He cannot be in earnest, he cannot intend to be so cruel to me."

"What shall you do, Julia? Do you wish me to answer William's letter? What do you wish me to say?"

"Edmund, I hope you will not think less of me, if I say these ridiculous, stupid conventions which prevent me from speaking plainly, directly and from the heart to the—to the person who loves me—these ideas are artificial and absurd. I suppose I am expected to say nothing, and to go up to my room, and do my needlework, and never, never, attempt to change his mind." Julia grew angrier as she spoke; her eyes flashed, and she paced up and down, speaking in a fierce whisper so that the servants should not overhear.

"Well then, Julia—speaking plainly, can you think of any reason why we should not go to Portsmouth? I can write to our Aunt Price, and say we are coming for a brief visit to pay our respects. You have never met her, and I am sure you would wish to make her acquaintance and to meet the rest of the family. Susan would be happy to receive a visit from you, no doubt."

Julia stopped her pacing and stared at her brother with wild surmise and dawning hope.

"You would not object to being absent on a Sunday?"

"I daresay my parishioners would not. A little variety would be interesting for them. I will ask my friend Richard Owen to fill the pulpit for me."

"Indeed, I'm sure Mr. Owen would enjoy some time in the countryside exceedingly!"

"I only hope he will consent to let me pay him a fee for his services—he is very much in need of it, but he may feel some awkwardness in taking monies from a friend."

"You can pay his travelling expenses, at least, and see that Mrs. Peckover feeds him well. And why do you not invite his sisters as well? They can use my room while I am away. As I recall, you said the Miss Owens are excellent singers—very accomplished." And Julia continued to enumerate all the reasons why it was desirable that the Owens should enjoy a brief sojourn in the countryside—fishing—long walks—horse-riding—country air—until it appeared that she and Edmund were removing themselves to Portsmouth for their friends' benefit.

"We are agreed, I think," Edmund concluded. "I will speak to Mrs. Peckover about it. So, would you like to go to Portsmouth with me?"

Julia knelt at Edmund's side, and laid her head in his lap.

"Dear, dear Edmund. My excellent brother! In spite of everything that has happened to you, you are still a friend of forlorn hopes. Take me to Portsmouth, please."

*   *   *   *   *   *   *

Autumn had never been a favourite time of year with Fanny Price. Of course the changing colours of the season were delightful, especially at Mansfield Park. In Camden Town it was a different matter. September brought mud, and dark clouds, rain, and more rain. But her dislike of autumn was not owing to the weather, or the lack of sunshine. It was rather that, during her childhood, the end of summer signalled the departure of her cousin Edmund for school,

74

and she would be without his company, often until the Christmas holidays. She associated the shortening days and the lengthening nights with loss, and loneliness and had to struggle against a tendency to lowness of spirits.

Her friend William Gibson did not call upon them at Mrs. Butters' house so frequently as they could wish, for he was almost entirely taken up with reporting and writing for the political periodicals, and spent most of his days in the gallery at the Parliament and his evenings penning long articles in his modest lodgings. He had sent several friendly notes, but she had not seen him, in fact, since the disastrous encounter at Lady Delingpole's reception. She wished that Mrs. Butters might think of taking a trip into London, especially to meet with their friends, but she was too timid to propose it, and the older lady was disinclined to go anywhere in the pelting rain, preferring to nurse her aching joints by the fire at home.

Fanny was not the only one whose prospects were blighted by the inclement weather. Inexperienced as she was in mercantile affairs, she could not help but observe that matters were not faring well on the first floor. Fashionable ladies were putting aside their summer muslins in favour of silk and velvet, but few of them chose to make the journey from London to Camden Town. The decline in revenue was a source of anxiety for everyone, as the continued existence of the academy depended upon the success of the dressmakers' shop.

Fanny, thinking of how she had made doll's clothes out of small pieces of discarded fabric in Bristol, asked Mrs. Blodgett for the trimmings of silk, lace, and ribbon from the third floor, for her pupils.

"And why should we do that, Miss Price? We sell them to the rag-man, and we need every shilling."

"If I had the scraps of silk and bombazine, I could give them to the girls to practise upon before we entrust them with an entire skirt panel. And, we could make doll's clothing with the thinner fabrics. A piece of fabric, sold to the rag man, is worth only a penny to the pound, but if we were to make doll's clothing—"

"No one has requested any doll's clothing."

"I meant to suggest, ma'am, the doll's clothing be put up for sale, as a —"

"Who buys doll's clothing? I am sure I never did."

"But I believe, ma'am, that you had no daughters?"

Mrs. Blodgett frowned. "We have not enough students to be setting them to additional work. Usually two or three girls are missing every day, complaining of illness, or their mothers are lying-in and they are needed at home, and so forth."

Fanny was silenced, and went off to meditate on the inconvenience and vexation of working with someone who always said 'no' to any new proposal—until it suddenly struck her that, she herself had also been described by her cousins, as just such a person! The thought surprised and humbled her, and she resolved to be more patient with Mrs. Blodgett, and firmer with herself.

* * * * * * *

When Mary Crawford Bertram visited her friends in London, she was under the necessity of satisfying those vulgarly curious persons who enquired about her long separation from her husband. This she did by hinting at the tragic reasons she had fled from Northamptonshire—reasons which delicacy forbade her to broach. Her wistful countenance, her tremulous voice, her averted gaze, her insinuation that there was more to be told, could she bear to tell it—all served to leave the intended impression. Many persons—particularly those who had never met Edmund Bertram—concluded she must be the injured party, and pitied the beautiful young wife, who was able to effect her independence because she had kept control of her own fortune upon marriage.

Now, Mary's acquaintance buzzed with the news that she had lately received, after a long silence, a brief, cold letter from her husband the clergyman, forbidding her to come home until Miss Julia Bertram were married.

"Miss Julia Bertram has a tolerable dowry, but nothing out of the ordinary," Mary confided. "She is still a beauty, though approaching three-and-twenty. She is the daughter of a baronet—although the name is *somewhat* tarnished. Her sister Maria threw herself at my poor brother and disgraced herself, and then her father lost his fortune.

"Rich tradesmen are the natural prey of girls in Miss Bertram's situation. There are no small number of men who, having secured their fortunes through trade, seek to acquire a gloss, a polish, on their unfortunate origins. It would be folly, absolute folly, for Julia to give her hand to anyone for less than three thousand a year, and *I* am inclined to believe she could find a mill-owner or merchant with an even heavier purse, especially if she is not exacting as to his youth or appearance. In fact, *entre nous*, the older the better— look at my friend Janet Fraser! Only a few years more, and she will be wearing black ribbons, I think, and a very wealthy widow she will be!

"My friend Julia should do very well for herself. I am only saying what all the world knows, except for foolish girls who read novels."

This latest embellishment concerning her in-laws, her new assertion that the Bertrams sought a mercenary match for their daughter, aroused no scepticism amongst her friends.

Mary Bertram could still command a home with her friend Janet Fraser whenever she was in London. Janet had captivated the widowed Mr. Fraser four years before, but choosing a much younger lady for his second wife had not, as he perhaps intended, successfully arrested the passage of time. Mrs. Fraser lived for society, bustle, and consequence, and showed no indication of tiring of London life; her husband more and more came to prefer their quiet country home in Twickenham. He complained of her extravagant spending and her flirtations, while she protested that she did not make allowance for her vivacity and youth.

Mrs. Janet Fraser's step-daughter Margaret, as yet unmarried, and viewed without disguise by Mrs. Fraser as an encumbrance, was another source of discontent in the union. Margaret, an earnest, bashful young lady, was only two years younger than Janet's friend Mary Bertram, but worlds apart in sophistication and ease of address.

Since Margaret was no sparkling wit, and was too short and plump to appear to advantage in a ballroom, Mrs. Fraser held her step-daughter very cheap, and noisily despaired of Margaret's ever making a good alliance, however many balls or soirees the girl was dragged to. It was a grievance Janet Fraser resorted to frequently, even when her friend Mary was sitting at her harp.

"Ah, Mary, if only Mr. Fraser had consented for Margaret and me to stay with you in Brighton," Janet exclaimed. "I told him it was for Margaret's sake! We might have found her a husband!"

"I could hardly have exerted myself for her in Brighton," replied Mary, placing her hands flat against her harp strings to silence them, "for I was excessively unwell the entire time I was there. Lord Elsham was so insistent I should go, but I have inherited my late aunt's prejudice against the sea. The sea air—which everyone claims to find so invigorating—is vile! Rotting mussels and seaweed! Why not bring Margaret to Bath instead? There we may husband-hunt in some comfort."

"You know why not—Mr. Fraser, that tiresome man, refuses to stir anywhere, not even to Bath, which might do *him* some good. But, so soon as I propose a thing, he is certain to refuse it."

"You have made the most elementary error, Janet, in promoting the scheme yourself. I blush for your simplicity. Ask his physician to advise it to him, ask one of his friends, ask his valet, ask the man who lights the street lamps, and he will be ordering the carriage 'round. He will be announcing it to *you* — 'we had much better go to Bath, Janet,' —even if he directly refused you, his own wife, a fortnight before. I believe this rule was formulated by Mr. Newton, or it ought to have been, because it is just as reliable as one of his theorems."

"Until then, Mary, and now that you are back, you must help me take Margaret about. Could you not display her at Lady Delingpole's weekly receptions?"

"I did not realize our little Margaret was interested in political gatherings."

"Who cares what might interest her? Whig or Tory, what does it matter? I have had word of a gentleman newly arrived in town, from Bristol—a Mr. Meriwether. He is a widower, with a very handsome fortune. In the wine trade, I believe. He is making a lengthy stay in London and my friends tell me he is looking for a wife!"

"Janet! What luck!"

"Please watch out for him, and make his acquaintance if you can."

"Of course, my dear Janet. It would be my pleasure to help in any way I can."

"How glad I am to have you back in London, Mary! I began to be quite jealous of your friendship with Lady Delingpole, and suspected you loved her more than me."

"Well, supposing I do, dear Janet, you will be happy to know that Lady Delingpole has no plans to return to Wales until next summer, and therefore cannot tempt me away from you."

Mrs. Fraser smiled. "You will not be surprised when I hint to you, that some persons wonder if *Lord* Delingpole does not admire you even more than his wife does."

Mary laughed. "Only someone unacquainted with Lord and Lady Delingpole could surmise such a thing. I do not object to gossip, but there should be some ingenuity behind it. This is the laziest sort of speculation. Simply because I spent several months in Wales—"

"More than *several* months!"

"Very well, but I do assure you that the chief attraction for me is not dear old Lord Delingpole."

"Did I say that? Don't be so cunning, Mary. I hinted that you are a prime attraction for *him*."

"Oh! Of course he admires me. But no more than I require, I assure you. Shall I disappoint you dreadfully if I confess that, while in Wales, I devoted myself to the serious study and collection of Welsh harp music. As I would be happy to demonstrate. This piece is called 'Morfa Rhuddlan'."

* * * * * * *

The younger Mrs. Butters continued to be a frequent patron of the academy, if "patron" was a fit description for someone who did not expect to pay for the services she enjoyed. In addition to wanting a full wardrobe of riding habits and pelisses, as well as the usual morning frocks and evening gowns any lady requires to make a creditable appearance, she had three young daughters who were growing rapidly, and they needed new clothes and alterations not infrequently.

Fanny was not surprised to observe that generosity was not met with gratitude. Cecilia Butters held the view that since 'the work was done by charity cases,' the cost must be negligible.

Fanny was personally altering a bodice which Mrs. Butters had brought back, with the complaint that it was ill-fitting, when Mrs. Blodgett entered the classroom with a busy clacking of heels and a breathless air.

"Oh, what do you think, Miss Price! The Prime Minister's wife and a deputation of Tory ladies will be visiting us in a se'ennight, to examine the good work we do here! Mrs. Perceval herself! Think of it! How excellent this will be for drawing business our way!"

"How wonderful, ma'am," answered Fanny, rising from her seat. "There must be a great deal you wish to do in preparation."

"Indeed, indeed! How can we obtain some flowers to decorate the room? They will be so dear at this time of the year, and we cannot appear to be wasteful and extravagant! And refreshments— we must have refreshments! Oh, heavens!"

"Perhaps there ought to be an oration, an address of welcome," suggested Mr. Edifice, who, as usual, had found some reason to linger after his morning's labours were done. "With some flattering allusions to Mrs. Perceval, from the classical authors, as representing the spirit of Benevolence. Or Athena—she was the patron goddess of needlework, as perhaps you were aware, Miss Price."

"Yes!" exclaimed Mrs. Blodgett. "What a fine suggestion, Mr. Edifice! My husband can give a welcoming address to Mrs. Perceval when she arrives. And we must have all the members of the ladies committee here, of course. We need to let them know straight away, Miss Price! Oh! But what to do about the flowers!"

"Mrs. Blodgett, if you will permit the academy to use all the trimmings of fabric and ribbon from the cutting room, I believe I can instruct the girls in making artificial flowers. And ma'am, you may recall that I wished to use the scraps to make—"

"Yes, yes, Miss Price, if the work is done well enough. We have not much time to prepare, so see to it immediately!"

So Fanny went to work, showing her students how to make artificial flowers with paper and taffeta to transform the schoolroom, sewing decorative sashes for the committee ladies, and explaining to her students what a Prime Minister was.

From the charitable ladies came the proposal that the pupils sing 'Rule, Britannia' but only one trial of their abilities was necessary to establish that, while a few of the girls could carry a tune, the majority sang badly or not at all.

"Well, this is most disappointing, girls," sighed Mrs. Blodgett. "I do wish we could have something more by way of entertainment. Mrs. Perceval is also bringing some of her young daughters with her as well."

Instead of a musical interlude, Mrs. Blodgett accepted the kind offer of Cecilia Butters that she and her daughters display themselves, wearing the fashionable attire made for them at the academy. There was, alas, insufficient time to prepare entirely new ensembles, but Cecilia Butters consented to choose something from her wardrobe, and her daughters likewise.

Mrs. Butters and Mr. Gibson were to attend on the day; she as an honoured founder of the academy, and he to report on the proceedings for the Society for Bettering the Condition and Increasing the Comforts of the Poor. Fanny was determined to make amends for her unfriendly behaviour on the last occasion she had seen Mr. Gibson—the disastrous reception at the Delingpoles—and her pleasure at the thought of seeing her friend, more than overbalanced any anxieties she felt about the visit of so august a person as Mrs. Perceval.

CHAPTER SEVEN

MR. AND MRS. PRICE eagerly anticipated the arrival of their oldest son, William, and in particular, they looked forward to showing him their copy of *Amongst the Slavers,* sent to them by the author himself, and inscribed "For Miss Betsey Price, my fellow story-teller, with kind regards, Wm. Gibson," on the flyleaf. In this precious volume their boy was immortalized.

When the book was not in Susan's hands—for she was often called upon to read the passages involving William aloud to the family circle—it rested in a place of honour on the mantelpiece and was pointed out to every visitor, no matter how many times that same visitor entered the parlour.

"And to think, when William brought Mr. Gibson in from the *Derwent*, as yellow as butter and thin as a skeleton, I packed him upstairs to the attic!" exclaimed Mrs. Price regretfully. "If I had known he was going to become famous, and say so many handsome things about our William, I would have turned Tom out of his bed for him, you may be sure."

"This should do our boy no harm at the Admiralty," Mr. Price reflected with satisfaction. "This fellow Gibson has run up the signals for William, very handsomely."

Mr. Gibson had remained in Betsey's memory as the most unusual adult she had ever met, because during the time of his convalescence in the attic, he spoke to her courteously, listened to her politely, and regaled her with tales of Africa and monkeys and crocodiles. She had been a most indifferent student, but when Mr. Gibson's book arrived, she applied herself to learning how to read, so she could make out Mr. Gibson's inscription for herself.

Wanting for nothing to experience perfect felicity but the return of her favourite son, Mrs. Price was surprised and vexed to receive a letter from her nephew Edmund Bertram, announcing an intended visit from himself and his sister Julia, to pay their respects to her. This surprise provoked more than it than gratified, as her niece and nephew would be underfoot just as William's ship was expected to return! As she expostulated aloud on the inconveniences and undoubted expense entailed by this un-looked honour, she noticed a conscious look crossing Susan's face. Mrs. Price pounced on the girl, and would not relent until Susan confessed William's affection for his fair cousin.

Let any romantically-minded reader who might censure a girl of sixteen for betraying her brother's secret, remind themselves that they never spent an evening unable to escape a poky little parlour and the tireless questioning of a Mrs. Price.

*   *   *   *   *   *   *

The appointed day, upon which so many solicitudes, alarms and vexations had been expended, finally dawned. The charitable ladies, the Blodgetts, Mrs. Butters, her daughter-in-law and her grandchildren were all assembled in the shop. As a light but persistent rain had fallen all morning, Mr. Blodgett, Mr. Edifice and Mr. Gibson waited outside with large umbrellas to assist the guests upon their arrival.

The sympathetic reader no doubt will share in the quiet exultation felt that morning by Mr. Edifice, for, despite the preference given him by his wife, Mr. Blodgett declined all ambition for rhetorical greatness and resigned the honour to the curate, and so the danger that Mrs. Perceval and her entourage would be greeted by a second-rate orator, was happily averted.

"Unfortunately, Miss Price is not permitted to listen to the address with us," Mr. Edifice remarked to Mr. Gibson, as he looked over his notes one last time. "Mrs. Blodgett thought it best for Miss Price and her pupils to remain upstairs, so as not to overcrowd the shop. I did show her the early drafts of my speech and she was most encouraging. I know it would have given her no small degree of satisfaction to hear the finished effort."

"I do not doubt it, sir."

"Of course," Mr. Edifice smirked, "I could not venture to say whether she most admires the *speech* or the *speaker*, for she has more than once commended me on my vocal abilities. I have the happy knack of being able to raise my voice for extended periods, without succumbing to hoarseness."

"You should feel all the compliment of it, sir, for Miss Price is a most discerning critic."

"She is, isn't she? You will not find me to be one of those men who hold that the acquirement of knowledge is unnecessary or even undesirable in females, Mr. Gibson. Of course, there are limits, there are boundaries, but, as the young ladies of our nation will be, in the fullness of time, our helpmeets, our wives and the mothers of our children, they must not be entirely ignorant."

"An enlightened viewpoint, indeed, sir."

"Naturally, Mr. Gibson," the curate added, moving yet further away from the others, and lowering his voice confidentially, "in choosing such a companion, any gentleman would need to rationally consider the fact that Miss Price, however amiable, possesses only a small inheritance of three thousand pounds. There are good connections on her mother's side, but her father is merely a lieutenant of marines."

Can Fanny possibly be entertaining thoughts of this fellow? Can he be forming designs on her? Mr. Gibson thought irritably to himself, and ventured: "But good connections alone will not provide the means for embarking on married life, will they, Mr. Edifice. I quite agree with you, sir, it would be folly for any self-respecting gentleman to form an alliance that was ill-supported financially. Pure folly."

"There is another possibility which you may have overlooked, Mr. Gibson," another quick glance over his shoulder— "in my opinion, Miss Price might expect to be enriched from another connection. Her patroness, Mrs. Butters, is exceedingly attached to her."

"Ah, so you have some information?"

"I do not know it for a fact, Mr. Gibson, but it is not at all unlikely, in my view, that Miss Price may build upon some fair prospects there."

"Has Miss Price herself hinted this to you?"

"Oh, heavens no! No, no, not at all. You cannot be so well acquainted with Miss Price as I, otherwise you would know her notions of propriety are so very strict that she would never allude to such a thing. I only speak of what I have observed, and have inferred. I only say, I think it is quite probable, and as more and more time passes, it will only become more probable—in fact, I may say, expected—by their mutual acquaintance."

"Mrs. Butters *is*— but here sir, I think I behold the arrival of our distinguished guests. Do not permit me to abstract you any longer. The *éclat* of our proceedings rests very much upon your shoulders, I think."

A small procession of carriages drew the august visitors to the doors of the academy just as the men finished their private colloquy—which was not entirely private as Ethelinda, the eldest of Cecilia Butters' three daughters, wishing to be the first to see the Prime Minister's wife, had also waited outside the shop and so had overheard the conversation.

Jane Perceval, accompanied by two daughters out of her numerous family, along with an equerry and several other wives and sisters of distinguished parliamentarians, were bowed across the threshold.

"Madam," Mr. Edifice began, "It is impossible to receive so signal an honour—"

"*Hssst!* Mr. Edifice! Wait until she is seated!"

Having shushed the curate, Mrs. Blodgett directed her husband to escort Mrs. Perceval to a chair which had been thickly festooned with fabric rosettes. The lady seated herself and looked around, with an encouraging smile.

"Ahem! Madam, it is impossible to receive so signal an honour as that which has been conferred upon us, and not experience the warmest sensations that gratitude can inspire. Distinguished as you are, by every virtue which can do honour, and add lustre to your rank, compassion for the disadvantaged is by no means the least amiable or prominent feature in your truly estimable character. Indeed, the words of the poet are very apt here: *Non minus sanctitate quam genere nobilis*, 'no less good than great.'

"Just as Athena, the exemplar of wisdom and womanly virtues, who, rendered by the artist's hand in eloquent marble, presided over her temple in the city which bears her name, so, indeed, we invite you to preside, as our very own patroness of the needle arts, over the city of Camden—which unfortunately does not bear your name—but Camden, we are told by the antiquarians, must take its meaning from the Latin, *campus*, meaning, *field*, and therefore we may draw the parallel between pastoral fields, and fields of industry, and the strewing of benevolence, further tended by the charitable exertions of the Society..."

Mrs. Perceval listened with every show of sincere attention, but a more discerning orator than Mr. Edifice might have perceived that his audience was beginning to stray as he moved from invoking Athena, and went on to the Nine Muses and the Three Graces and the Vestal Virgins and Britannia. Madame Orly was hopping back and forth from one foot to the other, for her boots were pinching her toes, and little Isabella Butters wanted a glass of water, and Mr. Blodgett had stopped listening altogether and was thinking about fishing, until finally an especially ornate rhetorical flourish from Mr. Edifice signalled to his listeners that his address was reaching its conclusion.

"...We are justly fearful, ma'am, lest we offend your modesty by expressing the character of your worth. We foresee also how needless any encomium will be of your merit. You have most excellently deigned to take notice of the humble efforts of the Camden Town chapter of the Society for Bettering the Condition and Increasing the Comforts of the Poor, and it is our most fervent wish that you will be pleased with what you find here at Blodgett's Sewing Academy."

Upstairs, Fanny and Matron could hear the low babble of voices through the floorboards. They heard the sonorous tones of Mr. Edifice, and the polite applause which followed. Then, Fanny knew, Mrs. Perceval would be invited to admire Cecilia Butters and her three daughters. And soon after, the prime minister's wife would be among them! She smiled and gestured to her pupils to be quiet and listen carefully for the applause and sounds of admiration as the three Butters girls each came forward in turn to curtsey to the visiting dignitaries. Unseen by the waiting students above, Ethelinda and Rosamunde displayed their pretty frocks, and little Isabella was a charming miniature of her mother in a riding habit. But Fanny had arranged for an additional surprise—the Butters girls presented a doll, dressed in the latest fashions, to each of Mrs. Perceval's daughters, a gift that had been prepared by Fanny and her pupils.

Fanny was gratified to hear a general hubbub, female voices predominating. Something, or perhaps everything, was meeting with great approbation below.

After a few moments, a shuffling of feet and a shifting of chairs signalled the end of the ceremonial portion of the program. Matron, unable to hold still for nerves, slipped upstairs to the cutting room to confirm everything was in readiness—spotless white cloths laid upon the cutting tables, all covered with cakes and fruit and sandwiches and cold chicken and soda water and punch, courtesy of Mrs. McIntosh and her housemaids.

The students were all commendably silent, listening intently for the tread on the staircase which would herald the arrival of Mrs. Perceval. Some of the girls had imagined that a prime minister's wife would wear a coronet and an ermine robe, or cloth of gold spangled with jewels, and more than one was quite disappointed when a petite and elegant woman, in perfectly ordinary and sombre clothing, at last appeared at the head of an equally staid entourage.

Mr. Edifice and Mr. Gibson brought up the end of the procession and stood next to Fanny. They had time only to exchange smiles and nods, before the doings of Mrs. Blodgett and Mrs. Perceval claimed their full attention.

Matron and Fanny were presented, and they curtsied, and Mrs. Perceval expressed her surprise that the charity employed only one teacher. "This young lady is your only sewing instructress, is that correct?"

"At present, ma'am, the returns from our enterprise do not allow of engaging more," explained Mrs. Blodgett, "but we trust, when more ladies visit our establishment and order their clothes from us, we will be in a position to employ more experienced teachers."

"Ah!" remarked Mrs. Perceval, as Fanny, being powerless to say anything, silently absorbed the slight. "The distance from the shopping district is something of a drawback, perhaps."

Mrs. Blodgett opened her mouth, as though to contradict the prime minister's wife, closed it again, and nodded submissively. "This way, then, ma'am."

Mrs. Blodgett had decided, for reasons which eluded Fanny, to show Mrs. Perceval the counting room and the embroidery frames and the cards of thread and every inanimate object in the place, before presenting the actual students to her.

"We have had this little dumbwaiter installed, which is very convenient for sending and receiving materials between the floors...."

"Your suggestion, as I recollect," Mr. Gibson whispered to Fanny.

"...and here, over here, ma'am, as you will observe, we have buckets of sand, always ready in the event of fire, in every corner of the room."

"These buckets? The large red ones, marked, 'Fire'?" Mrs. Perceval asked composedly, and Fanny and Mr. Gibson had to bite the insides of their cheeks.

Their honoured guest was at last free to turn her kindly gaze upon Fanny's pupils, and Fanny held her breath as Mrs. Perceval made her inspection, with a smile and a nod of her head for every little sempstress, from the tallest to the smallest, from the boldest to the most timid.

When the august visitor had completed her circuit of the classroom she was met by Tansy, the youngest student, who presented her with a small bouquet of silk violets tied together neatly with white ribbon. There could be heard amidst the ranks of the pupils, a soft intake of breath as Tansy commenced her low curtsey, and upon her successful re-ascent, two score girls exhaled in relief.

"Oh, how charming!" exclaimed the lady, admiring the bouquet. "These flowers are cunningly made indeed—I assume your students made them all! How well done! Their little fingers are so nimble!"

"And these lovely, colourful sashes," she added, addressing herself to Mrs. Blodgett, "which all of your committee ladies are wearing—these also were created by your students, were they not?"

"Indeed yes, ma'am," Mrs. Blodgett responded with visible pride. "Every sash is made of multiple pieces of fabric, as you can see, skilfully pieced together, and embroidered with a variety of stitches, spelling out the initials of our Society for Bettering the Condition and Improving the Comforts of the Poor. Our girls are perfecting their talents while making them, using the leftover scraps from our enterprise, and many are now sufficiently skilled to ornament the gowns for our customers."

"Very commendable, Mrs. Blodgett. Your program reflects great credit upon your instructress," Mrs. Perceval added, and this was accompanied by a kind smile and a nod of the head to Fanny.

Fanny curtsied, and could not help beaming at her students with pleasure and triumph. Something about Fanny's sweet smile appealed to Mrs. Perceval, and she took a step nearer to her and murmured, "You know, being in this place brings back many irresistible memories. Mr. Perceval and I began our married life together above a carpet shop, in a warehouse like this. How we froze in the wintertime!"

Fanny smiled and curtsied again, but Mr. Blodgett, standing nearby, whispered to Mr. Gibson, "And now they have a dozen children—not difficult to guess how Perceval kept the lady warm!"

Unfortunately Mr. Blodgett's voice, in the large, bare, high-ceilinged room, carried a little farther than he intended. Mrs. Blodgett shot her husband a piercing look.

"And if you will follow me, ma'am, we may now examine the upstairs cutting and sewing room, and then we will enjoy a cold collation. This way, Mrs. Perceval, ma'am."

CHAPTER EIGHT

IN THE TIME that had elapsed since Edmund Bertram's previous visit to his Price cousins, two more sons, Sam and Tom, were gone—Sam, to serve as a midshipman, while Tom was bound apprentice to an apothecary. Distressed as always for money, the Prices had removed themselves to smaller quarters. Susan and her younger sister Betsey shared a tiny garret bedroom, the door of which could not even be opened entirely because the bed blocked the way, and the room which served as both parlour and dining room barely accommodated their old table and chest of drawers. Mr. Price nevertheless took his same favourite spot in his armchair by the fireplace, and the servant had to push past him to get back and forth from the kitchen. Fortunately he spent his time abroad more often than at home, in the company of old comrades at the docks, but upon his return, his booming voice reached to the attic, in competition with the noise of Charles and little Betsey, who had never been taught to regulate their voices or their movements, to discriminate between being indoors and out.

Edmund still recollected the limited accommodation and unlimited anarchy of the Price household, and took rooms at the Crown for himself and his sister. No sooner did they arrive, however, than Julia clamoured to be escorted to her uncle's house. She had never been to Portsmouth and was determined to like it. She pronounced the dirt, the smells, and the noise to be 'colourful, boisterous and charming.' The winding streets through which Edmund escorted her, were 'quaint and interesting,' and the Price's home itself was 'cosy and home-like.'

Julia arrived with gifts; there was a tin of tea, and a large box of beeswax candles, and new bonnets for Susan and Betsey, and a book on navigation for young Charles, the last boy still at home. She received the kindest reception from her girl cousins. Susan was pleased to improve her friendship with Julia, and Betsey was in awe of the tall, fair-haired beauty. But alas! the salutation from her aunt Price, the woman she hoped to call her mother-in-law, was more restrained. There was no knowing glance, no special smile reserved just for her, no affectionate squeeze of her hand.

"This is very good of you, Miss Julia, I must say, to bring us these lovely little gifts," she said. "And I expect my sister Norris has a message or a parcel she has sent by you?"

"Indeed ma'am, we came away so quickly, we did not inform our Aunt. I am afraid we were very thoughtless," said Julia.

"Ha! She would have tried to travel as ballast with you, to save herself the cost of the fare! You did well to slip your cable so quietly, and have my hearty thanks for it," cried Mr. Price, who had vivid memories of a prolonged visit from his sister-in-law in the recent past.

After tea, Mr. Price offered to take Edmund for a tour of the docks, in a manner that did not allow for the possibility that his guest might not be interested, while Julia remained behind in the hopes of recommending herself to William's mother. She was taken aback, however, when Mrs. Price directly declared, "So, you fancy yourself in love with my William, do you?"

Susan, her face betraying a guilty conscience, dragged Betsey to the hallway to try on their new bonnets before the little mirror, and then led her outside. For Betsey, the pleasure of showing off her new bonnet before her friends won out, but narrowly, over her urge to crawl under the table to listen to the interesting conversation.

Alas, Julia would not find in Mrs. Price a champion of romantic attachments. Although Miss Frances Ward had disobliged her family to marry a lieutenant of marines, she did not endorse a similar course for her oldest and favourite child.

"I haven't forgotten, Miss Julia, what it is to be carried away by love. Nature plays a cruel trick on us, when we are young—our passions run so high..." Mrs. Price closed her eyes, briefly, remembering. "Happiness—very happy indeed, we were. Then came the hard times. Another baby every year. And opening your eyes in the morning, to the sound of a baby wailing in its cot, and the only thing you can think about is how in the name of heaven were you going to pay the bills and feed the children, the worry and the endless work, until you fall into bed exhausted at the close of the day."

"My dear Aunt Price... I hope that the help you received from my parents... My father's assistance... And of course, taking Fanny to live with us..."

But Mrs. Price was in a bitter mood and would not be placated. "Oh, yes, I was bewildered when they proposed to take *Fanny*, and not one of my boys. My oldest girl gone, and Susan barely old enough to fetch and carry. I was left with six small children, and another on the way, without Fanny to help me! You cannot begin to imagine! Well, Miss Julia, shall this be my reward—for you to steal William away from me as well?"

"Oh, but of course not, Aunt Price. I know he loves you exceedingly."

"When I was *your* age," continued Mrs. Price, ignoring her, "I never dreamt I would grow old one day. We none of us intend to. Once, I was considered to be something of a beauty, like yourself. Once, my hair was the same beautiful colour as yours. I had pretty dresses to wear, and a little pink parasol, trimmed with lace. And I went with my sisters to the assemblies at Northampton, in my white gown, and wearing little dancing slippers with rosettes on them. And I never sat down, let me tell you, for want of a partner.

"Yet, here I am, with half of my teeth out of my head and my back aching so badly that some mornings I can barely get out of bed. So please tell me, Miss Julia, if you take William from me, what am I to live upon in my old age, after losing my health in rearing up ten children? After I have buried my husband? Where shall I live? Where shall I go? If you have no consideration for poor old widows, I am sure my son William does! He knows what is due to his mother! He is the oldest son, and he will be the head of the household one day, responsible for Susan and Betsey as well, if I should lose Mr. Price."

Julia was mortified. In her world, money was simply something which flowed out of her father's purse, as needed. She and her brothers and sister were secure in the expectation of handsome dowries and settlements. In none of the genteel families of her acquaintance were the children responsible for the maintenance of the parents.

"But—but—I am sure dear Uncle Price is very hale, and you need not have any concerns on that score, Aunt Price? He looks very well, indeed," Julia said uncertainly, recalling her uncle's short, thick neck, the large bulbous nose marked with blue veins, and his ample belly. "And, should the worst occur, naturally my father would make some provision for you."

"How generous you are with other people's money! As though I had any expectations of your father!" Mrs. Price tossed her head proudly. "And my William will do very well for himself—if, that is, he does not make a foolish marriage.

"Tell me, miss, what can *you* do for my William? You cannot help him in his career—you have no relatives with influence at the Admiralty. Rather, you will only hold him back. You have some monies from your father, I suppose, but you will be used to living as a great lady, at a high expense, and your expectations will far exceed your income—you will plunge him into miserable debt."

"Aunt Price," Julia stammered and blushed. "Please, I am by no means extravagant in my expectations. A large income is not necessary for my happiness."

"No? Perhaps you should look carefully around you, before you decide how large an income is necessary for your happiness," Mrs. Price snapped.

Julia was very quiet when Edmund came to escort her back to the Crown Inn.

* * * * * * *

The *Crocodile* anchored safely at Portsmouth and the cold sleet and grey skies of England were a foretaste of paradise for the survivors of the journey. Thirty-four of the crewmen had perished of the fevers which haunted the African coast. William Price became first lieutenant when Captain Columbine's wasted body, wrapped in his shroud, went over the side.

The news of Edmund and Julia's visit brought the most acute sensations of pleasure and pain. It could only mean Julia had been informed of his determination to relinquish his courtship of her, and further, that she disagreed. While a conviction of her indifference might lessen the grief of giving her up, he found he derived the sweetest satisfaction from knowing she still esteemed and loved him.

He doubted whether he could even endure to meet with her under his parents' roof. Pride as well as delicacy militated against it. Julia already knew that he came from humble circumstances, but to *know* a thing and to *see* it with one's own eyes were two different matters. He hated to think of beautiful, elegant Julia entering those cramped quarters which, despite his sister Susan's best efforts, could not appear as anything but shabby. He was glad he was not there when she walked into their tiny parlour for the first time, to witness the look of surprise, or consternation, or worse—even distaste—that must have crossed her face. He could not sit with Julia, nor greet her calmly, or converse as though they were merely cousins, with the eye of every person in his family upon them!

Fond as he was of his father, William knew him to be uneducated outside of his profession, coarse and ungenteel, while his mother was vocal in her opposition to the match—he cringed to think of the welcome Julia must have received from them.

William resolved to keep to his duties while Julia was in Portsmouth, and spend as much time as possible away from his home, afraid that seeing her would weaken his resolve.

The day after his return happened to be Sunday, and the Prices and their unwelcome guests were all to attend church at the Garrison Chapel together.

William had sometimes pictured in his mind the day when he would take Julia's hand at the Garrison Chapel. It would be a beautiful day, with a mild, freshening breeze, sunny but not too hot. The minister would pronounce them man and wife. His entire family, his brothers and sisters would fill two pews, and his brother officers would form a guard of honour outside the church, and he and Julia would run under the arch of their outstretched sabres. That was how it was to be.

But instead, this cold and blustery day, he sat, highly conscious of the presence of Julia and Edmund in the pew in front of him, and he tried to keep his eye fixed on the pulpit through the entire service, and did not raise his voice to sing the hymns, but only mumbled under his breath, the better to hear her sweet voice. Afterwards, his mother went for her usual walk, and the rest of the family followed.

A brisk and near-freezing wind greeted the family upon their exit from the chapel, and Julia naturally turned to William, and held out her arm for his escort. Edmund gave all his attention to Mrs. Price, and the young couple soon fell behind the others.

Although they were in a public place, there would be no more opportune time, or place, for William to repeat what he had already written, and so, with a voice trembling with emotion, he said: "Miss Bertram, I asked you to wait for me, without making a proper

94

proposal for you. I was wrong—selfish. I never should have asked it of you. Years may go by before I might be able to make a home for you, and no matter what, I will always be plain William Price, and you are Sir Thomas Bertram's daughter, and I ought never to have formed expectations on you."

Julia looked at him, pleadingly, as he continued: "So I must release you from your promise, and I want you to meet—" he blinked back tears which the cold wind was starting from his eyes," —meet someone you could care for. You needn't regard what we said to each other when we were just a boy and a girl. It was like a type of play-acting, amongst the hedgerows, it wasn't real, and we mustn't bind ourselves to it."

"William," exclaimed Julia, shaking her head in disbelief. "It is not the custom in this country for a man to propose marriage and then withdraw the offer. It is too cruel, it is—it is dishonourable!"

"Miss Bertram," William repeated more firmly. "I am sorry you will think so much the worse of me, but perhaps it is for the best. Perhaps in the end, you won't regret giving me up, if you don't think of me as a gentleman. My feelings—" but he broke off. It would only be increasing her pain, and his, for him to tell her how much he loved her.

"*You* are making the choice for me, William! Do you not think I know, do you not think I understand, what it means to be a sailor's wife? I am a grown woman now, and I know my own mind. It is not for you to determine what I can endure and what I cannot."

"But *I* could not endure it, Julia, *I* could not!" William burst forth. "I could not bear to force you into a life of anxiety and loneliness, watching and waiting for me to come home—or worse, take you with me and expose you to danger and hardship. You are the daughter of a baronet, and I am merely a lieutenant, with no-one to help me rise through the ranks. You deserve a better life than the one I can offer you, and there is the end of it."

"William," Julia whispered with passionate intensity. "You do not persuade me. You cannot prevent me from loving you. You cannot prevent me from waiting for you. You can only break my heart, or come back for me one day."

William had to turn away to collect himself. The urge to take her into his arms, to kiss and comfort her, was unbearably painful.

"I release you from your promise, Miss Bertram, for I had no right to ask it of you. I wish you every happiness. I pray you will allow me to return you to the inn. God bless you."

He gestured, to invite her to resume walking, but he did not take her arm. Her shoulders slumped for a moment, then she drew herself up and walked briskly toward the Crown, he following just half a step behind, to shelter her from the wind.

CHAPTER NINE

BY MUTUAL but unspoken agreement, Edmund's "brief visit" to Portsmouth was concluded the day after Julia and William's conversation on the Ramparts. He and Julia returned to Thornton Lacey; she far too oppressed in spirits to improve her acquaintance with the Miss Owens, or to properly admire half of their accomplishments, and the charitable reader is asked to leave her in solitude, to nurse her broken heart, for some weeks.

Lieutenant William Price spent much of his remaining leave time in Portsmouth in colloquy with his brother officers, listening especially attentively to any tales of faithless sweethearts, and men who came home after being away for several years to find a baby in the household cradle. What was once a source of japery and amusement to him was now a matter of painful reflection.

Domestic life offered few of the consolations of the past. He was more aware of the dirt, noise, and vulgarity of the crowded street in which the family resided; the smoky, cramped rooms of their home where his sister Susan valiantly tried to keep order. No wonder her temper sometimes frayed.

Had he, William Price, changed a great deal, or had everyone around him changed? A few years ago, he had thought himself enamoured of all the Gregory girls, especially Lucy, who had turned up her nose at him when he was merely a scrubby midshipman.

He met the Gregory girls again, now as a first lieutenant—they greeted him warmly and made much of him, but how differently did they now appear to his eyes! Pert, showy, and gaudily dressed in cheap and loud fashions, chattering without pause and laughing too loudly, captivated by nothing so much as their own reflections in the shop window, ignorant of the world, and ready to jilt one suitor as soon as a better prospect appeared.

Julia, with her superior education, elegance, and manner, had spoiled him for the brash, simple girls from his old neighbourhood. He did not expect to ever meet her equal, nor did he think he could ever deserve her.

His resolution made, his heart in rebellion, William paced the docks, anxious to be at sea again. In October, his next-assigned ship, the *Kangaroo*, made port. William was there to greet his new

97

commander when Captain Bradley stepped ashore. He met a desolate widower—the captain's wife had sailed with him to Jamaica, and died upon the return voyage.

A parcel arrived from Thornton Lacey shortly before William's departure—it proved to be a large quantity of dried rose hips. Two years had gone by since that October day when he and his sister Susan had been guests at Mansfield Park, and Susan had proposed walking in the hedgerows to collect rose hips for tea. And he, anticipating a chance to speak privately to Julia, claimed to be extremely fond of rose hip tea.

In fact, he didn't much care for the taste at all. But he was a man in love, and he still loved, so he took the rose hips with him, and continued to drink a cup every day.

William continued to be his mother's pride and his family's boast, and all the neighbours knew that the oldest Price boy was returning to Africa as a first lieutenant. Young Betsey was excessively amused by the name of the ship. She had to laugh whenever she thought of it. "The *Kangaroo*! Bounding out to sea!" She exclaimed to her mother. "Over the bounding main!" And she and her brother Charles loudly bounded up and down the stairs, although Charles was now twelve years old and should know better.

"Betsey, my love, you are giving your mama a terrible headache," complained Mrs. Price. "I'm sure *Kangaroo* is as respectable a name as any other."

"Oh, no, it is not," cried Charles. "It is a silly name for a ship, ain't it, Betsey. A ship should be called the *Dauntless*, or the *Dangerous,* or the *Resentful*. Just think, when William tries to make those French ships heave to: *This is Lieutenant Price of the* Kangaroo! Those froggy sailors will be rolling all over the deck, laughing."

"Well, perhaps he will be promoted soon, and have a new ship."

"Like the HMS *Dormouse*," said Charles.

"No, like the *Monkey*!" laughed Betsey

"Or the *Hedgehog*!

"Children, I beg you!"

At any rate, reflected Mrs. Price, as she poked at the meagre fire, her dear boy William would soon be warm enough, in Africa, away from this miserable cold, these grey English clouds, this fine clinging rain and sleet, this damp chill that seeped into your bones.

She closed her eyes and imagined the fiery heat of the southern sun and the piercing blue colour of the African skies.

*   *   *   *   *   *   *

Stoke Newington was a small community, and it was inevitable that the servants of Mrs. Butters' household should learn, and disclose to their mistress, that her son, George Butters, was embarrassed for funds. The local tradesmen were refusing to extend any further credit to Cecilia Butters; her servants were still waiting for their quarterly payment from Michaelmas, and Christmas was not far away.

Mrs. Butters struggled with herself about assisting her family with their financial difficulties. She knew it to be a temporary, not a final, resolution; indeed, it would most likely result in a settled expectation, on the part of her daughter-in-law, for ongoing assistance; an *increase* in improvident spending, rather than a reformation.

"Cecilia is short of money, Fanny, without a doubt," she told Fanny. "But I do not understand why she feels she is entitled to *mine*. And if she did not spend every farthing that passed through her hands on her horses and her other animals, she would not be unable to pay her servants."

In the end, because Mrs. Butters did not want her son's household to raise a clamour, and because she shopped at the same butcher and greengrocer and poulterer who held the overdue accounts for her daughter-in-law, and she wanted no reproach attached to the fair name of "Butters," the kindly widow opened her purse again and discharged many of her daughter-in-law's household debts.

Her generosity was, as usual, not limited to her own family. As winter closed upon Camden Town, the charitable ladies of the Society for Bettering the Condition and Increasing the Comforts of the Poor discovered, to their dismay, that two small coal stoves were inadequate to heat the building.

Mr. Edifice could see his breath when he pronounced the morning prayer. The girls wiped their dripping noses on their sleeves and blew on their cold fingers. At Fanny's request the Blodgetts donated some lengths of stout flannel so the students might make themselves warm petticoats, and Fanny and Madame Orly sat and knitted fingerless gloves in the evening, until every girl was supplied.

The society ladies debated and consulted, and consulted and debated, about the problem, until Mrs. Butters took matters into her own hands and paid for the installation of some braziers, and ordered more coal. What a relief it was to Fanny to arrive the next morning and not suffer, for watching her pupils shivering with the cold!

* * * * * * *

The good people of Thornton Lacey, especially the mothers and daughters, had long pitied the situation of their minister, condemned to be neither a bachelor nor a husband, in the prime of vigorous manhood.

And likewise, of Miss Julia Bertram it was declared a mystery that such a handsome young lady, all of three-and-twenty, returned from her frequent visits to London still single, with no directions to Mrs. Peckover to prepare wedding cakes.

But what was to be done?

The same sentiments also disturbed the serenity of their father, Sir Thomas Bertram, in far-off Norfolk. Sir Thomas, of course, was above stooping to manoeuvring on behalf of his daughter, but he thought it not inadvisable to suggest that Julia and her brother Edmund attend the Northampton assemblies during the holiday season, giving as his reason the desirability of maintaining old and valued, but neglected connections. There were families, and persons, he wrote in his letter to Edmund, whom the Bertrams had not seen since he and his lady had exiled themselves; it was only fitting that he should deputize his children to pay their respects at Christmas-time.

Edmund and Julia went to Northampton, more to oblige their father than from any expectation of pleasure; their Aunt Norris, it somehow came about, was to accompany them, and her delight at resuming her old office of chaperone, and joining former acquaintance at the card tables must suffice—her happiness must be theirs.

"How are you, my dear Mrs. Owens? I see your daughters are here tonight—all three, still unmarried? My niece Maria was married a few years ago, I suppose you know, and lives in Norfolk. Your Sarah, I should say, is almost as beautiful as Julia—no, no, I do say it, and I am sure all of your girls are very accomplished. Everyone says so. How is your son? Still a curate? Edmund has been at Thornton Lacey these two years, but of course he cannot step into his rightful living at Mansfield until Dr. Grant takes himself away, more's the pity.

"Yes, dear Julia is over there by the fireplace. No, she has not chosen a husband, not just as yet. Naturally, she can be particular in her choice. Julia goes up to town frequently, and is very much admired there.

"How old is she? Err... about three-and-twenty, I believe. Now, who shall deal first?"

Julia had "come out" at the Northampton public assemblies six winters ago and she and her sister were then proclaimed the belles of the county, a circumstance which gratified but did not surprise either of the Miss Bertrams.

Julia blushed now, to recall the sentiments which animated her, the selfish ideas she entertained, the pride and the vanity which consumed her, those long years ago.

Most of the young ladies she had stood up with in previous seasons were married with children, and now, their younger sisters gathered expectantly, waiting for an invitation to take to the floor. She, who had nothing more to hope for, stood and watched while the dance went on without her. Her own season, her own brief time was over, but she took a wistful pleasure in watching the younger set rushing up to take her place, to experience for themselves the fleeting pleasures that bloom, youth, and beauty bring, when all the senses are alive, and so much meaning hangs upon a smile, a glance, the lingering touch of a hand. Thus was hope and love and promise perpetually reborn while she was left only with her memories and the purity of her constant attachment to a man who would not have her.

Her resigned, distant air and pensive smile rendered her a figure of some interest, and her high-flown meditations were interrupted by none other than James, Viscount Lynnon, the son of Lord and

101

Lady Delingpole, who asked her to reserve the last two dances before supper. She was surprised to be addressed by him, as she was a few years older than he; moreover, he was of noble birth, and every lady in attendance that evening was beneath his notice, unless he chose to take notice of them.

Lynnon was fond of dancing, excelled in it, and had resolved to take in the assemblies in a true spirit of egalitarianism. Julia enjoyed her turn with him, for the mere pleasure of dancing, and the viscount was not averse to conversation—rather, he seemed eager to engage her attention. No sooner had he seated his partner at the supper table than he began to outline the visions which teemed in his youthful brain.

"Only imagine, Miss Bertram. Imagine—there are no countries, no borders, and therefore, no causes of dispute. No more wars. And of course, no state-ordained religion, either."

"So all the people will live under one government?"

"There would scarcely be such a thing as government. No longer would we conduct our lives according to falsehoods and petty social dictates. No more hypocrisy and deceit. Perfect freedom for man—and for woman!"

"And your friend Mr. Shelley thinks this can all come about?"

"You may think him merely a dreamer, Miss Bertram, but he is far from alone in his views. I hope to persuade you to join us. No more ranks, no more titles, of course—Shelley will establish a community living in perfect brotherhood. It will be particularly advantageous to the lower orders, you know."

"This is rather confusing, sir. Will you surrender your title, and refuse to inherit your father's fortune?"

"Oh," the young lord waved his fork about cheerfully. "That's as may be. What matters is, how and where can I do the most good. If I can do the most good as a Lord, even in the House of Lords one day, Shelley says that's what I should do. I am no poet, like Shelley. I cannot write the way he does, don't you know. His own father has thrown him off, don't you know, for being expelled from Oxford. And eloping."

"Eloping! How romantic!"

"Do you think so? Actually, Shelley hates marriage, you know. That is, he believes it is a type of bondage. But there was this pretty girl, a friend of his sisters, don't you know, and he had to rescue her from the stupidity and ignorance of her father. They ran away to Edinburgh, but now they are settled in Keswick. They have barely a farthing to live upon, don't you know, so I have done what I can. Shelley has written me, many times, asking me to come and stay with them."

"I have heard that the Lake District is very beautiful. Does not the poet Southey live there?"

"Yes, I fancy that poets like Southey and Shelley need to have a beautiful place for inspiration, you know. But, we need more people for our scheme to establish a proper colony of free thinkers, living in absolute harmony and equality. So, what do you say, Miss Bertram? Why don't we elope and go there together?"

Julia was momentarily dumbstruck.

"You'd have to adapt to a vegetable diet, of course," he added, eyeing the slice of ham on Julia's plate. "Only vegetables, fruit and water. And bread. Shelley says, if all men stopped eating meat, there would be no more war. It's the consumption of animal meat which is the root cause of mankind's aggression. Brilliant, don't you know? Perhaps," he laughed, "I should not say *root* cause, you know? Hey, *root*?

Julia laughed, as she knew she must.

"But what do you say? Are you ready to cast off convention, all of the stupid antiquated doctrines, all the foolish constraints of society, and live a life of simplicity, answerable only to Nature's laws?"

"Sir, I am not certain, but did you just propose marriage? You are not one-and-twenty, I believe, and while I am greatly honoured, I do not think your parents would—"

"Oh, do not speak to me of parents! And a Scottish marriage—while necessary to establish our legal independence, would not confer ownership on me, nor constrain us—financially or, er.... any other way, you know."

Julia wondered if she ought to take offense, at being proposed to in such a fashion. Lynnon appeared to be assuring her, as though it were to her advantage and not his, that the role of husband imposed no responsibilities on him. She considered, and decided it was best to treat the whole matter lightly. He was, after all, the son of a very rich and influential man who was currently her father's tenant.

"Well, sir, I beg you will forgive me if I decline your interesting proposal at this time, although I am sensible of the profound honour you do me. And if I may be so bold, I think you would be well-advised to be guided by your father's wishes, at least until you attain your majority."

"Never! Never let it be said that I obliged my father!" Lynnon declared, his face flushing with anger, and Julia swiftly pushed a platter of carrots toward him.

"There, there. I am sorry for rousing your spleen, sir."

*　*　*　*　*　*　*

The young students of Camden Town no longer shivered, thanks to Mrs. Butters, but they were, nevertheless, quivering with excitement over the news which had thrown all of London into a panic—the brutal midnight bludgeoning of a linen-draper and his family on the Ratcliffe Highway.

Everyone took the keenest interest, mingled with horror and alarm, in the newspaper accounts, Fanny as much as anyone, for the killings had occurred very close to the Thames River police office where her brother worked, and in fact, one of their officers was the first to be called to the dreadful murder scene.

She sent John a brief note of enquiry, which was answered by an even briefer one, telling her on no account to come to Wapping until the murderer was apprehended, "for I have obtained extra work, patrolling the streets at night, for which I am to be paid twelve shillings per week, so I shan't have time to visit with you."

Despite her feeling such a personal connection to the horrible murders, Fanny felt it was her duty to suppress, so far as possible, the speculation, the whispers, and squeals of fright in her classroom—the older girls in particular delighted in horrifying the youngest students, by relating how the victims' skulls had been smashed in, except for the baby, whose throat had been cut so savagely its head was nearly severed from its body. Murders were not unknown to London, particularly not to the Wapping area, but these murders created an unprecedented general alarm and fright on account of their unbridled savagery. As well, there was no known motive for the crime—there had been no robbery. It was generally held that the killings were the work of a deranged madman. A foreigner, most likely.

The wave of fear spread through entire country. Honest merchants struck down in their own establishment, their brains splattered across the wall! Since the outrage had occurred in a linen-draper's shop, Mrs. Blodgett and Madame Orly were afraid that Blodgett's Academy might even be the next target of the killer. Mr. Blodgett attached extra locks and chains upon their doors, and kept a cudgel behind his shop counter. These precautions did little to allay the anxieties of Madame Orly. Madame had actually witnessed bloody violence with her own eyes; she had seen heads paraded on spikes, and crowds calling for blood, and no reassurances would erase those ghastly episodes from her memory, nor cause her to refrain from attaching the terror she experienced when a young girl in France, to the nameless dread which clung to every Londoner.

"Surely, Madame, we are at a safe distance, here at Camden Town," said Fanny, in an attempt to convince her friend of something which she herself could not entirely feel.

"*Non, non*, that is all the more reason to be alarmed!" Madame exclaimed, "Why should the killer stay in Wapping, where everyone is looking for him? He must have run far from there by now, he could be anywhere, anywhere at all!"

Fanny could not gainsay her friend's logic, and drew at least this comfort—if the madman had indeed escaped from Wapping, her brother John was only in danger of catching cold on his nightly patrols, rather than being dispatched into eternity with a blunt instrument or a razor to the neck. She sent him his Christmas present—a warm muffler—without waiting for the holiday.

* * * * * * *

At Mansfield Park, Lord Delingpole had done all that energy, skill and resolution could do to accomplish the crucial goal of chasing every last fox in Northamptonshire to the ground. Lady Delingpole had likewise found much to gratify in her new country residence, and the people of Mansfield had discovered in her, an intelligent and industrious patroness, who gave judicious relief to the poor and was prompt in settling her accounts.

The Delingpoles were not above venturing into the village to do some shopping, or just to go for a carriage ride in the neighbourhood. Shortly before Christmas, Lord Delingpole was to be seen guiding their gig expertly around the frozen ruts on the main road through Mansfield, with his lady beside him.

"The most extraordinary piece of news has reached my ears, dear. Apparently, our son proposed marriage to Julia Bertram at the Northampton assemblies."

"Did he, by gad. And one presumes the lady accepted—happy to catch at an Earl's son!"

"I am told she refused him."

"Excellent—we are spared the awkwardness of putting a negative on the match, at least." His lordship gave the reins an irritated shake, and the horses picked up their pace. "Why did he propose? Why did she refuse? Does she think she can do better than a Viscount?"

"I am not certain why James proposed, but his good friend Percy Shelley was married recently—to a tavern-keeper's daughter, of all things—and you know how our son emulates Mr. Shelley."

"So if our son was unsuccessful with Miss Bertram, is he in danger of proposing to the next young laundry-maid he sees?"

"Quite possibly. You'll have a word with him, dear?"

"That word being, 'disinheritance'?"

"If you think that would persuade him."

"So, why did she refuse him? Refuse our boy?"

Lady Delingpole laughed. "Are you affronted, as well as being relieved? When I next meet Miss Bertram, I will ask her. Let us call at Thornton Lacey on our way to town."

"Shall we return to town on Wednesday or Thursday, Imogen?"

"Thursday, I think. I wanted to listen to the children's choir practising at the church. Dr. Grant tells me they are quite charming."

"We should go up on Wednesday. I need time to consult with Perceval and Castlereagh before Parliament resumes."

"Why do you do that?"

"Why indeed, my dear? I sometimes ask myself the same question. The work of persuading people, while making them think it was their idea in the first place, is excessively tiring."

"I meant, David, why do you offer me a choice and then tell me what you have decided? If you need to be in London on Wednesday I have no objection, but why do you pretend to consult my wishes in the matter?"

"Did I? I was just thinking aloud, I suppose. Shall we return to the house now?"

"Yes—no—stop a moment. If you turn there, at the corner, we will pass the White House. We had better stop and call upon Mrs. Norris."

"Whatever for?"

"Because we cannot drop the acquaintance now, David. We must visit her to make our farewells before we leave Northamptonshire. Only a quarter of an hour, no more."

"Five minutes."

"That would be more insulting than not stopping at all."

"This is why you asked me to take you out driving today in the first place, isn't it? To hoodwink me into wasting half-an-hour with Mrs. Norris. You planned to do this all along, and never told me."

"Did I? I forgot to think aloud, I suppose. Turn here, please."

*   *   *   *   *   *   *

John Price had never heard Mr. Harriott sound so angry as he did that morning. The burly magistrate had been meeting in his private office for the last half hour with some justices from the nearby Shadwell public office. John and the other clerks, toiling away at their desks in the outer room, exchanged uncomfortable glances as their chief's voice grew in vehemence and volume.

John's was the first face that the chief magistrate saw when he threw open the heavy wooden door of his office in an explosion of energy which made even Mr. Laing, the head clerk, jump.

"You!" He barked at John. "Fetch the maul!"

"Sir? Fetch them all? Fetch who, sir?"

"The maul! Bring me the murder weapon, confound you! Are you a complete simpleton?" And Mr. Harriott flung a ring of keys at John, who awkwardly caught it. "The maul in the store-room. Bring it here!"

John knew better than to protest that he was not a judicial clerk—he ran to the back door and down the outside back stairs to the storage room and he fumbled with half-a-dozen keys before he found the correct one. As he prowled through the gloomy, low-ceilinged room, crammed with barrels and boxes, he heard Mr. Harriott's angry rumbling through the floorboards above his head and the exasperated replies of one of the Shadwell magistrates.

"Not our jurisdiction! Not our jurisdiction! Perhaps the Home Secretary would be so good as to inform me, what he thinks I ought to have done, when the murders occurred, sir, on our very doorstep! Mr. Horton was summoned to the scene before the bodies were warm! Should Mr. Horton have refused to respond? Should I have slept soundly through the night, while a deranged murderer stalked the streets?"

"The Home Secretary has only questioned the propriety of your issuing a proclamation and a reward, from your office, sir. The Shadwell office, Mr. Harriott, would not presume to offer a reward for a crime which occurred on the river, and in the same spirit—"

"And how do you know, sir, that this outrage was not perpetrated by a foreign sailor? What could be more probable? The very persons whom our office watches over, night and day, and keep in order. Shall I instruct my men to be deaf, dumb and blind, as they go about their duties, rather than offend the tender pride of your officers?"

"Every public office is apprehending and questioning suspicious persons all over London, and you are encouraged to continue to do so, Mr. Harriott. Your interest and cooperation has been highly valuable, sir, highly valuable, but the Home Secretary has directed that the Shadwell office—"

"With all due respect, the public is clamouring for every public official in England to involve himself in this affair! But it appears the Home Secretary is more taken up with humiliating and humbling me, than with finding a fiend lurking in our midst."

At last John, fumbling in the gloom, found and seized the maul, which had been placed on a high shelf. It was long, and heavy, and he had to set it down on the landing to re-lock the door of the storeroom. Taking it up again, he paused, out of overpowering curiousity, at finding himself holding something which had brutally ended the lives of three persons, and examined the weapon with fascination.

John noticed a small depression under the thick layer of dried blood on the head of the maul. He moistened his thumb in a puddle on the wet railing, and rubbed vigorously at the spot, revealing two initials punched into the metal: "JP."

"Mr. Harriott! Mr. Harriott!" he cried, running up the stairs. "Mr. Harriott, have you seen this, sir?"

Mr. Harriott and his visitors all crowded around and looked, and exclaimed, and someone said, "it is a very great pity, don't you think, that no-one thought to examine the weapon for such marks before now—it is a full week gone by—and you have only now discovered this?"

"I shall cause a new handbill to be issued, with a better description," said Mr. Harriott, but his earlier truculence was gone, replaced now with a conciliating and subdued manner.

"Do not trouble yourself, Mr. Harriott. We shall take the weapon with us and commission an accurate sketch of it, and issue a new hand-bill. This is a Shadwell matter. Thank you for your cooperation, sir. Good day to you."

And John dared not meet Mr. Harriott's eye after the other gentlemen took their leave, with the maul.

* * * * * * *

Mrs. Peckover heard a carriage stop before the parsonage-house. She reached the front door just as Lady Delingpole's footman was about to raise the knocker, and soon thereafter, Julia Bertram received her august visitor in the parlour, while his lordship waited in the carriage.

Julia enquired politely after Viscount Lynnon and learned he was gone ahead to town.

Lady Delingpole, with a smile, but with a manner not to be refused, motioned Julia to take a seat on a small settee, which was barely large enough for two persons. Lady Delingpole seated herself beside Julia and fixed her with a most significant look.

"And speaking of my son, Miss Bertram," said Lady Delingpole, fixing her with a most significant look. "Is there anything you would care to confide in me?"

109

"Oh! Madam, I think you must have heard—please do not alarm yourself, I had not imagined him to be at all—that is—there is nothing—"

Lady Delingpole patted Julia's hand. "You are a good girl, Miss Bertram, and too sensible to be affronted at what I am about to say. Of course you would be an excellent wife for James, or for any young man, I daresay."

"I have no expectations whatsoever, indeed, your ladyship."

"Have you not?"

"I venture to hope that your ladyship will not be offended in turn, if I say, though I am very fond of you, I do not wish to marry your son? And I am well aware he is too young to contemplate such a step, and even if he were not, I do not imagine..." she trailed off, too embarrassed to explain that Viscount Lynnon was attempting to assemble a harem of free-thinking women for his friend Shelley.

Lady Delingpole laughed. "Well, excellent. I was a trifle concerned that a coolness might arise between our families. We are still friends?"

"And honoured to be so, ma'am."

Lady Delingpole looked at her appraisingly for a moment, as though considering—then shook her head.

"When James is of the age to be married, his father and I will guide him in his selection, as we did with our daughters. The matter is too important to be left to his judgement alone."

Julia said nothing, but her countenance betrayed her disapprobation of parental tyranny. Lady Delingpole smiled.

"It was almost thirty years ago when I first met his Lordship—Viscount Lynnon as he was, just a week before our wedding-day. As I recall, when I was introduced to him I thought to myself, 'well, it could be worse,' and the look on his face pretty much said the same about me. He was five-and-twenty, I was seventeen years old and I had not set foot in England in all my life, and it was to be my new home, and with a stranger for my husband."

"Married at seventeen, ma'am! To a stranger, in a strange country!"

"To the man chosen for me by my parents," affirmed Lady Delingpole. "We would not have expected otherwise, in those days, and at our station in life. My parents at least chose a political household for me to marry into, for I was already an ardent Tory."

Warming to her theme, Lady Delingpole took Julia's hand.

"My dear, when you come to be married, you and your husband should share some of the same pursuits—apart from whatever children you give him, of course—having some interests in common is a better guarantee for marital happiness than mere physical attraction, for we are not young forever. Lord Delingpole and I have politics as our shared passion."

"Yes, ma'am."

"You must also have your *own* occupations and diversions. Nothing disgusts a husband so much as a wife who cannot entertain herself. If she sulks and sobs when he leaves the house, and falls upon him with complaints and upbraidings when he returns, he soon wants to avoid his home.

"Attend to my advice, Miss Bertram, for you will not hear anything more valuable, or to the purpose, when it comes to marriage."

"But....but what of love, your ladyship?"

"Did I just inform you that I loved Lord Delingpole at first sight?" Lady Delingpole rose, and, crossing to the mirror above the fireplace, adjusted her hat a little. "I think not. Beginning with fancying yourself in love is all very well—but it is no guarantee of future contentment. Even the most idle observations of our fellow creatures can tell us this."

Her appearance restored, she turned back to Julia. "Now, Miss Bertram, promise me you will call upon me when you are next in London, so that I may know you are in earnest when you say you harbour no resentment."

Just then, Lord Delingpole called from the carriage. "Imogen! It's time we were on our way."

"Of course it is," sighed her ladyship. "The time to leave is when our husbands are ready to leave. That is the correct time. Otherwise it is too early or too late." She pulled on her gloves just as Edmund Bertram arrived from the church, having been summoned by the manservant.

"Lady Delingpole, I am sorry I was not at home to receive you. Must you depart so soon?"

"You may escort me to my carriage and greet my husband at any rate, my dear Mr. Bertram. I am pleased we were able to wish you a Happy Christmas. Have you any note, any message, I can convey to town for you? No? Nothing? Well, my best wishes to you, for the New Year."

* * * * * * *

Cecilia Butters visited the academy shortly before Christmas, desiring a good lined cape with a hood. Mr. Edifice greeted her with his customary politeness.

"Dear Mrs. Butters has been extremely generous, has she not, ma'am? The highest praise could hardly exceed her just desserts."

Cecilia Butters was startled, and an angry flush rose to her cheeks. She believed the curate must be in the secret of her financial troubles; somehow he had learned of the assistance she had received from her mother-in-law. Who could have betrayed her most personal affairs? Who but Miss Price?

"Mr. Edifice," she began, with some hauteur, "I am not in the habit of—"

But Mr. Edifice was gesturing to one of the new braziers, and inviting her to come and warm her hands.

"Here we see her goodness toward all the children, and everyone who works here."

Cecilia Butters required but a moment to re-arrange her thoughts.

"I see. I see. Yes, very generous indeed."

"I hope ma'am, the next time you see your good mother-in-law, you may convey to her my sincere good wishes, compliments and thanks. Miss Price has often spoken to me of her generosity."

"*She* would have good cause to!"

This answer encouraged Mr. Edifice to hint, "Indeed yes, for I think Miss Price is almost like a daughter to Mrs. Butters, would you not agree? As dear to her as a daughter?"

This last suggestion once again plunged Cecilia Butters into the utmost perturbation and her mood was not improved, when in the next moment, Fanny appeared in high spirits, followed by two delivery boys struggling with a wicker hamper, which caused all of her students to shriek with excitement. They were certain that whatever was in Miss Price's hamper, must be intended for them.

They were not wrong. Fanny had given a lot of thought to what gifts she might give to her pupils at Christmas. Of course they would want enough quantities of sweets and candy to make them ill, but Fanny was not inclined to indulge them in this; especially as it would be contrary to Mrs. Butters' own strictures on the use of sugar.

Instead, Mrs. McIntosh had, at Fanny's request, baked many loaves of gingerbread, made with molasses and honey, but Fanny also wanted the children to have something even more substantial. She had thought of buying each of them a chicken, but upon learning that not all of the families had stoves capable of cooking a whole chicken, she had instead arranged with a local tavern to bake up a large quantity of meat pies, which she would make up into parcels with the gingerbread, in a length of clean muslin, which formed part of the gift. The cost had not been excessive, and she knew everything would be welcomed by the families of her pupils.

"Christmas!" exclaimed Mr. Edifice to Cecilia Butters, certain of her concurrence. "A time to consider our own blessings, and to generously give what we can!"

But that fair lady regarded the hamper with a frown. "How much did all of this cost my poor mother-in-law, Miss Price?'

"Pray do not alarm yourself on that account, ma'am," replied Fanny evenly, "for I have purchased these gifts with my own monies."

"Well... of course you have no living expenses, do you, thanks to my mother-in-law. You must have a good deal of pocket money to throw about."

"Yes, ma'am," was all Fanny would say; but inwardly she added, *what you call 'pocket money' is in my pocket because I earned it, all myself.*

Fanny very sensibly felt the great satisfaction she derived from being able to make choices with her purse, without being obliged to the generosity or caprice of anyone else. *This money was not given to me by anyone,* she thought, *I am beholden to no-one for it, and I can have no qualms in spending it, in exactly the manner I please.*

CHAPTER TEN

LONDON WAS SHOCKED again by fresh horrors, a few days before Christmas. A man, his wife, and their maid were slaughtered in the dark of night in their public house and as before, the killer escaped into the streets. Once again, the murders took place in Wapping and the residents of that area almost rioted outside of the Thames River and Shadwell police offices, demanding more police protection. But the renewed terror spread through all of London and beyond.

Many households armed themselves, and men volunteered for neighbourhood patrols. The girls of the academy were dismissed at dusk, so they could walk home before darkness fell. At Stoke Newington, Mrs. Butters' man-servants took it in turns to stay awake and guard the house all night and Madame Orly pushed her dresser in front of her bedchamber door before retiring for a restless night's sleep. Fanny too, checked and double-checked that her window-frame was locked and pulled her blinds tight every night. She felt a little foolish doing so, but the panic of fear was highly contagious.

It was impossible to escape the atmosphere of dread which hung over the metropolis as Christmas approached.

On Christmas Eve, Mrs. Butters found it advisable to visit her banker to review her quarterly accounts and adjust her investments, having laid out so much monies on the academy and her family. Together with her brother and her sister-in-law, she went into London, and Madame Orly and Fanny were obliged to stay a little longer at the classroom, before Donald McIntosh and the carriage would return to convey them back to Stoke Newington. This arrangement suited both Fanny and the lady's maid very well, as they wanted to put the final touches on their gift for Mrs. Butters—a new embroidered jacket—without her knowledge.

As soon as the students were dismissed, Master Blodgett, in the absence of his parents, quickly locked up the downstairs shop and went to spend the evening at a tavern. Upstairs, Fanny and Madame Orly pulled their chairs beside the stove and stitched and sewed and chatted amiably.

Half an hour became an hour, then two. Fanny set down her work and rubbed the back of her neck. "I hadn't realized how dark it has grown, Madame," said Fanny. "I shall fetch us some more candles."

"What time is it?" said Madame Orly, examining her pocket watch. "Can my watch be right? Is it six o'clock already?" She jumped up and looked at the classroom clock on the wall. "Yes, six! No wonder I am so hungry! Where is McIntosh? Where can he be?"

A look of dismay and apprehension crossed the Frenchwoman's face, and Fanny realized she was thinking of the Ratcliffe Highway killer.

Both women moved to the windows, hoping to see Donald McIntosh and his carriage. The streets were empty, and a fog had crept in with the dusk. One or two working men hurried by, shoulders hunched against the cold, faces down, guided through the gathering gloom by a few dim streetlamps. Though it was barely evening, the night sky was forbidding and cold. A man paused under a street light to fill his pipe—he looked up, idly and around, at the tall windows of the academy. Fanny and Madame Orly, with one accord, stepped back from the window.

"Would you like me to put the kettle on, Madame?" said Fanny. Will you have a little tea?"

Madame Orly shook her head. "Do not build the fire, I don't want anyone to see smoke from the chimney. I don't want anyone to know we are here—all alone."

Was it the chill from the windows, or was it the fear in Madame Orly's voice, that caused the gooseflesh to raise on Fanny's arms? Only a few hours ago, the classroom had been light, cheery, and filled with chattering girls, exclaiming over their Christmas presents from Fanny. Now a feeling of anxiety pressed upon her. Where was Mrs. Butters and the carriage? What had happened to them?

Fanny and Madame Orly worked together to pull the long, heavy curtains across all the tall windows, throwing the classroom deeper into darkened gloom.

They then unhooked and lowered the mirrored work-light chandeliers, so that they could be re-fitted with candles for the next day of school. Fanny had never noticed before how particularly unpleasant was the sound of the rattling chains clinking through the iron rings in the ceiling.

A scraping noise made Fanny jump, even as she realized it was only Madame Orly pushing aside a chair.

"Fanny, I have some bread and butter downstairs, left over from my dinner," the Frenchwoman said. "I will go and get it." Her voice sounded different in the echoing silence around them, pale and uncertain and small.

"I will rake the coals, and tidy up, Madame, and shall join you in just a moment," answered Fanny with assumed cheerfulness. Madame Orly picked up one of their two candlesticks, and disappeared down the stairs, leaving Fanny alone in the small pool of light, in the large empty room.

Fanny began quickly winding up her thread on its bobbin and arranging her sewing basket by the light of her remaining candle. She was accustomed to solitude, in fact had often sought it in the past, but now, all alone in the gathering darkness, the complete silence was unnerving. None of the homely sights of the classroom looked familiar now. Shadows loomed around her. Even her cloak with its hood, hanging on its peg, looked like a thief lurking in the corner. She could hear a shutter creaking in the wind somewhere, and a horse clip-clopping slowly up the street. It could not be Mr. McIntosh, for he had a pair of horses to the carriage. Where was he? Had anything happened to Mrs. Butters in the city?

Although she tried to reason with herself, the horrid details of the recent murders rose to her mind once again. Somewhere in the darkness there lurked a fiend in human form who stalked their streets, who moved silently in the black of night, who raised his arm and struck savagely and without mercy. He appeared from nowhere, he killed, and he disappeared into the darkness. He could be anywhere.

Don't be ridiculous, she told herself. *Even supposing the killer were to strike again, the chances that he would come here are extremely remote, one might say non-existent. And he kills at midnight—it is hours from midnight.* Yet, she hurried to smother the fire in the stove, and fold up her sewing work and stuff it into her portmanteau. Swiftly, she caught up her candle, and headed for the stairs, ready to join Madame Orly in the shop below where, she hoped, they would not have much longer to wait.

When she reached the top of the stairs, she heard the faint tinkle of the bell at the back door of the shop. *That's odd*, she thought, *why did Mr. McIntosh come to the back door?*

She heard Madame Orly say "Who is it? Who is there?"

Then Madame Orly screamed—but the scream was cut off!

A thudding noise—as though a body had fallen to the ground!

Absolute terror seized her. The fiend—was he here? Was he downstairs? Had he chosen this shop, had he been watching outside, did he know there were only two defenceless females within? Had Madame Orly herself, hearing a noise at the door, and supposing it was Donald McIntosh, opened the door to her murderer? All of these thoughts flashed through Fanny's mind as quickly as lightning.

She blew out her candle, and was enveloped in blackness, straining to listen, too frightened to move.

How could she escape? There was but one flight of stairs in the building, one that would lead her to the killer, or the killer to her.

Could she hide herself behind a screen? Under some bolts of fabric? To do so, she would have to move, and the creaking floorboards would betray her location.

She could hear footsteps which did not belong to Madame Orly. Yes, there *was* someone else in the building!

A man's footsteps. A slow, cautious step. Then another. Then another.

He was climbing the stairs!

Despite her terror of discovery, Fanny could not remain in the open classroom, awaiting her death. Instinct told her to run, to hide, in the darkest corner she could find. Groping her way through the darkness, she scurried to the dumbwaiter, opened the door, and climbed inside. Perhaps the killer would not be able to find her in the dark, although she feared he would be able to locate her by following the sound of her pounding heart.

The footsteps grew louder.

She sent up a silent prayer for herself and Madame Orly.

A man's voice calling hesitantly: "Hello?.... Hello?"

It was not Mr. McIntosh's thick Scottish brogue.

"Miss Price? Are you here? Miss Price?"

Joy! Utter joy and relief!

"Oh! Mr. Gibson! Mr. Gibson! Is that you?"

"Miss Price? Where are you?"

Fanny climbed out of the dumbwaiter as quickly as she had climbed in and moved blindly toward the sound of his voice, her arms outstretched. "I am here, Mr. Gibson. I blew out my candle when I heard the noises downstairs."

"Oh. Miss Price. I am so sorry, I must have alarmed you." His fingertips found hers, and somehow—she knew not quite how—she found herself wrapped securely in his embrace. Her fear disappeared, to be replaced by new sensations. She clung to his tall frame; he tightened his grip around her slender one.

"Miss Price, I—I—I am afraid we must hurry downstairs," he said. "Madame Orly has fainted."

Fanny looked up—she could barely make out the outline of Mr. Gibson's face in the dark. "Is she all right?"

"I trust so. I attempted to revive her—patted her hands and so forth, but she did not respond, so I thought I had better look for you, and see if you had any smelling salts. But the building was so silent and dark, I thought it impossible that you could be here. In the end, I appear to have frightened you both half to death."

Fanny and Mr. Gibson felt their way downstairs, while he kept his arm protectively around her waist. They were still in total darkness, because Madame Orly's candle had been extinguished when she fell to the ground. Fanny and Mr. Gibson, with one accord, sank to their knees and felt their way along the passageway until they found Madame Orly, lying where she had fallen. After an anxious moment, she responded faintly to Fanny's voice.

Once Fanny and Mr. Gibson assured themselves that Madame Orly was unharmed and beginning to recover herself, she, by anxious questions and he, through reassuring explanations, retraced the chain of events which had led to such profound, if brief, terror.

Mr. Gibson was indeed the source of the sound, the movement, the shadow which had terrified Madame Orly into insensibility, for he had tried the back door and found it carelessly unlocked.

"When I arrived, I saw no lights anywhere in the building, for the windows were shuttered," Mr. Gibson explained, "and it looked as though you had already gone—I thought perhaps you had found some other means to get home, but just in case, I bid the driver wait until I had looked inside, to be certain of you. We came up the alley, for Mr. McIntosh told me the front door would be double-bolted and padlocked, so I thought I would try the back entrance. I was on the point of knocking, when the door yielded and, the next thing I knew, I heard Madame cry out, and she fainted, and I was left in the dark. Pray, Madame, will you ever forgive me, for having frightened you so?"

"But what of Mrs. Butters?" asked Fanny. "Why did you come to be here, and not Donald McIntosh? Has anything happened to them?"

Mr. Gibson explained that one of Mrs. Butters' carriage horses had gone lame in London, and Mrs. Butters had sent a messenger to his lodgings to ask him to hire a hackney coach to hurry to Camden Place. "I came as soon as I could, for it was rather difficult to find a cab on Christmas Eve, and even more difficult to find a driver willing to come out to Camden Town—I thought I should have to walk here—and even now our driver is waiting impatiently without—allow me to accompany you safely home, ladies."

There was still some delay for the driver, however, for Madame Orly needed a glass of water, and their cloaks had to be retrieved, and the spare key for the back door taken from its hiding place, none of which was easy to do in the dark. Mr. Gibson found Madame Orly's fallen taper on the floor, and went outside to get a light from the cab-driver's lantern. When he returned, the sight of his kind, concerned, face, illuminated by the single flame in the darkness, was irresistible to Fanny, and now the fluttering of her heart had nothing to do with deranged killers stalking in the night, but with feelings of another order altogether!

Fanny would long remember that cab ride home to Mrs. Butters' house. The three of them were seated closely together on a seat intended for two persons, with Mr. Gibson in the middle, and his reassuring warmth, his solid presence, made her feel entirely safe, no matter how many insane murderers roamed the streets. Out of the window, she could see the homes and farmsteads they passed, all lit up and glowing warmly within. It was Christmas Eve, families were gathered together, all was right with the world.

"Oh! We are so grateful to you for saving us, *M'sieur* Gibson," Madame Orly exclaimed, forgetting, in her great relief to be alive and well, that there had in fact been no murderer on the premises.

* * * * * * *

By decree of Henry Laing, the head clerk, the office Christmas party proceeded as usual, despite the strains and additional labours of the preceding fortnight, and therefore John Price set down his pen as the clock struck twelve on Christmas Day and toasted his colleagues of the Thames River Police Office with a small glass of beer. But just as Mr. Laing loosened his cravat, a sure precursor to his breaking out into song, Mr. Horton came in from the street, with some fresh intelligence which made the revellers forget about their beer and Mrs. Laing's mince pies.

"The ownership of the bloody maul has been traced to a foreign sailor," Mr. Horton announced.

"There—a foreigner—I knew it!" cried another officer.

"No, this sailor is not the killer. He is far out at sea. He left his tool chest with his landlord, and the landlord positively identified the weapon, and says it went missing from his yard, and *another* one of his lodgers, another sailor, an Irishman—"

"There—an Irishman—I knew it!"

"This Irishman was questioned yesterday evening. He had a bloody shirt, and can't account for his whereabouts, and is being held at Coldbath prison."

A burly hand clamped down firmly on John's shoulder from behind, and John turned to see Mr. Harriott.

"We may congratulate ourselves, gentlemen, on our contributions toward the resolution of this terrible business. It appears we can expect little enough thanks and acknowledgement coming our way from the press or the public. However, the present mood of the nation, provides us with an opportunity for catching the ear of Parliament, to urge better funding for a professional class of police officers."

"Hear, hear, sir!" came the response.

John expected the trial of the Irishman to follow shortly, and wondered if he would be called upon to testify about his discovery of the initials on the murder weapon. The jury—and the public— would learn how this small, over-looked clue had been of the first importance in catching a killer.

CHAPTER ELEVEN

"Ah, Mr. Gibson! You're a grand sight for the New Year. Our first footer!" cried Mrs. McIntosh with pleasure. "Tall, dark-haired and bonny! And are ye bearing gifts as well?"

"Good fortune to this house, and all who dwell here," answered Mr. Gibson cheerfully, not at all inclined to cavil at Scottish superstition on such a fine winter morning. "Although I must disappoint you on the score of gifts. I am a hapless bachelor after all. I was rather hoping *you* had some of your good baking reserved for *me*, Mrs. McIntosh. I should think bringing bread to you is like bringing coals to Newcastle.

"Oh, that's right," he added, smacking his forehead. "I was supposed to bring you some coal, as well. At any rate, ma'am, no-one can bake a better scone than your good self."

"Flatterer!"

Just then Fanny, wreathed in smiles, came tripping through the parlour door to greet him, and he withdrew from under his arm a small roll of paper, tied up with a ribbon.

"But instead of the traditional gift of coal, I do bring for you, Miss Price, a printer's proof of my report on Mrs. Perceval's visit to the academy, which you may consign to the flames after you've read it. Or before, if you like."

The pure pleasure of the visit, alas, was clouded by Mr. Gibson's announcement that he must leave almost immediately for Portsmouth, to investigate and report on the tragic loss of several of the Navy's ships in severe winter storms in the Baltic. He was to attend the courts-martial and interview the few survivors for the *Gentlemen's Magazine.*

"No doubt you wrote your family before Christmas, Miss Price, but I should be happy to convey any message or parcel to them on your behalf. I am sure my little nursemaid Betsey has grown a foot since I last saw her."

"Betsey and all the family will be so delighted to see you, Mr. Gibson. I am only sorry to tell you, they have moved to a smaller household, for otherwise, they could have spared you a bedroom for your stay in Portsmouth."

Mr. Gibson had been very ill when he was an unwelcome boarder in the Price household several years ago, and his recollections of the food and accommodation were not very charitable, although he had formed an unlikely alliance with young Betsey, who had served as his nurse-maid. He had spent his days lying on his back in the Price's attic, watching the slow orbit of the sun from east to west across the dormer windows, and listening to the voices which echoed through the house—Mrs. Price, talking to herself in querulous tones—Susan, halloo-ing a command to the servant in the kitchen—boisterous Sam and Charles, and the deep bass rumble of Mr. Price.

The Prices were a rambunctious, harum-scarum sort of family, and Betsey's upbringing, for example, was as different as possible from the cold, austere, silent childhood that he had known, living with his clergyman uncle in Cambridgeshire. In his uncle's home, there was no toleration for noise or disorder or unpunctual meals.

Aloud, he said only: "Oh, I should not think of imposing myself on your good mother, Miss Price."

Mrs. Butters, for motives which will be intelligible to the discerning reader, did not immediately greet her guest, for she found herself to be unavoidably delayed by some household matters, leaving the two young people alone in the parlour. When she did make her appearance, the rest of Mr. Gibson's visit was given over to the topics of the day. The Prince Regent, his selfish extravagance and his lechery was vigorously dwelt on by their hostess, who denounced His Royal Highness as a libertine and a blockhead.

And of course, there was the outcome of the Ratcliffe Highway murders to be canvassed, lamented, and wondered at. The Irish sailor who had been the chief suspect hanged himself in his prison cell before he was formally charged with the crime. His suicide was taken to be a confession, and his body was paraded through the streets on a hurdle on New Year's Eve, with thousands gathered to watch, and he had been buried at a crossroad in unconsecrated soil; a proceeding, Mr. Gibson observed, which ought to make any rational Englishman blush for shame. "The authorities actually drove a stake through the wretch's heart. In front of thousands of ravening spectators! What barbarous superstition!"

Fanny and Mr. Gibson shook hands upon parting, she smiled, their eyes met, and he wondered if she, too, was thinking of that brief moment on Christmas Eve, when they had found each other in the darkness and he had embraced her fervently. He wished he could hold her again.

The too-brief visit was over, and Mrs. McIntosh saw to it that their visitor departed with some scones, wrapped up carefully with a pat of butter, while she sighed and laughed inwardly at the inability of two well-disposed young people to come to the point. What was all the fuss and pother about? When was that Mr. Gibson ever going to declare himself?

It did occur to Mr. Gibson—but only after he departed—that perhaps there was nothing particularly lover-like in talking over the state of the nation and the barbaric disposal of a wretched sailor, with the young woman he esteemed. Unfortunately, he thought, he hardly knew what else to talk about. Miss Price was as little disposed to be flattered by gallantries as he was adept at bestowing them.

I have written poetry, he thought to himself, *but none of it was love poetry. Should I try my hand at a sonnet? Somehow, I cannot think of it without laughing, and I think Fanny would laugh as well!*

He might have felt reassured had he known that, immediately after his departure, Miss Price sat down and read his article for the Society and was once again filled with admiration for her friend's talents with his pen. Anything that was awkward, tedious, or irksome about the day was smoothed away, every person appeared to best advantage, but without any obvious puffery. He described the arrangement of the classroom, the routines of the school, the "intelligent and capable" instructress—without of course, naming her—and he portrayed the young students in a kind and sympathizing light. Fanny felt very strange at first, to be reading about an endeavour in which she played so signal a part, but upon reflection, she was delighted that Mr. Gibson's words would convey immortality on the academy and everyone in it, in the next annual report of the Society.

On the following day, Fanny took Mr. Gibson's article with her, to share with Mr. Edifice. The curate was in no very receptive mood. It had dawned on him, when he was about half-way through the twenty-second chapter of Numbers, that the story of Balaam's ass was a poor choice for a bible reading for young students. He stubbornly carried on, ignoring the laughing and tittering, but the tips of his ears grew red and his temper frayed. Therefore he greeted

Miss Price with some asperity when she told him, "Mr. Gibson quoted quite extensively from your speech to Mrs. Perceval, and it will all appear in the annual report."

"Did he indeed?" Mr. Edifice replied disagreeably, to Fanny's surprise. "If he is appropriating my speech, over which I expended no small pains, it would seem only right I should be remunerated, would you not agree? Will I receive some portion of the fee Mr. Gibson was paid to write it? Why should I be pleased when he has profited at my expense?"

"Oh, but you are quite mistaken, Mr. Edifice. Mr. Gibson is not receiving any payment for writing this article, although of course he earns his living as a writer. But as this is for the benefit of the Society for Improving the—you know, the Society, he did not request a fee."

Mr. Edifice was visibly discomposed by this explanation.

"Really! That is—no, no, of course not. You are certain? Quite certain, then. Ah, yes, but as it's for the Society, after all, and neither would I ask the Society for any—that is, not any amount above and beyond my usual salary for my duties here—that is—how very generous of him."

He turned to leave, then paused and added, "I own that I assumed Mr. Gibson would expect to be paid for such a service—indeed, for any service. He told me most decidedly that no man of sense should venture upon matrimony unless the bride brought a substantial dowry with her, or something to that effect. 'Pure folly to do otherwise,' he said. As a result, I had put him down, perhaps wrongly, as being of a mercenary character. But, obviously Mr. Gibson has his charitable side. I should be sorry to think I misjudged him. Naturally, I am highly gratified to see my words in print, and I look forward to the publication of the annual report."

Fanny bid farewell to Mr. Edifice with her usual placidity but with great inner perturbation. After the curate left, she kept puzzling over his account of his conversation with her friend. She had often heard it said, that gentlemen spoke more candidly and revealed their true sentiments, in company with other men, without ladies present. Still, she could hardly credit the assertion that Mr. Gibson—who had always said money was of no consequence to him—would only consider matrimony if his bride were wealthy. The sentiment was completely at odds with what she knew of his principles.

But, after all, what did it matter—what *could* it matter, to her? So far as she knew, Mr. Gibson never intended to marry—he had said so, more than once. Still, she felt greatly dismayed, and she wondered how she might hint at the topic when Mr. Gibson returned from Portsmouth. But how? She blushed at the thought.

* * * * * * *

The *Kangaroo* had lost many weeks, tracking a wandering path down the coast of Africa, attempting to rendezvous with Captain Frederick Irby and the HMS *Amelia*, as per their orders from the Admiralty. Lieutenant Price and the entire crew scanned the horizon for the *Amelia* or the *Protector*, and they were still more vigilant in watching out for any slaving ships. The West African Squadron consisted of these three ships—*Kangaroo, Protector,* and *Amelia*—which were entirely insufficient to patrol the vast expanse of coastline, and the many wandering rivers and tributaries, out of which the evil trade continued, and for every slaver the Squadron encountered, at least a dozen slipped away with their freight of despairing Africans.

During William Price's previous tour of Africa, he had enjoyed the companionship of William Gibson, and he felt the loss of his friend's conversation every day. His fellow officers on the *Kangaroo* were not as congenial, and there was a tendency to complain and find fault with everything, that was as dispiriting as the sultry weather.

His fellow officers on the *Kangaroo* were not as congenial, and there was a tendency to complain and find fault with everything, that was as dispiriting as the sultry weather.

The voyage and a subsequent tedious month back in Sierra Leone, reinforced William's conviction that his late commander's dying warning was completely sound—he would not have wished the tedium and the misery, the heat, and the blinding rains, upon the woman he loved—not for any consideration, and not even for the consolation they might have found in one another.

At no time did this persuasion weigh upon him more profoundly than on a miserable day in mid-February, when he and some of the crew were assigned to paddle their launch to explore a tributary of the River Gambia. The endless creeks and twisting

125

rivers along the coast were home to the luxurious settlements of the slave-masters. The long caravans of men, women and children, chained together and driven through the jungle, were collected at these slaving establishments, examined, sold, and packed into canoes to be ferried to the waiting ships on the coast.

This was William's first opportunity to command a small expedition, charged with enforcing the will of His Britannic Majesty King George at the point of a bayonet, thousands of miles from home, and facing a wily and determined enemy hidden in the formidable jungle.

Price and his sailors were accompanied by half a dozen Africans of the Kru tribe; short wiry men with tattooed faces and sharp, filed-down teeth, naked save for their loincloths. The Kru were not as susceptible to the fevers of the coast, and of course they knew how to navigate the treacherous shoals of the creek while Price and his men watched the shoreline on each side, clutching their loaded muskets. An attack could come from anywhere, at any moment, as they made their way upstream; the jungle provided the most perfect cover for any armed assailant, while they were perfectly exposed in their vessel, and still the launch was reckoned the safest place to be, for the crocodiles awaited anyone foolish enough to jump overboard.

The sun blazed down unrelentingly on William and his crew, but he dared not order the rowers to move from the middle of the river to one of the shady banks, for there awaited swarms of mosquitoes and sand flies, whose torments rendered all the rest of their discomforts insubstantial.

The sailors were silent and sullen, aware that an expedition of this sort would in all likelihood be a death sentence for some of them, even if they never heard a shot fired. The pestilential airs of Africa, especially the shock of the night dews after a day of blazing heat, could strike a man down with fever in a single day.

The excursion was only moderately successful. They did surprise an American schooner in the act of loading some captives, and captured the ship and rescued the slaves on board, but the dozens of Africans still being held on shore in the long sheds, known as barracoons, were swiftly driven into the jungle out of their reach.

Their small victory came at a heavy price: No sooner had the expedition returned to Freetown, than William's men fell ill. Within a week, yellow fever swept through the crew of the *Kangaroo*. Out of 120 men, William Price was the only officer still on his feet, and only fifteen men of the company were fit for duty.

The invalids who appeared to stand some chance of survival were quartered in a hut by the beach, which was in fact more comfortable than the Freetown hospital, for the promise of an occasional breeze from the ocean.

About a fortnight after his return to Freetown, William rose early, to make an accounting of the convalescents. He awoke with a headache, and his joints ached, but he mentioned it to no-one. These were the first symptoms of the onset of the yellow fever but, he told himself, *perhaps I merely have a head ache.*

The sun, glancing on the water as his little dinghy was rowed to shore, was so bright as to sting his eyes, and his spirits and energy were very low by the time he reached the town. His limbs felt leaden, and his eyes burned.

Reaching the convalescent shed, William was greeted by a tall and angular Negress who, in contrast to many of the female inhabitants of Sierra Leone, was modestly covered from neck to ankle.

"Good day to you, sir. We lost no men last night, praise be to Jesus."

"Thank you, Ruth," the young lieutenant smiled at her nervously, recalling that she was an ardent Methodist. The Admiralty disliked Methodism and tried to discourage its spread amongst the navy, but William thought they were mostly harmless. "You have a new preacher for your church, I think? How do you like him?"

"We liked him well enough sir, but this here fever took him before he had been here a week. God's will be done."

Not knowing what else to say, William stepped into the hut, and was assailed by the smells of unemptied chamber pots and vomit. His stomach lurched, and the bile rose to his throat.

"Do you have everything you require to take care of my men, Ruth?"

"I need me two strong fellas to help me turn and wash everybody. They is being sick everywhere."

William pulled off his hat and wiped the sweat off his forehead. "I am afraid I cannot spare anyone from the crew."

Ruth's lips pouted out in disdain. "Don't put no Englishman on this job. Get me some Kru men, they do it."

"They won't like to work for a woman, I think."

"Ha! They do anything for money. Then they go back home and buys them another wife."

William promised to hire some helpers, then moved on to greeting the men who lay on narrow trestle beds, packed into Ruth's little one-room hut. He helped Ruth bring cups of water to parched lips, until a wave of nausea overtook him. He looked up and saw that the walls of the shack were undulating like a sheet hanging on a laundry line in a gentle breeze. He looked over to Ruth, but she was not alarmed by the strange sight, so he decided not to mention it to her.

William stepped out on the veranda and leaned against the door post, looking at the *Kangaroo* bob up and down in the harbour and listening, with failing spirits, to the murmured conversation of the sick men inside, whose discontents seemed to pull him down with them.

"Half of my best mates are dead and gone—and for what? Why did Tom and Pete and Benjy shit themselves to death, to save these black devils from being slaves on t'other side of the ocean, when they was already slaves here? Can you tell me that?"

"Our *own* people was being stolen right off of our shores by the Barbary pirates—"

"Aye, by the hundreds. Entire villages taken by the Moslem bastards, and free Irish men and women made into slaves, and made to row their boats, or serve in their hareems, and how many fooking ships did the Navy send to set *them* free?"

"That's right, Mick. And another thing—how many lads from my village are rotting sacks of dead meat, lying all over—what's that fooking country again?

"Portugal. It's where Port comes from."

"Aye, Portugal, gone to fight in Portugal so that we can free the Spanish whoresons from the French whoresons? They are all Catholic whoresons together, ain't they? No offense, Mick. They aren't worth the powder to blow them all to hell. Why are good Englishman dying, so as to save a bunch of greasy Spaniards?

Would any of them do the same for me and mine? Not a single whoreson would, I can tell you that for naught."

"Why are we here? Fook them all, that's what I say."

William realized that in addition to pouring with sweat, he was also feeling chilly.

"...Fook me," continued the lament from the hut. "I miss the cold. I miss the snow. I miss the rain and the sleet. I wish I could be freezing my balls off back in Ireland, damn me if I don't."

A tall, coal-black African, wearing only an old dinner jacket and nothing else, strolled by, saluted William, and gave him an appraising smile, his white teeth flashing against his dark skin. "Good morning, officer boss. You be lookin' mighty peaky, I am thinking."

William leaned over the railing as a stream of black vomit poured from his throat. His legs turned to water and he collapsed, insensible.

CHAPTER TWELVE

"PARDON ME, MA'AM. I am an experienced seamstress. Have you any vacancies?"

The young woman had somehow slipped past the watchful eyes of Madame Orly on the first floor, to enter the classroom, where she found Fanny. Her youthful prettiness was marred by blue shadows under her eyes. Her countenance announced intelligence, and her address was civil and calm, but her hands, Fanny observed, were so tightly clenched together that the knuckles were white. Her quiet intensity caught Fanny's interest.

"Business is slow at present, I am sorry to say."

"Yes, ma'am, times are hard. I owned my own shop in Liverpool. I expect you are aware of how bad things are in Liverpool, after the government stopped the slave trade. Few ladies can indulge themselves in new articles of dress, these days."

"And do you propose to settle in London?"

"If I can find steady work here, ma'am." The newcomer cast an appraising look over the rows of girls bent over their sewing. "To whom may I apply? Where is your manager?"

"What's this? What's this?" Mrs. Blodgett descended upon them. "Looking for employment?" the older lady declared peremptorily. "No, we have no need of you here. Take yourself off."

Fanny saw a look of despair flash across the young woman's face. An overpowering sensation of empathy impelled her to make a daring resolution.

"Mrs. Blodgett, I wonder if we might engage this young lady on trial for a month—"

"Whatever for?"

"Mrs. Butters thinks I should spend some time in the country. As well, Madame Orly will be accompanying her to Bristol for a few weeks. This young lady could substitute for both of us in our absence."

"Mrs. Wakefield said she would volunteer occasionally while you take your rest cure," Mrs. Blodgett said, in a tone of voice which implied Fanny must be some sort of a malingerer or weakling.

"Well, ma'am, if Mrs. Wakefield may donate her services, may I not donate my salary?" Fanny heard herself saying firmly but calmly. "Thanks to your sister's kindness, I have no living expenses. Therefore, I will pay for a month's trial period for Mrs.—Mrs.—"

"Bellingham, ma'am. Mrs. John Bellingham," the young woman looked anxiously from Fanny to Mrs. Blodgett and back again. "I would be exceedingly grateful, ma'am, to be given a chance to prove my worth to you."

"Do I detect an Irish accent?" Mrs. Blodgett's nostrils flared in distaste.

"I am of the Protestant faith, ma'am. My father was a shipbuilder in Belfast. I am married to an Englishman."

"A shipbuilder!" cried Fanny. "Mrs. Butters would look kindly upon this lady, ma'am, for she is from a shipbuilding family."

"Well! You do presume a great deal, Miss Price. Have it your way then, but you will be held answerable for the consequences." Mrs. Blodgett walked away, shaking her head, and talking to herself, and Fanny and the newcomer were left together. Fanny pretended not to notice the tears of relief in Mrs. Bellingham's eyes, as she led her to the counting-room for a cup of tea.

"Please excuse me, Miss Price, but I am very much overpowered," Mrs. Bellingham murmured, as she took up her cup and saucer with trembling hands. "You will find me to be, in general, a very straightforward, matter-of-fact person. Your kindness..."

"There is no need for you to apologize, or to explain yourself," Fanny returned calmly. "I fancy that you are like me, rather reserved by nature, and not given to exchanging confidences upon slight acquaintance. Let us focus on the work before us, and leave everything else to another time, shall we? After you finish your tea, I will show you around the workshop and you can meet our young pupils. My friend Mrs. Butters says teaching these girls is no more difficult than herding cats."

This won a smile from the new employee, and she relaxed something of her guarded countenance.

Fanny felt curiosity, no less than sympathy, for her new acquaintance. In her looks, air, and speech, Mrs. Bellingham seemed well bred enough, but Fanny's experienced eye detected that her gown was turned and carefully made over, and her half-boots, though well-polished, deserved to be retired from service. She was not dressed in mourning, but she appeared to harbour some deep private grief.

Fanny's own knowledge of struggling with hidden sorrows, urged her to protect and help her new acquaintance. She was gratified to have the means to do so, cost her what it may in discord with Mrs. Blodgett.

Fanny's intuition that Mrs. Bellingham would be a good addition to the academy proved to be correct. She was a good instructress, a good seamstress, and an good saleswoman, and before a fortnight passed, Mrs. Blodgett declared that she would stay on, even after Fanny's return from Northamptonshire!

* * * * * * *

William Gibson returned to London after his time in Portsmouth, to discover that his literary star had been dimmed by a new and brighter celestial apparition.

George Gordon, Lord Byron, was creating a sensation in town. His exceedingly handsome face, his licentious private life, and his menagerie of wild animals drew even more attention than his new poem. Everywhere he went, Gibson heard nothing but talk of *Childe Harold* and Byron.

Most reluctantly, Mr. Gibson realized that his own day of distinction was over. Yes, he would produce new books and articles, the future productions of his pen might be well-received—he had the highest hopes for his novel in progress—but never again would he experience the gratification of newly-acquired fame, of knowing that people of fashion and influence were asking each other, "Have you read Mr. Gibson's book?" as a first topic of interest.

However, as a single man, and moreover, a young, good-looking, and conversable man, his company was still highly sought at dinner parties when a hostess needed to even out her table. He might have received one invitation where Lord Byron received ten, but he still could dine out most evenings of the week, if he so chose.

Mrs. Janet Fraser often found herself in need of two or three extra gentlemen, for she was still burdened with her step-daughter Margaret, and her friend Mary Bertram was staying with her again. It was Mary who suggested the name of "William Gibson" as an amusing dinner guest. Janet Fraser, hearing Mary's description of him, agreed he would be very eligible in that capacity, but, alas, could not be added to the list of potential husbands for Margaret because he was merely a writer, barely a gentleman, and she was the determined supporter of everything mercenary and ambitious, provided it be only mercenary and ambitious enough.

Janet Fraser still pinned her hopes upon Mr. Meriwether the wife-hunting widower from Bristol, and he headed her invitation list.

Mr. Meriwether had risen from humble circumstances, and apart from the loss of his wife in childbirth some years ago, good fortune had blessed all of his endeavours. At eight-and-forty, having grown wealthy in the wine trade, he had the means and the inclination to pursue interests long denied to him by the press of business. He enjoyed engaging in political debates, all the arts were delightful to him, and he scarcely ever ventured out of his home without acquiring more books for his rapidly-expanding library.

Thus, in arranging her name cards, Janet Fraser sat Mr. Meriwether next to Margaret. Her sister Lady Stornaway and her noble brother-in-law would have the seats of honour; Mary Bertram, Mr. Gibson and three other fashionable couples filled out her table.

As he entered the drawing room, William Gibson recognized only Mary Bertram, who directly attached herself to him, and then pulled him into a corner, to ask, with a smile which belied her professions of concern, what news he had of their mutual acquaintance, Miss Price. "I must apply to you, Mr. Gibson, for I have heard the most *alarming* reports of her. I have heard, though I can hardly believe it, that she is working as a sempstress in some warehouse in Camden Town! Can she have fallen so far in the world?"

"You will undoubtedly be relieved to know, ma'am, that Miss Price is in fact serving as the head instructress at a sewing academy under the sponsorship of the Society for Improving the Condition and Increasing the Comforts of the Poor."

"Aaahh, I see. She's a Clapham Saint now. Well, that would suit her very well. Fanny was never one to hide her light of benevolence under a bushel. What do you think, Margaret?" She turned to Margaret. "Can you conceive of some way to make ourselves half so useful? Can you not think of some scheme by which we may revel in the plaudits of our fellow men?"

Before Margaret could reply, Mary went on: "Well, despite what the fashionable world may think, I am happy to hear that Fanny has found some occupation. When one scheme of happiness fails, after all, human nature turns to another; if the first calculation is wrong, we make a second better. Did you know Fanny previously had designs on my husband, and actually hoped that the son of a baronet would marry the daughter of a marine officer, or whatever he was? You look surprised, Mr. Gibson. You did not know of dear Fanny's vaunting ambitions?"

"Mary, you speak as though she only wanted to marry him for his rank," protested Margaret. "Mr. Edmund Bertram is a very good, honourable, sensible man. Why should Miss Price not genuinely esteem him, growing up with him, as she did?"

"Oh yes, my husband is a paragon, Margaret. A paragon of goodness and virtue. But when did you study his character? I was not aware that you and he had ever exchanged more than 'how do you do's'?"

It was Margaret's misfortune to look guilty here. Mary had long suspected, but had no proof, that it was Margaret who had secretly informed Edmund Bertram of his sister Maria's clandestine meetings with Henry Crawford. "We d-did speak—just a little."

Mr. Gibson, seeing the cold expression on Mary's face, put an end to further enquiries by offering Miss Fraser his arm, and asking her to show him a large oil painting of a rugged seacoast at the other end of the room. He swept her away and they tenaciously discussed the painting, while his mind was busy.

He had known, from the time he met Fanny, that she had loved someone. She had never named him, had only hinted enough for Mr. Gibson to understand that the love match could never be. He had assumed it was a case where a difference in rank made a match improbable, if not impossible. Now here was confirmation that Fanny loved her cousin—had grown up loving him—had loved him

134

for years—perhaps could not help always loving him. And she was about to go visit and live with him, in Northamptonshire.

It was not an easy matter to absorb this information, while trying to soothe an agitated Miss Fraser, and while gesturing at a large painting and saying, "Waves... the waves... don't you think? Yes, the waves are very... wave-like."

Mr. Gibson was to lose his youthful partner when dinner was announced, for Janet Fraser saw to it that Miss Fraser was escorted into the dining room by Mr. Meriwether, and Mr. Gibson's arm was assigned to bring a different lady safely from the drawing-room to the table.

The change of rooms and company brought a change of topic. Janet Fraser, her sister Lady Stornoway and all of her female friends, were entirely taken up with Lord Byron and his new romantic poem, and could speak of nothing else.

"*Childe Harold*, I think everyone must acknowledge," Janet Fraser declared, "is something new and bold, something completely romantic. His writing is so very forceful! Cowper or Pope seem quite old-fashioned now, in the comparison."

"Is it 'child' with an 'e' or Harold with an 'e'?" asked another fair guest. "I can never recollect."

"I can commend any young man, born to wealth, rank and ease, who has exerted himself to write and publish," said Mr. Meriwether. "But only time will tell if the author will join the first ranks of our poets."

Mrs. Fraser shot Margaret a piercing glance.

"How interesting!" said Margaret. "Pray, go on, Mr. Meriwether."

"As a travelogue," continued Mr. Meriwether, "The poem is interesting enough. Byron's descriptions display talent and spirit, but I find his medieval language to be quite affected and ridiculous—with his 'lemans' and his 'lays' and his 'wights.'"

"If I must say what I think," Mr. Fraser said, "*Childe Harold* is a somewhat vulgar publication. It has no moral tendency."

"Anything that is so honest, so revelatory of the heart of an ardent young man," countered his wife, "cannot be considered vulgar." She recited, with great feeling: "*Ours too the glance none saw beside, the smile none else might understand, the whispered thought of hearts allied, the pressure of the thrilling hand!*"

135

"The poem may not be suitable for young persons," said her husband, "but it does not follow that it is of interest to adults."

"True, Mr. Fraser," answered his wife. "In fact, I doubt that it can be properly appreciated by any person in whom all youthful passions have been extinguished."

"It is his youth which tells against him," added Mr. Fraser with some asperity. "He labours too hard to display his classical learning, and he is altogether too self-important."

"Mr. Meriwether," Margaret interposed, for she was thoroughly weary of the familiar squabbles between her father and mother-in-law. "Did you use your own horses for the journey from Bristol?"

The conversation turned to horses for a time, and from there to long journeys, and then to travelling abroad, which recalled Janet Fraser to *Childe Harold*.

"*The torrents that from cliff to valley leap,*" she declaimed, rolling her eyes expressively. "*The vine on high, the willow branch below, mix'd in one mighty scene, with varied beauty glow.* How exquisite! It is seldom one encounters such passionate sensibilities in a man—and such poetic gifts!"

"What do you think, Mr. Gibson?" Mr. Meriwether nodded across the table. "I fear we need to reform ourselves if we are to win the notice of the fair sex in the future. We must wear our shirts open at the neck, and take care that our hair curls loosely over our foreheads."

"And you must always look distracted, as though you were composing some tragic sonnet," Mary Bertram cried. "And eat only biscuits, and drink only soda-water."

"Now there is a sacrifice I am not prepared to make," Mr. Meriwether laughed.

The ladies took their solicitude for Lord Byron with them when they retired to the drawing room, and Mr. Gibson enjoyed conversing with Mr. Meriwether about mutual acquaintance in Bristol, and the recent meeting of the African Institution. But upon re-joining the ladies, the gentlemen re-joined their praise of the poet and his poem:

"...All *I* know is, Byron is the very handsomest man I ever saw."

"Oh! Did you really see him in person?"

"Yes. I was riding on Rotten Row, and he was there, in Lady Melbourne's carriage."

"How tall is he?"

"What was he wearing?"

"Did you catch his eye?"

"Oh! There is something very—how shall I say—not quite polite about him."

Janet Fraser detached herself from her female guests, came eagerly forward and took Mr. Gibson's arm.

"Mr. Gibson, I am told that you read aloud beautifully."

"Thank you, madam."

"Could I venture to ask—would you not object to reading to us now? We would all be most excessively delighted if you would."

"I am at your service, ma'am, if the rest of the company is in agreement. Would you care to hear some short portion of—"

"Oh thank you! Thank you! Here you are, Mr. Gibson. Here is my copy of *Childe Harold*." And the volume was placed in his hands.

* * * * * * *

The season, the month, the time had arrived for Mrs. Butters to pay her annual visit to her niece Honoria Smallridge in Bristol. The signifier for this journey was not the sound of birdsong or the flowering of the forsythia shrubs, but the growing restlessness and irritability of Mrs. McIntosh, the housekeeper.

"Mrs. McIntosh must commence her spring-cleaning now, Fanny, or I shall not be answerable for the consequences if she is prevented, for one more day, from making a start. She must pull all the furniture out of the rooms, take down all the portraits and the curtains and set the housemaids to beating the rugs," explained Mrs. Butters. "I take myself well out of her way at this time, and you must do likewise."

Donald McIntosh, who also found it prudent to be out of his wife's way when it was spring cleaning time, drove the party to Oxford, where Fanny affectionately parted from Mrs. Butters and Madame Orly. Fanny was confident about completing the trip to Mansfield without an escort; after all, she had made the journey once before, when she was even younger and more inexperienced.

The following day, Fanny stepped down from the coach at an inn on the outskirts of Mansfield, the same establishment wherefrom she had run away from home, three years before. Her cousin Julia was there with a pony cart to take her to Thornton Lacey. "I am learning how to drive, and I am exceedingly fond of it, so I begged Edmund to let me retrieve you. Welcome, Fanny!"

Fanny rejoiced in her return to her beloved countryside at a time of year in which a receptive mind may contemplate the triumph of the revolving year over the dead hand of winter, and wonder at the tenacity of nature. The soft pale green buds, revealing that life pulsed within the dead-seeming branches of the bare trees; the tender purple crocus under the hedges, all caused her to marvel once again at the method by which a kindly Providence has designed these first effusions of spring to be enchantingly lovely to human eyes.

Julia maintained an eager flow of conversation on the ride from Mansfield. Fanny, always a courteous listener, was interested in hearing about the new house—which she had not yet seen—Julia's garden, and Julia's frequent visits to London. She would have liked to hear Julia's opinion of Edmund's health and spirits, but her quiet enquiry was met with: "Oh! Yes, Edmund is very well, he is always walking and riding about. Did you know that I lost my dear old mare, Lady, this past winter? I cried and cried over it, for I have had her since I was fifteen or sixteen, I think..." and Fanny contented herself with waiting until the pony cart pulled up at the elegant parsonage-house, and she could see Edmund for herself.

Edmund was more than a little surprised when he first beheld Fanny after such a long separation—At first, he thought her much altered in her looks, then decided it was her manner which had undergone the greatest change. His quiet cousin was still very demure, still more fitted for a listener than a talker, but her movements, her glance, her air, while tranquil and graceful, were all decidedly more assured and mature.

He, no less than she, had altered a great deal in the past few years. While his marriage had brought disillusionment, his occupation had strengthened him. In assisting his parishioners, he had also enriched himself. He was better acquainted with the hopes, sorrows, and fears of his fellow man, and also understood more of their self-deceptions and weaknesses. He had held bereft and weeping fathers who had to bury their little children. He had whispered hope and encouragement to a young boy living with a tyrannical father. He had pretended he hadn't seen the look of naked longing in the eyes of a young widow. He had joined couples in marriage, and a year later—or sometimes much sooner—baptized their first born. He had stood and intoned the service for the dead as the cold wind whipped his cassock about him and the leaves whisked around the graveyard, flying in and out of the freshly-dug grave like a swarm of restless souls. He had mediated in disputes between neighbours, between mothers and daughters, and pleaded leniency for poachers and thieves, and scolded drunkards and bullies, and praised the patient, quiet, hard-working men and women who toiled without ceasing, just to keep their families fed.

Edmund had always been his father's pride, owing to his upright nature and his strict sense of honor and decorum. But to this he added a new humanity which softened his character. From better understanding the private burdens of his parishioners, and on account of his own errors, he had learned humility, and was now more inclined to pardon and excuse, than remark and condemn.

Fanny could not but perceive the changes which time and experience had wrought in Edmund. She admired him all the more for his goodness—so evident by the respect and affection which the villagers showed for him—his kindness to Julia and his composure in the face of private sorrow.

Edmund appeared to derive as much pleasure as she from the resumption of their old habits of talking, reading, and riding together, he the chief speaker, she the chief listener.

But their renewed avowals of friendship, however sincerely made, could not completely restore the intimacy of the past. *She* was not a sheltered naïve girl looking up to Edmund as her only arbiter of truth and knowledge. *He* was occupied with his duties in the parish, and he was more taciturn and withdrawn than in his youth, which she could not wonder at. He was an excellent master to his servants, an excellent vicar, a good friend, a kind brother, and he would have been, thought Fanny, the best of husbands and fathers, had his marriage prospered well.

Fanny also observed that the reverses endured by the Bertrams in the past few years had improved Julia's character. She was no longer the same self-satisfied Miss Julia Bertram of Mansfield Park.

Her first acquaintance with sorrow had come when she realized that Henry Crawford was not in love with her. Then came the loss of her family's fortune and the removal from their home, a reversal which Julia bore with a self-possession that surprised Fanny.

Resentment against her cousin for past slights and neglect was no part of Fanny's nature, and she was happy to be acknowledged by Julia both as a close relative and a friend, while Julia learned to respect her younger cousin as she had never done before.

When a girl, Julia had been guided by her older sister Maria in everything, including Maria's tendency to be condescending towards Fanny. Now, Julia saw and admired Fanny's quiet self-discipline, her fund of literary knowledge, her unfailing thoughtfulness. Fanny had asked Edmund more questions and took a warmer and more sincere interest in the poor cottagers of Thornton Lacey than Julia had ever done. Observing Fanny sit down and write a long and affectionate letter to Lady Bertram, Julia's mother, living in far-off Norfolk, Julia realized that Fanny had been a more faithful correspondent to her mother than she herself had been. And upon Fanny's mentioning Miss Lee, Julia blushed to realize it had never once occurred to her to write to their old governess, while Fanny wrote to her regularly!

Despite this better understanding and higher opinion of each other, the two young ladies could not be said to be on newly intimate terms. Fanny had once suspected that her own brother William was very fond of Julia, and that Julia was not entirely indifferent to him, but she never supposed that Julia would seriously entertain the idea of becoming a mere "Mrs. Price," nor that her brother would risk his own happiness in forming such a design. With that in mind, she never raised the subject of her brother during her visit. Julia made no communication, and Fanny took no liberties. Fanny had never betrayed her affection for Edmund to anyone. They were two solitary sufferers, or connected only by Fanny's consciousness.

*　*　*　*　*　*　*

William Price's knowledge of the yellow fever, its commencement and progression, told him that, however wretched he may have felt, his case was not a fatal one. He was young and healthy; he had acquired no vicious habits to undermine his constitution, and he knew that bed rest, boiled water and a simple diet were his best preservatives. He refused all other treatments, having developed no faith in their efficacy from his own observations.

He knew he was feeling better when, after some days and nights of being indifferent to his surroundings, he found himself aware of a persistent and irritating noise. Turning his head on his pillow, he saw a man of middle-years, lying on his back, in the adjacent cot, his long and noble nose pointing skyward, and his mouth hanging open.

Apart from counting the cracks in the plaster of the ceiling, the snoring of his roommate was about the only thing Price could focus on, as he drifted in and out of sleep.

An orderly, coming in with a bowl of mush made from boiling water and pounded ship's biscuit, informed Price that his noisy room-mate was Captain Frederick Irby of the *Amelia*, the new commander of the West African Squadron, likewise convalescing from fever.

In the following days William, able to leave his bed for brief periods, assisted the orderly in taking care of the Captain, and showed him every attention and courtesy within his limited power. The irksome confinement of their joint convalescence was made more tolerable by their conversation—William, on account of his extended service in the African Squadron, was able to satisfy many questions put by Captain Irby as to the coast, the climate, the amenities in Freetown, and the efforts of Irby's predecessors, while Irby for his part was not loath to recount the details of his career in the Navy and his engagements with the French.

The reader will not be surprised to learn that Irby was favourably impressed by the conversation of the young lieutenant, seeing in his remarks the proof of good principles, professional knowledge, energy, courage, and cheerfulness, everything that could deserve or promise well.

"We'll have work for you, Price, by and by," said Irby. "I am fitting up that schooner you captured near the Gambia to scour all the slavers from the Pongus river."

"Yes, sir."

"Our information is that two of the slavers are British subjects. Apprehend them if you can. They will be tried under the new felony laws, and transported to Australia."

"Indeed, sir. And sir...."

"Yes, lieutenant?"

"A schooner and a few jolly-boats, working together, might more effectually carry the message to the slaver settlements. On the previous expedition, I did not wish to put my entire crew at risk by taking the launch ashore to fire the barracoons, as I wished. But a small party could detach from the main—only a few men, some torches and a quantity of gunpowder would be all that was necessary—"

"Yes, of course, Price. I see your point. And we can fit small cannons on the schooner to provide cover for the fire-team. Excellent suggestion. The slavers on the Pongus shall learn that you come with fire and sword to execute judgment upon them."

* * * * * * *

A mild spring morning shortly after her arrival saw Fanny seated next to Julia, as the young ladies jounced along the road to Mansfield in the pony cart.

They were paying a visit to their Aunt Norris, who of course Fanny would on no account avoid or neglect, for she truly believed the young owe a duty to their elders, even disagreeable elders. Thus could Fanny set out on the seven mile ride with Julia with no expectation of pleasure whatsoever, but with a serene conscience and a nicely worked cushion cover to present as a gift. The ride proved to be both diverting and entertaining for, in addition to admiring the beauties of the countryside, Fanny heard from Julia all the details of her encounter with Viscount Lynnon at the Northampton assemblies, and his Christmas-time proposal, and Fanny was excessively diverted.

"Julia, I fancy that a great many girls, when finding themselves proposed to by a viscount, would accept him immediately, and be in a carriage on their way to Gretna Green within a quarter of an hour!"

"You are asking me if I was tempted? Fortunately, I refused him before I had the opportunity to think of what it might mean—

that I could be the wife of an Earl one day. And I am not so vain as to suppose that Viscount Lynnon has a partiality for me—he was collecting disciples for his friend Shelley, and I happened to be at the Assembly that night."

The spirit of mutual confidence impelled Fanny to disclose that she, too, had a suitor—Mr. Edifice. "And I am also certain that, were we not thrown together every day at the academy, he would never have thought of me! One does want a proposal of marriage to be based on more than mere convenience!"

"One wants," said Julia softly, "a declaration from the person that one loves best in all the world. Wouldn't you?" She looked at Fanny gravely.

Fanny hesitated, startled. Was Julia speaking of her own wishes? Was she thinking with regret of William? Or was she hinting that she knew of Fanny's love for Edmund? How might she reassure Julia—and herself?

"But—but—many, many people are disappointed in their hopes, so far as a first attachment is concerned, if their affections are not returned, or, or they have not money to marry upon, and so forth. Still, it need not follow that their lives must be entirely blighted. Especially, I think, if one *resolves* to seek happiness. Those persons who have struggled with disappointment must think of their duty to their family and friends. I am sorry to take such a moralizing strain, but I believe it to be true."

"And many of these people go on to be happily married in the end?" asked Julia.

"Yes, of course, they do." said Fanny. "Many of them."

"Miss Price? Is that our own Miss Price?" a familiar voice exclaimed from the roadside, and Fanny recognized Christopher Jackson, the old carpenter on the Mansfield estate. Her interesting dialogue with Julia must be set aside at their approach to the environs of Mansfield.

The respect and affection in his voice, and the courteous way Fanny asked after Mrs. Jackson and young Christopher and the other little Jacksons, struck Julia most forcibly. It had never occurred to her to ask the Mansfield servants about their families. She did not know the names of their children. She was a "Miss Bertram," who would have spurned any over-familiarity from a servant or from anyone of the lower orders. They greeted her, Miss

Bertram, with a nod of the head, quite properly and politely, and yet—she would have liked for her old retainers' faces to light up at the sight of her, as they did for her cousin Fanny.

As they proceeded, Fanny viewed with great interest the changes to the familiar landscape, and to her surprise and delight, other passers-by recognized her. Julia had to rein in her horse more than once, so that Fanny could receive their greetings.

Here was Fanny being acclaimed by an old widow, whom she had aided with many charitable visits in the past, and here was a young boy from a poor family who, Fanny declared, had grown two feet since she saw him last. The material comforts that aided these families had come from Sir Thomas, but the food, clothing and monies had been brought round to their cottages and distributed by Fanny's hand.

Julia had, in the past, preened herself on the generosity and benevolence of her father toward the deserving poor, and, by extension, thought well of herself. Her father's generosity was a credit to her family and the name of Bertram. But she, she herself, had idled away most of the days of her youth in amusing herself, and had bestowed little time and effort upon others.

She silently resolved to do better in the future, to be more aware, to be more helpful in assisting her brother Edmund. "You have certainly not been forgotten, Fanny," was all that she said, once the last villager had patted Miss Price's hand, and said, "God bless you, my dear," and waved them on their journey.

"This is very gratifying, I will own—but, this is largely because of our Aunt Norris—"

"Aunt Norris!"

"Yes, Aunt Norris, for, whatever else we may say of her, it was she who taught me my duty to the poor, and always kept the poor-basket, and took me with her on her charitable visits," said Fanny.

Yes, thought Julia to herself, *and I always contrived to be elsewhere or doing something else, while Fanny had to struggle along carrying a basket half as big as she was!*

And here was another lesson for Julia, for in a few moments they were in Aunt Norris' parlour in the White House, and she was a witness to Fanny's polite and unfeigned solicitude despite her aunt's unfriendly reception! Julia had been accustomed to thinking of Fanny as weak and over-yielding, but surely there was a hidden

144

strength here; a higher species of self-command, a just consideration of others, a principle of right, which Fanny had imbibed as a child and practised every day.

But alas! Aunt Norris had not forgiven nor forgotten Fanny's role in delaying Henry Crawford's marriage to Maria, and the disastrous consequences that had followed. Her fond display over Julia was in marked contrast to her manner with Fanny.

"How very well you are looking, Julia! I always said, you and Maria were the handsomest young ladies in the county. And... no news? You have nothing to confide in us?" Mrs. Norris smiled archly and heaved a sigh, for, with few other cares to occupy her days, Julia's failure to find a husband was an increasing object of solicitude.

This, Julia reflected, was as unjust as it was irritating, because her aunt herself was nearer to thirty than twenty when *she* became a bride. Resolving not to be rude, but unable to answer as mildly as her cousin, Julia answered: "Please do not despair, dear aunt. I shall go up to town in a fortnight, and pass the Easter holidays with our cousins in Bedford Square, and no doubt the suitors will be buzzing around me like a swarm of bees!"

Julia spoke with a lightness, an irreverence, that she could hardly feel, and then, to Fanny's mortification, she impulsively added, "but don't you know, aunt, you will be able to congratulate Fanny before long, for she has an admirer, and he is a man of the cloth, just like dear Uncle Norris! I am sure you will approve."

"Oh!" Fanny exclaimed. "Please, Aunt Norris, Julia is speaking in jest, in jest only. There is no—"

"The sooner you are married Fanny—if someone will have you, which I cannot but doubt—the better. I do not know which is more disgraceful, the fact that you are working for money or the— the other business," declared her aunt.

Julia, nettled on behalf of her cousin, replied, "Mr. Edifice is also employed at the academy, and he esteems Fanny very much, doesn't he, Fanny? He doesn't think less of her for earning her own bread, and neither do I."

"Well Fanny, you must do as well for yourself as you can," returned Aunt Norris. "With all the advantages that I and dear Sir Thomas gave you, rearing you up at Mansfield Park, I trust you can make amends for your follies and your scrapes by marrying respectably!"

"Yes ma'am."

*   *   *   *   *   *   *

Their visit with Aunt Norris concluded, Julia and Fanny rewarded themselves by calling on Dr. and Mrs. Grant, at Mansfield Parsonage. Mrs. Grant was half-sister to Mary Crawford Bertram, but this did not alter the respect and affection both girls felt for her; she was a good and kindly woman, seeing the best in everyone dear to her, and unable on that account to cast off a beloved sister, while at the same time feeling, in the most acute terms, the scandal and disgrace which Mary had brought to Mansfield, the Bertrams, and everyone associated with them.

Dr. Grant was likewise well-disposed toward both Miss Bertram and Miss Price, as being pretty, civil young ladies, who provided a welcome diversion during the too-long interval between his breakfast and his dinner.

Mrs. Grant took a warm interest in Fanny's charitable work at the academy, and had many questions to pose as to the regulations of the school, the modes of instruction, the aptitude of the pupils, and Fanny's predictions for their future, all of which caused Julia to realize that she had not felt or shown half so much genuine solicitude for Fanny's doings in London as was demonstrated by Mrs. Grant. It had not occurred to her to ask Fanny about it!

What an admirable quality it was, Julia reflected, to be unaffectedly interested in the doings, cares, and concerns of others. And not as a gossip, or a pry, still less for the purpose of uncovering fault and weakness, but to rejoice in their successes and commiserate in their difficulties! Julia privately resolved to be less self-centred, to pay more attention to the claims of others upon her time and thoughts.

Mrs. Grant also asked very particularly after Edmund, lamented that they saw him so seldom at Mansfield, and upon Dr. Grant's leaving them to attend to some correspondence, added quietly: "I cannot suppose that either of you girls are in communication with my unhappy sister. Mary spent the winter months in Wales but is now in London, so you might see her, Julia, should you go to town this Easter as you intend."

"Indeed, Mrs. Grant," said Fanny, out of the goodness of her heart, wishing to reassure the feelings of a loving sister, "I did see her briefly last autumn, and she looked to be in excellent health."

"Thank you, Miss Price," came the reply, with a tremulous sigh. "You are very kind. I miss Henry and Mary—so very much! She is as lost to me, as though she were also on the other side of the grave! What I would not give to have us all as we were before! But pray, do not mention what I just said to your brother. I cannot expect Edmund to—even though he is the kindest and best of men. He has not exposed her to scandal and exposure, and himself to contempt and ridicule, by asking for a divorce. I bless him for it, and hope..." but there she trailed off, for what hope could there be?

An uncomfortable silence followed, until Julia, rising awkwardly, proposed that dear Mrs. Grant show them the growth and progress of her rose garden and her shrubbery.

* * * * * * *

Of the dozens of calling cards on display on Janet Fraser's mantelpiece, the one which took pride of place was that of Patrick, Lord Elsham, the particular friend of Mary Bertram.

It was well known that Mary Crawford had charmed the Earl, when he first met her at the home of her uncle, the Admiral. He had campaigned for a long time to make her his mistress; she had resisted, so it was said, and went in to Northamptonshire with her brother.

But when Mary Crawford, now Bertram, returned to London shortly after her marriage, she admitted Lord Elsham as a visitor to her town home, in defiance of public opinion, and she vacationed at Brighton at the same time as he—without, of course, the company of Lady Elsham.

London gossips said that Lord Elsham had tired of Mary and abandoned her, leaving her without a protector. But his curricle, with its coat of arms and a full complement of groomsmen, pulled up outside of the Fraser's town home one day that spring, and his Lordship requested and received a private audience with Mrs. Bertram.

Margaret Fraser, who tended to wander around the house like a ghost, unheard, unnoticed and unwanted, could not resist pausing outside, and she heard much, but not all.

"Mary, why did you think I could be so easily imposed upon? Do you think me a simpleton, easily flattered, easily misled?"

Alas, Margaret could not distinguish Mary's softer tones in reply.

"Does Lady Delingpole know of this?"

"No—no—Patrick, of course not. No-one knows of it. Can you not forgive me? Can you not understand?"

"I should have known that a woman who would deceive her husband, would also deceive her lover."

"Patrick, I do regret it." Mary's voice grew louder, she had lost her composure, an unusual thing with her. "Please do not betray me—if my husband should ever learn—"

"He *shall* learn of it—from me."

"No, dear Elsham, I beg of you. You would not be so cruel as to expose me publicly. It will kill me, I swear it. You would not take such a terrible revenge against—"

"Mary, see to it. Tell him yourself. I will not wait forever."

Margaret heard Mary begin to weep, and Lord Elsham made an impatient noise.

"Well, then. Well then, madam. I think you understand me. Good day to you, then, madam."

And Margaret softly scampered away for fear of detection.

* * * * * * *

Fanny accompanied Edmund, at his invitation, for long rides to explore the countryside around Thornton Lacey. Julia generously gave her new horse over to Fanny as often as she wished.

Although Fanny had grown up at Mansfield, she had seldom been included in the frequent exploring-parties in which the young people had indulged in the past, even though she was better formed to enjoy and profit from such excursions, having a keen eye and a fund of poetry and prose at her command to bring forward when a new vista, or a secluded spot, brought to mind some favourite encomium on nature. Therefore, everything that Edmund showed her was new to her, though all in the environs of Mansfield, and no detail was too small or prosaic to capture her interest. She entered into his concerns, approved of his projected plans, and sympathized with his little vexations.

"Here, Fanny, here is the boundary of our parish—my little empire is not very extensive, but I hope that I have helped to materially improve the lives of the villagers here. My glebe land is more productive, thanks to the reforms I have instituted, and some of the younger farmers have undertaken to follow my example. We have planted fruit trees, and have got up a committee to improve the roads, and another to bring relief to the poorest of the cottagers."

"You are doing just as you said you would do, Edmund—living amongst your parishioners, showing yourself to be their well-wisher and friend, and they, knowing you, and knowing your good conduct and principles, are the better for it!"

Edmund smiled. "That is to say, everybody knows everybody else's business here in the country. It is no small advantage to the churchman, for in addition to his own remonstrances, when a man drinks too much and neglects his labours, or a woman is too harsh to her children, the malefactor knows that all their acquaintance have discussed and condemned their behaviour, and it is human nature to want the approval of our fellow-creatures. If a man chooses a wife from this village or the next, and treats her unkindly, he must consider what her brothers might have to say about it, or if a son fails to assist his widowed mother, all the other mothers will tell him of his fault.

"But," he concluded, "living in each other's pockets, as we do here, is not a congenial mode of life for everyone, we must allow."

"I can imagine no felicity superior to this!" Fanny answered. "To live in such a lovely spot of countryside and to know that you have done so much for your fellow creatures! We cannot cure all the sorrows of the world, but, as Voltaire said, we can cultivate our own garden, and avoid evil and vexation. Oh, cousin, who would *not*—" and she broke off, conscience-stricken, as she recalled that Edmund's wife so despised country life, that she had done the unthinkable and left her husband.

Edmund smiled sadly. "Fanny, I know what you are thinking. Of whom you are thinking. It should not surprise you to know that I think of her every day, every morning and every night. And I haven't forgotten, either, that you tried to warn me that she was not what she appeared to be. But I was too readily seduced by my wishes—by what I *wanted* her to be."

He turned to look at her, and Fanny thought that he had never looked so handsome as he did now, with the rays of the late afternoon sun lighting his face.

"Fanny, I fear that I must leave Thornton Lacey, before long."

"What! Leave! Why? Is Dr. Grant retiring? Are you returning to Mansfield?"

"No. I received a letter from Mary, asking me for a reconciliation."

"You intend to—to take her back?" Fanny managed to stammer, her breath catching in her throat.

"Yes, Fanny. Irrespective of my inclinations, I believe it is my duty to redeem her, if I can. She is my wife. It must begin with my forgiveness."

Fanny looked away, unable to meet his eye, unable to speak, as a sickening feeling stole over her. She could never forgive Mary—not for winning Edmund's heart, not for breaking it. He must still love her, in spite of her treatment of him. He was still bound to her.

Fanny attempted to push down her own feelings and force herself to attend to what Edmund was saying:

"...I have contemplated this question many times and always end up with this conclusion. But there are many difficulties in our way. It is impossible that she return here. It would not be tolerated, not by my superiors nor by my parishioners. I doubt that Mary Magdalene herself would get a better reception from any of them."

"Then, cousin," Fanny said with a detachment she did not feel, "if you were to resume living with her as husband and wife, you would have to leave this lovely place, and perhaps go somewhere... somewhere where no-one knows your history?"

"Yes, someplace very distant, Fanny. But where? Some little crofter's cottage in the Scottish Hebrides? St. Petersburg? Calcutta?"

"Pardon me for observing that none of those places seem calculated to satisfy Mary. A place remote enough for discretion's sake, would be a good deal too remote from the fashionable world for *her*."

"Indeed. And how shall I support us? Shall I become a Methodist and preach in the fields? Or collect beaver furs in Quebec?"

"It must be faced up to, I suppose," Fanny sounded unconvinced.

"I am hardening myself, gradually, to the necessity of leaving Thornton Lacey, for Mary's sake. Please say nothing to Julia just yet. Nothing has been resolved upon."

Fanny nudged Julia's mare up next to Edmund's horse and reached out to touch his arm. "Cousin, you know that whatever happens, you will always have my loyal friendship. I hope you will be content."

"I am lonely, Fanny," he suddenly confessed. "Very lonely. I fear Gray's ridicule applies to me, these days...

Poor moralist! and what art thou?
A solitary fly!
On hasty wings thy youth is flown;
Thy sun is set, thy spring is gone—

Fanny's eyes flooded with tears and she quickly looked away. To tell him that she would gladly have been his lifelong companion, would only bring further distress to them both. He had chosen another; he belonged to Mary. If only Mary could make herself worthy of such a man!

"I think—" she stammered, "I doubt— that you will find an effusion upon spring, that does not end with some reference to fleeting youth, and the limits of mortality. Poets," she attempted to laugh, "would not think themselves worthy of the name if they could contemplate the season with anything less than melancholy."

Both were silent for a time, struggling to contain their emotions. The silence between them seemed to grow more eloquent, and Fanny feared she might betray the secrets of her heart, locked inside for so many years.

Fortunately, Edmund was the first to regain his composure, and with a smile, he said, "What would content me the most at this moment, Fanny, would be a good dinner. Shall we return home?"

"Certainly, cousin."

CHAPTER THIRTEEN

WILLIAM GIBSON'S confidence in his abilities as a writer were but briefly shaken by the advent of the flamboyant Lord Byron. He resolved to leave off poetry and concentrate on prose. Since his return from Portsmouth, he had been hard at work on his first novel, a fantastical tale of the future, which he hoped would equal or surpass the success of *Against the Slavers*. He also continued to pen reviews and articles for the *Gentlemen's Magazine* and other periodicals. His diligence left him little time to call upon Fanny in Stoke Newington, but she played no small part in his imaginings.

Not long after making the acquaintance of Miss Fanny Price, he was wont to say to himself, "I am not the marrying kind, but if I were, Miss Price is the type of person who would do well for me, I think." His mind admitting this much, over many months and many involuntary, idle musings, and without his intending it whatsoever, he began to sketch a future in which Fanny became established in his imagination as his partner.

He now acknowledged to himself that in the scenes his fancy painted, he and Fanny lived together in a comfortable little house on the outskirts of London, close enough to Fleet Street but far enough away from the smoke of the city so she could breathe fresh air and walk through the fields with him in the morning. Fanny would read his first drafts, encourage his efforts, and pour scorn his critics.

Although Fanny's relations had given her a better home, in material terms, than her old home in Portsmouth, *he* would be the one to give her a home she could truly call her own, in which she could exert her own tastes and preferences, where she would be respected by her friends and neighbours.

When Mr. Gibson first realized Mr. Edifice was his rival for Fanny's affection, he had laughingly dismissed the possibility that she might ever bestow her hand upon the self-important cleric. He had hinted the question to Mrs. Butters, and she too, had laughed at the idea. But in the following weeks, his doubts kept recurring— *surely Fanny would prefer a man in holy orders rather than me, a Free Thinker?* And... *say what you like about that Edifice fellow, he does recognize Fanny's worth*, but... *Edifice says he will not take her without a handsome settlement*, still... *if he did propose, would*

*she accept him? Would she value the stable, secure kind of life he
could offer her, instead of casting her lot with a writer?*

At least, if Fanny were considering matrimony—with anyone—he ought perhaps to think it an encouraging thing; it meant that her heart was detaching itself from her cousin, her first hopeless love.

He wondered if he should speak now, even before his novel was published—for he depended upon the success of that novel to provide enough income to afford a modest home. But was it not presumptuous and rash to offer matrimony before he was in a position to support a wife? To ask her to bind herself to him, before the future was certain?

But, consider as he might, he could think of no way to hint at matrimony with Fanny without actually coming to the point. How to prepare her to take such a step?

He agreed, along with Mrs. Butters, that her first answer was likely to be 'no' —not out of any feminine caprice or disinclination for him or for the state, but out of an apprehension of anything new, untried and unknowable.

In the meantime, and unable to answer the question to his own satisfaction, he concentrated on his journalistic career. The losses to English merchants, owing to the collapse of trade around the globe, was the story of the season, and Gibson frequently attended Parliament, which was also much taken up with the unrest in Manchester, where over one thousand stocking looms had been smashed by bands of angry unemployed weavers.

He was in the public gallery, watching the debate late one afternoon, when another spectator quietly applied to him. "Sir, pardon me, but are you familiar with the persons in the House?" Gibson turned to behold a man of middle years holding a pair of opera glasses over his long, aquiline nose.

"I cannot name every member of the House, sir," Gibson returned. "But there you may see the Prime Minister, just leaving the chamber, and there is the Home Secretary."

"Aha. I am obliged to you, sir." The stranger then moved along and Gibson heard him repeat the same question to others in the gallery.

The debate on the house floor devolved into a dreary going-over of accounts, and Gibson, always bored by money matters, could not attend to it. He decided to go in search of Lord Delingpole, who was a reliably candid source of information for the behind-the-scenes struggles of the Tory government.

He found the earl in a passageway, disputing vigorously but with good humour with some other peers, but upon spying Gibson, Delingpole broke off and grabbed his arm, dragging him along the corridor, and pushing against the tide of men who were leaving the house chambers to return to their meeting rooms.

"Gibson, you scoundrel! I've been told you are writing for the *Edinburgh Review* now! Why are you scribbling for a Whig publication! Are you for sale to the highest bidder? Shall we see your name listed in the next directory of the Covent Garden *filles de joie*? "Tall, fine figure, brown haired, good teeth, enjoys saucy *repartee*?"

Gibson repressed the urge to retort that the appellation bestowed upon him by Lord Delingpole might more accurately be applied to politicians, and said only, "Your Lordship, I have never claimed allegiance to either Tory or Whig, only to the cause of abolition, which happily has distinguished adherents on both sides. I was asked to write a refutation of a recent publication which defended the practise of slavery."

"Well then, well then. How was your trip to Portsmouth?"

"When it wasn't tedious, it was horrible."

"Yes. I shan't forget the poor old First Lord, with tears in his eyes, unfolding the matter in the House."

"Having been on service in Africa, and having been faced with the prospect of dying far from home, I too was particularly affected by the unhappy fate of our sailors in the Baltic."

"But... do you agree with the verdict of the courts-martial that the tragedy did not come about by any negligence or error on the part of the Navy? Your article will not be critical of the administration, I presume?"

"The fleet was advised that no one should attempt the voyage after the first of November, and the convoy set out almost three weeks after the deadline. I shall report the Navy verdict: the capsizing of the ships in winter storms was an act of god."

"You are well aware, I am sure, the delay was occasioned not by the Navy, but by the merchant ships they were escorting."

"So the god in question is Mammon."

"Very well. You may stay with me, for here comes the prime minister, and if you can keep a civil tongue in your head I will present you."

Gibson had barely time to express his thanks when a slender man of middle age, dressed all in black, paused to greet Lord Delingpole. Gibson had seen the prime minister from the gallery on numerous occasions, but he was inwardly surprised upon meeting him in the flesh. Most political leaders, like Lord Castlereagh or Lord Delingpole, commanded whatever room they entered. Heads turned, conversations paused. By contrast, Spencer Perceval was quiet and unobtrusive, and had Gibson not known he was, in fact, the prime minister, he might have taken him for a minor functionary about the House of Commons.

"Mr. Perceval, may I present to your notice the writer, William Gibson, the author of *Amongst the Slavers.*" Gibson straightened up from his profound bow and realized that he towered over the diminutive prime minister. Gibson was also struck by the man's pallor—his skin was nearly translucent—but he wore a serene expression. The weight of his responsibilities must be crushing, Gibson thought to himself. The nation was in its eighteenth year of war with the French, the national debt was fathomless, and the population was dangerously restless—how did the man maintain such an appearance of tranquillity?

"I am most gratified to meet you, Mr. Gibson. I have read your account of your adventures in Africa with the greatest avidity. The portraits you painted of the sufferings of the unhappy Africans cannot fail to sway opinion in favour of the abolitionist cause."

"Sir, you do me great honour."

The prime minister raised his voice, so that it echoed all along the corridor: "We will continue to prosecute the war against slavery, if I may so term it, with unremitting zeal. The trade embargoes, we trust, shall not only fatally wound the French adventurer but put a stop to the commerce in human souls."

Satisfied, Perceval allowed Lord Delingpole to take his elbow and steer him away from the others, while Gibson followed.

"The upcoming debate is a critical one, sir," Delingpole said quietly. "The Whigs have public opinion with them. The problem is—how to persuade our own men to vote against the best interests of their constituents? To align themselves in favour of measures which are bringing economic misery to hundreds of thousands of our fellow country-men?"

Perceval nodded and smiled. "We know the trade embargo must be maintained, ere the Lord of Hosts brings His chastisement to this fallen nation. As the prophet said, 'For, behold, the Lord cometh out of his place to punish the inhabitants of the earth for their iniquity.' The Scriptures reveal the hand of God in everything which has transpired."

"Everything, sir?" Gibson could not resist asking. "Do you contend, sir, that the Bible predicted everything, including our defeats and losses in Europe?"

Perceval's smile never wavered. "Mr. Gibson, you will be familiar with chapter eleven of the Book of Daniel, which speaks of war between the king of the north and the king of the south. 'So the king of the north shall come, and cast up a mount, and take the most fenced cities; and the arms of the south shall not withstand, neither his chosen people, neither shall there be any strength to withstand.'"

"Sir?"

"Wellington's massive fortifications in Portugal—he has 'cast up a mount,' indeed. And Wellington will lay siege to the fortress cities. He has taken Ciudad Rodrigo, he will attempt Badajoz and Salamanca. The prophet assures us of complete victory. 'The arms of the south shall not withstand.'"

Perceval tapped Gibson's waistcoat for emphasis.

"This is why I resist the misguided advice, pressing upon me from all quarters, to withdraw Wellington and our forces from the field in Portugal. God will provide the victory and in the meantime, the evil scourge of Popery will be swept away in Spain. Even Napoleon is a tool in His mighty hands. The Corsican is suppressing the worst excesses of Catholicism, and throwing down the regime of the corrupt priests with their archaic superstitions, and then we, in turn, will defeat Napoleon. 'And at the time of the end shall the king of the south push at him: and the king of the north shall come against him like a whirlwind, with chariots, and with horsemen, and with many ships; and he shall enter into the countries, and shall overflow and pass over.'"

"You are—that is, England is—the king of the north?"

"As foreseen by scripture. All will be well. Good day to you, gentlemen."

Gibson was much struck by the light of certainty beaming from Perceval's mild eye as he bid them both farewell. The writer followed Lord Delingpole through the busy corridors, saying nothing, until the opportunity arose for them to have a few quiet words in a gallery overlooking the lobby.

"The king is mad, your Lordship, and now I have met his Prime Minister."

"Well yes, Perceval can be a little eccentric, I grant you, but only he was able to raise the funds to continue the war, so we need him in place."

"With all due respect, your Lordship, he is making decisions of state, and spending almost all the national purse, upon the authority of verses written by some unknown scribe in a distant desert, some aeons ago."

"Are you opposed then, to the prosecution of the war against Napoleon? Are you so naïve as to urge, that if we let him alone, he will leave us alone as well? You might just as well be a Whig."

"I mean, your lordship, that when debating and arriving at the correct course of action, an Englishman expects the decision will be made by the collective wisdom of Parliament, not by one religious fanatic's interpretation of a bit of Old Testament prophecy—so-called."

"You speak a little too warmly, I think, sir. You do not want to join Mr. Finnerty in prison, now do you?"

"In these times, sir, any journalist who has not been convicted for libel could hardly respect himself, or be admired by his peers."

Lord Delingpole only laughed, then nudged Gibson in the ribs and nodded in the direction of a man who was slowly climbing the steps from the lobby, closely followed by a small retinue of clerks and society ladies, who were all eyeing him with something very much like veneration.

The man was tall, and strikingly handsome, indeed, so very handsome as to cast a sort of enchantment on the observer; his looks and his air signified not merely nobility but some rare and special alchemy of genius and feeling. Gibson did not need an introduction to understand that here, he beheld George Gordon, Lord Byron. The broad brow, the dark and curling hair, and his slow progress up the stairs, owing to his misshapen foot, told Gibson everything he needed to know.

"There is that tiresome show-off Byron," muttered Lord Delingpole, springing down the marble steps to intercept him. "I must take him down a peg. Follow me, Gibson." And he loudly accosted the poet in the middle of the flight of stairs, so everyone above and below could hear them.

"Your Lordship!" Delingpole's voice echoed throughout the stairwell and the lobby. "May I present Mr. Gibson, the author of the celebrated account of the West African Squadron. Mr. Gibson, I think Lord Byron needs no introduction. All of fashionable London is speaking of him."

"Your servant, sir," Byron inclined his head. "I have read your excellent narrative with great interest."

"And yours, sir -" Gibson was about to politely lie in return, when Delingpole intervened.

"I recommend Mr. Gibson's work to all my friends, and I only regret that I will never have the pleasure of reading your new effusion, sir, for I cannot bring myself to spend so large a sum on a single book."

"You surprise me, sir!"

"Do I? How much do you pay your scribes to write out the complete poem? To say nothing of copying the illustrations. Your book must cost several hundred pounds, does it not?"

"Scribes? Sir, I do not understand you. My poem was published by John Murray."

"John Murray? But surely he produces books by means of a printing press?"

"Of course, sir."

"A printing press? A machine? How can this be? Only a few weeks ago, sir, you spoke so eloquently in the House against mechanical looms, which were depriving the weavers of their livelihood. I had assumed you applied the same elevated principles to the conduct of your own life. How can you live with yourself, sir, knowing how many men might have been employed in copying your doggerel? You have condemned hundreds of scribes and their families to starvation, have you not?"

"Your lordship is jesting, surely."

"I am in earnest, sir. By what right do you condemn the mill-owner for doing what you yourself have done? Or are you, as I suspect, sir, a hypocrite, a *poseur*, and an ignoramus?"

Byron's handsome brow flushed, and he glowered up at his critic. "You make light of the matter, sir, but it is *you* who have made criminals of these desperate men. You have hung them from a gibbet for the crime of attempting to feed their starving families!"

"What do you call a man who assaults and even murders his employer, who smashes his machines and foments revolution, if not a criminal? You have not answered my question: can you enlighten me, sir, why it is that *you* may profit by selling books made by machines, but the mill-owner may not sell his stockings?"

"As I said in the House, sir, it is also the case that the stockings produced by machine are of an inferior quality."

"What is that to you, sir! If a man wishes to purchase a pair of ill-made stockings at a lower price, instead of buying hand-woven stockings, it is his own affair entirely. What a feeble argument! Shall you dictate to your fellow Englishman what they shall sell and what they shall buy? A Whig who calls himself a friend of humanity is always a despot in disguise."

Byron was formulating his reply but Delingpole would not wait. "Cat got your tongue, sir? Well, we shall meet again at White Lodge, I expect. As long as you've no objection to the wheel, that is, and can take a carriage to Richmond. Good day to you, sir!"

With an air of triumph, Delingpole swept Gibson down the stairs to the lobby.

"Yes, but the weavers..." Gibson protested feebly.

"The weavers will have to find new employment, just as the scribes must have done," answered Delingpole brusquely. "Your great-grandsire wore a ruff around his neck, and your father wore a wig, but you wear neither. And yet I did not have to step over the desiccated bodies of any ruff-makers or wigmakers on my way to the House today—did you? And any rogue can write a book. No offense, Mr. Gibson."

"Oh, none taken, sir. I am a lazy rogue, and I own it. Or rather, I aspire to be a gentleman, and to not have to work at all. What would be the consequences for society if machines could replace all human labour? You have given me a lot to think about, your lordship."

* * * * * * *

The academy had been in operation for almost a year, and its routines were well established. The long broad tables had gone upstairs to the cutting room, where they were needed, and small round tables brought in instead. Fanny had prevailed in her desire to arrange the students in small groups, with the most skilled girls keeping an eye on the younger ones; and when Matron or Mrs. Blodgett were called away, they knew they could talk quietly amongst themselves, without reprimand from their instructress.

Looking back upon her earlier apprehensions, recalling the fears and self-doubts which had assailed her before the academy opened, Fanny acknowledged that Mrs. Butters had been right; she was not only able to be a sewing instructress, but was able to perceive and suggest many small improvements to the efficient management of the enterprise.

Upon her return from her fortnight in Northamptonshire, Fanny, Matron and Eliza Bellingham all worked together in the most amicable fashion. The results, Fanny thought, spoke for themselves.

William Gibson had brought Fanny a paddle-shaped fan from China, which he had purchased from a sailor in Portsmouth. It was made of tightly stretched silk, fine enough to be semi-transparent, and upon which some skilful hand had wrought a delightful specimen of embroidery. Fanny imagined that the court ladies in Peking might refresh themselves on a warm day with just such a fan as this.

She brought it to the academy to show to her pupils, showing them how the portrait was equally flawless on both sides. Thousands of tiny stitches rendered the needles of a contorted pine tree, in whose branches perched a golden bird with colourful feathers, which Mr. Gibson confirmed was the mythical phoenix.

This gift, which Fanny treasured, spoke to her of her friend's esteem and his respect for the artistry, patience, and skill of those who created pictures with needle and thread. As Fanny remarked to Eliza Bellingham, while it was true that only men had the ability to erect structures made with marble and wood, women, feebler in strength but perhaps no less lacking in imagination and the desire to gratify it, were also creators, even though they only worked with fabric and thread.

"Very true, Miss Price," was the answer, "and a bonnet or a lady's gown is constructed, no less than a building is. Not only that, we dressmakers can make a lady appear larger, or smaller, or taller, than she really is!"

"And look at the miracles stay-makers accomplish with lady's bosoms!" laughed Fanny.

The most gratifying aspect of her work was the undoubted success of the introduction of doll's clothes to the shop. Even when customers did not indulge in new outfits for themselves, they were nevertheless often persuaded to buy a doll for their daughters, and these dolls, as Fanny put it, were like little ambassadresses for the Academy, a gentle reminder for the more fortunate families. Perhaps the parents might think, now and then, on the little girls who toiled all day in Camden Town, while their *own* daughters were free to play with dolls.

Shortly after Fanny's return, the following colloquy was heard in the cutting room on the highest floor of the building.

"I hope to receive this order before Easter, Mrs. Bellingham. My girls will be excessively disappointed if they do not have their new frocks by then," said Cecilia Butters as she drew on her gloves.

"Yes ma'am, I will see to it personally."

"And my bonnet? Can it be re-trimmed to match my new dress?"

"Certainly, Mrs. Butters. I am a milliner by training. Rest assured, your bonnet will look completely new once I have done with it."

"That's good to hear. Mrs. Bellingham, I must say I am quite satisfied with your services. You understand my tastes very well."

"I thank *you*, ma'am. And it is a great pleasure to fit up your charming little daughters as well, as I myself have three sons, and no daughters to dress."

"What!" Cecilia Butters exclaimed. "You have children? Three sons? And how can you endure to be without them while you are at work? Who, pray, takes care of them? It is not fit. It is not natural."

Mrs. Bellingham wrung her hands nervously.

"Oh! Ma'am, they are presently in Liverpool, living with my aunt and uncle. My husband is unable to work, and I must earn a living, so that I may be able to pay for their education."

"Oh. Well. How very unfortunate."

"Ma'am, you are exceedingly kind to take such a warm interest, but I trust I will be reunited with my family before long. Necessity compels me to work for the present."

"For the present? I should be sorry, after all, to lose your services."

"Oh... Yes, thank you indeed, ma'am. Good day, ma'am."

Cecilia Butters withdrew and descended the stairs to the classroom.

"Good day, Mrs. Butters," said Fanny.

"Miss Price."

"Good day, Mrs. Butters," said Mrs. Blodgett.

"How are you today, my dear Mrs. Blodgett? I am exceedingly pleased to discover that Mrs. Bellingham is a milliner as well as a seamstress. Now I can bring my bonnets here to have them all re-trimmed."

"It would be our pleasure, ma'am, I am sure."

"And, ma'am, if you are satisfied with our services," Fanny added, although a little startled at her own boldness, "we would be very much obliged if you could kindly inform your friends, so as to encourage more customers at our establishment."

"Of course, Miss Price. Of course. You must keep your eye upon the money, mustn't you? Good day to you, Mrs. Blodgett. I will be returning on Tuesday afternoon. Please remind Mrs. Bellingham."

"I will ma'am, though I warrant there is no need."

"Indeed not, only my girls would be excessively disappointed if they do not have their new frocks for Easter. But you are correct—I may rely upon Mrs. Bellingham."

Fanny got up to escort their visitor downstairs, but Cecilia Butters waved her away.

"I can find my own way, thank you, Miss Price. You may as well stay at your employment. Good day."

A moment's silence, and then—

"Oh, that odious little creature! Poor Harriet is sadly put upon," sighed Mrs. Blodgett.

Fanny could not contradict her companion's estimation of Cecilia Butters, but only laughed and went to assist a girl in choosing her colours of embroidery floss for her project.

A few moments later —

"Where are my scissors? My good scissors?" Mrs. Blodgett exclaimed.

"Ma'am—"

"Who has stolen my scissors?"

"I think, ma'am—"

"Miss Price! Miss Price! Close the door! Search the cloakroom!"

"Ma'am, I believe your scissors are downstairs in the shop. Shall I fetch them for you?"

Fanny hurried down and searched behind the counter for Mrs. Blodgett's scissors. Madame Orly, seeing her, rustled up to her confidingly.

"*Que le bon dieu vous bénisse, Mademoiselle Price, pour nous avoir donné cette Madame Bellingham! Elle est un trésor!*" Madame Orly exclaimed. "*Et, savez-vous pourquoi?*"

Madame Orly often spoke to Fanny in French in front of the Blodgetts, because they did not understand French and she enjoyed hearing them grumble about it.

Fanny smiled and replied in English, "I think I can guess why you are so pleased with Mrs. Bellingham. I believe she has bestowed a great deal of time upon Mrs. George Butters and her three daughters, has she not?"

"*Mais oui!*"

"For my part, I am happy to know I was able to render assistance to a respectable young woman in a desperate situation. She is very patient with the customers, is she not?"

"Patience! As patient as.... as the dear saints! Not I—not for Cecilia Butters. *Non*, not another moment can I speak to that dreadful woman! She has only just left us— 'Be certain that my new gown is ready for Easter, do you hear?' And out she goes! Do you know, Monsieur Blodgett sends all the bills to our Madame Butters, and the dear old woman pays for it?"

Fanny could only smile and shake her head. "I confess, I often need to bite my tongue when I am in company with Cecilia Butters."

"But, she likes our Eliza Bellingham. I have told Madame Blodgett that we need Madame Bellingham's assistance in the shop every morning, and Madame Bellingham, she says she would like to work the longer hours, as many hours as we can give her, but *hélas,* that obstinate old woman—"

"Oh! Perhaps we had better speak in French, Madame," whispered Fanny.

CHAPTER FOURTEEN

IN OBEDIENCE TO her parents' wishes that she place herself in the way of as many eligible bachelors as possible, Julia Bertram returned to her cousins in Bedford Square, who brought her to one of Lady Delingpole's Wednesday afternoon receptions.

Julia knew there was a chance, more than a chance, of encountering Edmund's errant wife. But she was still discomposed when Mary Bertram pushed her way through the throng and saluted her with every evidence of affectionate regard. Julia was at first unequal to meeting her sister-in-law with anything approaching civility, let alone warmth. She might even have turned and walked away, had not Margaret Fraser and another unknown gentleman accompanied Mary, and Julia did not wish to create a public scene.

"Ah! My dear Julia! It has been an age! You are more beautiful than ever, I see, is she not, Miss Fraser?"

"Hello, Miss Bertram, so pleased to see you again," Miss Fraser said, and if the poor girl did not really feel the pleasure she professed, the reader is asked to forgive her, for she sensed that whatever was about to transpire would not be to her benefit.

Mary Bertram chattered gaily for another moment, with civil nothings and polite compliments, while Julia regarded her silently. Suddenly, Mary recollected the gentleman hovering patiently at the edge of their little circle, and exclaimed, "Ah, where are my manners? Allow me to present Mr. Nathaniel Meriwether to you. Mr. Meriwether, this is Miss Bertram."

Julia knew she was being rude, but she could not bring herself to acknowledge Mr. Meriwether, seeing him as a confederate of Mary, with more than a slight curtsey. She remained silent, hoping that Mary would take herself and the others away. Then Mr. Meriwether bowed gracefully and said, "Miss Bertram, your servant, ma'am. It is a pleasure to meet you indeed. Mrs. Bertram has informed me, we have some mutual acquaintance. I have the honour of knowing Mrs. Butters, whose late husband was a friend of mine. I was a wine importer by profession, and he built my company's ships."

He sounded so sensible and his manner was so engaging, yet so proper, that Julia found herself unbending, and she replied, "Oh yes, dear Mrs. Butters. She has been very good to my cousin, Miss Price."

"And as well, she is a good friend to the unhappy Africans, is she not, Miss Bertram? I admire her extremely."

"Well!" said Mary Bertram brightly. "I shall leave you two to talk about absent friends, and slaves, and things. Come along, Margaret." And she took Miss Fraser by the arm—the girl seemed loathe to leave—and pulled her away.

To her surprise, Julia found herself falling into easy conversation with Mr. Meriwether. Even such trite enquiries as 'had she been long in London' or 'was she well acquainted with their host and hostess,' were not disagreeable because the older gentleman appeared to listen with the most unaffected, sincere interest in everything she said. She in her turn politely enquired into the wine business and unexpectedly found the topic was rather interesting.

"Unfortunately, Miss Bertram, between the risks attendant in obtaining a decent product, and the taxes and duties charged upon it, a great many persons have turned to smuggling, and of course they may sell at a lower price than the legitimate trader."

"The temptation to do so must be considerable for many, I imagine."

"Which is why a government which imposes high import duties must acknowledge it creates criminals out of ordinary men. Having said so much, I do not argue against all taxes, of course. If something must be taxed, wine seems to be an eminently fair item, enjoyed as it is by the more prosperous households."

"You would not resort to smuggling yourself, sir?"

"I could not answer to my conscience if any persons in my employ were apprehended in the act of bringing a contraband cargo onshore."

"I believe I have read that higher taxes do not always result in more revenues, is that not so? Most gentlemen stopped wearing wigs, for example, when the government put a tax on hair powder."

"You are quite correct, Miss Bertram. In the same vein, imports of wine from Portugal this year will scarcely be half of what was brought in two years ago. The apprehension that the French will destroy all the vineyards in Portugal—but forgive me, this is a topic upon which I fear I often weary the patience of my friends. I suppose a lady so young as yourself cannot recall a time when we were not at war."

"Oh, you flatter me, sir, for I do remember when my old nurse told us about the poor queen of France."

"Yes, of course," Mr. Meriwether shook his head and smiled. "And when *I* was young enough to have a nurse, she was telling me about Bonnie Prince Charlie! If not the new play being put on by that Shakespeare fellow down at the Globe!"

"Oh, I think not, sir," Julia laughed, "but you must have had the pleasure of travelling in Europe before the war."

"Indeed I did, and it is a great pity you have not been afforded the opportunity of crossing the Channel in a fair breeze, and landing at Calais or sailing south to Bordeaux, as I have done!"

Mr. Meriwether spoke so well, with such wit and spirit, of travel, of the valleys of the Loire, of hills covered with grape vines or blushing purple with lavender, of picnics amongst the fallen stones of ancient abbeys, of eating old cheese and young wine and fresh bread, that Julia found herself quite entranced, and longed to be upon the sea, and travelling to new horizons.

Since Mr. Meriwether was almost old enough to be her father, Julia saw no harm in bestowing her attention on a man of such intelligent and pleasing address. She was careful not to behave coquettishly; she knew some Society ladies of standing viewed her with suspicion because her older sister had sacrificed her virtue before her marriage. Smiling, talking, and laughing with an intelligent well-informed man was an unlooked-for pleasure, and Mr. Meriwether's age, relative to hers, ought to shield her from any remark.

Julia and Mr. Meriwether at last parted with declarations of satisfaction in having made each other's acquaintance, and on his side at least, with an additional private wish of meeting the young lady again soon. Julia, in a good humour, was preparing to ascend into her cousins' carriage, when a hand on her arm detained her. She turned, and was again face-to-face with her sister-in-law Mary Bertram, who looked as calm and composed as though they had been frequent and friendly companions for the past twelvemonth.

"Julia, perhaps we may speak—it has been an age, has it not?" Mary began, confidently drawing her aside from the departing throng.

Julia looked at her coldly. "I believe the time passed by very slowly for my poor brother, when he was waiting in vain for a word from you."

"Yes, Julia, I have been a fool, I freely own it, and have been unjust to one of the finest men in England. I should be excessively grateful and humbled if his family would assist my efforts to restore Edmund and me to the happiness we once knew."

"I will support my brother. Whatever constitutes his happiness will make me happy as well."

Mary's face lit up. "Indeed? And so you understand how important *your choices* are? Edmund has spoken to you about it?"

"I do not understand you, ma'am."

"I mean, Edmund will not permit me to return to him until you have taken a husband. He and I are *longing* to be reconciled but his sense of duty to you is such that he says he will not take me under his roof while you remain there."

"What!" Julia gasped. "I do not believe it! I do not believe *you*!"

"Can you mean—has Edmund said nothing to you? How I honour his discretion and his high-mindedness! How like him. He did not wish to cause you a moment of guilt over the fact you are standing in the way of his happiness."

"I—standing in the way—?" Julia clenched her fists at her sides, so that she might not rake her nails down her sister-in-law's face.

"Yes, to protect your reputation, he will not allow me to return to my home until you are gone from under my roof. So, you do understand why I enquire with more than passing solicitude—Julia, are you engaged? Do you have an understanding with anyone?"

"You are presumptuous, madam," Julia was provoked into saying.

"Oh, this is no time to be coy, dear sister. I know you have developed a passionate interest in the navy, especially in the West African Squadron. But, my dear Julia, it is time to put aside childish dreams and consider your duty, is it not?"

"*You* speak to *me*, of duty, madam?"

"After Maria's folly, your own reputation will always be in doubt—"

"I am not obliged to punish myself for her sins!" Julia exclaimed with irritation.

"Oh, of course not," Mary assured her, then lowering her voice and glancing about her, she continued: "But surely you see why you must be extremely prudent in your choice of a husband. Throwing yourself away on a poor lieutenant is a heedless act. And what a connection! If you had met your future father-in-law, as I have, I am sure you would think better of it. A horrid, coarse, disagreeable man."

Julia flushed angrily, not deigning to correct her sister-in-law.

"Life is not always fair, Julia," Mary continued with a sympathetic smile. "My inheritance gives me the capacity to manage my own affairs. But you—you are dependent upon your father, on your parents, and they have fallen *far* in the world—besmirched by your sister's scandal, caught out by the ban on the slave trade, your family home now occupied by others. I see no other course for *you*, my dear, than to marry to your best advantage."

"I can only say, that you are the last person on earth from whom I would take advice on matrimony, ma'am, considering how you have dishonoured the state by leaving my brother."

"If you are determined to remain in single blessedness, why cannot you go and live with your Aunt Norris, and leave Edmund free to do as he chooses?"

Julia sighed. She did not wish to explain the truth—her father no longer trusted Aunt Norris' judgement. Her chaperonage of Maria, when she was in London, had not protected her sister from being seduced by Mary's brother. She said only, "I would vastly prefer to stay with Edmund."

"Your loving feelings for your brother are quite understandable. How much, indeed, *do* you love your brother? Do you love him enough to bring his current suffering to an end?"

Julia turned away, unable to compose herself. Mary, sensing that she had hit home, pursued the subject further.

"You should ask yourself—how can you put your own happiness, which is itself a matter of chance, ahead of the welfare of your entire family?"

"Why do you say happiness is a matter of chance? Because of your own unfortunate experience?"

"Julia, happiness in married life *is* purely a matter of chance, or good fortune. Do you believe a marriage of attachment will guarantee perpetual happiness? On what evidence do you rely? Only look about you—how many husbands cease to love their wives? How often does devotion sink into indifference, or worse? How many wives place a cuckoo in their husband's nest? As for your sailor sweetheart, he appears to be a lovely boy, but what if you marry the son, and he grows up to be like his father?"

"I could not be so taken in as to his character, although my poor brother was deceived as to yours!"

"Are you so naïve as to think that yours is the only pretty face he has noticed? Have you not heard the saying, 'every sailor is a bachelor past Gibraltar?'"

"First you speak to me of duty, then of constancy—this from *you*, madam!"

"So cold! So distant! You affect to despise me, but you must know I come to you as a true friend, Julia. I am well-connected here in town and could procure you many useful invitations. Your poor mother and father deserve the comfort of seeing you happily settled. And for how much longer do you intend for Edmund to postpone his own life, while you wait for your lieutenant to return from the sea? Two years? Five years? Seven? Ten?"

Here, Mary was on surer ground. The imputation of selfishness had penetrated Julia's defences—Mary saw the younger woman flush and chew her lip unhappily.

"Your *entire* family, Julia, on the one hand, hoping and expecting you to do your duty by them," Mary repeated, "and on the other hand, a hopeless dream. A dream that the *other* party has probably forgotten by now. Is it not possible that he is in fact, regretting the youthful impetuosity which tied him to you? After all, what can you do for *him*? You cannot help him advance in his profession. True love, I have always heard it said, is unselfish. "

"Enough! I think you have said quite enough, madam." And Julia fled to her carriage.

* * * * * * *

It is a reliable maxim that the true heroine should be utterly surprised by the revelation of a suitor's affection, and completely astounded by his proposal of marriage. But Mr. Edifice's attentions, always persistent but formal and polite, had become so pointed, that Fanny actually wondered if he was forming expectations on her. At the risk of denigrating the intelligence of other heroines, Fanny had sufficient penetration to understand the meaning of Mr. Edifice's compliments and his gallantries; his smiles when he greeted her, and his sighs upon departing. These attentions could tend in only one direction. The only aspect of his conversation which perplexed her was, his frequent enquiries after Mrs. Butters, his lavish praise for her philanthropy and her generous nature, and his remarks on the evident fondness of the older lady for Fanny.

Mr. Edifice lingered in the school room every day, waiting for her arrival; he followed her, and commended her work, her patience, her artistry, and her resourcefulness, seemingly oblivious to the sly grins and smothered laughter of the pupils.

He gave every impression of being a man who wanted only a little encouragement to declare himself. She felt it would be best, of course, if he never proceeded so far. She was sorry—for his sake—that she could not like him better than she did, but she could *not* like him well enough to encourage him. But how to gently dissuade him? She had not flirted with him, she had always received his attentions calmly, and sometimes even went so far as to tell him, "excuse me, Mr. Edifice, but I must be about my duties now. Good day to you."

No heroine, not even Fanny, could prevent herself from meditating on the differences between the attentions paid to her by Mr. Edifice, who she spent time with six days out of the week, and Mr. Gibson, whose visits were rare, brief, but looked-for and remembered with fondness. There was, on the face of it, nothing lover-like in Mr. Gibson's conversation.

Though she had tried, Fanny could not dismiss Mr. Edifice's assertion that Mr. Gibson wanted a wealthy wife. At first, she told herself she was disappointed only because she regretted that a man of Mr. Gibson's elevated principles should, in the end, have a mercenary turn.

But—was this the only reason for her dismay, for the strange pangs of regret that she felt whenever she recalled Mr. Edifice's words? Would Mr. Gibson overthrow his intention of remaining single, if he met with a wealthy young lady? And, Fanny knew, he was meeting eligible young ladies constantly, as he dined frequently in Society.

In the meantime, she had to contend with Mr. Edifice, her unwanted suitor. But Fanny was no judge of her own manner. Her address was incurably gentle and polite; and she was not aware how much it concealed her indifference to him.

Mrs. Bellingham's knowing little smile when she saw Mr. Edifice hanging over Fanny, told Fanny that she would welcome a confidence. Fanny was equally curious, if not more so, about the state of her new friend's marriage.

Mrs. Bellingham had mentioned that her husband lived in London, but she herself took the cheapest possible lodgings in Camden Town. She spoke of her children, her three little boys, and her failed business in Liverpool, which she greatly lamented, but said very little about her husband, except for one day when Fanny happened to remark that the "afternoons were now much lighter, and the days growing longer," and Mrs. Bellingham replied: "Oh, Miss Price, as for long winter days—that winter I passed in St. Petersburg when my husband was— away from me! The darkness, the endless darkness and the cold while I waited for John to come back to me!

"And I was all alone! I could not afford the candles to work by! I remember standing by the window in the morning, scraping the frost off the glass, watching for the sun to rise on the horizon, and trying to keep up my cheer for the sake of little James..."

She shook her head. "It was so dark and so cold, Miss Price, you would not believe how cold. When you stepped outside, the cold snatched your breath away. The snow was piled high in drifts on the streets and the ground was still frozen as hard as iron in April! Why anyone would want to be born in that miserable country, I have no notion."

"You must be so pleased to be back in England again," Fanny exclaimed sympathetically.

"Oh indeed yes, Miss Price."

Mrs. Bellingham's lips curved into a smile but her eyes, Fanny noted, were blank and sad.

*　*　*　*　*　*　*

Julia dined in company with Mr. Meriwether on a few occasions following their first meeting. After her return to Thornton Lacey, she was surprised to receive a letter from him

She was even more astonished to find it was an offer of marriage, very handsome in its terms, exceedingly generous in the amount he would settle upon her; there would be a house in town and an estate in the country, pin-money, jewels, carriages, and travel. Mr. Meriwether was a widower, but there were no step-children to resent her introduction into their home. He promised her security, loyalty, and affection, and added the highest praise of her temperament, her beauty, and her well-informed mind. He attested that his health was excellent, and his yearly income exceeded even her idle speculations. His language was that of a man of education, feeling, and sense. No objection could be raised to the letter in point of style, and he wound up the whole by asking to be permitted to attempt to create an attachment on her part.

Here was a sincerity, a frankness, a worth not to be held lightly. Julia was genuinely gratified and honoured by Mr. Meriwether's application, as she respected and esteemed him. But how to reply?

Julia spent an hour alone in her garden, sitting and standing, pacing and pausing, pondering what she should do. She had no dislike for Mr. Meriwether. And she thought herself peculiarly well-suited to become the mistress of an elegant town home in London, with carriages, servants, and horses. With his wealth and her breeding, they would establish a new family, respectable, genteel, liberal, and prosperous. She saw herself as the hostess at an elegant table, surrounded by friends, she imagined herself shopping for new clothes and jewels with little to restrain her, she thought of welcoming her sister Maria from her seclusion in Norfolk, and of being, for once, the sister who came first in consequence and fortune; she thought of the charities she could sponsor and the kindnesses she would bestow upon the deserving poor, she pictured a nursery full of lovable children—and then she thought of a well-appointed bedchamber, and she quailed.

Mr. Meriwether was by no means repulsive in appearance. He was affable, but not handsome, well-built, with a trim and active figure. A woman calling herself Mrs. Meriwether could repose every confidence in his understanding and his placid temper.

But—Julia knew what it was to feel passion. When she was younger, she had been almost seduced by the skilful, furtive embraces of Henry Crawford, which at the time had left her distracted, weak, powerless to resist and yearning for more. Even now, the thought of how his hands had roamed freely over her, how his lips left a trail of kisses that blazed like fire, raised uncomfortable and irresistible sensations within her.

But that remembrance was nothing to the memory of the day she had kissed William Price, and had pledged herself to him, and felt his strong arms about her, and seen the devotion shining in his eyes. How was this to be thrown away and forgotten, and how was she to give her hand without her heart?

Many young ladies, Julia knew, had renounced a first love, even a partiality toward one gentleman or another, and married for sensible considerations, rather than romantic ones. They had given themselves to men chosen by their families. And in some cases, the marriages prospered well. At least, husband and wife became good friends. She thought of Lord and Lady Delingpole—a true partnership, he a leading man in government and she, an avid political hostess. And in fact, she privately acknowledged, it could be contended that her own father, captivated by the beauty and complacent manners of her mother, had not chosen so wisely for himself as Lord Delingpole's parents had chosen for their son.

Duty and expediency all pointed in one direction, but alas! her inclinations pointed in another.

Restless and half-unawares of where she walked, Julia crossed the fields which separated their home from the village. She became aware of the rhythmic pounding of hammer upon anvil. The blacksmith's shop, as yet partly screened by a row of newly-planted trees, was so close to the parsonage that the noise from that establishment frequently reached their ears.

If their blacksmith had the power to marry persons using his anvil for an altar, as was done in Gretna Green, she could accept the rash offer of Viscount Lynnon, and marry the heir to the Delingpole Earldom! A title and a massive estate in Wales might well lessen the pain of relinquishing her lieutenant. But nothing could have justified an acceptance of Viscount Lynnon's proposal—there was no mutual esteem to speak of, and her motives would have been entirely mercenary.

Her attention returned to the letter in her hand, and she re-read it carefully. She was struck, quite forcibly struck, by the propriety of Mr. Meriwether's language, which testified to a man who had risen far above his humble origins through intelligence and application. It was a most unexceptional offer.

Julia retraced her path homeward and regained her garden. The sun was setting, and Edmund had lit some candles in his study. She saw him through the window, sitting at his desk, nodding over a book, but—and the picture struck at her heart—alone, all alone, and condemned to remain so.

Julia recalled the visit from her cousin Fanny, earlier in the year, which had illustrated to her the beauty and virtues of an unselfish character. She had then privately resolved to think of others more, and less of herself. Was this not a case in point? Was she being selfish? Not only foolish, but selfish—clinging to a forlorn hope?

Mrs. Peckover appeared at the top of the path. "Miss Julia, the damps of the evening are rising. I'm sure your brother would want you to come inside now."

Julia swiftly assented, and without saying a word, hurried in and went upstairs to her own room.

Mr. Meriwether must be answered. It would be uncivil to keep him waiting for her reply—she owed him that much, at least.

Julia began her letter with the usual thanks—for indeed she could express, without any trace of affectation or false humility, the extent of her surprise, her gratitude, her sensibility of his great merits, the honour, and *et cetera*. But she paused over her conclusion. Should she invite him to continue his suit? Ask for time to consider? Or, should she peremptorily decline and not hold out false expectations?

Complete darkness and silence fell about the house and her letter remained unfinished.

At last, she decided to show Mr. Meriwether's proposal to her brother and talk it over with him. She took up a candle and crept down the stairs.

Julia found Edmund asleep in his study, with Milton's *Paradise Lost* open on his lap. She gently picked up the volume and saw it was open at the passage describing Adam's resolve to follow Eve out of paradise, and share her fallen fate:

How can I live without thee, how forgoe
Thy sweet Converse and Love so dearly joyn'd,
To live again in these wilde Woods forlorn?
Should God create another Eve, and I
Another Rib afford, yet loss of thee
Would never from my heart; no no, I feel
The Link of Nature draw me: Flesh of Flesh,
Bone of my Bone thou art, and from thy State
Mine never shall be parted, bliss or woe.

Everything, it seemed, conspired against her. Edmund was longing for Mary and she was keeping them apart. William had told her, most definitely, to abandon all hope. She could not deceive herself that her parents would rejoice in a match with her cousin.

And Mr. Meriwether appeared to be a good man.

Julia went back upstairs and concluded her letter by telling her suitor to apply to her father, Sir Thomas Bertram, at Everingham Lodge, Norfolk, "without whose approbation I would not permit myself to contemplate any attachment."

Her father might object to the match, and spare her the misery of deciding.

The note was despatched the following day, and she tried very hard not to think about it.

*   *   *   *   *   *   *

One April morning when Fanny arrived at work, she saw Eliza Bellingham in the downstairs shop, talking earnestly with a well-dressed gentleman with a benign expression and a handsome aquiline nose. He was smiling as he spoke, but Eliza appeared to be by turns exasperated and apprehensive, in great contrast to her usual composed manner with customers. Fanny decided she had better intervene.

"May I be of some assistance? Mrs. Bellingham, what can we do for this gentleman?"

Eliza Bellingham jumped at discovering Fanny at her elbow. "Miss Price! Miss Price, may I introduce my husband, John Bellingham," she offered, and Fanny thought she detected some reluctance, some discomfiture, in her friend's voice.

"Miss Price, your servant," Mr. Bellingham bowed low over her hand.

"I was just asking my husband to depart, Miss Price. He can have no business here which he and I could not discuss—"

"I *am* come here on a matter of business, Eliza. I require an alteration to my coat" —he indicated the article in question, folded neatly over his arm— "and as you refuse to live with me or perform any of those little offices a wife ordinarily performs for her husband, I am come to this academy, for I understand your fees are very reasonable."

"This is a ladies' establishment, Mr. Bellingham," Fanny interposed. "I should think you would wish to consult a tailor for alterations to your coat," and Eliza Bellingham cast her a grateful glance.

"No, but I only require this—" and Mr. Bellingham held up an oblong piece of paper. "I only wish for a pocket of these exact dimensions to be sewn inside my coat. I could almost do the work myself, except I have other demands upon my time."

"Show me, sir, where you wish the pocket to be placed."

"I wish it attached firmly to the lining of the coat, just here, on the left, so that my right hand can access it easily. It should be able to bear some weight."

"And you wish the pocket to be the dimensions of this paper? And placed so low, below the waist? Will it not affect the hang of the garment?"

"Perhaps, but I am no dandy."

"Are you not, John?" asked his wife. "You have a new hat and breeches, I see, which is more than—"

"I require the pocket for carrying copies of a pamphlet I have written. I am distributing copies to every member of Parliament, as well as to every gentlemen of influence whom I come across—"

"John, how could you! How many pounds did you spend on printing pamphlets? When I had to take James out of school for lack of money to pay the fees!"

"Everything I am doing, I am doing for you and our dear children, Eliza. You must trust me."

Mrs. Bellingham closed her eyes and rubbed her temples. "Forgive me my outburst, Miss Price. I do apologize." Turning to her husband, she added: "John, not here. Not now. Please go. Leave the coat with me and I will attend to it."

"Why should you attempt to silence your own husband? What have *I* to be ashamed of? It is rather, the Prime Minister, and his detestable minions, who ought to feel shame. Young lady," he went on, addressing Fanny, in his calm, quiet voice, apparently oblivious to his wife's frowns. "You see before you a victim of one of the most monstrous injustices which ever befell an Englishman. Robbed of the fruits of honest enterprise, slandered, and imprisoned for years in a foreign country, deprived of the ability to provide for my family, I am now endeavouring to obtain redress for the unaccountable neglect and malice of the English ambassador to Russia. I have petitioned Mr. Perceval, the Privy Council, the Foreign Office, and the Prince Regent himself, to address the terrible wrongs done to me. To call my story one of misfortune does not begin to explain the whole. When I lay all the facts before you, I am convinced you will agree, it can be seen in no other light than that of conspiracy—a conspiracy against me and mine. Financial restitution of course, will be forthcoming, but also, there must be an apology, a public acknowledgement, that the British government failed me in my hour of extremity—"

"Oh, please, John—Miss Price is not at liberty to stop and listen to everything relating to our misfortunes." Eliza looked pleadingly at Fanny.

"Indeed sir, I regret that your wife and I must return to our duties. Perhaps sir, it is best for you to consult a tailor, for the work on the coat," Fanny offered. "Our academy is intended for training young girls, and therefore our work proceeds more slowly than you may desire."

"Indeed, I had hoped to have the work accomplished as soon as possible. Good day, Miss Price. Good day, my dear. Be of good cheer. All shall be resolved very soon."

As she watched her husband depart, Mrs. Bellingham sighed, evidently relieved that he was gone, but she was at the same time barely maintaining her composure. Fanny wordlessly took her arm, and led her upstairs to the privacy of the counting room, and sent a girl for a cup of tea.

"Oh! Miss Price," whispered Mrs. Bellingham, wiping tears from her eyes. "What must you think of me. I am humiliated beyond words to have to explain my situation. That was indeed my poor husband, John Bellingham. I told you he was unable to work, which is not a lie, but I was too ashamed to reveal the whole truth of it. John has been..." she searched for the right words, "...he believes that our government will restore some considerable financial losses he suffered in Russia a number of years ago, and nothing I, or anyone can say, will put the notion out of his head. Indeed, he has sometimes promised me, to leave the past behind and find some kind of employment, but when I followed him to London I discovered that he had been lying to me."

"My dear Mrs. Bellingham, if you would rather not speak of it, now or ever, I will honour your discretion. But, if confiding in a friend may bring you some relief, please consider me as your true friend."

"You have been a friend, indeed, Miss Price. And you deserve an explanation, as well."

"What was the injustice of which he speaks?"

Mrs. Bellingham smiled wanly. "He *has* suffered. That much is true. My husband was working at Archangel—I suppose you know, Archangel is a Russian port, up north, and the only place where English ships can land to trade with Europe since we started fighting the French. At any rate, John was an insurance agent for the shipping and he had some trading affairs of his own. But he fell out with another merchant—I still do not understand it all, but it seems this merchant was charged with making a false claim on his insurance, and he believed it was John who betrayed him to the insurance company.

"The merchant caused my husband to be arrested on false charges of unpaid debts. He was kept in prison, in the vilest conditions, unable to bring the matter to trial! He lost his employment of course, and his ventures failed. I was only twenty years of age, with an infant at my breast and another child expected, when John was taken away. When he was finally freed, after almost six years, John was a changed man."

Fanny murmured sympathetically. Mrs. Bellingham absentmindedly twisted a bit of ribbon in her hands, not meeting Fanny's eyes, as she continued the tale:

"Miss Price, he may appear calm and reasonable, but do not be deceived. All he can think about is how he begged the British embassy in Russia to help him, when he was imprisoned, but in vain. 'He was in a foreign country, and subject to their laws,' was the only advice he received.

"On all other subjects he is as rational as you or I, and you can see he is not loud or violent, but, I fear that in relation to our misfortunes, he has lost his reason entirely. He is not the man I once knew."

"This is a most affecting tale indeed, Mrs. Bellingham. You have had much to bear."

"At the time of his imprisonment, not knowing if or when he would be released, Miss Price, I did not know *how* I bore it, but I had to preserve my health and spirits for the sake of my children, as I still do today. My own resolution is, that I must support my sons by myself, for I can never hope to rely upon him in the future."

"Oh, my dear Mrs. Bellingham, how I do admire your fortitude! I wish there was more I could do to assist you! I wish Mrs. Blodgett would consent to retain you for more hours of work here"

"You have already done so much for me, Miss Price—I could never thank you enough."

"I wonder if my friend Mr. Gibson could investigate this case. He is always alive to questions of injustice. And he has many powerful friends in the government."

"Alas, I doubt Mr. Gibson could do anything, Miss Price. There are cases of injustice everywhere in this world. I have urged John that it would be best if he could endeavour to put the past behind him and work on rebuilding his fortunes, but, he will not, he cannot. I can see that now. I do not know what is to become of him. He is now notorious to half of the politicians in London. He is forever haunting the Parliament, watching from the gallery, button-holing anyone he can in the lobby. How it will end, I cannot say, but—" the brave woman's voice quavered. "But he believes he will succeed, even when everyone has told him 'no' to his very face! At any rate, I dare not rely on his coming to his senses. And I dreaded his visit here, for I feared he would demand all my wages—thank heaven he did not and I may keep them for my children! I am afraid he is running up more debts here in London—we are destitute, Miss Price, I cannot bear this much longer!"

Mrs. Bellingham's feelings gave way and she began to weep. Tears came to Fanny's eyes as well. Fanny placed a sympathetic hand on the poor woman's shoulder and let her cry softly for a while. Finally, Fanny said: "I understand why you did not confide in us before now, Mrs. Bellingham. I believe I should have felt and acted likewise, in your position."

"Alas, now you know why I have had so little to say about myself! I was ashamed to be so guarded with you, and with everyone here, when you have all been so kind to me. It is a torment to know he is speaking of our financial failures all over London, and telling everyone about his distress for his poor wife and children—yes, that is what he says, even when I, his wife, have begged him to leave off. He told me he would, he promised he had—but he lied to me. I am resigned—he *cannot* stop himself."

Fanny debated within herself, wondering if she could provide some consolation to her new friend by sharing her own story. Fanny was not in the habit of speaking about herself; she was reticent by nature. But her newfound intimacy with Eliza, and her compassion for the afflicted woman's feelings, moved her to set aside her own habitual reserve.

Warmly, impulsively, sympathetically, she began: "*I* understand, as perhaps few could, the fear of notoriety, Eliza. But, if my own experience can provide any consolation, I will confide that I, myself, was featured in all the newspapers two years ago. How dreadful it was at the time! But now, other stories and scandals have supplanted it. If it is any encouragement to you, Eliza, this trial will pass eventually, mustn't it? At worst, we are the topic of a brief hour and then are forgotten."

And to gratify Mrs. Bellingham's curiosity and to distract her, Fanny confessed that she was the once-notorious 'Miss P,' who had pretended to be married to the late Henry Crawford, or as the newspapers had called him, 'the well-known and captivating Mr. C.' As she had intended, her friend was distracted from her own sorrows by the astonishing revelation.

"What an extraordinary tale! Yes, I think I remember reading about 'Mr. C' at the time. A reckless, rich, well-born gentleman pretending he was married, so as to avoid getting married to another young lady. And you were truly 'Miss P,' his pretended wife? Nay, I cannot believe it."

"It was misrepresented in the papers," Fanny said hastily. "But of course it was not in my power or my inclination to come forward to correct the misapprehensions of the public. It was reported there was to be a duel, fought over my honour. But my honour—".

"Oh, my dear Miss Price, do not imagine for a moment that I, knowing you as I do, could conceive of you doing an immoral or a wanton thing! Really, you need not explain yourself—no explanation is necessary—I have absolute faith in you."

"I *did* do something wrong, Eliza, I let the world believe I married Henry Crawford. It *was* wrong of me, very wrong. Do not suppose I am comparing your blameless conduct with mine, in any way. It is not generally known abroad that I am 'Miss P' and as the memory of the scandal fades, I grow more secure on that account."

"Of course! But, my dear Miss Price, I am certain you must have had your own good reasons for doing what you did."

"Will you not call me 'Fanny'?" asked Fanny diffidently.

Eliza's eyes watered anew: "I can never forget your goodness to *me*, not so long as I live... Fanny."

Fanny waited in sympathetic silence while her friend composed herself. In a few moments, Eliza was able to say, "Let me go and wash my face and return to my duties. Thank you, Fanny. Whatsoever may occur, please know how grateful I am."

CHAPTER FIFTEEN

WILLIAM GIBSON, flattered by Fanny's appeal for his help, and quick to oblige, arranged to meet John Bellingham in a public house in Fleet Street. When he went to keep their rendezvous, Mr. Bellingham was already there. Gibson recognized Bellingham as the man he had seen haunting the galleries of the Houses of Parliament, asking for the names of the important figures to be pointed out to him.

Mr. Bellingham had already laid out upon the table, a considerable mass of papers, letters, and publications. At first Mr. Gibson was reluctant to read and absorb all the details of what looked to be a complicated and tedious narrative, and in the poor light of the public house, it was a struggle to take in all the documents which Bellingham kept thrusting under his nose, all the facts and details which the aggrieved man could recite from memory.

Then, as the writer began to understand the hardships which the composed and well-spoken man sitting opposite him endured in Russia, he grew indignant. Clapped up in a cramped, foul prison crawling with lice and bedbugs. Fed only sour porridge and wearing the same clothing for months on end. Paraded in shackles through the streets with the most brutalized common thieves and cut-throats—thrown to the mercy of the Russian wolf by a dilettante English ambassador who was absent from his post for months at a time—it was a story to rouse the spleen of any proud Englishman.

But, as one hour stretched to two, then more, Gibson first grew restless, then impatient and then to his own surprise, irritable. Mr. Bellingham was a foreigner in Russia and had fallen afoul of their laws, not British ones. Mr. Gibson was surprised to learn that, at one point, Mr. Bellingham had been released, but instead of returning to England, he stayed in Russia and brought a lawsuit against the Russian government, who responded by promptly throwing him back into prison again.

Freed at last, the angry businessman expected Parliament to pay him one hundred thousand pounds for his losses and suffering—a ludicrously high figure. Gibson could think of many families who had suffered as much or more than Bellingham, who were brought to destruction precisely *because* of the policies of their own government. What about the fellows who'd signed up to fight for king and country three years ago, and shipped out to Europe under incompetent leaders who encamped them in a Dutch swamp, where they perished with fever? Where was the redress for the 4,000 dead soldiers? What did their families deserve?

Or, what of the merchants who, owing to the global trade blockade and counter-blockades, were bankrupted, with warehouses full of goods they could not sell? What about the potters, the weavers, the lace-makers whose materials sat unsold? The prosecution of the war worked directly against their interests. They were impoverished by the very government which taxed the rest of what little they had. There wasn't enough money in all of England to repair every injustice. Yet Mr. Bellingham droned on.

"Finding myself thus bereft of all hopes of redress, my affairs ruined by my long imprisonment in Russia through the fault of the British minister, my property all dispersed for want of my own attention, my family driven into poverty, my wife and children needing support which I was unable to give—I ask you, Mr. Gibson, as a man, what would you not be willing to attempt, in your efforts to obtain justice on behalf of your children?"

"Your children? Pray, Mr. Bellingham, what are the birthdates of your children. How old are they?"

"Their birthdates? Well—what— James is eight years of age, I suppose, and John is six years old by now, and little Henry.... Henry is... You are not suggesting anything about the constancy of my wife, are you?"

"No, no, Mr. Bellingham. But you refer so repeatedly to your manly distress on behalf of your children. I find myself wondering what you actually know about them. Their birth dates, for example."

"That is nothing to the purpose, Mr. Gibson. Nothing to the purpose at all."

"I think it is to the purpose of testing the sincerity of your arguments."

"Well, if you think my head can retain such trivialities, you cannot understand my hardships, my sufferings, the outrages—"

"If I cannot understand after listening to you talk for three hours without ceasing, I fear I shall never understand, Mr. Bellingham. I am sorry to say, I agree with your friends—had you employed as much industry, ingenuity and energy toward repairing your fortunes, as you have done in resenting the past, you and your family would be in a better position than you find yourself in today."

Mr. Bellingham drew himself up, and scowled.

"Sir! I am sorry to discover in you, another one of those toad-eaters who will not speak up against this administration. You will curry favour with the powerful rather than help the oppressed."

Another man might have resented the slur, but Mr. Gibson only laughed. "Indeed, Mr. Bellingham. You have sketched me perfectly.

"Sir," he added, rising and offering his hand. "I wish you well. I wish you very well, and prosperous, and happy. And if I can do you any good turn, it would be my pleasure to do so, for the sake of your family—for young James, John, and little Henry. I shall not forget your story, but I can make no promises of any kind toward obtaining redress for you. Good day, sir."

"If my own government refuses to do me justice, Mr. Gibson, I will act as an honest Englishman. Soon I shall force the government to give me a hearing. Good day to *you*, sir."

* * * * * * *

Lady Delingpole, relaxing in her chamber, engrossed in her novel, suddenly became aware of her husband's voice and realized he was at her elbow.

"....So—are you at home for the gentleman? I almost said 'yes' on your behalf, knowing you to be very fond of him, but thought I had better confirm."

"I regret I was unable to give you my full attention at the very instant you wished to claim it, dear, but, as you *may* have observed, I was looking at a book, and, as you *might* have surmised, I was in fact, *reading* the book, therefore, you must give me a moment—of whom am I fond?"

"Oh—I must start again, must I? Well, William Gibson has called, and wishes to present you with a copy of the annual report of the Society for—-confound it, you know, that society that Wilberforce and his Clapham Saints set up for the deserving poor."

"Oh, excellent! Yes, I shall see him directly. Ring for Andrews, will you?"

William Gibson had not long to wait—not more than half an hour, indeed—before Lady Delingpole was graciously able to receive him.

"I wanted to thank you again, your Ladyship, for using your influence to arrange the visit from Mrs. Perceval to the academy. Our mutual friend Mrs. Butters also wishes me to convey her thanks. As is so often the case where you are concerned, your hand, the hand that guided events, was invisible. I am sorry to say, your name does not appear in my article."

Lady Delingpole laughed. "I did hear all about it though, from Jane Perceval! I cannot wait to peruse your account of the proceedings!"

"Unfortunately, ma'am, propriety and discretion compelled me to leave out the most interesting parts."

"Still, I am confident that Mrs. Perceval's patronage will benefit your enterprise. I am always ready to assist such worthy causes as this. Now, this is the one in Camden Town, is it not? And run by Mrs. Butters' family from Bristol?

"Yes ma'am, and the sewing instructress is Miss Price, a niece to Sir Thomas Bertram."

"Of course. I think I once met Miss Price, very briefly. A pretty, civil-behaved young lady. Ah yes, I have heard about this niece to the Bertrams. I suppose Mrs. Butters will need to find a new instructress soon."

"Ma'am?"

"Miss Price's aunt—the other one—not Lady Bertram—what is her name—lives at Mansfield—"

"Her aunt?"

"Oh yes, Norris. Yes, Mrs. Norris. She told me Miss Price will soon marry a curate—in fact the curate engaged by the academy. It must be the same curate who gave an interminable speech when Mrs. Perceval visited. Mrs. Perceval told me about the curate, too! 'An unforgettable oration,' I think she termed it. You look surprised, Mr. Gibson."

"Ah... perhaps I am, a little, your ladyship. When did you learn this news?"

"Only last week, when Lord Delingpole and I were last at Mansfield. Mrs. Norris said the Bertrams would be well pleased if Miss Price could marry so respectably. Well, I wish them both very happy, of course. Not every woman would care to be married to someone who so loves the sound of his own voice, but there you are."

"Yes. Yes, indeed ma'am. There I am."

* * * * * * *

Of all the duties which Lieutenant Price had undertaken in Africa, none pleased him so much as the expedition up the Pongus River, with a small detachment of British and African sailors, to destroy every slaving station they found. Confronted with William's schooner, armed with two small cannons and a crew of torch-wielding Kru tribesmen, the slave-masters abandoned their houses (some astonishingly large and luxurious). Their homes and their warehouses were set ablaze, the slaver's crews were overcome, the slave masters taken as prisoners, and their captives released.

William had seen action against the French, but the pleasure to be had in visiting sheer destruction upon one's enemy was a new sensation for him. When the fires consumed the thatched roofs of the barracoons, when they collapsed in a roar with a shower of sparks, and the Kru men ululated and exulted, he very much wanted to join in their war cries, to pull off his uniform and dance naked upon the deck of the schooner as they did. When he watched the reflection of the flames on the sluggish river, he thought it was no unfair representation of the state of his soul; externally placid, he was in tumult inside himself; angry, rebellious, and resentful at being denied his best chance for happiness in this world.

He thought back to his Latin lessons with his friend William Gibson; to his efforts to gain education and refinement, to his wish to become an acceptable son-in-law to Sir Thomas Bertram! And now here he was, covered in soot and sweat, speaking the crude patois of the Sierra Leone colony, eating, sleeping, and working with half-naked savages. So far away from tea and cucumber sandwiches on soft white bread, and croquet on the lawn, and talking about the weather: "Would it rain? Perhaps a little? Ought we to venture out?"

At Mansfield Park he had sometimes felt like a graceless, ignorant, clumsy imposter. Here, in charge of his schooner and his little crew, in the middle of the jungle, he felt strangely at home. Here was reality. "Detached service" they called it, and it was a fitting signifier for William's state of mind; detached from his past, detached from all he knew and loved.

Africa was no kinder to the ships of the West African Squadron than it was to their men. The sails rotted in the humid air, the hulls became fouled with worms, the beer went sour and the butter rancid. Upon his return from the Pongus River, William joined the men invalided off the *Kangaroo*—that is, those well enough to stand up without holding on to something, who were all pressed into service to help repair the HMS *Protector*.

Captain Irby, delighted with the intelligence, bearing and resourcefulness of the young lieutenant, requested William's transfer to the *Protector*, and so it was that William departed Sierra Leone to make one more patrol for slaving ships. The subsequent capture of the Portuguese slaver *Maria Primero* off of St. Thomas and the rescue of almost five hundred Africans was a handsome reward for the crew.

In March, the *Protector* took on six tons of elephant tusks to be imported to England, and William left the African coast only eight miserable months after he had sailed out of Portsmouth on the *Kangaroo*. He had done well in the way of prize monies, and might be supposed—by some—to be eligible to address the daughter of a baronet. But he clung to his fears for Julia's safety, and the dying words of his captain, and refused to consider the idea.

And further, he told himself, a young lady as amiable, as beautiful and accomplished as Julia must by now have found new admirers; gentlemen of education, birth and refinement, whose claims would render his own pretensions worthy only of mockery.

CHAPTER SIXTEEN

JULIA TURNED THE LETTER from her father over and over in her hands. Had Sir Thomas found some just objection to Mr. Meriwether, or did he approve of her suitor? Her imagination could not supply the answer, but she knew what she wished it to be.

She left the breakfast table without saying a word to Edmund. Outside, in the solitude and tranquillity of her little garden, she found the courage to open the note.

My dear Julia,

You will not be surprised, I believe, to learn I have received an application of a most particular kind, from a gentleman who seeks the honour of your hand in marriage.

May I commend what I conceive to have been your conduct on this occasion. The fact that you referred Mr. Meriwether to me, without reference to your own inclinations, confirms me in my hope that you have profited from the unhappy lesson of your sister, and have forsworn any tendency to that independence of spirit which prevails so much in modern days, even in young women. I am greatly gratified you have recollected your obligation to defer to those who have some right to guide and advise you. In his letter, I might add, Mr. Meriwether paid the highest tribute to your modesty and propriety.

I have informed Mr. Meriwether by return of post that once I have satisfied myself as to the veracity of his representations of his background, conduct, and fortune, I could perceive no grounds upon which to oppose his paying his addresses to you. He has assured me he takes no offense at the natural solicitude of a fond parent, and in fact he invited me to freely put any questions to him, or to his friends and associates.

The match may not be, in all of its particulars, what I and your mother had projected for you, when you were in your cradle. Still, despite what we owe to ourselves in upholding the dignity of the name of Bertram, I have never been one to deny the just claims of merit, endeavour, application, and worldly success.

However unexceptional this match may appear to be from a pecuniary point of view, dear Julia, I need hardly add that your happiness and credit in life is of the greatest importance to your parents. If you sincerely believe you can be happy and honourably married to Mr. Meriwether, despite the differences in your age and the still greater differences in your rank in society, I shall have no objection to make.

Experience as well as conviction leads me to assert that your own happiness will be increased by entering the married state, and if the strength of my affections alone could answer my wishes, you would be very happy indeed. I need hardly add, that to behold you honourably and properly settled would be greatly to the satisfaction of,

> *Your devoted father,*
> *T. Bertram*

* * * * * * *

It was late on a Friday afternoon, and Fanny and Eliza Bellingham were in the counting office, going over the accounts for the store and the academy.

"How extraordinary—a scrap of fabric, rendered into an evening gown for a doll, gives us a better return, yard for yard, than a full-size gown for our real flesh-and-blood customers!" Eliza Bellingham gestured at her calculations. "Mr. Blodgett told me he will order more dolls for us to dress, and is giving over more space in the shop window for them! If only I'd done this in Liverpool! I should have made sweet little bonnets for heads that are made of china, not heads which are stuffed with—-"

"Sawdust?" suggested Fanny.

"I was not speaking of *dolls'* heads, and you know that, Fanny!"

"Eliza, why do not you and I draw up a memorandum for presentation to the committee, explaining the profit to be made from the sale of dolls' clothes? Indeed, could we not emphasize to our customers the fact that the clothes are made by labouring children, for charitable purposes?"

"That's a wonderful idea, Fanny! And, why should we sell them only here in Camden Town? Perhaps we could find other shops willing to sell them in London?"

"Yes, of course! Heavens, Madame Orly went into London with Mrs. Butters this morning—I wish I had thought of sending some samples along with her."

"Mrs. Blodgett!!"

Fanny and Eliza heard Cecilia Butters' raised voice, and after exchanging perplexed glances, they both hurried out to the classroom to behold an indignant Cecilia Butters bearing down on Mrs. Blodgett.

"Mrs. Blodgett!"

Four and twenty little heads looked up, four and twenty pairs of hands froze in mid-stitch.

"Mrs. Blodgett, I have learned there is a most unsuitable person in your employ here."

"Whatever can you mean, ma'am?" Mrs. Blodgett was both alarmed and affronted.

"I mean, a notorious, scandalous woman has been allowed to work here, to associate with *my* children, to spread her polluting influence. I should have thought, Mrs. Blodgett, that solicitude for your own reputation and the safety of your pupils would ensure you would hire only persons of the most unimpeachable character! Did not the charter for this school specifically state that only gentlewomen of pious and decent character be engaged?"

"Whomever can you be referring to, ma'am?"

Fanny cast an anxious look at Eliza, who covered her face with her hands and retreated back into the counting office. Fanny stepped forward, prepared to defend her friend, even if it meant encountering the full force of Cecilia Butters' anger.

"Do you recall a scandal about a *Mr. Crawford* a few years ago?" Cecilia Butters continued, her words echoing about the room. "Do you recall there was a woman who passed herself off as his wife, lived with him at his estate, and then, when he left her, forced her cousin to fight a duel over her? The newspapers called her 'Miss P.' Do you know, who is 'Miss P'?"

Cecilia Butters turned and pointed to Fanny, who froze in horror and shame.

"It is she! It is none other than Miss Price! Miss Price!"

Four and twenty heads swivelled and looked at Miss Price with expressions ranging from confusion, to surprise, to wonder.

"Can this be true! Good gracious! How could my sister-in-law have permitted this! No, she could not have known of this disgraceful affair, or she would never—have you, Miss Price, deceived Mrs. Butters as to your character?"

"I have not, Madam," said Fanny. "And there was no duel—I never—"

"Can you deny that you called yourself 'Mrs. Crawford'?" interposed Cecilia Butters. "And that you and he lived together in Norfolk?"

"No, ma'am, I cannot, but—"

"Please! Miss Price! Think of the young persons present! How dare you!" Mrs. Blodgett drew herself up and pointed to the door. "You are discharged, as of this instant. Leave these premises—at once!"

It was futile to argue. Fanny turned, her eyes swimming with tears, and stumbled back to the counting office to retrieve her bonnet and shawl.

"Oh, Eliza—" she began to exclaim, then stopped in confusion.

Eliza Bellingham, with a conscious and guilty air, turned away from her.

Then the answer came to Fanny, with the force of a blow—Eliza Bellingham, for whom she had done so much, had betrayed her!

Fanny gasped in surprise, but no words came. She tied on her bonnet with trembling fingers, picked up her shawl, then turned and walked numbly to the staircase, conscious of four and twenty pairs of eyes watching her hurry away.

Fanny gained the street and paused to wrap her shawl around her, wondering if any of her students had hopped down from their stools and pressed up against the window to catch a last glimpse of her. Overcome by feelings of humiliation, she could not command herself to turn around and look up, but instead walked on, hardly knowing where she went, only wishing to be out of sight of the academy. Later, she heartily wished she had waved good-bye to her students.

She had poured so much of herself into the school, into the pupils, and now she was leaving without a backward glance, without a word of thanks or acknowledgement, but rather, with her reputation in shreds.

Fanny walked blindly down the street, grateful for the close brim of her bonnet which shielded her face from the few passers-bye. But after a few moments, the tears welled up, and she could no longer compose herself—she must give vent to her feelings.

Through tear-filled eyes, she fled down the lane to the peaceful old St. Pancras church. She slipped inside and took a seat on a wooden bench, just as the full force of her grief burst forth.

The unexpected betrayal of Eliza Bellingham was severely hurtful. Fanny thought of Eliza as a true friend, an intimate friend. How often had Eliza expressed her gratitude to Fanny for what she had done!

She had championed Eliza Bellingham at the academy and had even paid for her first month's salary—she had asked her friend Mr. Gibson to do what he could, to help Eliza's unfortunate husband. She had confided the story of her secret past with Henry Crawford with the purest of motives; to offer sympathy while her new friend underwent a gruelling ordeal. And this is how she was to be rewarded!

Fanny covered her face with her shawl and tried to muffle her sobs. Composure and self-command fled her entirely for a time.

"Miss Price? Oh, pardon me.... I do not wish to intrude. May I be of assistance? Are you unwell?"

A wave of humiliation washed over Fanny as she recognized the voice of Mr. Edifice and she became aware that the curate was hovering over her, looking distinctly uncomfortable.

Fanny dabbed her tears with her shawl. "Thank you, Mr. Edifice, for your kind concern." She sighed, trying to find the words. "Mr. Edifice, there has been a... a problem at the academy... and I am discharged. You will soon hear all the details, I have no doubt. There was an episode in my past which—is difficult to describe, and perhaps impossible to justify. Mrs. Blodgett has decided I can no longer work with the students."

Mr. Edifice's brows shot up with astonishment.

"You, Miss Price? Compromised in some way? I had not thought—that is, I am quite taken aback. I must infer that you were harbouring secrets from—from all of us? I had thought better of you, Miss Price, as I think you were not entirely unaware. This is a most disheartening revelation, to be sure."

Seeing Mr. Edifice's evident discomfiture almost helped Fanny regain her own composure. *He only wishes to be rid of me now*, was her thought, and out of the goodness of her heart, she obliged, leaving the church, and crossing the fields so as to avoid re-passing the academy. She walked briskly, weeping occasionally, all the way to Stoke Newington, finally arriving, worn out in body and spirit, at Mrs. Butters' house. She let herself in—Mrs. McIntosh was snoring gently in an armchair in the back parlour—and she crept upstairs, to reach the sanctuary of her bedroom, where she collapsed upon her bed.

Finally able to give vent to her emotions, she allowed herself to succumb to a tide of humiliation, resentment and sorrow.

She was not surprised at the petty vindictiveness of Cecilia Butters, nor the unthinking condemnation of Mrs. Blodgett. Their characters had long been known to her. But she felt exceedingly hurt by Eliza Bellingham's betrayal.

She could draw no moral lesson, no ethical adage, from the episode. What had she done, which, in hindsight, could be faulted as imprudent or unkind? Should she have turned Eliza Bellingham away at the door, when the desperate woman had come looking for work? Was it foolish of her to have shared a confidence with a woman sorely in need of comfort?

What of all the additional hours, thought and care she had devoted to the concerns of the academy? Was she a good person, or a fool, to have invested so much of herself in an enterprise which tossed her aside in an instant?

She must have finally fallen asleep, for she awoke late on Saturday morning, unrefreshed and still sunk in an abyss of misery. She decided to allow herself twenty-four hours to indulge in feelings which she would not want to harbour in her breast when she went to church on Sunday morning.

"I believe I shall go for a long walk, Mrs. McIntosh," she told the housekeeper.

Mrs. McIntosh's face reflected her disapproval. "After no supper and less breakfast? Will ye no sit doon, Miss, and have something to eat before ye go scampering about, or a stout wind may carry ye away, or ye may faint and drown yourself in the river."

Fanny obliged her, not sorry to have someone show solicitude for her well-being, and delayed her walk until after she attempted to eat some soup and soft rolls which tasted like clay in her mouth.

The news of her abrupt dismissal must by now have been relayed to the charitable ladies of the Committee. Would any of them question Mrs. Blodgett's decision? Would any of them take a moment to say, 'hold, have we done justly by this young woman

194

who has worked so hard for us?' Would they perceive that the vindictive nature of Cecilia Butters and the self-interest of Eliza Bellingham was at the heart of the matter? Or would the committee ladies take the easier path, and forget there ever was such a person as Fanny Price?

Mrs. Butters and Madame Orly were expected to return from London late that afternoon. She knew they would be highly incensed on her behalf, but she had no thought of asking Mrs. Butters to intercede and restore her to her employment. On the contrary, Fanny was coming to the reluctant conclusion that she could no longer live with the kindly widow. Mrs. Butters' granddaughters would never be permitted to visit their grandmama, not so long as she was there—Cecilia Butters would be adamant on that point. In losing her job, Fanny had lost her home, as well.

She knew it was her duty to exert herself, to cease indulging in such black thoughts, but oh, how painful was the effort to subdue her feelings of misery and yes, resentment!

The quiet, solitude and shade of Abney Park was well-calculated to help Fanny compose her spirits. As a result of her dismissal, she thought, she now had the leisure to contemplate nature, rather than toil in a warehouse.

She thought of her friend William Gibson. Perhaps by now he had received word of what had happened. *There*, at least, she could be sure of sympathy, and the thought calmed and supported her a great deal.

And—it does appear that I must abandon all hopes of Mr. Edifice! She thought, and even laughed a little.

After her return to the house, a scruffy little boy came to the door with a bouquet of forget-me-nots in a small crockery vase wrapped with a bit of old ribbon.

"My sister Martha goes to your school, Miss," the boy stammered. "And they all said to tell you as how they will miss you very much."

The little bouquet cost her more tears. She thought of the girls gathering the flowers from the fields around Camden Town, and one of them contributing the jar, and another the ribbon, and the lengthy walk for the young messenger, who was thanked with a glass of lemonade and some meat pie.

Fanny sat with her bouquet as the afternoon shadows fell, comforting herself by thinking of what she had been able to accomplish in her brief time at the academy. A teacher's knowledge is diffused slowly, from one person to another. Her old governess at Mansfield Park, Miss Lee, had taught Fanny how to do fancy-work, and she in turn had passed on her skills to the four-and-twenty girls of the academy. They would be able to earn their own bread, even if it was just a pittance; thanks to Fanny, they need not exist in utter poverty or abject dependence. It should be enough; and she hoped that with time, the sweetness of these reflections would outlive the disgrace of her dismissal.

CHAPTER SEVENTEEN

WILLIAM PRICE WAS back at Gibraltar once more, but this time as an officer, instead of as a lowly midshipman. It seemed another life since he had first marvelled at the sight of the massive pinnacle and the fortress when they appeared over the horizon, or when he had cheerfully risked his neck to scramble along the narrow paths which overlooked the churning seas far below.

The temptations of Gibraltar; the women from many nations beckoning from upstairs windows, the jewellery-sellers and the conjurers and the fortune-tellers; the opportunity, seldom passed up, of getting into a fist-fight; all of this was the same as he remembered, but he had no spirits to venture out with his fellow shipmates, no desire to lose in a few hours the coins which took weeks to earn, no wish even to drown his thoughts in the oblivion of strong drink.

But the Governor and his wife were holding a grand reception at the Clubhouse Hotel, to celebrate Lord Wellington's victory at Badajoz, and William was amongst those invited to attend.

So inadequate was the room and so numerous was the crowd, with so many persons swarming here and there, in quest of a better seat, or a lost comrade, or a glass of punch, that only a person utterly determined to take pleasure in the event, could have done so. And William, in the dejection of his spirits, shying away from seeking out any old acquaintance, and lacking ambition to make any new ones, allowed himself to be pushed about, as unresisting as a piece of flotsam pulled along in a strong current. And as a piece of flotsam, when carried past a turning in the fast-flowing stream, will be caught in an eddy and be left behind, so William found himself elbowed into a quiet alcove, unregarded by the passing throng. Without caring what he did, he took possession of an unoccupied chair and silently regarded the revellers pushing to and fro.

When a cheerful-looking older woman, likewise buffeted by the current of humanity, chanced to come his way, he swiftly stood and surrendered his chair. The lady seated herself and, smiling broadly, declared she would not let form prevent her from making the acquaintance of such an amiable young officer. Her alert and intelligent countenance was more effectual than mere beauty, in banishing the unsociable spirits of the lonely lieutenant.

197

"The roof will constitute an introduction, I think. I am Mrs. Croft, wife to Admiral Croft."

"Your servant, ma'am. I am William Price, First Lieutenant of the *Protector*."

"You have done your duty and made your bow, Mr. Price," said she with a merry laugh, "So, I will not take it amiss if you look about you for better company. My husband went to speak to the Governor and he asked me to wait for him, so I shall stay here until he finds me."

"It will be my honour to remain with you, Mrs. Croft, and my great pleasure as well. Or, may I fetch you some punch?"

"I think the prize would not be worth the effort, Mr. Price, there are so many people prepared to celebrate our victory over the French by stamping upon a toe to gain a cup of punch or a slice of cake! Pray, stay by me and tell me about yourself."

William fell into easy conversation with the lady, whom he judged to be some years younger than his own mother.

"I need not enquire what you have been up to, sir, for your fair hair and darkened skin speak for you—you have been in the horse latitudes for an age! Africa or the West Indies?"

"Africa, ma'am. With Captain Irby, and prior to that, I served under Captain Columbine."

"Ah yes, Edward Columbine, a good a man as ever there was! Rest his soul. I knew him when my husband was stationed in Bermuda."

"Really, ma'am? You were in Bermuda?"

"Oh yes, I have crossed the Atlantic four times with Admiral Croft," she smiled and nodded in affirmation.

William spoke as he felt: "Captain Columbine was of the opinion that it was too dangerous for wives to accompany their husbands to sea."

"And, true enough in his case. My brother says the same. He declares we ladies should not live on board with our husbands. I despair of ever seeing him married! However, I do not know that navy wives are *more* prone to dying on their watch than are wives back home in England. Consider, your own Captain Irby lost his wife whilst he was serving on shore, in charge of the Sea-Fencibles in Essex, poor fellow. For my part, I can declare that the happiest part of my life has been spent on board a ship with my husband.

Thank God! I have always been blessed with excellent health, and no climate disagrees with me. Life is uncertain, wherever you are, and so, persons as fortunate as you and I must be very sensible of it."

"As... you and I, ma'am?"

"What! Young man, are you not fortunate? You are young, you are English, you are handsome, and you have survived your service with the West African Squadron. Your blessings lie upon you as thick as the hairs on your head, sir."

William grinned, and felt a little of his old lightness of spirit overtake him.

"You are quite right ma'am, and I will not forget it again, I promise you."

"Now, here is my husband, with your Captain Irby, if I am not mistaken."

"Sophy!" exclaimed the Admiral with disarming familiarity. "I should have sent out a search party for you in a moment, but Irby spied Lieutenant Price from across the room. And he told me he had a particular message for Mr. Price, and said I might want to stay within hailing distance, as it would give me pleasure to watch the lad receive this bit of news." And then in a whisper which was quite as audible as his every day voice, he added, "Dispatches from the Admiralty, you know."

William looked from his captain to the admiral and back again, not trusting his own ears.

"It's true, Price. I have just received the assignments for our convoy. You, Lieutenant—nay, *Commander* William Price, are assigned to the HMS *Protector*..."

A sudden pounding in his chest and a loud buzzing in William's ears prevented him from comprehending what Irby was saying. He saw his captain's lips move, and the Admiral and Mrs. Croft were both smiling, and Irby was nodding his head emphatically, but William could not make it out.

"I—I beg your pardon, sir. Could you repeat what you just said?"

"Too much sun," Admiral Croft said, shaking his head wisely. "It disorders the brain. He should be well enough in time, we hope."

"Price, I was informing you that after we put in to Portsmouth, you will be assigned as commander of the *Protector*, and you will perform convoy duty between Portsmouth and Cork."

William looked all the amazement that he felt, and Captain Irby, laughing, held out the orders so he could confirm the fact for himself.

"I, Sir? Made Commander? When there are so many of us—I mean we—lieutenants? I must be powerfully obliged to someone for their kind interest on my behalf."

Captain Irby agreed that William was indeed extraordinarily fortunate, and gave his opinion that William Gibson's book played no small part in elevating humble William Price from amongst the many other deserving candidates for advancement. The young commander now numbered some of the leading figures in Parliament amongst his well-wishers—Wilberforce and Stephen in the Commons, and Delingpole in the House of Lords. "Further, the public, I've no doubt, will be pleased to read of your elevation, while I will be exceedingly sorry to lose such a capable officer. I trust you have done well in the matter of prize monies?"

"Very well indeed, I thank you, sir—once the Admiralty gets around to distributing it."

"I dare say a young chap like yourself would rather join in the war effort than chase after slavers," said the Admiral. "And you will be putting in to shore quite frequently. You can court an English *and* an Irish sweetheart, eh?"

Mrs. Croft fixed a shrewd look upon William. "Perhaps he has only one sweetheart in mind."

"Then, this news will gladden her heart! Happy for you, man!"

"Alas, my dear Admiral, his old captain, our friend Captain Columbine, counselled him against marriage!"

"Every man must decide for himself, to be sure," said Admiral Croft. "But a captain cannot hold his ship back from battle, for fear he may come to grief, and I trust that you, Commander Price, will be as bold and resolute on the seas as your nation expects of you, though you may choose to be more timid in your own affairs."

"The Admiral," said Mrs. Croft with a smile, "is not comparing marriage to a naval engagement in any particular way. But the same principle applies—our fears of the worst should not prevent us from acting in a manner which would best constitute our own happiness.

Forgive me for my impertinence, Commander Price, it is none of my affair, and I will only add, I wish you continuing good fortune, and the wind at your back."

Admiral Croft clapped William heartily on the shoulder.

"Hasten home, my boy, hasten home, and claim your prize. What is there to wait for?"

*   *   *   *   *   *   *

It was a Sunday afternoon, and Julia and Edmund returned from morning services and finished the basin of soup which Mrs. Peckover had left for them. Unlike Dr. Grant, for whom the Sunday dinner at Mansfield Parsonage was a reward for the exertions of his eloquence in the pulpit, Edmund had established the Sabbath as a day of rest for even his own household servants, and he and Julia enjoyed their quiet Sundays together.

After they ate, Julia went upstairs to change to a simple house dress. From out of her window she saw Edmund, his bible tucked under his arm, walking back to the church to conduct a baptism. He looked so alone, thought Julia. And how did her poor brother feel when he took the infants of the parish into his arms, and pronounced their names, and beheld the pride and happiness of their mothers and fathers? He, who would have been a most excellent father...

Julia realized with a start that a full year had elapsed since the time her brother Edmund had received the letter from Mary. Matters had remained in suspense between them—another twelvemonth gone by—and there was no resolution. Julia had spent the same year waiting for a reversal of fortune that prudence told her could not rationally be expected.

Edmund had said nothing to her, had not so much as hinted of his dilemma, but it struck her forcibly that day—her presence at Thornton Lacey prevented Edmund from reuniting with his wife.

"He will not leave Thornton Lacey for I have no other home to go to," she murmured aloud to herself.

How selfish it was to continue in her present state, and keep Edmund from Mary. How futile were the hopes she had cherished! How pointless to hope in vain!

A sudden resolution seized her. She fetched some writing paper from her brother's study and sat at the dining table. A soft breeze fanned the window curtains as she wrote.

Dear Mr. Meriwether, she began:

After much reflection upon my readiness to enter the married state, I write today to assure you that I am extremely gratified and honoured by your proposal of marriage, which has also received the approbation of my beloved parents.

Therefore, my dear sir, I accept your proposal, being fully assured within myself that in pledging my hand to you, I embark upon matrimony with a man in whose character, honour, and temper I may rely...

The letter was sent to the post the next morning and she knew he would be reading it by the following day.

I will grow accustomed, she told herself. *I will grow resigned. I will be content.*

* * * * * * *

And what was Fanny thinking and doing that same Sunday afternoon, two days after her dismissal? Thanks to the return of Mrs. Butters and Madame Orly, she was feeling much better. They were of course more indignant on her behalf than she was for herself, and Madame Orly was all for resigning her position at the shop in protest, but Fanny urged against it. She was touched by the affection which prompted the offer, but feared that the gesture would only harm the charitable efforts of the school. For the same reason, Fanny counselled restraint when Mrs. Butter penned a long, stern letter to the ladies of the committee. "They after all have contributed their time freely," said Fanny, "it would be unkind to upbraid them."

"Does my sister-in-law suppose, does Mrs. Wakefield suppose," answered Mrs. Butters in an angry tone, "that I would carelessly foist an immoral person into a place wherein the welfare of young people was at stake? Or do they think that I, having had you as guest in my home this twelve-month and more, must be entirely in ignorance of your character? Am I blind, deaf and ignorant? Or worse, do they think me mendacious and abandoned in my principles? Or not worth consulting, before they took this absurd decision? As for Cecilia—well—I cannot trust myself there!"

It was not in Fanny's nature to listen with satisfaction while Mrs. Butters inveighed against her sister- and daughter-in-law. She could not rejoice in family quarrels, but at the same time she derived great comfort in these proofs of affection and loyalty. They helped to compose and she knew they must, in time, reconcile her to her new situation. The affectionate support of her friends, combined with intervals of quiet meditation, had materially restored Fanny's mind to some measure of tranquillity.

Fanny was preparing to go out for another long walk when a hackney coach stopped in front of Mrs. Butter's house. To her surprise and pleasure, William Gibson alighted along with her brother John.

"I thought you could do with a diversion," Mr. Gibson announced cheerfully. "And your brother has never seen the north of London, so I proposed that we all go exploring together."

William Gibson let her know, by way of a feeling glance, that the unhappy news had indeed reached him. Fanny was grateful—grateful and much struck by his prompt response, and the kindness and delicacy of his conduct. Her brother John, being himself and therefore unobservant of the emotions that roiled in the breasts of other mortals, was in his own way a good companion for a sister who wanted to put her sorrows aside.

With the highest feelings of gratitude and affection both for her brother and the man who had delivered that brother to her, Fanny joyfully acquiesced, and she joined them in the coach, pointing out spots of interest on the drive from Stoke Newington to Primrose Hill, where Fanny expressed a wish of climbing to the summit, to take in the view of all London and the surrounding countryside.

William Gibson continued to be all that was considerate and entertaining as they made the ascent. The young writer was clamouring inwardly to know whether the rumour about Fanny's understanding with Mr. Edifice could possibly be true. Fanny being entirely in ignorance of the tale, did not know with what self-denial he awaited an opportunity to speak to her privately.

Fanny, for her part, was eager to speak with John about the progress of *his* career, and to reflect on the murders which had so terrified London last winter.

"I should think there must be a better way of examining for clues, when a crime has occurred. And people should not be permitted to go through the place where the murder happened, gawping at the dead bodies. Thousands of people went to the draper's shop, Fanny, to see the Marr family laid out on their beds. There were people lined up down the street, even ladies of fashion, waiting for their turn to see a mangled corpse. What if one of those people had picked up some important clue? Mr. Horton found the maul, but the killer also used a razor to slit throats with. That has never been recovered."

"Did the police not search the lodgings of the killer?" asked Mr. Gibson with interest.

"They did... a full week after he hung himself in prison! Why had no one thought of doing it before?"

"Indeed!" agreed Fanny. "Perhaps every police office ought to compile a list of hints for police officers, to remind them of useful actions to take."

John sighed. "I wish I could be an investigator. I want to get out behind my desk. I want to look for the clues."

"I am sure you will be promoted, will you not? I am certain Mr. Harriott recognizes your good qualities."

"Oh, there. Mr. Horton is to receive ten pounds reward for finding the maul at the draper's shop—as though there were any merit in spotting a three-foot long implement covered with blood, lying next to one of the victims. While I.... *my* name has not been put forward for a reward, although it was I who spotted the initials "JP," which led to the identification of the owner."

Fanny and Mr. Gibson were both warmly sympathetic on John's behalf.

"I think it is because I embarrassed Mr. Harriott in front of the other magistrates. I did not intend to. I was just looking at the maul."

They had nearly gained the top, and Fanny was congratulating herself on her improved strength and stamina, when she was alarmed by the sound of two pistol shots in quick succession.

"Do you hear that?" she asked.

"Primrose Hill, I have heard, is a place where gentlemen go to have duels," said John, not recollecting that the word "duel," merely the word, was unnerving for his sister, let alone the contemplation of being near a duel in progress.

"Unlikely on a Sunday afternoon. I fancy someone is just testing their pistol, or practising their aim," Gibson gestured uphill, from where the sounds appeared to be coming. The trio looked around alertly, Fanny with some trepidation, and they advanced slowly toward a copse of trees until they spied a man seated on the stump of a tree, composedly cleaning a pistol.

"Miss Price, your eyesight is better than mine, I think," said William Gibson. "Doesn't that fellow look amazingly like..."

"Yes, it does look like Mr. Bellingham," Fanny concurred. "But perhaps it is only because the Bellinghams have been much upon my mind of late."

Just as they were close enough to make him out, and conclude that it was indeed John Bellingham, he was seen to replace his guns in a small wooden case, and begin his descent from the hill. He had not appeared to notice that he was being observed.

"He looks familiar to me as well," John said. "He looks like a fellow who came around to our office a few weeks ago. I asked him if he was reporting a crime, and he said yes, a crime had been committed against him by the government. Mr. Laing told him we did not deal in cases of that sort, and sent him on his way. He left a pamphlet."

"Do you still have it?" asked William Gibson.

"No, I looked it over, and so did Mr. Harriott and Mr. Laing, and then someone used it in the necessary."

"We will mention no names," said William Gibson.

"Whoever last had the petition before him, put the petition behind him," returned John.

"Poor Mr. Bellingham! That is his fate, it seems," Fanny sighed.

"Crimes committed in Russia are not in our jurisdiction," John said defensively.

"No, of course not, Price, no-one is accusing you of indifference."

"But—John—I suppose it is not out of the ordinary that a private gentleman should have a pistol. However, if you knew Mr. Bellingham, I believe you would be alarmed by the fact of *his* being in possession of one."

"Your sister is quite right," said William Gibson. "We are well enough acquainted with Mr. Bellingham to say that we cannot repose any confidence in his judgement. I fear, if he has a pistol, he intends to use it. At the risk of being accused of having a wild imagination, I think the prudent thing to do would be to speak to someone in authority about this."

"As I recall from his pamphlet, he chiefly blames the English ambassador to Russia for his troubles. Would not that person be his first target?" asked John. "What was his name?"

"Leveson-Gower. Lord Leveson-Gower," Gibson recalled the name from his lengthy interview with the aggrieved Bellingham. "This person is the target of his ire, would you not agree, Miss Price?"

"Yes, Mr. Gibson. He spoke about him with great resentment. I wonder, is the ambassador still at his post in Russia?"

"I can make enquiries," said John. "If he is still abroad, he is safe, at least for now. Here we are at the top! How excellent! I hadn't thought you could climb so far, Fan!"

"Let us find a seat so your sister can rest herself before we descend again," Gibson suggested.

The trio sat together and took in the scene of tranquillity and prosperity spread out before them, while they discussed the possibility that John Bellingham was contemplating murder. How other-worldly, thought Fanny, to sit under a calm blue English sky, with good and true companions, and canvass such an atrocity! If it were not for the recent Ratcliffe Highway murders, she would have found it impossible to entertain the idea that a civilized man could contemplate such a barbaric deed.

"Unlike some people," said John, with a significant look at his two companions, "I have regular employment and cannot come and go for my own pleasure. But as it happens, I worked extra hours all last week, and I believe I could obtain permission to take a half-holiday tomorrow. Tomorrow morning, I will make enquiries about the whereabouts of our Lord Leve-what's-'is-name, and we could all meet again and confer on what to do next."

The resolution taken, Fanny proposed they all walk down again and return to Mrs. Butters' house for some refreshment. She took Mr. Gibson's proffered arm as her brother, lost in his own thoughts, walked on ahead of them.

"I could not part from you today, Miss Price," said Mr. Gibson, "without expressing my deepest indignation concerning the way you have been treated. Forgive me, but I must relieve my feelings on that score."

"The certain knowledge that *you* would sympathize in my distress," Fanny responded shyly, "I must own—I must own, I have thought of it, and relied upon it, and it has comforted me a great deal. And Mrs. Butters of course, and dear Madame Orly, are also very kind. May I ask, how did you come to hear of it—and what did you hear?"

"I was informed by Mr. Wakefield, who had it from Mrs. Wakefield, who had it from Mrs. Blodgett, that you had been dismissed for improper conduct. And I owned to him, I was surprised—extremely surprised—that the committee is evidently content to accept your dismissal, without conducting an enquiry or speaking with you directly as to the veracity of the accusations. It is a violation of the fundamental rules of natural justice. They repose greater confidence in Mrs. Blodgett's judgement than I had thought would be..."

"They cannot be bothered to exert themselves, that is all," Fanny said, not attempting to hide the sadness she felt. "It is too much of an effort. Mrs. Butters has written to them. She is insisting they acknowledge, in writing, that the worst accusations against me are untrue."

Indeed, merely to allude to the idea that she, Fanny Price, had lived with a man without benefit of clergy and had instigated a duel, was excruciatingly embarrassing for Fanny. She rushed on: "But—but I have this comfort— the pain that this has occasioned is more strongly felt by me, owing to a good and growing tendency in my nature. I mean to say, had this occurred to me several years ago, I should have thought I was too lowly and unimportant to protest. Now—you may laugh—but I *do* think better of myself, I *do* deserve to be treated with more consideration, more respect. I am *not* the lowest and the last."

"'The lowest and the last'? Whoever would dare to call you the lowest and the last?"

"When *you* say it, Mr. Gibson, you make it sound so ridiculous, that I can laugh at it now. The point is, because I have lived out in the world for a time, I have more confidence in myself than in—my earlier life.

"What truly pains me though, is there is no acknowledgement of what I have done, what I *did* accomplish, at the academy. I never thought I should be forced to leave so abruptly, without a word of thanks. I deserved better than to be addressed in such a fashion, in front of my pupils. It was wrong."

"Indeed you *did* deserve better! Your abilities, your contribution, will only be appreciated after you are gone, not that any of them will have the decency to acknowledge it, I fear."

"So you see, I *can* console myself with this thought—as compared with the past, I now value myself, my own worth and dignity, more highly than before."

"Still not so highly, I think, as your true friends value you."

Mr. Gibson felt Fanny's slender fingers wrap more securely about his forearm. He hesitated, then ventured: "*I* would be your partisan, Miss Price, if I could presume myself to have the right, the privilege, of speaking on your behalf. But, perhaps... surely Mr. Edifice... what does Mr. Edifice say?"

Fanny looked perplexed, then laughed. "Mr. *Edifice*? Why Mr. Edifice?"

"Pardon me if I am being indelicate, but I would have expected Mr. Edifice to have entered the lists for you—in fact, I should say he has a particular motive for defending your reputation."

Fanny was silent for a while, then replied, "I will not pretend that I do not understand you, Mr. Gibson. I am astonished. You are labouring under an extraordinary misapprehension. I cannot imagine how you formed such a mistaken notion."

"Truly, Miss Price? I had it on what I thought was very good authority. Your Aunt Norris, in fact."

"Mr. Edifice!" Fanny repeated, bemused. Then, she began to laugh, almost recovered herself, then laughed some more, for she could not bring herself to act affronted.

And Mr. Gibson thought, *so this is what walking on air feels like.*

The gentlemen escorted Fanny by cab back to Mrs. Butters' house. They were welcomed in for tea, and all disagreeable topics, such as unjust dismissals and attempted assassinations and mistaken rumours, were put aside in favour of happier conversation.

Mrs. Butters greeted John Price with especial kindness. Fanny had never presumed to invite him to her benefactress's home, and

John was somewhat abashed at being in genteel company, but his reserve could not long withstand Mrs. Butters' cordial and frank reception. While at first, he sat rigid and immobile, afraid he would break one of her teacups or commit some other vulgarity, he soon relaxed, especially when Mr. Gibson began recounting his humbling experience at the "Childe Harold" dinner party, omitting only the identities of everyone involved, and his tale had them all laughing immoderately.

"Oh dear!" exclaimed Mrs. Butters, wiping her eyes. "Aha! A salon full of society ladies, swooning over Lord Byron, in front of their own husbands. What is this world coming to? And you, my poor Mr. Gibson, how very mortifying for you!"

"You tell a story against yourself very wittily, Mr. Gibson," smiled Fanny, "but I cannot help being a little indignant on your behalf. And as well, I suspect at least one of those ladies you describe was attempting to annoy her husband, to make him jealous. If so, it is behaviour unworthy of a wife."

"I am glad to know you think so, Miss Price," answered Mr. Gibson, "and I will add, that this rule of conduct applies to both sexes. No *man*, worthy of the name, would ever treat his wife, in public or private, with anything less than the respect she deserves."

Mrs. Butters turned away to fuss with the tea things, so that Mr. Gibson might give Fanny a look full of eloquence and devotion.

"Is there any more apple tart, Fan?" asked John.

CHAPTER EIGHTEEN

"MARGARET!" EXCLAIMED Janet Fraser, holding out a note written in an elegant hand. "My sister informs me that Mr. Meriwether proposed marriage to the younger Bertram girl—and she has accepted him!"

"That would be Julia," Mary Bertram offered, reaching for her coffee with more calm languor than she felt. "So, I should fancy they will be marrying soon? Nothing to wait for?"

Margaret, already dismayed at finding Mary Bertram at the breakfast table with her step-mother, twisted her hands in her lap and waited for the reproof she knew was coming.

"This is the *second* time you have allowed a Bertram girl to steal a suitor away from you, Margaret!," exclaimed Janet Fraser, throwing the note down on the table in disgust. "First you lost Mary's brother, after I had moved heaven and earth to bring you two together."

"Although to be fair," Mary added, "many young ladies had hopes of Henry, but he never had a serious thought of Margaret."

The memory of Henry Crawford's attentions, his flattery, his whispers, his secret caresses and stolen kisses, all came upon poor Margaret in an instant, and she flushed to the roots of her hair. She had believed him to be in love with her. She had been miserably undeceived.

"But," continued her step-mother relentlessly. "I *had* supposed our Margaret might have succeeded with Mr. Meriwether—he was actually looking for a wife. Of course, it all comes to nothing once again."

"But what was *I* to do, ma'am?" said Margaret mournfully.

"You have no spirit, Margaret, no character, no fire!" Mrs. Fraser scolded. "What are we to do with you? You are almost three-and-twenty! And still behaving like a child!"

"Mr. Meriwether *was* kind to me, ma'am, but then Mary introduced him to Miss Bertram, and he p-p-preferred her to *me*!"

Janet Fraser looked at Mary and raised an eyebrow. "Have you been fishing in my pond, Mary?"

"I do feel for you, Janet dearest, but—"

"Ah! My dear Mary! How slow of me! If Miss Julia *Bertram* is to be married, then, your husband may at last condescend to take you back under his roof? Is it not so?"

"Yes, so naturally I did nothing to stand in the way of Mr. Meriwether's preference for Julia. Had it been otherwise, of *course* I would have done everything in my power to help Margaret catch him—and perhaps even she will have the goodness to acknowledge my *many* efforts on her behalf these past months," —this last, with a sigh and a scowl at Margaret.

"May I congratulate you then, on the fulfilment of your ambitions, my dear Mary? When shall you re-join that handsome husband of yours?" Mrs. Fraser was struggling between the remains of resentment, and pleasure for her friend, but Mary thought that loyalty to friendship was winning through.

"We have only to decide where we are to live, which is no small matter. He will need to leave his profession, and I must reconcile him to it, for his own good. I have been speaking to Lady Delingpole about the possibility of moving to Ireland."

"Ireland! Amongst the savages! No, no, my dear friend, that cannot be. You cannot leave me!"

"Lady Delingpole assures me it is not so dismal there as one might suppose."

"How I admire your fortitude, Mary! The thought of leaving London fills me with horror!"

"It seems I must make the sacrifice, my dear Janet, if I am ever to have a home to call my own again."

Margaret muttered something under her breath.

"What did you say, Margaret?"

"Nothing, mother."

"You are not even a good liar, Margaret."

"Oh, I do believe our Margaret can show cunning," said Mary. "She is no sorry, helpless, little creature. She is capable of betraying a friend to satisfy her urge for revenge."

Margaret coloured. "I do not understand you, madam."

"I think you understand me very well. It was *you* I have to thank for betraying my brother—you told Edmund that Henry was meeting with his sister Maria in secret. And as a consequence, Edmund nearly refused to marry *me*. Your useless jealousy and spite over my poor brother cost me dearly in my husband's eyes."

"B-because he learned that *you* had been deceiving him, you mean?" Margaret shot back, too miserable to care. "Such a pity he did not profit from the lesson! And what could I tell your husband now, madam, about Wales!"

"How dare you! To what do you refer?"

"But—as your p-poor husband was foolish enough to marry you in the first place, let him remain a fool! And take you with him to Ireland, or g-go jump in the sea!"

And Margaret fled to her bedroom, weeping.

"Wales?" asked Mrs. Fraser. "My dearest, most intimate friend, whatever happened when you were in Wales? How could you have kept a secret from me? What is the little fool talking about?"

"I have no notion, Janet. Truly. But the surest way to punish her is to ignore her."

* * * * * * *

John stood in front of the police office, breathing in the familiar, ripe smells of the ebbing tide. The Thames was crowded with shipping as usual; the forest of masts, their sails furled away, waved restlessly back and forth as ships settled in their berths, the curlews and gulls circled and swooped to plunder the rubbish exposed by the receding waters. The rising wind plucked at his clothes and his hair like so many nagging thoughts.

Mr. Laing, the head clerk, had given him the afternoon off. John was not supposed to be there, lingering in front of the office— all staff were to come and go by the back door—but Mr. Harriott always came in at the front door, and John wanted to speak to him privately.

'Mr. Harriott! Sir! A moment of your time, sir, if I may."

The magistrate paused. "Well, what is it, Mr. Price?"

In a low voice, John reminded the magistrate of the recent visit of John Bellingham, and his complaints of ill-usage by the English ambassador to Rome.

"This ambassador, sir, I have learnt, is now in London. Lord Leveson-Gower. He is now a member of Parliament, sir, and lives on Stanhope Street, near Primrose Hill."

"And? What does this have to do with our office?"

"Indeed, sir, this is not in our jurisdiction, but I have information—I fear—that is, my friends and I are quite certain—Mr. Bellingham intends some outrage upon Lord Leveson-Gower. You will recall, sir, when Mr. Bellingham came to our office—"

"Ahem! Yes, now I recall the gentleman. You need not concern yourself, Price. The authorities are well aware of him. This Bellingham fellow has been everywhere, including Bow Street. And Bow Street contacted the officers at Parliament. So everyone who ought to be informed, has been informed, and is fully aware of this man's eccentricities and his discontents."

Mr. Harriott made for the front door, but John persisted:

"Would it not be better to arrest Mr. Bellingham and bring him in for questioning?"

"Questioned about what? He has broken no law. He has not threatened violence against anyone. He has not said or written anything of a seditious nature, to my knowledge."

"He is exceedingly angered sir, he is quite taken up with his grievances. My friends and I think he is not in his right mind."

"The law does not give me license to apprehend a gentleman, even a nuisance of a gentleman, for petitioning his government. He is exercising his ancient rights and liberties."

"But, only question him, sir—speak to him—ask him what he is about. I am certain he is bent on mischief—more than mischief."

Mr. Harriott waved John away impatiently. "It would be highly injudicious for me to intervene. The Home Secretary made it clear that he does not want humble John Harriott sticking his nose into matters which don't concern him. I do not care to expose myself to further mortification of the sort I endured, when attempting to protect this neighbourhood from the Ratcliffe killer." Again Mr. Harriott's hand went to the door knob, but he added, "We must take into account places, persons, and prerogatives, Mr. Price. You and I are not answerable for Mr. Bellingham's conduct, according to the Right Honourable the Home Secretary."

"Yes sir, but may I add, that Mr. Bellingham has been seen firing a gun on Primrose Hill. And Primrose Hill is very close to Stanhope Street.

Mr. Harriott paused. "Hmmm. I would not, on any account, alarm Lord Leveson-Gower unnecessarily, but if this is indeed the case, I may send a note to him. Thank you, Mr. Price."

To spare Mr. Gibson the expense of another trip to Stoke Newington, Mrs. Butters asked Donald McIntosh to drive Fanny into town, where she met with her brother and her friend at a tea-shop on Broad Street in the early afternoon.

"This morning I confirmed Lord Leveson-Gower *is* here in England. He is a member of parliament now," John reported. "And he lives with his family on Stanhope Street."

"Stanhope Street—isn't that near Primrose Hill?" asked William Gibson.

John looked grim. "Indeed it is. Very near. That may mean something, or nothing. But, listen to this—we would not be the first to share our concerns with the authorities. About the same time that Bellingham came to our office, he also applied to the Bow Street Magistrates, and they told him off just as we did. And he sent them a letter, very ominously worded, saying if they did not get him the hearing he wanted, he would *execute justice himself.*"

"'Execute justice himself!'" Fanny exclaimed.

"Yes. So of course Bow-Street took the letter to the officers at Parliament, but *they* dismissed it as just another meaningless threat from an eccentric. There are, after all, a great many people disgusted with the government nowadays—the weavers, the merchants, the slave-traders, the Catholics, everyone who is sick of the war. If they arrested all the people who hate the authorities, why, at least half of the country would be locked up."

"But are we three still persuaded that he may be capable of a violent act?" Gibson asked, looking at John and Fanny in turn.

"I am," answered John shortly.

"And so am I," added Fanny. "And he will act very soon, I believe. Mr. Bellingham talks as though he has no time to lose. He wished an alteration done to his coat, for example, and wanted the work done in a day."

"What manner of alteration?"

Fanny indicated with her hands. "In the skirt of his coat. He wanted a pocket sewn on the inside."

"A pocket he would access with his right hand?"

"Yes, he said he intended it to store papers."

"Most men keep papers in their waistcoat, not down in the skirts of their coats." Gibson mimed the action of reaching across

214

his chest and reaching down to pull something out of his coat. "What would he be using the pocket for? A flask? Sandwiches? Or—Miss Price, what size of pocket?"

"Oh, I should say about nine inches deep and not quite as wide."

"Deep enough to hold a pistol?" John asked.

Fanny and William looked at each other in alarm.

"And are we reasonably certain the Ambassador is his target?" asked Mr. Gibson.

"Oh—that's right," John recollected. "In his letter to Bow Street, he also said, 'Soon I shall play a court card.'"

"So, you suspect he might be referring to the royal family?"

"King, Queen, or Jack. Or George. And still, the authorities ignored him."

"We have good reason to suspect he is on the verge of doing something desperate, something violent, involving some politicians or public men," Mr. Gibson said. "If the authorities cannot be persuaded to act, then we must have a word with the fellow. If we were to confront him, then surely he would abandon his schemes, knowing himself to be under suspicion."

John nodded his assent, and Fanny did likewise.

"Miss Price, did you ever learn where Mr. Bellingham lives in town?"

"Yes, I did hear of it because he was two months in arrears on his rent and Mrs. Bellingham had to ask her uncle for monies to send to the landlady. I saw the receipt. He lives at the corner of Ormond and New Millman Street."

"Not far from here!" cried John. "Gibson, let's put a stop to him today. Shall you and I pay a visit to Mr. Bellingham?"

"We would need to escort your sister back to Stoke Newington first."

"Why?" asked Fanny. "You would only incur needless delay and expense. Mr. McIntosh will pick me up here with Mrs. Butters' carriage at five o'clock. We have time to visit Mr. Bellingham's lodgings before then."

And to Fanny's surprise, her brother added: "I think we should bring Fanny along with us, Gibson. He knows her."

"But *we* know he carries pistols, and is steeling himself to commit murder—I won't have your sister exposed to such danger."

"I think John is right, Mr. Gibson. Mr. Bellingham has been very civil to me, and furthermore, his wife told me he always makes a point of being courteous to the ladies."

Mr. Gibson still looked doubtful, and Fanny had a sudden thought, and her countenance lit up in pride and pleasure: "Think of what this could mean for *you*, John. If you were to prevent a terrible crime from occurring, if Mr. Bellingham was to confess his plot to you and Mr. Gibson, what a good thing it would be!"

John looked at Fanny as though seeing her for the first time. "Indeed, Fanny, if we apprehended Mr. Bellingham, and saved Leveson-Gower's life, well, it would be such a triumph for me! Catching pickpockets in the taverns is nothing to it!"

"And," he added, aware that he was guilty of thinking only of himself, "it is good for you to stay busy, as well, Fan, so as to keep your mind off the fact you were dismissed from your employment in disgrace."

Mr. Gibson scowled.

"What? Did I say something amiss?"

"'Tis no matter, John," Fanny laughed. "Now, what shall we do?"

"Confront Mr. Bellingham at his lodgings—right now—if he is there."

"What shall you say when you knock on the door, Miss Price?" asked Mr. Gibson. "On what business do you wish to speak to him? What will you tell his landlady?"

"Here," said Fanny. "John, I have your mended shirt with me in my carpetbag. I shall say, 'here is a shirt for Mr. Bellingham, from his wife.'"

"Very well, but if your masquerade is successful, what becomes of my shirt?"

"I shall make you a new one, I promise! And if Mr. Bellingham isn't at home, I shall offer to take his mending up to his room myself. And if I spy the case of pistols, I shall put them in my carpetbag."

"Miss Price, you can't be serious."

"Gibson's right, Fan. The plan is an excellent one, and does you credit, but there is one small objection which you may wish to take into account first. If someone catches you stealing pistols, you could hang by the neck for theft."

"Oh! Gracious, yes, I do not think I am hardened enough to risk that. But I can still enquire if Mr. Bellingham is home. He would come to the door for me, without the least suspicion."

"And if the man *is* at home, Miss Price, please be very cautious and let your brother and me engage with him."

John hailed a cab to Ormond Street and instructed the driver to stop a short distance away from the lodging-house. Fanny stepped down from the cab with her small carpetbag in her hand. Mr. Gibson and her brother watched as Fanny plied the knocker.

Mr. Bellingham *was not* at home, the maid who answered informed her; he had walked out, along with her mistress, to look at the paintings at the European Museum.

"Did he indeed? What a kind gentleman!" offered Fanny, who, now that she was actually putting her plan into action, felt very self-conscious and foolish, and even began to wonder if she and her companions had let their imaginations run away with them, as she had at Christmas-time, with her fright over the Ratcliffe Highway killer.

Oh yes, the maid affirmed, Mr. Bellingham was a most courteous gentleman, and Mrs. Robarts thought very highly of him.

"As he is not here at present, I shall deliver his shirt. Pray, which is his room?"

But the maid would not permit Mr. Bellingham's room to be trespassed upon, and with no further ado, the carpet bag was pulled out of Fanny's hands, the door was closed in her face and she had lost her opportunity and her brother's shirt. Thus ended Fanny's first attempt at spycraft.

She hurried back to the cab for a hasty conference.

"This is actually quite fortunate," Mr. Gibson suggested. "If Mr. Bellingham is escorting a lady, it seems impossible that he should be intending to commit any desperate action today. No one is in danger, at least not immediately. Well done, Miss Price."

"Going to gawp at a bunch of paintings is a desperate act enough," said John. "Only a woman could have proposed it to him."

"Do not you think it would be most unlikely for Mr. Bellingham to have taken his pistols with him on such an outing," said Mr. Gibson, lowering his voice so that the cabby might not overhear them. "Therefore this may be the ideal time to confront him with some measure of safety—and in a public place, where, if he has any care for his reputation, he will not create a commotion."

"But what should we say to him?" asked Fanny.

"I think we should give the impression that we have more information than we do," offered John. "We will tell him we know what he is about, which may be enough to bring about a confession."

"And even if he denies any hostile intentions, I think we can, with good conscience, go on and warn Leveson-Gower, at the very least," Gibson added.

John enjoined the cabdriver to hurry to King Street, but no driver could make the Piccadilly Road traffic disappear for the convenience of his passengers, and Fanny and her companions did not arrive at the doors of the museum until quarter past four. The trio stood, uncertainly, in front of the entrance.

"I shan't want to pay a shilling for each of us to go in, only to discover he is not in there," complained John.

Fanny read the sign posted at the door. "It seems we are too late to buy a ticket, at any rate. The museum closes soon, and everyone will come away."

"Why don't we just wait out here, then?" suggested Mr. Gibson.

"Except—Donald McIntosh will be waiting for me with the carriage on Broad Street at quarter to five. What should we do?"

"There is time for one of us to walk back to Broad Street and ask him to come here," said John. "Gibson, why don't you go?"

"On the other hand," Mr. Gibson said, "I know Mr. Bellingham very well by sight. You have only met him the once, and might lose him in a crowd."

"But Fanny knows him very well, too. She will spot him, certainly!"

Mr. Gibson gave John a significant look, with a quick side glance at Fanny.

"What?" said John.

"John," said Fanny, "you are the youngest. Won't you oblige us and go find Mr. McIntosh?"

"Very well, it will be me, then. The only one with police office experience. I'll go and leave you two amateurs here."

They watched the slim figure of John as he trotted back towards Piccadilly, retracing on foot what he had just travelled by cab, then Fanny gestured to St James's Square, down the street. "I fear that if we went to sit on a bench in the Square, we might miss seeing Mr. Bellingham when he comes out. I think we had better stay here at the entrance."

"You will not be too tired, I hope, Miss Price?"

"No, we will not have to wait long, I am sure."

"Well, if you will permit me—may I take advantage of the moment to enquire, Miss Price, have you confirmed any plans, as to the future? You are quite determined—you will not return to the academy? No? They do not deserve you, at any rate. How much longer will you reside with our friend Mrs. Butters?"

Fanny shook her head regretfully. "I am exceedingly fond of dear Mrs. Butters. If it were not for the animosity of her daughter-in-law, I should be very content to stay with her. But, I will not become another bone of contention between Mrs. Butters and her family. If Cecilia Butters is convinced I am a fallen woman, she will never visit, nor allow Mrs. Butters to see her granddaughters again. I must go, and soon."

Mr. Gibson was silent for a moment, waiting for her to say more. "Then... *where* will you go, may I ask?"

Fanny sighed. "I can visit with my family in Portsmouth. I should like to see my aunt and uncle Bertram, although it would be... excessively awkward to go to Everingham."

Indeed, thought Mr. Gibson. *To return to the place where you pretended to be the wife of Henry Crawford! To encounter the same villagers, the clergyman, the winking servants! To hope for a welcome from the cousin, who loved and lost him!*

And, what about your cousin Edmund?

"No doubt you would be pleased to visit Northamptonshire again, as well. You have often praised its beauties."

"Yes..." said Fanny, and Gibson heard the reluctance in her voice, but could not be certain what that reluctance meant.

"Miss Price, may I express the hope that you would return frequently to London, to see your friends here?"

He glanced at her, thought that he saw the tears threaten, and carefully looked away, as she replied.

"I *have* been very happy, Mr. Gibson. Very happy indeed. It was so delightful to observe the success of your book. And—I think *I* have done some good as well, at the academy."

"Of course you have, Miss Price. And... Fanny..."

"Oh, look! Mr. Gibson! There he is!" Fanny grabbed Gibson's arm and pointed to the door. In the midst of a throng of persons departing the museum, there was Mr. Bellingham, cheerfully escorting a middle-aged lady in widow's garb, and a little boy.

"Oh dear, I did not know Mrs. Robarts had brought a child with her. The maid said nothing about a child. Indeed, Mr. Gibson, I suddenly feel quite abashed. I should not wish to speak of pistols and murder in front of the landlady and her son, now that I see them. How in the world does one introduce such a topic!"

"Yes, I understand your feelings, Miss Price. Why don't we follow them—what do you think?"

"Yes, let us follow and see whether they are heading back to Ormond Street. I fancy that they are. If John and Mr. McIntosh overtake us, the two of you could still confront him."

Mr. Bellingham and his companions walked along King Street and turned in the direction of Piccadilly. Fanny and William Gibson followed half a block behind, trying to conceal themselves behind other pedestrians. Mr. Bellingham and Mrs. Robarts were chatting genially, but Fanny observed that the lady was leaning rather heavily on his arm. At length, they all turned into a small lace and ribbon shop just off the main thoroughfare.

"Mr. Gibson, I have a suggestion," said Fanny. "I think the landlady is growing weary—and if I should enter that shop, as though I were going shopping myself, and see and greet Mr. Bellingham, he would naturally introduce her to me. And I could offer her a carriage ride home. There would be enough room in Mrs. Butters' carriage for myself, the lady, and her son. I would leave Mr. Bellingham behind. And then you and John could confront him, take him to Bow Street or Bedlam or whatever you think best."

"You make it all appear very plausible, Miss Price," Mr. Gibson answered reluctantly. "But the carriage—I fear I may have to leave you, and go back to St. James's Square to find your brother and Mr. McIntosh.

"I think I can say to Mr. Bellingham, quite naturally, that the driver let me down at the shop so I could buy some lace, and he that is returning for me soon. I shall be perfectly safe, Mr. Gibson—we know he can't have his pistols with him today, whereas, if we let him go, he may carry out his purpose the next time he goes abroad."

"Very well, Miss Price. I do think the plan is a sound one and you shall be safely in the carriage with Mr. McIntosh before John and I attempt to apprehend him. I shall turn back then. Good luck to you, and we shall meet again in a quarter of an hour."

Fanny walked to the shop, and discovered that Mr. Bellingham and his companions were the only other customers in the small, over-heated premises. Mr. Bellingham instantly recognized "Miss Price," and Fanny was introduced to Mrs. Robarts and her young son—the latter, after looking at paintings for an eternity, was clearly dismayed to find himself in a place which held even less interest to a young boy.

Fanny, looking about, uncovered a chair hidden under a rumpled pile of velvet cloth and said, "Pray, Mrs. Robarts, won't you take this seat?"

"Oh, I surely will—thank you, Miss Price. What a prodigious amount of walking we have had today! Mr. Bellingham and I walked all the way from Ormond Street, then dawdled about looking at paintings for two hours, and now here. I must have a little rest before we walk home again."

"Ormond Street, madam? Why, that is on my way home, and the carriage is coming to fetch me shortly. I should be delighted to convey any friend of Mr. Bellingham."

Everyone's face brightened, including Mr. Bellingham's.

Her plan was unfolding so smoothly that Fanny briefly thought back to the day at Mansfield when her cousin Tom asked her to take a part in some amateur theatricals. Fanny had refused, out of shyness and disapproval of the play, and had brought the wrath of her Aunt Norris down on her head. *If Aunt Norris could see me now*, she thought to herself. *Acting! Acting a part quite voluntarily. I almost feel I owe my cousins an apology!*

"I would be very much obliged to you, Miss Price," said the lady. "I trust we would not be inconveniencing anyone? You have sufficient room?

"Oh yes, I came alone. There will be plenty of room for you and your son."

"That would be capital, Miss Price," said Mr. Bellingham. "How very good of you. You just came out to town to do some shopping?"

"Yes—the coachman let me down here briefly, because I had heard this shop had an excellent selection of fine lace."

"They do indeed," affirmed Mrs. Robarts. "But that clerk is taking his own time in the back, fetching something out for me."

"There is another store-room in the rear of the building, Miss Price," said Mr. Bellingham, "stocked with goods for those who are professionals in the trade."

Turning to his landlady, Mr. Bellingham explained, "Miss Price is an instructress at a sewing academy. Isn't that so, Miss Price?"

"Indeed, Mr. Bellingham. And in fact, my errand today is on business. I never could afford to buy so much lace for myself," and Fanny emitted what she hoped was a natural-sounding laugh.

"Pray, Miss Price," said Mr. Bellingham genially, lifting a hinged section of the counter so that they might walk through. "Allow me to introduce you to the owner. His office is through here. He is a good friend of mine and I undertake to guarantee, he will give you a generous reduction on anything you desire, for so worthy a cause as your academy. Mrs. Robarts, kindly rest for a moment."

Continuing to play her part, and hoping she would not have to lay out monies on lace, Fanny followed Mr. Bellingham through a fringed curtain, down a long dimly lit corridor, and then, to her surprise, through a door which opened on a dark, narrow, alley-way.

"Where is the office, Mr. Bellingham?"

"There is no office, Miss Price." His hand slipped into the skirt of his coat, and he pulled out a short-barrelled pistol and pointed it at her.

"You were telling me falsehoods, madam. You and Mr. Gibson were following me from the museum."

Fanny felt the blood rush from her head and the ground swayed beneath her feet.

"You did not arrive at the shop by carriage, and you are no longer employed at the academy. But I don't have time to listen to your explanations or any further falsehoods. I have urgent business which cannot be delayed another moment. Where is Mr. Gibson?"

"Mr. Gibson—Mr. Gibson—he will be returning shortly, with the Bow Street Runners!"

"Do not attempt to deceive me. You are a poor liar, Miss Price. I trust you understand the unfortunate consequences should you try to step away from me, or summon aid."

He grabbed her arm tightly—she could not prevent a little cry of fright from escaping her lips—and he pulled her close to his side, as though they were lovers.

"You observed how quickly I was able to draw out my pistol, Miss Price. I am putting it back in my pocket but pray believe me, I will not hesitate to shoot you if you impede me or attempt to escape. Come along."

And he drew her, with great rapidity, down the alley and then circled back toward St. James's Street.

So *this* was real danger—not the foolish pretended fright she had given herself at Christmas-time, when she thought the Ratcliffe killer was stalking the academy! Yet, although her heart was pounding rapidly, and her breath came in faint gasps, Fanny felt strangely detached, oddly numb, and disbelieving, as though she were watching a play. This could not really be happening. Could she really be the captive of a deranged man with a pistol?

Fanny was too overcome to speak for a few moments, and soon rather too breathless, but she managed to say, "Mr. Bellingham, does this have anything to do with your... with the injustices you have suffered? Is that your urgent business?"

"Why do you enquire?"

"Because, sir, many of us who—who have been taken into your confidence concerning that unhappy matter are—are—concerned, very concerned, you are about to do something rash and desperate."

"Rash? Desperate?"

Oh no, thought Fanny to herself. *I have offended him.*

"When I appealed directly to Downing Street, and some government lackey dismissed me, and I asked them what in heaven was I to do next, he said—and I quote—'I should take such measures as I deemed proper!' I take them at their word."

"Oh heavens, Mr. Bellingham," Fanny murmured. "What steps? What are you going to do?"

He looked at her with his familiar mild smile. "I will inevitably be given the platform they have so long denied me. I will be able to present my case to His Majesty's Attorney-General, a judge, a jury of my peers, and the public. Of course no jury will convict me in a cause so righteous."

Fanny looked around in vain for her brother and Mr. Gibson. Mr. Bellingham warned her to look only straight ahead and continued his painful grip on her slender arm.

He swept her along swiftly, and in a few moments, they reached the broad avenue of Pall Mall and her captor pulled her in the direction of Carlton House. Mr. Bellingham was breathing heavily and sweating freely, looking neither to the right nor left, and a thrill of horror shot through Fanny at the sudden suspicion he intended to harm the Prince Regent himself. *No, it was madness even to suppose...* She had no intention of asking him and perhaps putting more insane ideas into his head.

They passed by several late afternoon loiterers, but Fanny was speechless, unable to signal her distress.

"I remind you Miss Price, I *will* shoot you on the instant if you make a noise or make any sign of alarm," Mr. Bellingham said quietly, and she was suddenly filled with the conviction that the Prince Regent *was* his target. Fanny tried to console herself with the thought that no-one could just stroll into the grounds of Carlton House and shoot the Prince. Surely, someone would intervene. But perhaps Mr. Bellingham had a reason for being here, at this particular time. Perhaps he had some information, maybe the Prince was about to exit the gates in his carriage. Then, it would be all too easy to step right alongside and shoot him.

Oh, dear Heaven! What was she to do?

Surely, she must do something! And if it was her moral and civic duty, regardless of her sex, what would be best to do? Should she refuse to let him drag her along? Should she start screaming and cause a commotion? If Bellingham made good on his threat and shot her openly in the street, wouldn't that guarantee his capture, and prevent him from killing someone important?

On the other hand, nobody likes the Prince Regent, including you, a cool voice inside of her head argued.

But, whether she liked the Prince Regent or no, was it not her *duty* as his subject to prevent an assassination? What the merest foot soldier in the Army would be expected to do? She thought of her brother William, who would not have hesitated for a second to put his own life in danger to save the Prince Regent.

The thought of William steadied her as nothing else could. Although she was breathless, and the blood pounded in her ears, she promised herself—should Mr. Bellingham try to enter Carlton House, she would struggle and scream for assistance.

And so she could not help thinking; a few more steps might end her life, in the few dozen yards still to traverse, this could be the last sight she beheld, these handsome white columns fronting Carlton House, these lovely, lovely trees lining the Mall, leafing out in pale green, and lit by the rays of the late afternoon sun. Never had the world looked so incandescently beautiful, so pulsing with life. A favourite poem sprang into her head:

There was a time when meadow, grove, and stream,
The earth, and every common sight
To me did seem
Apparelled in celestial light,
The glory and the freshness of a dream.

Yes, yes, she thought. *The world is beautiful. And I may be about to leave it, forever.*

Her captor continued to walk rapidly with her arm locked in his grip, his other hand in his pocket, and Fanny kept pace with him, afraid to look at the guards on either side of the entrance gate, standing at attention in their sentry boxes. *A few more yards, just a few more, and we will be clear of Carlton House, and I will not be forced to risk my life, not quite yet, not now...*

They were at one end of St. James's Park, and Fanny saw small groups of people strolling about the lawns, a young boy rolling a hoop, and Mr. Bellingham hurried her on, past the Horse Guards, toward the Birdcage Walk.

* * * * * * *

"Here, Mr. McIntosh, draw up here, before we reach the shop," Mr. Gibson, sitting beside the coachman on the box, laid a hand on his arm. "Mr. Price and I need to make ourselves scarce first."

Before the horses had even stopped, the carriage door swung open and John Price jumped out on to the pavement.

"Now, Mr. McIntosh, if you could kindly watch the door of that little shop there, and wait for Miss Price. Miss Price should be walking out with another lady, and, if all goes well—"

"Miss Price?" said a voice at John's elbow. He looked down and saw a young boy. "Is this Miss Price's carriage?"

Mr. Gibson, watching from the box, inwardly cursed the mischance that brought the landlady's son out to the pavement, to overhear them. "Why, hello there..." he began uncertainly.

"Is Miss Price coming back, then?" the little boy asked. "I should like to have a carriage ride!"

"'Coming back?' What do you mean, 'coming back'? Is she not in the shop?" Mr. Gibson asked, climbing down swiftly.

The little boy pointed down the street to the intersection. "I saw her. Her and Mr. Bellingham. They were crossing the street together."

"Are you certain?" asked John.

The boy nodded.

An icy hand grabbed Mr. Gibson's heart.

"Which way did they go?"

The boy pointed toward Pall Mall.

John said, "I will look in the shop, in case the boy's mistaken."

"Yes. Yes. That's wise, Price. I shall pursue them on foot."

"What's this?" demanded Mr. McIntosh. "What have ye done with Miss Price?" But Mr. Gibson was already running down the street.

"Gibson!" called John after the retreating form, "if you do not see her, keep widening the search, keep going in wider circles! We'll search with the carriage!"

"Can I go in the carriage now?" said the boy.

* * * * * * *

Her first trial had passed, but she was not out of danger.

If the Prince Regent was not his target, surely he was drawing ever closer to his real one. And that person or persons must be within walking distance.

Was he headed to Parliament? Or had they guessed wrongly? Perhaps his target was even closer, and someone would die, because she was too afraid to do anything. She greatly regretted not

226

screaming for help when they passed the sentries at Carlton House and she berated herself for her cowardice. She was panting and holding her hand to her side now, struggling to keep up with Mr. Bellingham as he sped her along.

"A forced march is a most unpleasant thing, is it not, Miss Price? Imagine, if you were not strolling along this lovely, tree-lined walk, but instead, you were in St. Petersburg, possessing only the filthy clothes on your back, unable to clean yourself or make a decent appearance, and being compelled to march in miserable sleeting weather, through puddles and slush and mud, in company with the most degraded ruffians. Imagine yourself being laughed at and abused by the passers-by. Imagine yourself passing by the home of His Excellency the Ambassador, not once, but several times, and crying out in despair for his assistance, and receiving none. Imagine yourself running, fleeing, and escaping through the gates of his home, rejoicing in reaching safety and sanctuary at last, only to be returned—yes, returned by force—to the Russian bear!"

Fanny wondered, *must I accept the fact that these are the last few moments of my life?* She tried to prepare herself for the possibility and discovered she wanted to live, very much indeed. Even if she was cried up as a heroine after her death, even if they put up a plaque somewhere, she thought she would prefer not to die.

Fanny resolved to choose a moment to call for help when there were sufficient crowds nearby—when there were enough people to witness and hear and, she hoped, prevent Mr. Bellingham from escaping, if he made good on his threat to shoot her.

They were approaching a small crowd of men and boys gathered together on the pavement, some elegantly dressed, some of the labouring classes. She reckoned her best time had come, although her mouth was so dry from fright she thought she could barely speak to be understood.

"Mr. Bellingham!" She struggled and stopped walking.

"Miss Price, I believe I already explained to you the necessity for your silence."

"Mr. Bellingham, I do not believe you are going to shoot me. You would not shoot a harmless, defenceless woman."

His large hand, wrapped around her slender arm, tightened so much that she gasped in surprise and pain.

"You are correct, Miss Price, I would not *ordinarily* do such a thing, but these are exceptional circumstances."

"Will you not confide in me? I know you have been sorely mistreated, but perhaps something can be done, even at this late hour."

"Something *will* be done, Miss Price. *I* will do it. *I* am the instrument of justice. All will be well." He jerked her arm. "Be silent and come with me. I am already late."

"No, no I won't, Mr. Bellingham," answered Fanny with a quavering voice. "And if you do not stay with *me*, I will scream, loudly. And those men up there will come to my assistance."

Mr. Bellingham glanced in their direction, then laughed. "Those men up ahead are gathering to watch a cockfight and I think they would be not at all interested in leaving off their entertainment to intervene in a dispute between us."

"Well," said Fanny, feeling extremely foolish. "Perhaps some of them will."

"It pains me to be under the necessity of having to explain this to a lady, but the fact is, they will assume you are a whore, trying to gull me out of more money. Are you willing to risk your life upon their chivalry? I *promised* you, Miss Price, that if you were to impede me, I would shoot you."

Indeed, had any passer-by closely observed them, they would have concluded that the lady was obviously in the grip of some strong emotion, perhaps even on the verge of hysteria, and the gentleman was only trying to reason with her. Fanny felt overwhelmed with despair at the conviction that what he had said was true—she had chosen the wrong time and place—those men would not come to her aid.

Fanny stood, hypnotized with horror, as Mr. Bellingham levelled the pistol in his pocket at her midsection and poked her with the barrel.

"The bullet to this pistol is half an inch wide, Miss Price. I fancy the wound will be so comprehensive, that you will expire quickly with little pain. I cannot say for certain, though."

Fanny shook like a leaf. *Will this be the last thing I see? The last thing I hear?—*

She took a deep breath and closed her eyes, and screamed. Her scream was a weak and kittenish one, because after all, she had never in her life really screamed before, and never would again.

A paralyzing force slammed into her. She felt herself falling, and the world went black.

CHAPTER NINETEEN

"THE ORDERS IN COUNCIL and the American embargo threaten British commerce with complete and utter destruction. To prosecute the war in Spain against Napoleon, the government has beggared our Treasury, poured out the lives of our brave soldiers, and they hesitate not to neglect every interest, every domestic tie—to cripple, oppress, starve and grind down our own people."

Lord Brougham, a leading Whig, with the wind of public opinion at his back, demanded that the House of Commons rescind an order by the Prime Minister to boycott all trade with France and her allies. The war against France, prosecuted for so many years, had exhausted the treasury but worse, involved all the western nations of the earth in blockade and counter-blockade. The public was thoroughly weary of war and angry at its leaders. Manufacturers suffered, merchants suffered, ships were idle and factories silent. Because so many people were affected, the debate brought a larger-than-usual audience to the House.

Brougham was youthful, handsome, eloquent, and ambitious. He had his witnesses at the ready, and the statistics at his elbow. The public gallery was packed with his supporters, as well as reporters from the daily gazettes, who hung on his every word as he described scenes of privation from all over Britain.

James Stephen, sitting opposite the speaker, glowered impatiently, while murmurs of approval for Lord Brougham floated down from the galleries above his head.

Stephen was an influential member of the government party—in fact, it was his book, *War in Disguise*, which had introduced the idea of capturing American merchant ships as part of prosecuting the war against France, a strategy which led to the global trade war. And now, America was on the brink of declaring war against England as well.

Brougham will let Napoleon take over the world, so long as he can buy some good French Burgundy, Stephen thought contemptuously.

But he was worried. Lord Brougham had arranged for representatives of the various British industries—pottery and plate, weavers and metalworkers, to testify in Parliament about the desperate hardships the government had imposed upon its own people. Stephen knew the Whigs believed they could pick off enough wavering Tories to call for a non-confidence vote and bring down the government.

"And where is their leader?" Brougham demanded, scanning the half-empty benches opposite him with contempt. "Where is the man whose policies have brought such disaster upon his own countrymen? Why is he not here to give an audience to their cries for assistance? Is his faction so indifferent to the just claims of our citizens, that they will not even deign to give them a hearing?

"Where indeed?" muttered James Stephen to himself. He had been assigned to cross-examine all of Brougham's witnesses, as though it was possible to deny the misery and hardship which stalked the land. If ever there was a thankless task, this was it. And while he faced down the angry crowds, and righteous members of the opposition, where was his chief? Still taking tea in Downing Street?

Stephen dashed off a short note and gave it to a messenger. "Tell the Prime Minister to come here immediately. Tell him to hurry. He must show himself if we are to survive."

* * * * * * *

"Miss Price! Fanny!"

Fanny's eyelids fluttered, and she became aware of William Gibson's face peering closely into hers. She next realized he was lying at full length above her, but bracing himself to keep his own weight off of her.

"Fanny! Fanny! Please answer me."

"Oh! Mr. Gibson! Oh!"

"Fanny! Thank heaven! You're all right!"

"I must have fainted for a moment."

"Several moments, actually." *The worst moments of my life*, Gibson thought to himself. "Pray, allow me." He winced as he rolled to one side, got up slowly and clumsily, then extended his hand to help her off the ground.

"What happened, Mr. Gibson?"

"You were speaking so intently to Mr. Bellingham you didn't see me running across the park. Just as I caught up with you, I saw him point a pistol—at least I think I did—" Gibson stuck his hand in his own pocket and mimed the action. "That, and your scream, convinced me he was about to shoot you. I thought if I fell on him, he might discharge his pistol, even accidentally, so I decided I had better fall on you instead. Pray excuse me."

Fanny began to shiver uncontrollably. Mr. Gibson had used his body to shield her from being hit by a bullet.

"Did he hit you? Oh, Mr. Gibson! Have you been shot?"

"No—that is—I don't think so. I imagine it is the sort of thing a person takes notice of. I felt a heavy blow to the back of my head—I think he hit me with his pistol-butt. I am still seeing stars." He felt the back of his head and winced again. "I shall have a considerable goose egg back there.

"Oh dear! I am so sorry!"

"Still, better than being shot, I fancy."

"And where is Mr. Bellingham now?" Fanny asked anxiously, looking around.

"He ran. He turned and ran, that way," Gibson gestured toward Westminster Cathedral.

Fanny clutched his arm. "Oh no, Mr. Gibson, we must stop him. He is about to kill someone, I know it."

"Yes, he was about to kill you!"

"Yes, but you see, I refused to go with him. He wanted to prevent me from raising the alarm, so he couldn't leave me at the shop. But I—I didn't—I wanted to stop him, so I refused to go any further—"

Gibson looked at her in wonder. "Do you mean to tell me, you were deliberately trying to stop him, in spite of the fact that he threatened to shoot you?" He formed each word very slowly and carefully.

"Well, because... I thought he was going to shoot the Prince Regent, and that would never do, and then he didn't stop at Pall Mall, but he came walking along this way, and I didn't know when he might reach his target, so…"

Gibson turned visibly pale, closed his eyes, and wavered back and forth. "Fanny," he said. "Fanny."

Fanny felt chagrined. "Perhaps I acted very foolishly but— but— my brothers would have done the same. Or something even better."

Gibson swallowed and nodded. "Would you mind—my hat—over there, on the ground."

Fanny stooped and retrieved his hat, which he held in his hand rather than try and force on his aching head.

"By now, perhaps he has reached his real target. Did he say anything to you about his intentions, Fanny?"

Fanny closed her eyes, trying to recall Bellingham's exact words. "He said, 'I am already late,' as though he had a specific rendezvous or opportunity in mind. And he said, 'I am the instrument of justice. All will be well.'"

"Already late—he is most likely bound for the Houses of Parliament—they begin their sessions at four-thirty. Miss Price, I think you did it—you succeeded in making him late and you've prevented him from reaching his target in time. But I must follow him." Gibson grabbed her by the arms and pleaded, "Fanny, please go back—quickly as you can. Your brother and Mr. McIntosh are searching for you. If you do not find them, then hire a cab and go home. Promise me. Do not linger in the park, it is no place for an unaccompanied lady."

"But you are injured! Are you well enough to go in pursuit, Mr. Gibson?"

"I am sorry, but I must leave you. I must run!"

Fanny knew she was no runner, and could not possibly keep pace with Mr. Gibson's long legs as he raced down George Street, to the palace of Westminster. Fanny stood and watched him until he disappeared from sight before turning to re-enter the park. She realized she was trembling like an invalid and her legs would hardly obey her. She pushed on, holding her shawl tightly around her, eyes downcast, looking at no one, for she did not know what she might do next—faint, or fall into hysterics, or just cry. She tried to draw long, deep, calming lungsful of air, but the housemaid had laced her stays particularly tightly that morning, and she could only take tiny shallow breaths.

She was terrified of the danger William Gibson was running toward, if he caught up with John Bellingham. Bellingham was insane, had two pistols, and was sturdily built. Her heart beat wildly in her chest, and she came over in a cold sweat.

Where is Mr. Gibson now, and what is happening? She murmured to herself. *Oh merciful heavens, if I could only know what is happening. I cannot endure the thought that he may be harmed.*

She could hear someone running up the path behind her. Frightened, she grabbed her skirts and began to run in earnest, and the footsteps followed in pursuit.

"Fan! Fan! Stop, for heaven's sake! What's happened! Where is Bellingham?" There was her brother, red-faced and panting, at her elbow.

Fanny turned to him pleadingly. "Oh, John!"

The world started spinning and she collapsed into John's arms.

It was late at night when William Gibson appeared at Mrs. Butters' house and despite the hour, he was eagerly admitted inside. By then, all of London had heard the news. In fact, many of the common people were overjoyed. There had been bonfires, singing and dancing and drinking in the streets.

"My dear fellow," Mrs. Butters welcomed him in, both arms outstretched, overcome with emotion. He allowed her to embrace him like a fond mother before he sank into an armchair by the fire. Fanny pulled up her own little chair to sit beside him.

"I ran," he said at last. "I ran toward the Houses of Parliament. I thought— 'If he was planning to shoot someone as they walked into the House of Commons, he is indeed too late, for the session has begun.' I thought, 'surely, he cannot enter the floor of the chamber, someone would stop him. Perhaps we have succeeded in thwarting him. Perhaps all will be well after all.'

"Then I thought, that's what Bellingham would always say, 'all will be well.' But I remembered that someone else said the same thing recently, and it was at the Parliament, too. 'All will be well.' The prime minister.'

He looked away as Mrs. Butters covered her face with her handkerchief to smother a wrenching sob.

"I was almost at the entrance at St. Stephen's door," he said quietly, leaning forward, his head bowed, his elbows resting on his thighs, his hands clasped tightly. "Almost. And I heard the shot.

CHAPTER TWENTY

AUNT NORRIS WAS visiting with Edmund and Julia while her home received a fresh coat of whitewash and new wall-paper in the dining room. Prevented from engaging in her usual occupations, and energetically spurned by Mrs. Peckover, Aunt Norris had little to do apart from making useful suggestions for the upcoming marriage of her niece.

"My dear Edmund, my dear Julia, how happy I am to be with you when you read the banns for the first time this Sunday!"

"This Sunday, Aunt Norris? So soon?" Julia asked with alarm. "do you really.... I mean, I believe I need some more time to grow used to the idea of getting married."

"But, my dear Julia, you should reflect and consider Mr. Meriwether's situation. He is so much older than you— he must feel the passage of time more acutely than a young person like yourself. Since Mr. Meriwether has asked, and you have agreed, I think there can be no reason for delay."

"Except, of course, May is held to be a most unlucky month for marriage, is it not? We should wait until May passes, at least."

"True, it *is* held to be so—by foolish, ignorant and superstitious people, none of which we are."

Julia could not answer the arguments of her aunt, and gave her consent that her brother should read the banns. Julia spoke of her happiness and satisfaction, but she spoke with calm reserve. There was no glow of spirits, no heartfelt smile. Though outwardly complaisant, she was still inwardly doubtful, and as Sunday approached, she felt entirely worse—uncertain of herself, guilty towards Mr. Meriwether, and resentful of her aunt. Her bonnet shielded her from the eyes of the villagers as her brother announced, "Nathaniel Robert Meriwether, resident of Hotwells Parish, Bristol and Julia Ann Bertram of this parish," and asked if any parishioners knew "cause or just impediment. This is the first time of asking."

"You can leave everything to me, dear Julia," her aunt assured her as they left the church, amidst the smiles, nods, and winks of the villagers. "I shall arrange all the details—the wedding breakfast, and corresponding with your father about the marriage articles. It will be no burden to me at all, I assure you. My own labours, I never regard. How delightful it will all be! Mr. Meriwether is certain to make some very handsome gifts to you. Where is your presentation gown, the one that you were never able to wear at court, owing to the fire at the palace? Is it in Norfolk? I shall write to your mother this very day and have it sent to us. We will want to have it altered slightly, of course—remove the hoops—but it should do very well for you as a wedding gown, and it cost dear Sir Thomas a very considerable amount of money, and it would be inexcusable in us to think of buying a new gown when you never wore the other!

"I was never able to assist your sister in this fashion, which was most unfortunate. And oh! You can include a visit to Everingham on your honeymoon journey! Be sure to propose it to Mr. Meriwether! Or, I can suggest it myself, when I meet him. As obliging a gentleman as he is, I am sure he can have no objection. I should very much like to see Everingham myself, of course. Are you going to take a bridesmaid with you? Fanny, I suppose. But, all things considered, perhaps I ought to also accompany you. I am sure Mr. Meriwether's carriage is large enough for four persons, and it has been an age since I saw my dear sister Bertram and dear Sir Thomas."

And on and on the good lady spoke, and one might have thought that she was better acquainted with Mr. Meriwether than Julia was, when in fact she had never laid eyes on the gentleman. But she enumerated his good qualities with confidence and enthusiasm—'generous, liberal-minded, clever' —while Julia was silent.

"Only think, my dear Julia! Two more Sundays and there will be nothing more to wait for!"

* * * * * * *

The public rejoicing amongst the lower orders over the assassination of the Prime Minister was greatly alarming to the authorities, who feared a general insurrection. The terrors of the guillotine in Paris were very much in the minds of England's leaders. The militia and the Foot and Horse guards came out to patrol the streets, until the government was satisfied that an English Revolution was not about to follow the French one.

The three friends—William Gibson, John Price and Fanny— all lamented, severally and individually, the failure of their efforts

236

to forestall the catastrophe. Fanny blamed her female weakness for obstructing and delaying Mr. Gibson—had he not been so concerned for her well-being, he might have apprehended the killer before he struck. John wondered if he would ever again be given so fair an opportunity to prove his worth to his superiors, and Mr. Gibson had the additional, private, reproach, that although he had known Mr. Bellingham to be a dangerous lunatic, and he was determined on all accounts to keep Fanny safely away from him, he had permitted the swift unfolding of events to overpower his caution, and the woman whom he most particularly wanted to protect and cherish was brought into mortal peril.

Some justifiable reproach would always attend their recollections, but the man who had struck down Spencer Perceval must ultimately bear the blame. The inquest, trial and execution of Mr. Bellingham swiftly followed, one upon the other. Fanny used her enforced leisure and nervous energy to sew while Mrs. Butters read aloud from the newspaper accounts, and she dispatched a new shirt and some cravats to her brother before the week was out.

If Eliza Bellingham had continued her employment at the academy for many years, perhaps she would have overcome the guilty conscience which she bore, for conspiring with Cecilia Butters to have Fanny Price dismissed. But her triumph was short-lived—she held her new position for only two days, when the shocking news that her husband had murdered the prime minister burst upon her. She fled back to Liverpool to be with her children. She was greatly afraid of being despised and persecuted, but she was in fact much pitied and a public subscription was taken up for her support.

"To which our Fanny anonymously gave five pounds!" exclaimed Mrs. Butters to Mr. Gibson, a week after the dreadful event. The generous widow had done the same and more, but she shook her head fondly at the thought of a girl who could never harbour resentment against anyone. "Although, when she returns from her walk, I would suggest you not mention it to her. You know how she is disconcerted by praise."

"Fanny no doubt excused the lady on the grounds that she was driven by necessity," returned Mr. Gibson. "Eliza Bellingham had three children to support, and a worthless husband. Poor woman. I still think the jury ought to have found him insane."

"But he refused to admit that he was mad," Mrs. Butters said, as she re-filled Mr. Gibson's tea cup. "I have read all the newspaper accounts. And he worked against his own lawyers, who tried to make out the case for insanity. I have no pity for the man."

"And there was no need to hold the trial so swiftly," continued Mr. Gibson.

"I expect the authorities felt it was for the best, to clear the matter up quickly. There was, after all, no question but that he shot the prime minister. Why waste your compassion on him, Mr. Gibson? Think on poor Mrs. Perceval, left with twelve children. Heaven support her!"

"Yes ma'am. I do not mourn for Mr. Bellingham. I mourn for British justice."

"Yes, of course you do, dear. Will you have another sponge-cake?"

"Thank you, yes. May I dip it in my tea? You will not object to the sailor's habits I acquired whilst on board the *Solebay*? Yes, to return to John Bellingham's widow, I do admire Fanny's capacity to forgive."

"'Fanny?'" Mrs. Butters raised an eyebrow and smiled. "No longer 'Miss Price,' but 'Fanny,' I perceive."

"She has long been 'Fanny' to me, you know very well, ma'am. And as we are sitting together so comfortably, there is something I want to consult you about. This business has created something of a dilemma for me."

"I am all attention, Mr. Gibson!"

"It was my purpose, Mrs. Butters, so soon as I had acquired sufficient capital, to declare myself to Fanny. I need not ask," he laughed, "if my plan meets with your approbation—unless your feelings on this point have changed very materially!"

"Unchanged as the North Star, my dear Mr. Gibson! I wish you joy!"

"And now Fanny must remove herself from under your roof, is that not so?"

"Unfortunately, my daughter-in-law has... it is an awkward situation, Mr. Gibson. But nothing has been resolved upon yet. I urged Fanny to make no hasty decisions. The dreadful shock to her system—first her disgraceful treatment at the academy, and then, being in London on the very day that Mr. Perceval was killed!

When she came home, I could see that she was terribly affected—pale as a ghost and very distressed."

"Indeed, ma'am."

"And they hung Mr. Bellingham this morning! She had met the man, even conversed with him! However one might try to drive the disagreeable picture from one's mind, we can't help thinking of him, dangling from a rope at Newgate and then given to the medical students! Anyone's constitution might give way under the strain of such things," said Mrs. Butters placidly, choosing a muffin and applying a goodly layer of butter. "I have ordered Fanny to rest and not to worry about the future for now."

"You are kindness itself, my dear madam, but, sooner rather than later, Fanny must leave you. I see the necessity for it. She has, in consequence, no home. There are some relations who might take her under their roof, but who is to say she will be greeted with the affection she deserves? But there—" he shook his head, as though to clear away some disagreeable thoughts. "I mean to say, I wish, most earnestly, that I had made my proposals to Fanny before this unexpected crisis. Do you see?

"And to ask her to take my name, when her own good name has been attacked—perhaps I am being overly nice here, but to offer her a home, when she is in need of one, might cause her to doubt her own disinterestedness—or worse, cause her to suspect I am acting out of motives of pity, and not true affection."

"And our Fanny is apt to question and doubt and hesitate at any rate, when faced with such a momentous choice. But," Mrs. Butters laid a reassuring hand on his arm, "my dear Mr. Gibson, this is but a passing regret. After five, ten, fifteen years' happy marriage, what will it matter? And, I know you do not mistrust Fanny's integrity, you only lament the appearance of things. You cannot imagine for a moment she would accept you, merely for the advantage of acquiring a home when she is in want of one. That is not the Fanny we know."

"Indeed not. Still, I wish I had spoken to Fanny a long time ago. It would have spared me more than one alarm and vexation. As it is, I am still anticipating the success of my novel—without it, we shall have a fairly narrow income to live upon."

"When will you speak? Today?"

"I think I need to prepare the ground first, and I have been racking my brains as to the best approach. May I enlist you as my confederate in my schemes?"

Just then, Fanny was heard in the ante-room, returning from her walk, so Mrs. Butters hardly had time to assent to Mr. Gibson's request that they meet tomorrow morning, and that they all take the air together in her carriage.

Fanny was agreeably surprised to see Mr. Gibson when she came in from her walk, the more because she had been attempting to harden herself to the likelihood that she would be leaving London very soon, and she did not know when it would be in her power to see him again.

"Your walk has done you good, Fanny, I see," said Mrs. Butters, and Mr. Gibson, as usual, wondered if he ought to join in praise of her person, to remark how the fresh air had brought the bloom to her cheeks.

"Mrs. Butters, I intend to write to my mother today, and propose a visit to Portsmouth," said Fanny with calm resolution, after seating herself and accepting a cup of tea.

Mr. Gibson frowned. He knew that Mrs. Price's household management left much to be desired—in fact, he feared that, although he had survived the experience, he could not be so sanguine about Fanny's chances! But he could not denigrate Fanny's parents to her face, nor could he offer an immediate alternative.

"But, my dear Mrs. Butters," Fanny continued, "I find that it eases my mind to know I have my own monies—monies which I have earned and saved, thanks to you, as well as my settlement from Mr. Crawford. How utterly cast down I should be, if I were to be completely dependent upon my relations for charity, as is the case with so many other females in my situation!

"Now, I am spared from feeling myself to be an encumbrance on my family—for I can and will contribute my share to the household. This will be different, so very different, from...." and Fanny waved off the rest of her thought, not wishing to complain of the years at Mansfield Park and her aunt Norris's endless reminders of the gratitude she ought to feel for the generosity shown to her.

"I quite understand you, my dear," nodded Mrs. Butters. "My late husband always acknowledged that I had been his partner in everything, in building our business together, and he always said, everything we had was as much mine as his, and he trusted me with it altogether."

"The occupations open to women of gentle birth are so few, and the pay, I have observed, is so miserably low," said Mr. Gibson, "that I suppose not one lady in a thousand could command enough monies to support herself in tolerable dignity, even supposing she were so inclined."

"Very true. And," Fanny said with a sigh, "because of my past folly, I cannot return to my old occupation of governess. My character is too compromised. But I was wondering, Mrs. Butters, if you could speak to some of your charitable acquaintance on my behalf? Perhaps there is some other benevolent scheme in which I might find employment. Caring for the elderly, perhaps, or maintaining a linen-service for lying-in mothers... really, I could go anywhere, if need be..."

Mrs. Butters shook her head regretfully. "If the times were better, Fanny, that is—but if you were to accept such a position, you would be taking it from someone who is worser off. You have your own little income from your savings. You are not destitute."

Fanny could not deny the justice of this. "Of course, it is only right that positions like this are bestowed upon gentlewomen who are in true distress, for whom the wage, paltry as it is, suffices them to keep body and soul together. The Miss Owens are a perfect example. My cousin Edmund's friend, Richard Owen—his father died last month, and his mother and sisters have hardly any income whatsoever and he must try to keep them on a curate's salary. I would not be so selfish as to put my claims above people like the Miss Owens."

"I know nothing of the Miss Owens," said Mr. Gibson, "but for their sakes, I am sorry for the fact that, should they take up some employment, they will be paid but a fraction of what a man is paid, and will be despised and pitied by their friends, who will think they are not entitled to be called gentlewomen."

Mrs. Butters could not resist, and hinted, "Fanny, I feel very certain that matters will arrange themselves—pray, do not worry about it—an entirely new occupation will be found for you, I've no doubt!"

"We will keep pondering the matter, Miss Price," said Mr. Gibson cheerfully. "Have you ever thought of writing a three-volume novel?"

And the rest of the visit was agreeably taken up with sketching out a fantastical plot, with a heroine of unimpeachable virtue and unsurpassed beauty, whose safety was threatened by the machinations of a ruthless villain, whose evil character the heroine manages to redeem, but only after enduring tragic vicissitudes and thrilling dangers, while travelling over the mountains of Switzerland and passing through the seraglios of Turkey.

"A story with nothing of nature or probability in it!" laughed Fanny.

Mrs. McIntosh was surprised when Mr. Gibson took every last piece of her baking with him, more than two dozen little cakes and other good things.

"The cheek of the man! He is tall and spare enough, to tuck away all that provender, to be sure! He certainly loves my cheese scones," she remarked to her husband later.

Donald McIntosh smiled, for he knew what Mr. Gibson had done. The coachman had been called out to drive him back to the city, and Mr. Gibson had requested that they stop in Camden Town. Mr. Gibson slipped into the shop and sprang up the stairs, two at a time, and surprised Mrs. Blodgett in the midst of berating the students over some dereliction.

"Good afternoon, girls," he announced. "Miss Price wishes to thank you, very kindly, for the lovely flowers and your message. It meant a great deal to her. She will remember you all, with the greatest affection. She asked me to tell you that she is very proud of each of you. And she wishes you to enjoy this."

He laid the parcel down on the table and left, before Mrs. Blodgett could say anything.

CHAPTER TWENTY-ONE

CHARLES AND BETSEY PRICE waited for hours, jumping and skipping by the sally-port, watching for their brother William, and when he at last appeared, they each took one of his hands and ran him home through the streets, leaving the porters to follow with his luggage. His parents were both standing in the doorway eager to greet him, to hear of his exploits and to exclaim over his new prosperity in the way of promised prize-monies.

"We'll toast you tonight with some good claret, see if we don't," exclaimed his father, and in his parental pride, he emptied William's pockets for the monies to purchase the celebratory bottle then and there, while calling out an injunction to the servant to prepare an especially good dinner. "And tell that rascally butcher he will be paid, indeed, now my boy William is home!"

The news of his promotion danced on the tip of William's tongue, but knowing of the exceeding joy he would be bringing them, William resolved to save the intelligence until the family was all seated together at dinner, so that he could watch each of their countenances as the revelation burst upon them.

Feeling restless and abstracted, William asked for a kettle of hot water, took it upstairs, packed his lieutenant's uniform away, washed himself and put on his civilian clothes. He next meant to go to the post office and send an express message to Julia, and he had been composing and re-arranging the words in his head.

Dear Miss Bertram, I pray this letter finds you well...

Dear Julia, I have some interesting news...

Dear, dearest Julia, please say you are free to marry me...

A bit of Shakespeare came to him—*love's heralds should be thoughts, which ten times faster glide than the sun's beams...*

He had returned home from Gibraltar, at the speed of the wind which filled the sails of the *Protector*. Now he was on land, and his yearning could travel no faster than a post-chaise. Could Julia sense, could she feel, how he longed for her? Could she know he was now in England?

No—if Romeo and Juliet could not send a message by sunbeam, and not avoid a fatal misunderstanding—but perhaps it was bad luck to think of that pair of lovers in particular! He was half-exultation, half-panic, fearing his happiness could still slip

243

through his fingers, despite the extraordinary turn of fortune in his favour.

Upon descending the narrow staircase, William encountered his sister Susan, who had been watching and waiting for him.

"There's something you need to know, William," she whispered. "And I thought it best to tell you, privately. Miss Julia is to be married, very soon. Our aunt Bertram has written and told us so."

William was down the stairs and out of the door in an instant. He ran without pause to the naval pay office and shouldered his way past the ordinary seaman who were queuing up, and addressed the nearest pay clerk, a harassed-looking young man whose bony wrists protruded beyond the frayed cuffs of his jacket.

"Mr. Dickens! Mr. Dickens! You must assist me! I must leave Portsmouth immediately, there is no time to lose! I require some funds for my journey."

"Now, Mr. Price, you know the regulations. We haven't yet received the authority for disbursement for your crew, and without the proper authority, we cannot venture so far off the pay schedule. No exceptions can be made, not even for an officer. We don't have the correct paperwork in hand yet. I don't have the full declaration of your abatements yet, so we must have that to start, and we have to reconcile them with the Admiralty ledgers, and then it has to be signed off by your captain, and then be submitted to the—"

"Hang the paperwork, Mr. Dickens!"

"Do not ask me to break the regulations, Mr. Price. I dare not risk my job here." Dickens sniffed and snapped down the lid on his inkpot. "The wife has given me another baby, and I cannot afford to lose my employment."

"A new baby! Congratulations to you, Mr. Dickens. Will you not allow me to make you a gift in celebration?"

"That would be most handsome of you, sir. We clerks can barely make ends meet."

"Yes, I know, Mr. Dickens. It would be my pleasure. Three guineas, shall we say? Five? Now then—now that we are good friends again, I know you will do what you can to assist me, won't you?"

William Price was gone out of Portsmouth, by post chaise, within the hour.

* * * * * * *

Even a girl so modest as Fanny could not deceive herself. Both yesterday and today, Mr. Gibson's attentions had been very pointed. At first she laid his behaviour to the recent calamity; it was not surprising that he should be solicitous of her well-being after she had first lost her employment and nearly her life, all within a few days. But there was a pronounced tenderness which threw her into confusion. She could not forget with what pleasure, with what satisfaction, he heard the news that she was not engaged to marry Mr. Edifice.

He had sat with her and Mrs. Butters most of yesterday afternoon and, upon Mrs. Butters' invitation, was to join them today for an airing at Kensington Park. Upon their arrival, however, Mrs. Butters, professing a disinclination for a long walk, remained in the carriage and went on to pay some morning calls.

A few words between Fanny and her companion sufficed to decide upon their route. She took his arm and they walked in comfortable silence for a time. Fanny was about to make some commonplace remark about the gardens, when William Gibson addressed her thus: "Miss Price, I wish to obtain your thoughts. I have been thinking seriously about the hardships any wife of mine would be forced to endure."

"Mr.—Mr. Gibson, you surprise me! I thought you had determined against matrimony." Fanny began to feel a little light headed, and hoped she would not start speaking nonsense.

"That, Miss Price, was many, many years ago—well, two years ago, at least. For some time now, I have been of a different frame of mind."

Fanny was all agitation and flutter; all hope and apprehension.

"I have compiled a list of my faults, which I hope you will do me the kindness to review along with me, so that you might include all the other drawbacks which have escaped my observation, but which will naturally occur to you."

"My friends all assure me that I am a very good listener, Mr. Gibson, so please begin." Fanny said, her mind and heart racing. She kept her gaze resolutely on the path ahead of her, although she listened with all her heart and soul to what he had to say.

245

"Ahem! Very well. First, I am exceedingly irregular in my hours. My wife could not expect me to always join her for breakfast, not when I have been awake half the night writing. Even worse, I am impulsive—the kind of fellow who will, on the spur of a moment, invite half-a-dozen strangers home for dinner, or empty his pockets for every beggar he sees on the street. I could not be trusted to manage money—all of the household accounts would have to be in my wife's hands, or else certain penury would be the result.

"As well, I need hardly dwell upon the miserable lot of the woman married to someone who depends for his livelihood upon the notice of the public. I seek acclamation, even when it comes in the form of beguiling females. My wife will accompany me to receptions and dinners and perhaps I will be monopolized by some beautiful woman, and my wife will be forced to watch it all with a tolerant smile!

"And yet, had I a hundred such ladies throwing themselves at me, no amount of praise and fame will satisfy a public man.

"The care and feeding of my vanity will be a greater labour for my wife than stocking my pantry or seeing to my wardrobe. She must soothe my wounded ego when I receive a bad review, and condemn the reviewer for a philistine and a blockhead, and she must read and be in raptures over all my new productions.

"And do not forget how I pique myself on my intellectual rigour and my rectitude. No day is complete for me unless I can point out the moral shortcomings of others. I did so well at making enemies in Bristol that, as you know, I was hauled off the streets and pressed into the Navy. It takes a special aptitude for outraging public opinion to end up with a press gang sent after you.

"My wife will soon discover that while I espouse the deepest regard for my fellow creatures and while I present myself as the champion of the downtrodden, the people I most neglect and abuse, are, by no coincidence, the people I profess to love most dearly. For example, if some public matter commands my attention, it absorbs me utterly, so that if my wife were to set herself on fire at the aforementioned breakfast table in an effort to get my attention, I would probably not even look up from my newspaper and merely ask if she had burnt the toast. As to remembering birthdays or anniversaries, who would expect such prosaic behaviour from an intellectual? Certainly not his wife.

"And, the most painful thing of all for my wife, is she would have to resign herself to the fact that I am not a believer. I suspect a great many others observe the outward forms of religion, simply because it is expected. But my vanity is such that I cannot be a play-actor in what for me are empty mummeries. My wife would have to content herself with the thought that her husband has tried to be a good man during his time on Earth.

"What do you think? You have known me for several years now, what have I forgotten?"

Fanny felt her face must be scarlet. Thankfully, she was able to turn her head away a little, and the brim of her bonnet shielded her countenance from scrutiny. At last, she commanded herself enough to respond.

"Theoretically, Mr. Gibson, I believe a wife will endure many little faults in her husband if she has respect for his character and his principles. Observation has convinced me that respect is the foundation of matrimonial happiness. A wife wants to look up to her husband, and if she cannot, she is the most unfortunate of creatures."

"If only you meant 'look up to' literally and not figuratively, Miss Price. I could set my mind at ease at once, for the top of your head barely comes up to my shoulder."

Fanny suddenly recalled what Mr. Edifice had said—about Mr. Gibson's determination to marry an heiress—and she was now thoroughly confused, not daring to believe what she was hearing.

"Miss Price, please, stop for a moment. Here is a little grove of laurels, will you step this way with me, so that I may speak to you privately." His hand at the small of her back guided her off the main pathway to a smaller path which terminated at a little bench, surrounded by shrubbery.

"When opportunity serves, Miss Price, I can go down on one knee, as the proper form requires, but even a man as love-struck as I cannot enjoy the thought of kneeling in this gravel for any length of time. The occasion and my sentiments impel me to speak, although the place may not serve us so well. Please, take a seat, and if I may, I will do likewise."

Fanny did not dissemble, did not murmur, "oh! But this is so unexpected, sir!" in the fashion prescribed for virtuous young heroines, although she was, in fact, completely surprised. While reason told her she could not be in error—Mr. Gibson was going to propose to her—her timidity and modesty still kept her in anxious suspense.

Retaining her hand, while she maintained the privilege of breathless silence, Mr. Gibson went on: "What I meant to say, Miss Price, is that I believe it is best to be as fully acquainted as possible with the faults of the person with whom you are to spend the rest of your life. Don't you think this is the soundest way to proceed? Then, should discord arise in the future, the other party can say, 'but you knew that when you married me!'"

"You have given the matter a great deal of thought, Mr. Gibson," said Fanny, still at a loss for what she ought to say. "But... you say you are speaking theoretically?"

"Correct. This is not a proposal of marriage, merely a preamble. And why? Because your understanding is so superior, Fanny. May I not call you Fanny?"

"Of course. You earned the right to call me Fanny when you saved my life." She managed to glance up at him briefly.

A grateful smile answered her, and he squeezed her hand. "What a good thought. I am not above acting upon your feelings of gratitude when the time comes to make my proposal. Yes, that would be very prudent on my part. Something like, 'pardon the moan of pain which escaped me when I knelt down just now, my dear Fanny, but I am still a trifle stiff and sore after knocking you to the pavement last week.'"

"You took a tolerably severe blow to the head as well, Mr. Gibson. I trust that you are thinking clearly."

"A fair question. But my faculties have never been so acute, Fanny, nor have I ever been so certain of my purpose. Oh! And I forgot. An addendum to the list of my faults: I am a most indifferent dancer."

"Oh please, Mr. Gibson!"

I never thought I would be suppressing the urge to giggle at a time like this, Fanny thought to herself, as she stole another quick look at her suitor's earnest, beautiful face, before once more turning away.

"Sorry. But it's true."

"I hardly know whether you are being serious or if you are teasing. Perhaps, when it comes to proposals of marriage, I am more conventional."

"Remember we are only discussing theoreticals today. Whatever form of marriage proposal you desire, you shall have from me, Fanny. I believe I can carry off any style with some credit—romantic, or business-like, or pitiable, abject pleas—you have but to indicate your preference. The thought of someone liking me well enough to marry me does fill me with amusement and wonder, Fanny. That is why it is difficult for me to be serious, you see.

"I want to give you time to consider the idea, Fanny. Do not answer me now, for I haven't asked you yet! Please think upon it. May I call upon you next week? Be sure to provide a cushion for my knees. They are rather bony. Do you object to bony knees? Another mark against me."

Fanny was now too overcome for speech, and William saw he had teased her too much. In a more gentle tone, he murmured, "May I speak to you in... a week?"

With her face still averted, she shyly nodded 'yes,' and in the warmth of his feelings, William might have started his proposal then and there, despite the inconvenience of the gravel walk, but he recognized that Fanny would not appreciate a declaration in such a public place, and he sincerely wished to give her time to think about the prospect of marriage before he asked for her hand. He did not wish her, in the first flurry of anxiety and doubt, to answer 'no,' even if the 'no' was later followed by a 'yes.' He wanted to hear 'yes' in the first instance. He stood, bowed, and offered his arm to escort her back to meet Mrs. Butters' carriage.

And Fanny, he thought to himself, *there is another question only you can answer—have you overcome your feelings for your cousin Edmund? Can you give your heart to me? Or will you find yourself married to one man and still loving another?*

* * * * * * *

Sunday morning came again, and the banns of marriage would be read for the second time. Julia had been feeling tolerably

249

composed. Mr. Meriwether had sent her a very handsome necklace and a long and affectionate letter. He was to visit them next week to sign the marriage articles. He was a good man, and she was a lucky young woman.

But she woke up early on that Sunday, several hours before she and Edmund and her aunt would sit down together for breakfast. However she tried to suppress her true feelings, they would surface at this hour, as sunrise lit the horizon and she was alone in her room and just regaining consciousness after a night of troubled dreams.

All brides feel apprehensive, her aunt had told her. It was only to be expected. Why, if she were not, it would be rather shameful and indelicate.

Her misery and agitation grew until she felt unequal to being in company with either her aunt or her brother and she resolved to go for a long walk, hoping to exercise her body until she became too fatigued to think. She managed to dress herself and crept downstairs. She could hear Mrs. Peckover raking the fire in the kitchen stove. She let herself out of the front door, then crossed the yard to the well and drew up a dipperful of cool water. Wiping her lips with her shawl, she hurried through the gate to walk to Sandcroft Hill and back before it was time to get ready for church.

The chilly morning air and the freedom of the outdoors only intensified the feeling of panic rising within her. As she paced along briskly, she revolved in her mind all the conversations she had had over the past year, all the reasons why she should forget about William Price. But what her head and conscience had approved of and marked as prudent and dutiful, her heart now rebelled against!

She wondered if certainty and calm would replace fear and panic as her wedding day drew closer. For if she continued to feel worse, she did not know how she could enter the church, and place her hand in Mr. Meriwether's, and pledge to be his wife. But oh, the scandal if she were to throw him over, after accepting his proposal, and the disappointment for Edmund, who was waiting to be free to reconcile with his wife!

She walked faster and faster, her eyes fixed upon the horizon.

The appearance of a solitary rider in the distance, cresting the hill, awoke her from her reverie. She realized she had been walking rapidly for over a mile, as though in a trance, almost heedless of everything around her. She prepared to school her features into

250

some semblance of indifference, and tugged her bonnet over her forehead so that her face might be shielded by its brim.

As the rider drew closer, her feelings revolted at the thought of being observed by any other human being. Although whoever he was, he ought to be at least as self-conscious as she. He must be a common farmer or labourer, for his face and hands were brown-skinned from hours in the sun, and he was riding bareback upon an old pony and hanging over its neck, clumsily trying to direct it without a bridle. He looked very ungainly and awkward, with his long legs dangling astride his low mount. Just like Sancho Panza in *Don Quixote* except that this rider was not short and stout like Sancho Panza, but quite tall, and—now that she stole another glance—rather well made. Rather like...

"Julia! Julia!"

She stopped.

"*Julia!*"

She was more than half-convinced that she was dreaming, that she had conjured his figure out of thin air, from pure longing and desire. But, if she had gone mad and was seeing phantasms, why had she placed the man she loved on a little brown pony, instead of a white stallion?

"*Julia!*"

He waved, he halloed. He smiled. It was William.

She ran toward him.

William jumped off his pony and ran to meet her. He was thinner, and very tanned. His bright blue eyes, searching earnestly, gazed into hers.

"Julia, are you to be married? Is it so?"

Julia's eyes filled with tears, and she nodded. "I am to marry Mr. Meriwether in a fortnight."

"Well then, God forgive me, and Mr. Meriwether too, but I cannot bear that you should do it. Julia, I want you for my wife. I love you, I have loved you since the hour I first saw you. Please forgive me for hurting you with my doubts. Please say you will marry me, my darling Julia."

He might have said more, but there was no need, for Julia was in his arms.

"William, are you really here? Am I dreaming?"

His lips, closing on hers, answered her question.

The lovers walked back to Edmund's house, William leading the pony by the halter, and holding his sweetheart's hand.

"I went post chaise from Portsmouth," he explained, "and travelled all night to Newbury, then to Mansfield, and was expecting to go on to Thornton Lacey, but when we reached Mansfield just after the sun came up, there were no more fresh horses to be had and the coach master refused to lend me a horse to ride here, though I offered him almost the price of a horse to borrow one for a day! So, I resolved to walk to you, and set out through the town, but as I passed by Mansfield Parsonage, I saw this pony—"

"Oh! Yes, now I recognize him! He belongs to Dr. Grant! It's the one he sends into town to fetch the mail!"

"Now, do you suppose if I let this poor old pony go, he will find his way home again, as he does from the post office? No matter, I shall return him myself and make amends to Dr. Grant so soon as I can. Because when I saw him nibbling dandelions by the side of the road—the pony that is, not Dr. Grant—I grabbed his halter and pulled myself on him and off we went! I could not wait another moment to see you, Julia. I was in dread, in case I should hear the church bells ringing this morning, and for aught I knew, today was your wedding day...."

"My wedding day is today, William, if Edmund will marry us!"

Fortunately, there was no one else on the road, and he could kiss her to his heart's content.

CHAPTER TWENTY-TWO

WHEN A YOUNG LADY has just experienced a most ardently desired, but unlooked for, lover's reunion, she might be forgiven for quailing a little when she subsequently realizes the first witness of her happiness would to be—Aunt Norris.

But even if Julia had wanted to withhold the news from her aunt, the faces of the two lovers as they entered the yard, transfigured by love and happiness, testified for them.

Mrs. Norris never cared to have anything she endorsed to be changed or re-arranged, and "what of Mr. Meriwether?—the disappointment—the scandal—the banns—the gown—the neighbours—the imprudence—" made all of the conversation for the first quarter of an hour.

Edmund was also perturbed for Mr. Meriwether's sake, but loyalty to a man he had never met, stood little chance when confronted with the happiness of a William Price, the cousin he knew and esteemed highly. When William told of his promotion and that he was to have command of his own ship, assigned to duty near England's shores, Edmund had nothing but the heartiest congratulations for them both.

Edmund could not help feeling a pang of envy when he saw his sister with the man she loved, as secure in the knowledge of his affection, as she was confident of her wish to return it, while he, Edmund, had allowed his desire for Mary to overcome his scruples, and was paying a mortifying price. But of course he allowed nothing of his own feelings to cloud their happiness.

"Shall I read the first banns for you this morning, Julia?" he asked. "It is not every day I have it in my power to so thoroughly disconcert my parishioners."

Julia gave William a beseeching look and he, speaking for the first time on behalf of himself and his life's partner, declined the offer, explaining, "I must be back to Portsmouth in five days—and Julia is coming with me. We must swear our oaths and you must give us a license, Edmund."

"What!" exclaimed Mrs. Norris. "Julia, are you going to live in Portsmouth?"

"No, Aunt Norris, I shall go with William—aboard the *Protector*."

"Have you gone mad? Live aboard a ship?"

William's grin stretched from ear to ear, and he nearly smothered his aunt in an enormous hug, then picked her up by the waist and twirled her around in circles. "Yes, my dear auntie, by all that's wonderful, she is to run away with me to sea!"

He set her down again and she tottered about, momentarily silenced.

Edmund had the unhappy duty of bringing William and Julia down from their heavenly flight by saying, "My dear sister and my soon-to-be-brother, I am sorry, but I have not the authority to marry you by license. Only my bishop can issue a license, and he is in Peterborough."

"Well!" exclaimed William, "We are off for Peterborough, then."

"And a license may take as long as a week to arrange."

"But what about Maria?" Julia demanded. "You obtained a license for her in one day, when she married Henry Crawford."

"Not I—it was a special license from the Archbishop of Canterbury himself, through the intervention of some powerful friends in London. And I think, the payment of an extraordinarily large fee."

"There, you see," added Mrs. Norris, "the church is no friend of impetuous marriages!"

"But what about the bishop in Peterborough?" asked William. "Once we explain the situation to him, he would act swiftly for us, I am sure."

"I do not pretend to know the romantic inclinations of my bishop, but I can tell you that he is eighty-three years old and you will not find a tortoise with a greater fondness for studied deliberation than he."

Julia looked up at William with confidence; this was the first test of his ingenuity and resourcefulness as a husband, and she relied on him to discover a way to make the trip to Peterborough and back, with a license in their pocket, in time for him to report for duty in Plymouth. He paced, considering and calculating, and she saw with dismay that his shoulders slumped.

"I could not venture to risk it," he said. "I could not be certain of reporting back in time."

"Oh Edmund, what are we to do!" exclaimed Julia, turning to her brother. "It is very trying that you cannot marry us."

William paced about the parlour some more, lost in thought, then said, "Julia, I will not suggest a Scottish marriage. I want nothing underhanded or shameful about our marriage day. But what if you were to return with me to Portsmouth, and wait for me there? The *Protector* will be in harbour for several months, being fitted up for new service, before we sail for Ireland. We could have the banns read in Portsmouth. We could marry in three weeks, or rather, three Sundays' time."

Julia's smile and the conviction that there was no other alternative, served to resign William to delaying his marriage for a few weeks. He was on the point of bidding his future bride to pack her trunk when his aunt, clutching the back of a chair to support her—for she was indeed in danger of collapsing from shock—exclaimed, "What, Julia, are you going to travel unescorted? Can you possibly be willing to compromise yourself in this way?" And to William: "Young man, have you no care for the reputation of Julia and all her family?"

There was a moment's silence. William looked at Julia, and she at him, as the awful realization dawned upon them both. Julia could not accompany William to Portsmouth unless Mrs. Norris came with them. All the comfort and intimacy of their journey would be destroyed entirely. Their love had already endured so many tests—could it survive this latest hardship, as well?

"Julia," Edmund interposed calmly. "Perhaps you'd like to show William around your garden? And Aunt Norris, could you please go and ask Mrs. Peckover to lay another place for breakfast?"

*   *   *   *   *   *   *

"Imogen! I am waiting." Lord Delingpole's voice echoed in the cavernous lobby of their London mansion. He paced back and forth by the front door where two impassive footmen stood at attention. "The carriage has come 'round. It is time to depart."

Lady Delingpole's head appeared over the railing two floors up.

"You may recall, my dear, that I have spent the last hour helping you to arrange your papers and find that missing memorandum. And now I am writing a brief note to our son, and I have not finished dressing. I shall be ready to leave shortly."

Lady Delingpole returned to her dressing room to complete her note and her *toilette*. The Delingpoles were to spend a few days at Coombe House, the country seat of the new prime minister. Lord Liverpool had reluctantly agreed to take up Spencer Perceval's fallen mantle, but had come close to resigning several times since then. The tumult of the past fortnight had tried even the energy and resources of Lord Delingpole—fears of insurrection, rumours of a new French army massing in Europe, and the deterioration of relations with the United States, meant that the Tory government faced nothing but crises, at home and abroad.

"I have brought the letter from our son, do you wish to hear it?" his lady asked him, after she joined him in the lobby in her travelling outfit, and he gave her his arm to escort her to their carriage. "I think it will take your mind off your worries over Lord Liverpool."

Lord Delingpole sighed wearily, which his wife took as consent. He leaned back in his seat in the carriage and closed his eyes while she read him the latest hastily-scrawled note from Viscount Lynnon, from Oxford.

"*I must apply to you for more funds this quarter*—" she began.

Lord Delingpole groaned.

"Wait a moment, David. Just listen. *But I give you my solemn assurance it will be the last time I ask for additional monies—or at least, it will be the last time I will plead the situation of my former friend Shelley as the cause of my impoverishment.*"

"What's that? 'Former friend'?"

"Just listen! *I have paid off some of Shelley's creditors in Keswick and in London—he spent all his money on books and he ordered a pianoforte and a new carriage, which he cannot pay for, and has nothing to live upon!*"

"So I am the indirect patron of this scribbling fool, am I? My spirits are not improved by this news, Imogen."

"Just listen, dear! *When we last met, I asked him, 'you are always prating on about the hardships of the common man, so why do you run up bills with all the tradesmen and will not pay them?*

256

Are the tradesmen not common men? Why do you hide from your own landlady and abuse her as a stupid witch?' Shelley grew quite angry with me when I challenged him on this matter, and he called me a witless ass and a dwarf."

"Damn his impudence. We Delingpoles may not be towering oaks, but in point of intellect—"

"Just listen, dear. *Shelley was always wont to abuse you, father, and the Tories, in the most execrable terms, which I had always disregarded—*"

An angry splutter from his Lordship interrupted the reading, but his wife persisted.

"*—but on this occasion, I said to him, 'at least my father doesn't suffer common men to be beggared and bankrupted, but always pays his accounts like an honourable man.' And he flew into a fury. I now suspect that he did not esteem me as a friend at all, and was only interested in my purse.*"

"What's this? What's this? Is our boy finally undeceived?" Lord Delingpole opened his eyes and sat up.

"Yes, dear. He has broken with his former idol, and has, I trust, learnt a valuable lesson."

"Well then, Imogen, you may release some more funds to him—just this once."

"I already have, dear. I thought you might want to know of this, even as preoccupied as you are," said Lady Delingpole briskly, folding up the letter and turning from domestic cares to national ones. "Tell me, David, how is Lord Liverpool? Will he stick?"

"Yes, Imogen, I persuaded him to withdraw his resignation—for now. This government is being held together with straw and twine. Thank g-d the Prince Regent is standing by us, and is holding the Whigs at bay. I trust I can keep Liverpool from panicking this weekend and throwing everything over."

Lady Delingpole sighed. "Heigh-ho! Meanwhile, an insufferably tedious weekend for me, attempting to make conversation with Louisa, talking only of servants, and greenhouses, and needlepoint, while you plan the fate of the world with Castlereagh and Liverpool!" She glanced across, and saw that her husband looked unusually preoccupied and tired, and was in no spirits for their usual banter. "But never mind, my dear. She is a lovely, well-disposed creature. I shall be sure to convey to her the thanks of a grateful nation, and tell her how *indispensable* dear Lord Liverpool is, and so on."

To her surprise, her husband took her hand and lifted it to his lips. "The nation may not know all that you have done, and continue to do, on its behalf, Imogen, but I do, and I am very grateful." Lord Delingpole leaned back again and closed his eyes.

"Nor does England know all that *you* have done, David. Nursery maids frighten naughty children with 'Boneypart will get you,' but it is *you* the children should thank, for keeping despotism from our shores. You are not only holding the government together, you are holding everything together. I shudder to think what would happen to this kingdom if you stepped away because of the opprobrium, the slander, the lies, heaped on your head. So much depends upon you, my dear!"

"Imogen," said Lord Delingpole, with his eyes still closed. "I do not tell you this nearly so often as I ought. Of all of the blessings in my life, you are the brightest and the best. You do know, I trust, that there has never been another? Not since the day your father put your hand in mine."

"Ssssh, now dear. Get some rest. I will awaken you before we arrive."

* * * * * * *

When something intolerable is shown to be inevitable, we must find the fortitude to endure it, and so Julia and William made for Portsmouth with Aunt Norris.

Aunt Norris's habits of frugality made laying out funds for a journey exceedingly painful for her. As William and Julia were to discover, she tended to view the entire world and everyone in it—coachmen and innkeepers in particular—as being in a confederacy to defraud her, a desolate old widow, of the few coins she still possessed. The fact that it was William, not she, who paid for the coach, tipped the porters, and bought the dinners and the lodgings, failed to extinguish her zeal for detecting lazy service and sharp dealings. Happily, her complaints and suspicions served to vary her conversation, which otherwise alternated between lamentations over poor, ill-used Mr. Meriwether, and the reckless folly of marrying a naval officer in time of war.

Mrs. Norris's regrets over poor, ill-used Mr. Merriwether were borne submissively by Julia, at least, for she agreed with her aunt that she had behaved wrongly by him, and the long and penitential letter she wrote to him before leaving for Portsmouth, had done little to assuage her conscience there.

But a most unexpected benefit, a handsome compensation, awaited Julia and William in Portsmouth: Julia had been dreading encountering William's mother, but much of Mrs. Price's resistance melted away when she understood that her sister Norris was also opposed to the match—but for dear *Julia's* sake! Mrs. Price's resentment, her wounded pride on behalf of her son William, and her habit of routine opposition to anything her older sister said, caused her to almost receive Julia with civility.

Susan and Betsey were enraptured by the news, and even Charles was not insensible of the beauty and charms of his brother's betrothed.

For Mr. Price, the dual announcement of betrothal and promotion was of course an occasion for uncorking a bottle—at the dinner table, and another after dinner, and then, taking his bottle with him, he visited his friends, up and down the street, but not before making several coarse remarks and jests, which embarrassed Julia exceedingly.

He was still in high good spirits the following day; the staunchest advocate of the match, proud that his son should be marrying the beautiful daughter of a baronet, and entirely sanguine about their future prosperity.

"You knew that he would marry one day, Frances," he reasoned with his wife over a hearty breakfast, when William had already gone out to visit his beloved at the Crown. "A lad like that. It can't be helped, can it? A young man sees a beautiful girl with a face like sunshine, dancing and laughing at an assembly, let's say, and he thinks to himself, 'that girl, right there, if I could choose a wife out of all the girls in the world, she would be the one I'd choose,' can you blame him for wanting her? And if he was lucky enough to win her and take her home—Frances, you haven't forgotten it all, have you? No, I'm sure you haven't, however so long ago it was. Now, give us a smile, my good old wife, and let's hurry up to the chapel and tell the parson to read the banns this Sunday."

William Gibson allowed almost a full week to elapse before sending a message, asking to call upon Miss Price. The reply was from Mrs. Butters, affirming that she and Miss Price would be pleased to receive him on Saturday afternoon, and so he hired a cab and made the trip to Stoke Newington, in a fairly high degree of nervous excitement.

The speech he had prepared was overlong, he feared. Fanny wanted a proposal, not an oration, surely. But between his enumeration of her charms and virtues, and his own predictions for their perfect happiness, and his judicious forestalling of all of the objections which any rational person could foresee to the match, he had a pretty long speech composed in his head, and was running over it all the way from London.

He was met at the door, most unexpectedly, by Madame Orly, and he could not read the expression on her face, but he instantly feared that something was wrong.

"Good day to you, Madame Orly. Is Miss Price within?"

"Oh! *Non, non, Monsieur* Gibson. I am so very sorry. But you see, not an hour ago, Fanny set out for Wapping, for to fetch her brother John. And they are to go to Portsmouth, by the post."

At first Mr. Gibson was afraid Fanny had suffered such perturbation at the thought of his impending marriage proposal, that she had flown to Portsmouth as a form of escape. Madame Orly was holding out a note to him—could it be a letter from Fanny?

"Why has she gone? Is something the matter, Madame Orly?"

"Ah, yes, something of the most unfortunate. Fanny left me this letter, she said that you could read it all."

And William took the note, written in an awkward hand:

My dearest Sister,

I have some Awful News for you. This Morning at about 2:00 am our Father Died. He had come back from a walk with mother and sat down to eat a grand Dinner—for we were celebrating with William & Julia—& he was in the best of spirits, & ate & drank with as good an Appetite as always but he was seized of an Apoplexy while rising from the table. We call'd for the Apothecary but there was Nothing to be done for him. He did not regain his Senses & he Died.

Our Mother of course is in the most miserable State.

A great many of our Father's freinds have kindly sent their Regards & have said the most obliging things about him which will be of some comfort to his Sons no doubt.

William & Julia & Aunt Norris are here as you know. As for dear Sam & Richard—Heaven only knows when my Letters will find them so far out to sea & could you please tell John yrself? I think that would be the best way & wd save him a Shilling for the Post.

O Fanny I very much want you & brother John to come here & assist us. Do say that you can come quickly! He will be buried this Monday afternoon & unless John comes, poor William will have to go to the burial alone of the family.

Yr sister,
Susan

CHAPTER TWENTY-THREE

WILLIAM AND JOHN PRICE buried their father on Monday and John returned to London on Tuesday. Fanny remained with her family. Julia and Mrs. Norris stayed in the Crown Inn, but called upon Mrs. Price every day, a level of solicitude which was almost more than the desolate widow could well tolerate.

Fanny was staunch in her support for William and Julia's marriage to proceed as they had first intended, before the untimely death of Mr. Price. At first William, much stricken by his father's passing, condemned the idea as impossible—disrespectful—and was resigning himself to sending Julia back to Thornton Lacey. But after the passage of a few more hours, and a few more days, he reflected that, after all, his father had blessed the marriage, and he and Julia had already waited two years. And fortunately, everyone to whom he turned for advice—and perhaps he was more inclined to go for advice to some persons than others—counselled him to secure his own happiness.

"Our father would not have seen any impediment, I am certain, William," Fanny told him. "Sailors cannot be bound by the same rules as the rest of us, especially in a time of war. I know he would have said as much."

Our sentiments cannot always be vanquished by reasoning with them. Fanny resolved to make an offering of her service, a sacrifice to the altar of convention and duty. She would pay her respects to her father in every way prescribed by custom—she would wear mourning, then half-mourning; she would buy him a handsome gravestone, she would stay in Portsmouth and assist her mother and her sister Susan.

She did so, knowing that some months would necessarily have to elapse before an engagement with Mr. Gibson could be contemplated, let alone announced. She could not feel comfortable or at ease in doing otherwise; Duty must be propitiated, to protect the happiness of her brother and her cousin Julia.

This was her first impulse, her chief motive and aim; there was a secondary one as well. Fanny also hoped her strict adherence to the prescribed forms of mourning might awaken what she *ought* to feel at the death of a man who bore the name 'father.' She was reluctant to examine her own heart, to enquire how sincerely she mourned a man she hardly knew, and that little known, had not truly respected. The tears she shed were for her mother, and her brothers and sisters.

Coming into a household preoccupied both with a death and an upcoming marriage, she did not think it appropriate to speak of her attachment to William Gibson. She hoped that, on some not-distant day, her mother might compose herself long enough to look at her first-born daughter and say, "Thank you, Fanny, for everything—and how have *you* been?" She wondered if there might come a moment when her mother's attention lighted fully on her, and no-one else. The moment never came.

As the days went by she concluded that, even if her mother had not been recently widowed, she would have evinced not the least inclination to ask Fanny about her life in London. Mrs. Price's solicitude was reserved for herself, William, and Betsey, her favourite children. Fanny was not called upon to explain why she was no longer at her position at the academy, and her twenty-first birthday came and went without acknowledgement.

This utter lack of curiosity in the doings of a long-lost daughter, more than the cramped quarters and the privations of Portsmouth, made it impossible for Fanny to think or speak of her residence with her family as living at "home." She was not a part of them, they took little interest in her, save for Susan, but continued about their lives and occupations as though she was not there.

On her previous visits, her reception had been much the same. Her ways were not their ways. She had been raised and educated in a great mansion. Her delicacy and elegance, her well-organized work-basket, even the way she sipped her soup, was a reproach to the family's coarser, slapdash mode of life. Her quieter voice went unheard amidst the hullaballo—for even the death of their father did not diminish the vigour of Charles and Betsey, and the family was seldom in the habit of allowing one another to finish an utterance without interruption. Her opinions were unsought on any matter.

She observed all this, rather than felt it deeply. She *had* hoped to be more, much more, to her family, but she had been gone for so many years, that it was too late for her to re-join them. She knew this kind of estrangement did not arise in all families, where a long separation had occurred. Something was wanting, or lacking, in her own, or in her. She did not know how to amend it. She was resigned to deriving what contentment she could, out of making herself useful.

If Portsmouth could not be regarded as "home," and Mansfield Park was her home no longer, Fanny quite understandably began to meditate on a future home not yet in existence.

Fanny's greatest pleasure, and she indulged in it privately, was reading the long, amusing, affectionate letters which William Gibson sent her, which she fetched by herself from the post office. He intended to follow her to Portsmouth, and also was to stand up with Fanny's brother at his wedding. But the editor of the *Gentlemen's Magazine* had engaged him to travel to Glasgow to report on the new steam-powered ship, the *Comet*, now ferrying passengers on the River Clyde at a speed of five miles per hour.

Mr. Gibson asked Fanny for her permission to take the assignment, and undertook to come to Portsmouth immediately afterwards. Flattered at being applied to, and fully resigned to the realities of Mr. Gibson's profession, Fanny gave her consent, although she worried for his safety.

* * * * * * *

In the end, William Price and his bride did fulfil their promise to marry only after receiving the consent, if not the unreserved approbation, of their parents.

Sir Thomas was in fact disappointed, in point of dignity and fortune. He thought the match imprudent. If it were not for his knowledge of his nephew's excellent character, he might have withheld his consent. His affection for his daughter, however, was stronger than his inclination to ensure the correctness of his prophecy, by forcing further hardships on the young couple, which might indeed bring them to grief. He did not withhold his approval or Julia's dowry and he sincerely hoped that the youngest of his four children would know only perfect marital happiness.

Lady Bertram was not unduly discomposed by the thought of her daughter living on board a ship, being blessed with such a paucity of imagination that she could not long dwell upon the potential inconveniences or dangers, or even summon them up in her mind with any force or clarity.

Upon receiving congratulatory letters from her sister and brother-in-law, to whom she owed so much in the way of assistance to her family, Mrs. Price finally resigned herself to the wedding. The loss of her husband, followed by the loss of a beloved son to matrimony, gave her a distinction amongst her neighbours and friends—their respect for her sufferings was her finest consolation. The arrival of Julia's elaborate gown from Norfolk stamped the event as inevitable, although Mrs. Price, unlike Fanny, did not exert herself to help alter the gown in time for the ceremony.

Fanny was with Julia, in her room at the Crown, measuring the length of the skirt, when a commotion in the passageway announced Edmund's arrival from Thornton Lacey. The reunion of brother and sister, on the eve of such a solemn occasion, called forth a few tears of joy from the ladies. Edmund, with the patience and quiet kindness which so much denoted his character, listened as Julia pointed out all the features of her gown and accessories, and had he remembered to bring her best gloves, which she had forgotten to pack?

He brought the gloves and more besides, a very kind and conciliatory letter from Mr. Meriwether, expressing his disappointment, but wishing her every happiness, and even, most handsomely, urging her not to feel remorse over having broken her engagement to him. *"It is for the best,"* he wrote, *"that you examined your feelings and acknowledged your scruples before our wedding. Please rest assured, Miss Bertram, that I could never have been happy, knowing of your regrets, had you felt yourself obliged to marry me."*

The generous sentiments of this letter helped to lift a disagreeable burden from Julia's conscience, and there was nothing left for her to do but to be completely happy. In the fullness of that relief, she privately confessed to Edmund what she had kept secret heretofore—that Mary, his estranged wife, had been the one to introduce her to Mr. Meriwether, that she had promoted the match with every argument in her power, with the aim of removing Julia from Thornton Lacey.

Edmund heard her gravely and quietly, and said only 'he would write to Mary, and ask to meet with her.'

"I think she desires a reconciliation, Edmund—will you? Is that your wish, also?"

"I would be a contemptible hypocrite, Julia, if I did not give myself the same advice I am obliged to give to my parishioners. Our church teaches that marriage is indissoluble. And as far as the world is concerned, I want to avoid bringing any further scandal down on either of our families. Both of those considerations must come before my own wishes and inclinations. It will not do even to talk of what I may wish."

"Oh, Edmund," Julia exclaimed. "I promised myself I would not be so selfish, and would try to think of others—and now I am so completely happy, while you…"

"I think a young lady may be permitted to dwell on the fact that she is getting married in only two days! My dear little sister! May you draw wisdom from all the marriages you have observed, Julia, and may you enter the state with a clear head and a warm heart."

* * * * * * *

William Gibson also returned to Portsmouth later that same day, having finished his northern assignment. Fanny had told no-one of Mr. Gibson's intended courtship. He was still thought of, and spoken of within the Price family, as 'William's friend,' and 'William's benefactor,' on account of his book *Amongst the Slavers*.

It was Julia who, watching Mr. Gibson and Fanny together, and observing that even the cramped dimensions of the parlour could not entirely account for how closely Mr. Gibson sat next to Fanny, and how often his hand brushed hers as he helped her make the tea, decided Mr. Gibson must be an admirer of her cousin. And so she informed Edmund.

The news made Edmund uneasy; a perturbation which he, at first, interpreted as being concern on Fanny's account. The thought that this complete stranger should be a friend, a confidant and admirer of Fanny! Edmund needed time and reflection to better understand his own feelings. However, only hours after he learned of Mr. Gibson's affection for his cousin, Edmund was invited by William Price to the Crown to dine together with Mr. Gibson, a last bachelor's dinner before the wedding.

William Price could not know of Edmund's reservations, and he was likewise unaware his friend Mr. Gibson held all the

Bertrams, more or less, guilty of carelessness about Fanny's happiness, and deficient in respect and esteem for her. And Mr. Gibson knew that in Edmund, he beheld his rival for Fanny's affections.

Thus, William Price, with a disposition to think well of everyone, and congratulating himself on making an introduction between two men he expected to become good friends, was surprised to sense the reserve, to hear the quiet 'how d'ye do, sir' exchanged, and to see the very firm and prolonged handshake, which put him in mind of a wrist-wrestling competition on board ship! He might *almost* have thought that these two had resolved to dislike each other on sight.

The conversation began amicably enough—William Price asked Mr. Gibson about his voyage on the *Comet*, and steam and steamships and the potential uses of steam engines provided a source of mutual interest and intelligent conversation.

"I'm sure you have read about the improvements being made in the safety and efficacy of steam engines," said Mr. Gibson. "At some point, the mechanical power produced by the steam engine will more than compensate the labour and cost involved in constructing the machine, and collecting the coal or wood to heat its boilers. I don't speak of the enormous steam pumps used at pit heads. I foresee that in a very few years, we will see new and smaller models of steam engine, suitable for domestic use. I am working on a novel, in fact, set in the future, in which many mundane tasks are performed by steam-powered machines."

"Such a novel should help spur the imaginations of our inventors," said Edmund. "We have had the water-mill for centuries, but it is not portable. Perhaps a steam-powered machine, small enough to be transported to the fields, could be used to dig irrigation trenches, or bundle sheaves of wheat. Fewer men, women and children would be condemned to labour like beasts of burden."

"Exactly," said William Gibson. "Consider how many chores involve repetitive, simple motions. Could not the cleaning of chimneys be accomplished with a brush mounted on a revolving cable, powered by a hand-crank or a treadmill?"

"And machines are replacing the weavers already," said William Price. "But the more complicated tasks—these still must be done by human hands. A machine can't climb in the rigging on a ship. In your novel, can you conjure up a machine that can sew a suit of clothing as my sister can? Or do elaborate embroidery?"

At the mention of Fanny, Mr. Gibson turned to praising "Miss Price" for the excellent work she'd done at the Academy, at the innovations she had introduced, and the difficulties she had overcome.

Edmund was taken aback by the familiarity with which Mr. Gibson spoke of his cousin; this stranger evidently regarded himself as better-informed about Fanny's opinions, her wishes, her habits, her likes and dislikes, than her own family. Edmund thought this Gibson fellow was being a little too presuming, in his talk of 'Miss Price this,' and 'Miss Price that."

"As much as my cousin Fanny deserves praise, I must own, Mr. Gibson, her *family* has always been somewhat concerned that Fanny is too delicate to engage in any demanding occupation, as the instruction of young people must surely be. You did not know her as a child, as I did. She was rather frail. She grew up in the country, and I cannot consider the air in London, nor the confinement of constant employment, as being beneficial to her health."

"If I may offer some reassurance, I can attest that her health and spirits have been excellent this past year," said Mr. Gibson. "She was in the habit of visiting the great public parks in London, and she took regular walks in her neighbourhood. I am aware she was thought to be delicate, in the *past*. Perhaps there was something to be wished for in her situation, more than in her constitution."

"At any rate," said William Price, his eyes darting back and forth across the table at his two unsmiling friends, "Fan has said she will stay with our mother here in Portsmouth until at least the end of the year. And as for next year, Julia and I wonder if she might like to stay with us in Ireland. The funny thing is, Fan and I always said that we would live together in a nice cottage when we grew up. I have been thinking I ought to take a cottage somewhere, if, when—well, in the future, it may not always be suitable for Julia to live on aboard ship—that is, if she and I, of course, if she is—and then, it would be very agreeable to Julia, to have Fanny as a companion."

"Very agreeable indeed! But, her friends in London would not be happy to see Miss Price settled so far away," said Mr. Gibson.

"Moreover, she enjoys visiting the bookshops and sometimes she attends concerts, which she could not do if she was in a remote cottage in Ireland—or Northamptonshire, for that matter. To be consigned to a type of intellectual wilderness could not be pleasant for so well-informed a young lady as Miss Price."

"I believe, sir, in these modern times, the distance from the metropolis is no barrier to the dissemination of literature and knowledge," said Edmund. "I belong to two scientific and one historical corresponding societies, and the mail coach carries journals and new publications across the nation within a few days of their leaving the press. However, there are other advantages to life in the country. When one considers the proportion of virtue to vice throughout the kingdom, the countryside is to be preferred. We do not look in great cities for our best morality."

"That's true, Edmund," said William Price. "I remember that poem—'God made the country, and man made the town.' And also, there are more lunatics in the city. Why, the woman whom Fanny engaged at the academy—it was that very woman's husband who shot the prime minister! What might have happened if Fanny had ever met *him*! Too close for comfort!"

William Gibson was briefly silenced.

"So, how is your novel coming along, Gibson?" William Price ventured after a half a minute marked only by the sound of knives and forks scraping on plates. "Can you tell us anything about it? Julia says you had better include a romance. She says young ladies won't read a novel that doesn't include a love story."

"She is quite right, too! But since the novel is set in the future, the distant future, I have been speculating whether the condition of women in society will improve as much in the next hundred years, as in the last."

"How interesting!" exclaimed William Price, and to do him credit, he did not interrupt his friend with a panegyric on the perfections of the lady he was to marry on the morrow, and the absolute harmony subsisting between them. "What do you predict, Gibson?"

"I predict a prodigious change in the future. I predict that intelligent and well-educated women will have the freedom to choose their own abodes and control their own income. Women will cease to be the plaything or possession of men."

"Are your creations entirely the product of your imagination, Mr. Gibson?" asked Edmund.

"No doubt every writer owes a debt to those who have come before him, sir. As Dr. Johnson said, 'in order to write, a man—"

"—will turn over half a library to make one book," Edmund finished for him. "Oxford?"

"Cambridge."

"I look forward to reading your novel, Mr. Gibson, and examining your portraits of the man and woman of the future," said Edmund. "If I might venture to give a hint, supposing your aim is to hold a mirror up to human nature, I maintain that even an independent woman will not disdain the loyalty and affection of her oldest friends, and the privilege of solicitude conferred by long-established family ties. For example, I should not call myself a tyrant, simply because it matters a great deal to me where my cousin Fanny goes, or who she lives with, or associates with. I have been Fanny's constant friend since she was ten years old, when she first came to us at Mansfield."

"And she was only eighteen, I think, when she... departed." And William Gibson gave Edmund Bertram a direct look which said: *When she ran away, that is. When she was so miserable she ran away.*

"Well!" exclaimed William Price. "Time will tell where Fanny chooses to go in the future. Julia and I are very happy to have her here with us, for our wedding. And you too, my good friends."

This plea for peace and amity did not fall on heedless ears, and William's guests raised their glasses in tribute to the bride and groom and happy married love.

*　　*　　*　　*　　*　　*　　*

The wedding party set out from Mrs. Price's door in good time; Charles and Betsey, scrubbed up and coaxed into their best clothes, led the way. Fanny impressed upon the children the necessity for decorum and Charles only attempted to trip Betsey twice, and Betsey only squealed a few times. Then came Fanny and Susan; Susan self-conscious but happy in her new gown, and Fanny looking very well, even in her black gown and bonnet, for her heart was full of tender feelings for her brother and Julia.

270

Edmund Bertram escorted Julia, who was so completely happy that she sometimes neglected to keep her eyes downcast, as befitted a bride. She smiled, sometimes even laughed, as they walked to the chapel. Her beautiful gown, which cost more than the combined incomes of the local residents, was hidden under a light woollen cloak. Mrs. Norris and Mrs. Price brought up the rear, Mrs. Price absorbed in her thoughts, scarcely hearing the murmured commentary, predictions, warnings and expostulations of her older sister.

Naturally the wedding procession drew a great deal of attention—good-natured jibes and doffed hats, and the local children ran in excited circles around the family, not unlike the seagulls that swirled overhead. The young ladies of the neighbourhood, including Lucy Gregory and her sisters, were awe-struck at the bride and her finery. And waiting outside the Garrison chapel, there were also a dozen of the bridegroom's fellow officers, handsome in their naval uniforms.

All of them—children, old housewives, officers, and young ladies—were later to acknowledge, in tones ranging from envy to admiration to wonder, that Miss Bertram was the most beautiful, and the most beautifully attired, bride who had ever been seen—her golden hair, her tall and shapely form, and her fair complexion, mantled with blushes, drew all eyes upon her.

William Price and his friend Mr. Gibson were in their places inside the chapel, at the altar.

Fanny and Susan helped Julia to remove her cloak, and she paused for a moment, and hung upon her brother Edmund, who whispered some final words of affection to her. Mrs. Price, clad in her widow's weeds, and Mrs. Norris, whose severe expression might have been more fitting at a funeral than a wedding, took their seats with handkerchiefs at the ready and with Charles and Betsey pinioned firmly between them. Fanny and Julia had agreed that the glory and distinction of attending Julia was reserved to Susan; Fanny prudently devoted herself to watching and supporting her mother through the ordeal.

Fanny's happiness for her brother was complete, but she could not glance past him, at Mr. Gibson, standing soberly beside the groom, without feeling deeply conscious. As well, she could not conceive of being a bride like Julia, of being the object of so many enquiring eyes, so much noisy admiration from passers-by. She could not imagine church bells ringing loudly on her behalf, clamouring across the town, demanding that even strangers pause, and say to one another, "someone must be getting married to-day."

If *she* ever were to be married, there would be no row of officers, no archway of swords, no bead-encrusted silver gown, no long veils, no noisy crowds, no procession back through the streets—modesty and bashfulness was no affectation on her part; she had no desire for show and spectacle.

The only way in which she hoped her wedding would resemble Julia's, was in the expression of purest love and devotion on the countenance of the bridegroom, just such a look as illuminated William Price's face when he took the hand of his Julia at the altar—or so it appeared to Fanny, before the tears swarmed to her eyes.

* * * * * * *

The happy couple left for a brief honeymoon visit to the Isle of Wight, and Aunt Norris wasted no time in turning her full attention to an enquiry into her unhappy sister's finances, and was fully confirmed in her suspicion that the Price family's expenditures had always exceeded their income, and that Mrs. Price had not laid up some savings every year in anticipation of the widowhood which was now upon her.

Aunt Norris observed—more than once—that she had refrained from pointing out how foolish and improvident poor Frances had been; there was nothing to be gained, when it was all too late, to speak of the virtues of thrift and economy.

Edmund had also, in his own quieter way, enquired into the state of his widowed aunt's finances, and satisfied himself that although her income was now much reduced, her expenses were likewise, for Mr. Price's expenditures on drink and tobacco were not insignificant. Both Fanny and William were contributing to their mother's comfort, and Edmund's information, conveyed by letter to his father, naturally resulted in Sir Thomas bestowing a modest annuity on his sister-in-law.

On the first Sunday after the wedding; Mrs. Price took her customary walk on the Ramparts after church attended by all her family, along with Mrs. Norris and Mr. Gibson.

The day was warm and bright. Little Betsey attached herself to Mr. Gibson's side and demanded a story, and he was speaking to her of princesses in towers, and fire-breathing dragons, when Aunt Norris interposed and said, "we did not see *you* in chapel today, Mr. Gibson, and certainly when I was a child, we did not indulge in fantastical stories on the Sabbath."

To Fanny's part amusement, part dismay, Gibson doffed his hat and responded, "Well ma'am, in that case, I shall instead tell young Betsey a story about a man who was swallowed by a whale."

Mrs. Norris glowered and moved along, muttering to herself, Susan laughed heartily, and Mr. Gibson looked over at Fanny apologetically and mouthed the words, "I'm sorry." Fanny knew her aunt would not let such levity go unremarked.

In fact, Mrs. Norris did not even wait until Fanny had got her bonnet off, before accosting her in the passageway about her unsuitable sweetheart.

"Fanny, I have not one half-hour of leisure, since arriving in Portsmouth, being so entirely taken up with my poor sister's affairs, and with arranging everything for the wedding, but I see that in addition to everything else that has fallen upon my shoulders, I must speak with you about this Mr. Gibson. What are you about?"

Fanny did not answer, as she saw that her aunt had not done talking, so she waited patiently.

"He is being very insinuating with you—don't think you could hide this matter from my notice. Hadn't you better discourage him? Young ladies cannot be too much on their guard where young men are concerned, Fanny, and in your case, you must be extra cautious and circumspect. There is Mr. Edifice to consider. He is a man of the cloth; his intended wife must be above reproach. What would he say, if he had seen with what familiarity you allow Mr. Gibson to speak to you? And the way that you allow him to take your arm when we are walking together? The way that you laugh when he says something he fancies to be witty?"

Fanny tried to answer firmly, but the old habits of submission were difficult to overcome. "Aunt, Mr. Edifice is—he was not—

Julia was speaking only in jest. She did not really intend for you to think Mr. Edifice was paying his addresses to me."

As Fanny spoke, her courage rose, and she added a gentle reproach: "And indeed, I am sorry to know such a false report has got abroad."

"I told everyone in Mansfield it was a matter not to be talked of, for the time being. If people cannot hold their tongues, it is no fault of mine!"

Fanny smiled, and turned away to go into the parlour, but her aunt's voice pursued her.

"Stay, Fanny, you cannot suppose your family will approve of this Mr. Gibson, if they knew Mr. Gibson as I have seen him. You cannot suppose that *I* can ever come to approve of it. Mr. Gibson is evidently not devout, and I fear he may be a radical! He is unacceptable. You should consider what you owe to me, to your family. Your uncle (thanks to me) took you in and raised you to be a proper gentlewoman—is this how you requite us?"

Upon hearing, once again, the old demand for gratitude and thanks, Fanny turned and looked closely at her aunt. Here was the woman who had frightened and subdued her, throughout all the years of her childhood. Here was the woman who told her she was always to be 'the lowest and the last.' But Fanny was no longer a shrinking child, she was now as tall as her aunt—a little taller, in fact, for in the past few years, Aunt Norris had seemed to shrink a little, and had withdrawn into her clothing, her large neckerchiefs, her starched white caps. She was no longer the vigorous, intimidating Aunt Norris of old. She was smaller, frailer. Long years of scowling had etched deep lines into her forehead and her face, the skin on her hands and neck was wrinkled and papery, her voice had dwindled to a querulous bleat.

"You speak of the church, Aunt Norris, and of course you and I both hold clergyman in the highest esteem. But you do not know Mr. Gibson as I do—and I do assure you, he is a virtuous man, and bears a better character, than even some clergymen or some people professedly Christian. I do not need to denigrate anyone to defend my friend Mr. Gibson, although I might."

Mrs. Norris threw up her hands in dismay. "If you were only harming yourself, I might have done with it, but you may injure everyone connected with you, and cause us to lose what respectability we have left. But if you are determined to be foolish, Fanny, and obstinate, and to go your own way without any regard for those who have the right to advise and guide you, you can only reap the consequences. Do not be surprised if you completely estrange yourself from those to whom you are so much indebted."

"It seems to me that there are also consequences for the argument—no, the threats—that you are making, Aunt Norris," Fanny countered, to her aunt's astonishment. "I should be sorry for you, truly sorry, if your scruples have the result of estranging you from every member of your family. I have been a witness to the manner in which you speak to my mother, and she is now barely speaking to you. Julia tells me you have received no invitations to Norfolk—it seems my uncle and aunt and Maria can all endure the loss of your company. You were good enough to escort Julia to Portsmouth, but you scolded her, every day, for breaking with Mr. Meriwether and you have been excessively unpleasant to my brother William. Can you imagine that you will be a welcome guest in *their* future home? If they have a daughter, do you suppose they will name the child after you?

"I have often thought of you—more often than you might suppose—thought of you living in the White House, all alone and growing older, and thought, as well, of the probability that you will one day need someone to nurse you and care for you. Who do you imagine might come to your side? Your sisters? Maria or Julia? Who shall comfort and support you in your old age?"

Fanny saw that her aunt absorbed the full force of her meaning—and the young woman's resentment instantly gave way to pity. She took her aunt's hand and held it gently while she continued:

"Let me assure you, Aunt, that *I* shall come to you, if you need me, or I will take you in to live with me. And I will deal with you kindly and take good care of you, for I have my *own* convictions about respectability and dishonour. And I choose to forgive you, and to forget the past."

Mrs. Norris's lips quivered, she mouthed the word, '*forgive?*' but said nothing more. Fanny swiftly withdrew upstairs, to calm her own beating heart, and shortly thereafter she heard the front door open and close.

There seldom can be a perfect understanding, let alone a reconciliation, when two persons are so divided in their thinking as my Aunt and I, Fanny consoled herself. *I could not have expected anything more by way of answer. It was perhaps futile to speak what I felt, perhaps even ill-advised. But it was not wrong. I was entitled to speak plainly, just this once. I cannot regret it.*

* * * * * * *

Edmund could not leave Portsmouth, without first having a quiet word with his cousin Fanny, but it must be at a time when Mr. Gibson was not hanging about, as he—a man supposedly hard at work on a novel—so often tended to be.

On the day of his departure, Edmund called upon the Prices early, just as they were rising from breakfast, and invited Fanny for a walk on the Ramparts, away from the crowded family parlour. They walked slowly together, arm in arm, Fanny remarking with satisfaction upon the wedding, until she thought to say, "but I suppose, cousin, the repetition of such details cannot be of as much interest to *you*, as it is to a lady. I shall defer all of my raptures for my letters to your mother and to Madame Orly."

"Thank you, but I do believe, thanks to Julia, that I could specify to the last detail, the veil and the trimming," answered her cousin. "But I think you concur with me that oftentimes—and I by no means include our recently-married friends here—I speak in general terms—oftentimes, too much solicitude is expended on the *wedding*, and not enough thought given to the marriage. To marry, to be married—it is a serious business altogether."

"'And therefore is not by any to be entered into unadvisedly or lightly; but reverently, discreetly...'" said Fanny, "and what else?

"'...advisedly, soberly, and in the fear of God,'" finished Edmund. "Fanny, are *you* contemplating matrimony?"

"Many young ladies contemplate matrimony, Edmund, whether they will admit it or not! But in the sense that you mean—you know that I am in mourning for my father—it will not do to be spoken of, not at present."

Edmund ventured to hint that he still thought her too young, with too little experience of the world, to commit herself in marriage.

Fanny thanked him for his concern. But she could not satisfy his anxious solicitude, his curiousity, as to what she might do after the year was out. Fanny wanted to "wait and see" after her six months with her mother were completed. She might stay longer in Portsmouth, or she might find a new home elsewhere.

Edmund was eloquent in urging caution—great caution—and reflection, before she took any momentous step. "And you know, Fanny, you can always talk things over with me, and I hope you do."

"Of course, cousin!"

A short pause, and then: "Fanny, I understand.... that Mr. Gibson intends to make a visit of some duration in Portsmouth."

"Yes, he is busy finishing his novel."

"The life and income of an author must always be precarious, I suppose. He may invest a better part of a year on some production and see only a poor return for all his efforts, if it does not meet with interest from the public."

"I dare say it must. But on the other hand, there is much to admire in a person who can rise to distinction, without patronage, without family, without connections to assist him, with the power of his eloquence alone. He *has* written one very successful book, so I cannot imagine why he should not write many more."

"It is natural that you should be well-disposed towards him," Edmund conceded, "because of the service he rendered. It is no wonder you feel gratitude."

"Oh?" Fanny stopped and said anxiously, "who told you of it? I did not want you to know about Mr. Bellingham, because I did not wish to cause you any anxiety. In fact, my own family does not know anything about the episode—apart from John, of course."

"Mr. Bellingham? Episode? I was referring to *Amongst the Slavers*, which portrayed your brother in such a good light, and helped obtain his promotion."

"Oh! Yes, of course. Yes, we are all very grateful to Mr. Gibson. Yes." Fanny resumed walking, at a brisker pace.

"What was that you just said about Mr. Bellingham? Do you refer to the assassin of the prime minister? What episode?"

"It was nothing, nothing."

"Fanny!" Edmund was truly wounded. "Fanny, have we ever kept secrets from one another?"

Fanny looked away. "John would not wish me to describe the incident, and it is best forgotten."

Fanny smiled and shook her head and Edmund saw that she was unmoveable. "It is best forgotten."

* * * * * * *

Perplexed and not a little dissatisfied, Edmund caught his coach to London, which gave him some time for reflection.

Edmund caught his coach to London, which gave him some time for reflection.

The feelings of dismay which swept over him when Julia told him of Mr. Gibson—what did they mean? Edmund realized that he was being selfish; and he was ashamed at his selfishness. He should not wish for Fanny to remain single for *his* sake—because he resented being supplanted in her affections.

The day might come, most probably would come, when Fanny would say, "Edmund, I should like you to meet my husband," he would have to shake the hand of his new brother, and say 'congratulations' and speak of his happiness for Fanny, but Edmund knew his true feelings; he recalled how he had felt, when he first became aware of Mr. Gibson. And it was not only Mr. Gibson; he doubted the world could produce any suitor for his cousin whom he would accept with complacency.

Gazing out the window, occasionally rubbing his forehead with a distracted air, Edmund wondered if his affection for his cousin had a dangerous tendency. Could it threaten his peace, and could it threaten hers, if she were ever to realize the depth of his feelings for her, feelings he was only beginning to understand himself?

Perhaps it was better to keep his distance. He was a married man. He had a wife. He had no future to offer anyone. And he was now on his way to London to meet Mary, whom he had not seen for two years.

CHAPTER TWENTY-FOUR

EDMUND BERTRAM CALLED upon the Frasers at Upper Seymour Street and was shown into the parlour—the very room where he had proposed to Mary, three years ago.

Here, by this chair, right here, was where he had discovered she was lying to him about Maria and Henry, and he had turned to walk away; *here* she had stopped him, and he had been overcome by his passionate longing. Here they had embraced and kissed for the first time. Here he had asked her to be his wife, and she had accepted him.

And today—a few minutes, a few words from her, would determine his future course. Would he once again have a wife? Or would he part from her forever? He was resolved on one thing: she was not going to evade him, not overwhelm him, as she had done the day he asked her to marry him. He could not be so easily imposed upon, he thought, as before.

In times of great duress, he tended to speak like a solicitor, or like the chairman of the rules committee of a men's club. But that was his nature. If Mary knew and understood him as a wife should know her husband, she would recognize that beneath the carefully chosen phrases, the mask of composure, there were depths of anger, jealousy, love, resentment, and pain.

How often, since the day she disappeared from Thornton Lacey, had he pictured this day, this moment! Sometimes she begged him for forgiveness, in floods of tears. Sometimes she and Lord Elsham appeared together, and laughed in his face. Sometimes he had raised his voice to her, although doing such a thing in waking life would have been abhorrent to him.

He heard the parlour door open behind him.

"Edmund."

He turned, and there she stood, after an unnatural interval of two years.

Mary, usually so eloquent, so voluble, said only "Edmund," again, with tenderness and something like reproach in her voice. She studied his face intently. No doubt she was measuring his appearance today and reconciling it with the memory she had carried for these two years, for he was doing the same.

She was beautiful, perhaps even more beautiful than he recalled. To see each other again, to be in the same room again, exerted the most powerful sensations in his breast. There was a confusion of feeling between them, of love and bitterness, longing and anger, that Edmund felt must be almost visible.

She came slowly toward him. Would they embrace? Kiss? Did she want him too? He could not tell what she wanted; he could not even judge of his own feelings. She began to extend her hand, but paused when she saw him stiffen slightly. He gave her a slight bow, and she stopped in the middle of the room, and inclined her head in return.

Mary motioned him to the settee and she took a seat on the other side of the fireplace. A space of only five feet separated them.

"Edmund, I am happy to see you," she began.

"Thank you, Mary, for giving me this opportunity to speak with you."

He saw her react to the coolness of his address.

"Before *I* begin, Mary, is there something in particular you would like to say to me?"

"You look wonderful, Edmund, even more handsome than I remembered."

"Can that be all you have to say to me, Mary?"

"Oh no, of course not, but darling, you know I am never any good at serious moments. Are you not pleased to see me as well, Edmund? I think you are."

"Mary, on occasions like this, at the outset of their first conversation in two years, I believe a wife who has been unfaithful to her husband ought to apologize. I am not even speaking of the morality of the thing. I am speaking of common courtesy."

"Oh! Well, of course!" Mary leapt up from her chair, and knelt at his side, looking up at him with anguish in her dark eyes. "Regret! Sorrow! Edmund, could you not feel my despair, even when we were separated by hundreds of miles? You must know how often I laid in my bed and wept from remorse, and shame and grief, at having thrown away the best husband in all of England. Can you not imagine how I have passed the last two years, a miserable wandering spirit, with no place to call my own? My feelings have so overpowered me, all these months, that it seems incredible you should not know them. Could you possibly think me indifferent?

280

How could you not know my heart, after what we have been to one another?"

She looked up at him, beseechingly. Though he tried to shield his expression, a look of pain, even despair, crossed his face.

"Mary, please, take your seat again. Please."

She looked surprised, but nodded humbly and resumed her chair.

"Mary, I attended very carefully to what you said. Will you likewise give me all of your attention in return?

She tilted her head enquiringly, but remained silent.

"I *do* believe you feel regret, Mary. But I observed, while you expressed your sorrow for—for what has occurred, you spoke only of the difficulties it caused for *you*. You said nothing about me— no word of apology—or even acknowledgement, for what *I* have suffered. In fact, you reproached me, for not being sufficiently alive to *your* suffering."

Her eyes opened wide in consternation. She drew breath to speak, but he continued, calmly and deliberately.

"No word, about what your sudden departure meant to *me*. No reflection on what it must have been like for me, to take the pulpit every Sunday, one Sunday after another, to see the eyes of all the parishioners on me. *They* all know my wife left me, and *I* know they would much rather hear about the mystery of my unhappy marriage, rather than anything I had to say concerning St. Paul's epistle to the Galatians.

"It was a matter of no small weight with me to know if you were capable of apologizing to me, spontaneously and without equivocation. To *me*, Mary. In the event you do not recollect what you just said, permit me to inform you, that you *did not* apologize to me, and if it did not occur to you to do so on this occasion, what must I conclude?

"Although I had, upon our first acquaintance, given you credit for being a kind-hearted and thoughtful person, the first six months of our marriage did much to test the image I first formed of you. In fact I began to suspect that the woman I loved was, at least in part, a creature of my imagination. Now, it is unhappily plain to me that you are perhaps the most selfish person I have ever met in my life."

He would have said more, but she could remain silent no longer. The desperate calmness with which he spoke only provoked her to anger and impatience. "Of *course* I am sorry for everything that happened! How I wish none of it had happened! But—how am I more selfish than *you*, or anyone else in your family? If your cousin hadn't lied about being married to my poor brother, if *her* brother hadn't captured your father's boat and destroyed your family's fortunes! If *you* hadn't decided we should never return to Mansfield! We would still be together if not for—but I am the only one whose transgressions remain unforgiven."

Edmund took in one long slow breath, felt the exhalation through his nostrils, and slowly inhaled again. "There are two other points I must mention, because they weigh very materially with me. I came to London two days ago."

She raised her eyebrows at this, startled at the thought that he had resisted the urge to go to her immediately.

"I have been calling upon some of my acquaintance. They told me, most reluctantly, what I have long suspected. I learned from them—that is, I cannot own myself surprised to hear that you have represented the *causes* of our separation in a light most advantageous to you, to all of your many friends and acquaintance in London. We would all be guilty, I suspect, of excusing ourselves to some lesser or greater degree when describing matters we should rather not discuss. But I am, in short, not surprised to learn that in the eyes of many, I am a villain, and entirely at fault for the breach between us."

"And no doubt everyone in Thornton Lacey says you are an angel!"

"I am well regarded there, but it is not because I have hinted at the state of my marriage or denigrated the character of my wife. There is an embargo on the subject in Thornton Lacey, and whatever else you accuse me of, I think you will believe my assertion on that point."

"Of course, Edmund, of course." She blinked a few tears away. "You are a good, good man. Better than I deserve. Not one person in a hundred would have your forbearance. I am a mere ordinary—"

"The final matter I wish to lay before you, Mary, is that Julia recently confided in me, the extent to which you have interfered with her happiness."

"This is preposterous. Julia would say anything to excuse herself for jilting poor Mr. Meriwether."

"You cannot possibly attempt to deny the role you played there, Mary."

"Edmund! You told me yourself, in writing, that you would not live with me unless Julia were *married*! You made it a condition of our reunion!"

"I did not instruct you to pressure Julia to marry a man she didn't love—didn't even know. I did not ask you to give her advice which wracked her feelings, and which was a cruel and gross distortion of my father's situation and sentiments."

"My counsel was heartfelt, very sincerely meant, and anyone would have agreed my advice was sound! You cannot pretend that Julia has not made a very imprudent marriage, and one most likely to end in..." Mary trailed off, seeing the expression on Edmund's face. She was astonished that this conversation with her husband was unfolding so disastrously. A terrible fear clutched at her heart.

"In the long silence which followed your desertion of our home, Mary, I began to grow resigned to the possibility I would never see or speak to you again—"

"You never tried to contact *me*! Not once! If you truly cared about me, you would have!"

Edmund's neck flushed with anger, and he came near to losing his composure. "Where should I have sent the letter? To Lord Elsham? Or some other?"

Mary fidgeted, and tossed her head.

Edmund wiped his hand across his brow and calmed himself. "Pray, let me have done, Mary. In short, I think I was not unreasonable in wanting to hear you express some remorse for breaking your marriage vows. In that, I have been disappointed. It appears to be something you cannot bring yourself to do, not without excuses and equivocations. But, even if you were now to fling yourself to the floor at my feet and beg for my forgiveness— and pray, pray, do not do so—I have come to feel I could not repose any confidence in your sincerity."

Her eyes, swimming with tears, upbraided him for his coldness, as he remorselessly continued.

"In addition to being unfaithful to me, you have been disloyal, by spreading unhandsome insinuations about me throughout

London. And finally, your conduct toward Julia, your misapplication of the sentiments I expressed to you in my letter, indeed, all of your actions together, have served to strengthen my conviction that we were best to continue to live apart."

"So... you refuse to take me back? What will you do? What will *I* do?"

"I will be the vicar of Thornton Lacey. You, Mary, must decide for yourself. You retain your fortune, and your freedom."

"You allowed me to hope—for a year? You dangled the promise that I might return to you and now—you snatch it away?"

"There was no premeditation on my part, Mary. I give you my word."

She clasped her hands together, and shuddered, looking down at the floor. "I think I do understand, I do see. You used to like me, I used to amuse you perhaps, but now..."

"I adored you, Mary." This last was uttered in the same flat, clipped tone which he had employed almost throughout their interview.

Edmund's heart was withdrawn from her. Mary sat as still as a statue for a long moment, staring into space. With inward desperation she surveyed the ruin of her hopes and had to acknowledge to herself that, had she known the right things to say to Edmund, had she not so misjudged the situation, they might even now be embracing each other with rapture and relief. She wanted more than anything to lash out at him, to say all the scornful, biting things which rose to her mind. But for once, she dared not indulge herself. Anger, raging anger, struggled with anguish, and the need to do what must be done.

Then she picked up and rang a small silver bell sitting on a little table beside her. She remained silent until the parlour maid appeared.

"Yes, Madam."

"Please have Polly bring... you know."

"Yes, Madam." The door closed, and Mary addressed Edmund.

"Edmund, you will recall the happy summer and autumn we spent together, before you told me you would never leave Thornton Lacey? Do you recall the *nights* we spent together?"

Indeed, Edmund had passed many restless hours recalling those nights, longing to have her in his bed again, but he barely nodded in reply.

"All those nights as man and wife, Edmund, and did you never stop to wonder whether—? Two healthy young people coming together as often as we did? After I left you, I went to Brighton, but soon I was obliged to take refuge in Wales, to conceal my state."

"Mary!"

"The child was born in June of the year ten, and I thought I would die of the pain and suffering I underwent in bringing him into the world. And from the moment I held your son in my arms, I wanted only the best in life for him. That consideration will explain my subsequent conduct. You must acquit the mother, even if you condemn the wife."

"Madam?"

"Edmund, had you addressed me just now with any tenderness, with any forgiveness, with any consideration of what *I* have suffered, I would have, in return, spared you this additional revelation. At first, I kept you in ignorance of your son's birth because I had greater ambitions for him. The child would have better prospects if he was thought to be the son of an Earl, one of the richest men in England, even if illegitimate, than as the heir presumptive to your father's bankrupt baronetcy. Lord Elsham has no male heir, and so, in my ambitious delusions, I saw the baby becoming as important to Elsham as it was possible for him to be. So, I informed Lord Elsham that the child was his. Wait—wait—Edmund—"

Edmund flushed red, and his fists were clenched.

"—by the time the baby passed out of infancy, Elsham was undeceived. They share not a single feature, and he can consult a calendar as well as you can. We quarrelled, and we parted. I then attempted to reconcile with you, and sent you a letter by Lady Delingpole, but *you*—"

"And the child? The child? Is he well? Where is he now?"

"I kept him in the countryside, in Wales. But he is now—"

"Nearly two years old!"

The door opened, and a plump little nursery-maid came in, holding a sturdy young child in her arms, who wiggled and kicked and testified to his desire to be set down. She began to carry the little boy to her mistress, but that lady directed her by a motion, to go to Edmund, who tried to stand up to receive his son from his nurse's arms, but his legs had turned to water.

Edmund awkwardly took the boy upon his knee, and examined him. A baby version of himself looked back at him—the same curling locks, lighter than his own, but he, too, was fair-haired as a child. The same deep blue eyes, the same broad forehead, the same close-set ears.

"I wanted to name him 'Henry,' but of course your sister named my brother's son 'Henry.' It was only fitting. So I named him 'Thomas.' After your father."

The nursery-maid withdrew, and Mary's composure suddenly dissolved. Tears filled her eyes and spilled down her cheeks.

"I never imagined I could love anyone or anything as much as I love my child. By law, Edmund, you can take Thomas from my arms. He is yours, he belongs to you, and I have no rights over him. So when you told me we could not live together as man and wife until Julia was married..." her voice choked. "And Julia was determined to wait, year after year, for William Price! That, Edmund, is why I did everything I could, to encourage her to come to her senses. For my son's sake."

The little boy looked around the room, then returned his gaze to Edmund. The two looked at one another, equally fascinated. At last, the child gave a delighted smile, and Edmund's heart felt as though it would burst.

"I was desperate," Mary continued, through her sobs. "I was trapped. I wanted to tell you about Thomas, but I was terrified that if you learned about your son while we were estranged, you would take him from me and cast me out forever. Then Lord Elsham returned, and berated me for keeping the truth from you. He threatened to tell you himself, if I did not."

Little Thomas bounced up and down on Edmund's knee. "How do you do? Play horsey?" he said clearly.

Mary smiled proudly through her tears. "He speaks very well for one so young, doesn't he? I remember your aunt Norris once told me the same about you, that you could recite your alphabet by your second birthday, and name all the little wooden animals in your Noah's ark..." She began to weep aloud.

"And now—you condemn me—you say there is no hope for me. I have lost everyone—I ever loved in my life. Selfish—you called me. But this last—I will now do willingly—for our son's sake. I surrender him to you, Edmund—even if you never allow me—to see him again. I beg of you—acknowledge him as your son—and love him as I do—and save him from disgrace. He is coming to the age of reason—soon he will want to know who his father..." Mary broke off, unable to speak for her sobs.

And Edmund could not answer, for he was quietly weeping as well, and clutching the child to his chest.

CHAPTER TWENTY-FIVE

LADY DELINGPOLE DECLARED herself unsurprised that in the end Mary Crawford Bertram gained everything she wanted. Edmund Bertram could not preserve his son's respectability without also saving the mother.

In the space of a fortnight, Sir Thomas Bertram and his lady received letters informing them of the death of their brother-in-law, the removal of their niece Fanny to Portsmouth, the exchange of one bridegroom for another by Julia, the reconciliation of their son Edmund with his wife, and the acquisition of another grandson!

Mary Bertram sent them a long, dutiful, and affectionate letter, with a miniature portrait of young Thomas, which attested to his complete resemblance to his father. Nothing of course could repair Sir Thomas's opinion of his daughter-in-law, but the revelation of an heir presumptive, when it had otherwise appeared that the baronetcy must pass to their cousins in Bedford Square, kept him from expressing himself so often and so volubly as he might have done.

Julia Bertram Price and her husband, Commander Price, plying the waters between Ireland and England together aboard the *Protector*, were as happy and in love as it is humanly possible to be, and in fact regarded themselves as the happiest couple in the world.

Julia, it must be confessed, struggled a little with wounded vanity when she learned Mr. Meriwether's affection for her was not unconquerable. Not four months after she dashed his hopes, he led Margaret Fraser to the altar! The new Mrs. Meriwether, valued for herself, indulged and petted, was a very happy woman, and what is more, she made her husband very happy also. *His* contentment was increased by knowing he gave his bride a more loving home than the one he took her from.

John Price kept up with his wrestling lessons and continued in his ambition to be a judicial clerk one day, an aspiration which Mr. Harriott did not discourage.

Mrs. Laetitia Blodgett penned a short and despairing note to her niece Honoria: *You cannot imagine the difficulties into which I am plunged! After dismissing Miss Price, I thought we should do very well with Mrs. Bellingham—but you know what happened there. Then we engaged a new instructress, an older woman, and paid her much more than ever we had paid Miss Price, but I had to turn her off for drinking! The students are grown absolutely wild, and Mr. Edifice and I can hardly keep them in order for five minutes altogether...*

Edmund Bertram's departure from Thornton Lacey was the means of providing a living for his good friend and old school-fellow Richard Owen, the struggling curate. Mr. Owen was thereby able to provide a home to his widowed mother and unmarried sisters.

Mary Bertram regretted her husband's over-generosity in the matter of Mr. Owen's salary. She thought one hundred pounds a year would be more than ample, and Edmund offered more than twice that amount! And the house as well! But she magnanimously kept her thoughts to herself.

Through the interest of Lady Delingpole, Edmund Bertram started a new life in Ireland as headmaster of a boys' school. Despite owing his position to the patronage of the Delingpoles, Edmund Bertram soon established himself as a well-respected headmaster. He also enjoyed the wider circle of acquaintance and the variety of diversions which life in Belfast afforded him, which put him in danger of having to agree with his wife; his talents, personableness, and industry, in fact fitted him for a wider sphere than a country parsonage.

Mary Bertram revelled in the society and elegancies of her new home—she was a more prominent figure on the smaller stage of Belfast, than she had been in London.

Their little boy Thomas, a remarkably fine-looking and clever child, was the delight of them both. Mansfield Park remained, for the time being, the preserve of Lord Delingpole and his horses and hounds but Mary always felt a thrill of pride and anticipation when she thought of the day when little Thomas would take his place as Sir Thomas Bertram. In the meantime, a thickening of her figure betrayed the impending arrival of a little brother or sister, which also interfered with her ability to reach the furthest strings on her harp.

Aunt Norris left Portsmouth and returned to Mansfield, not comprehending that her disapproval of William Gibson did more to incline her niece to marry the writer, than her endorsement could ever have done.

Fanny trusted in her own estimation of Mr. Gibson. She prized his integrity, his adherence to principle, his disdain for hypocrisy and cant, and his genius as a writer. Most especially, she loved and admired the warmth, frankness and generosity of his character—even if he tended to impetuosity at times. His boldness would strengthen her timidity; her caution might add reflection, where it was truly warranted, to his impulses.

Fanny could not offer Mr. Gibson the innocent purity of a first love, of a newly-awakened heart. Other people, she knew, loved a second time. But Edmund was tied to her by an invisible cord of feeling, a cord never to be severed.

Hers was an affectionate heart, needing only an object to love—as Mrs. Gibson, she would have someone to whom she could devote herself—someone who in turn, esteemed and truly delighted in her company. After a childhood of feeling herself to be an encumbrance—unwanted—either at Mansfield or Portsmouth, this was a promise of felicity beyond her expectations.

Between her private daydreams about travelling on an extended honeymoon, and her reflections on a future world where mankind was freed from demeaning toil, and the thoughts of the novels he was to write about it all, to point the way for struggling mankind, and the certainty of the domestic paradise she would create for them both once they did settle somewhere, Fanny's mind was very agreeably engaged as she waited out the months of mourning for her father.

In her imagination, her husband would write, and she would make fair copies for him, and encourage him, and welcome his interesting friends to the house, and they would enjoy precisely that balance of solitude and sociability which represented the ideal existence for both of them. They would be very happy indeed.

Even practical-minded Susan gloried in the secret romance, and to Betsey, who already loved him, William Gibson continued to be a revelation. She was greatly benefitted by the advent of this new brother, this kind, patient, and intelligent man, in her narrow world.

Mr. Gibson enjoyed his visit to Scotland - enjoyed it only as much, that is, as a man very much in love and parted from his sweetheart, can be supposed to do. In his walks with Fanny, he was no less eloquent on the landscapes and beauty of that northern country as he was on the visions of the future conjured up by the steamboat *Comet*.

The pictures of the lochs and the crags which he sketched with words were delightful to Fanny, and of equal interest were his speculations about the epochs to come.

As well, he and Fanny were able to untangle some perplexing misunderstandings and talk over the blunders and delights of the past two years, and in fact traced and re-traced them together more than once.

"When Lady Delingpole told me you were to marry Mr. Edifice," he exclaimed in one such conversation, "I could not believe it—would not believe it—and yet, I feared it was true."

"I should have thought you knew me better than to suppose it!"

"You must account for the effects of jealousy and wounded pride, upon an otherwise rational man," Mr. Gibson rejoined, drawing Fanny's arm more securely within his own. "But you are so free from such petty emotions as jealousy—I dare say you cannot even conceive of the state of my mind at the time."

"Oh, but I have been jealous, very jealous!" Fanny confessed, and told him of the real reason she had fled the reception at Lady Delingpole's.

"Jealous of—of that woman!" Mr. Gibson exclaimed, shaking his head in wonder. "How I have blundered! I recall the occasion perfectly, for when I saw you in Mrs. Butters' carriage, and observed how you were behaving so coolly toward me—I was bewildered. I can still picture the way you turned away from me, and would not speak. But then I met you again at the academy, and to my great gratification, we were friends once more."

"When you came to Camden Town to report on Mrs. Perceval's visit, was this the first time you had occasion to meet Mr. Edifice?"

"The first and last, in fact."

"Oh..." And of course Mr. Gibson could not rest until Fanny explained the meaning of that one little sound, and gently prised from her the story of the day Mr. Edifice told her "Mr. Gibson only wanted a mercenary marriage."

Now it was her suitor's turn to look astonished, and to laugh. "No, Fanny, I was urging *Mr. Edifice* not to marry anyone but an heiress! Discouraging his designs on you! All is fair in love and war, you know. But," he added more soberly, "It *was* money—the want of money—which held me back and kept me from declaring myself.

"I had always seen myself, where you were concerned, as a sort of knight errant. From our first acquaintance, I wanted to assist you, to protect you. But how was I to do it? I had no money and no prospects. And then, instead of rescuing *you* from your situation as a governess, I was myself abducted into the Navy. But happily, this afforded me with the experience to write my book. So then, I began to hope I could acquire the means to support a wife."

"You rescued me at Christmastime," said Fanny. "I shall never forget the joy of hearing your voice in the darkness, when I was hiding in the dumbwaiter!"

"I shall never forget that moment either, Fanny. But you were not really in danger—not at that time, at any rate. It was I who frightened you nearly out of your senses.

"And," he added, with great emphasis, "Fanny, instead of keeping you safe from danger, instead of protecting you, I carelessly led you *into* mortal danger."

"Do not blame yourself for what happened with Mr. Bellingham!" Fanny assured him. "You know that I wanted to help John to prove his worth to his superiors, so even if you had forbidden me to follow Mr. Bellingham, I should have done as I did."

"When it comes to those you love, my dear Fanny, you are absolutely fearless. I have noticed. As I said, I had always longed to be your rescuer, to give you the comforts, the security, the protection you deserved. But perhaps you don't need a rescuer. You are so extraordinarily different from other young women. Quiet, but strong. Gentle, but firm. So superior in understanding, in integrity, but without vanity. Wise enough to see the foibles of mankind all around you, but too kind to make sport of them. Perhaps that is why I feel myself to be a better, stronger, man when you are by my side, when your arm is holding on to mine.

"But soon, Fanny, soon... when propriety and you permit, I will tell you everything I could not say before. And should you permit it—but, yes, I understand you Fanny," he stopped, when his fair companion shook her head. "I will honour your convictions in this matter. I will give your late father the respect he deserves. I will prove to you, I hope, that although our temperaments are dissimilar, and our beliefs are sometimes different, we can be a true partnership—my dearest one—my Fanny."

Mr. Gibson had no relations, no family connections, to bring to the proposed union, but that deficiency was more than made up by the hearty approbation of his many friends. And let no one attempt to describe the satisfaction of Mrs. Butters, in anticipating the fulfilment of her plans.

AUTHOR'S NOTE

As *A Marriage of Attachment* concludes, Edmund has resumed life with Mary, Commander William Price has won his bride, and Fanny and William Gibson look forward to a happy life together. Please stay tuned—there will be more twists and turns!

May I ask, if you enjoyed reading this book, would you kindly leave a rating and review at Amazon or Goodreads? Thank you so much, it means a great deal.

ABOUT THE AUTHOR

Lona Manning loves reading, choral singing, gardening, and travel. Over the years, she has been a home care aide, legal secretary, political speech writer, office manager, vocational instructor, non-profit manager and English as a Second Language teacher. She was born in Seoul, South Korea, where her parents were educational missionaries after the Korean War. In addition to her works of fiction, she has written true crime articles for www.CrimeMagazine.com. Visit her website at www.lonamanning.ca for updates about forthcoming publications.

Connect with Lona Manning:
www.lonamanning.ca
www.amazon.com/Lona-Manning

ACKNOWLEDGEMENTS

A big thank-you to my editors, proof-readers, and beta readers: Anji Dale, Cara Elrod, Sandra Fillmer, Joseph Manning, Susan Meikle, Lenora Robinson, and several more who chose not to share their names. Your contributions made a big difference.

I am very grateful to my fellow authors Mark Brownlow, Callista Hunter, and A.E. Walnofer for their insightful comments and warm support. I hope we can continue writing and sharing the journey.

In the days since my first novel, *A Contrary Wind*, was published, I have made new friends, such as author Kyra Kramer, who joined me in the online "Fanny vs Mary" debates, and received wonderful support from some old friends, such as Pam Penner and Peter Geoffrey Cassey.

Getting to know the international Jane Austen-loving community has brought me great pleasure and many new friends. I received a very kind reception from the online Janeite world, even though my heroine is Fanny Price!

I owe a great debt to Claudine Pepe of JustJane1813.com for her early encouragement and support.

Thank you to Christina Angel Boyd, editor and publicist extraordinaire, for inviting me to contribute to the Jane Austen short-story anthologies, *Dangerous to Know*, *Rational Creatures*, and *Yuletide*.

My thanks go to Tim Barber of Dissect Designs (www.dissectdesigns.com) for creating the book covers for both books. I'm looking forward to working on the next one!

Thank you for my husband Ross, for putting up with a wife who tends to obsess about things.

BACKGROUND INFORMATION

JANE AUSTEN LIVED during a fascinating and important turning point in history, an era that linked the Age of Enlightenment, with its great thinkers like John Locke and Adam Smith, with the dawn of the Industrial Revolution and the Romantic Age. On the one hand, she grew up reading and loving the measured, balanced phrases of Dr. Johnson and she imbibed the values of restraint, courtesy, and moderation, as embodied in her heroine Elinor Dashwood. But the new century also brought poets like Wordsworth, gothic novels, a fascination with the Orient and wildly sentimental novels, all of which are enjoyed by her heroines Marianne Dashwood and Catherine Moreland.

The Enlightenment brought some religious toleration to England; people were no longer being burnt alive as witches and heretics but it was still a very poor career move to declare oneself to be an atheist.

In addition, British attitudes about rank, the merchant class and society, were being challenged at the dawn of the Industrial Revolution. The life of the English farm labourer and peasant was upended when common lands were fenced in for farming and grazing. The rural poor were no longer able to turn their pigs out to graze in the forest or their cow to graze on common land. Poaching wild game in the forest was a capital crime. Many poor people migrated to the cities to compete for jobs in the factories. They became wage slaves, cogs in an industrial machine. Child labour, massive social upheaval, pollution, and "dark satanic mills," completes the picture of misery and exploitation that we associate with the Industrial Revolution.

However, the Industrial Revolution soon brought a skyrocketing improvement in living standards as well as the development of public health, law and order, public charity and a decrease in child mortality. As economist Gregory Clark wrote: "Jane Austen may have written about refined conversations over tea served in china cups. But for the majority of the English as late as 1813 conditions were no better than for their naked ancestors of the African savannah. The Darcys were few, the poor plentiful."

You can see a graph at this link http://bit.ly/2DFnRwX which shows the undeniable fact that the Industrial Revolution was unique in the history of mankind.

And while wages rose, the cost of every day necessities fell, over time. Take the cost of candles for light, for example. HumanProgress.org notes that: "The amount of labor that once bought 54 minutes of light now buys 52 years of light." Candles today are used for decoration and as a gift, are easily re-giftable. But Julia Bertram was being truly thoughtful when she generously brought a box of nice beeswax candles for Mrs. Price.

Lord Delingpole was on the right side of history. But of course poor and dispossessed unskilled farm labourers and workers needed charity and many people were involved in providing it. The Society for Bettering the Condition and Increasing the Comforts of the Poor—known as The Bettering Society for short—really existed and their annual reports are available on Google Books. (There is no article from William Gibson about Mrs. Perceval's visit to Camden Town, however.) What is notable about this Society is that they were earnestly interested in looking for the most effectual ways to aid the poor. They did not believe, as we say today, in "throwing money at the problem," or being sentimental about the poor, and they were certainly not inclined to excuse anti-social behaviour. They studied poverty and its causes in a cool-headed way, for all that they tended to be fervent Evangelicals.

The Romantic poets Shelley and Byron, especially Shelley, were also taken up with the plight of the poor in England and Ireland, but they led with their hearts, not their heads. As Paul Johnson demonstrated in his scathing biography in the book, *Intellectuals*, Shelley was an utterly self-indulgent man-child of colossal ego. Shelley wrote grandiose manifestos on the human condition, such as his youthful poem *Queen Mab*, and he believed that everyone would read it and see that he was right. He would take up a cause, such as Irish emancipation, with passionate enthusiasm and outrage, and then grow bored or frustrated and move on to some other cause, which, not coincidentally, was also how he treated the women in his life.

He was also a consummate hypocrite, in that, as his disillusioned friend Lord Lynnon points out, he left trails of debts behind him, and his inability to pay his rent, his servants and his bills was one reason why he moved about so frequently. His modern counterpart is the celebrity who lectures the public on global warming while traipsing around the planet on private jets and luxury yachts.

Shelley was a champion of "free love;" and thought that marriage was a form of tyranny. However, in the days before birth control, penicillin, and state-enforced child support laws, "free love" was a very bad idea for women, something to bear in mind when revisionist feminists focus solely on the restrictive and oppressive aspects of the Patriarchy. Mary Wollstonecraft's experiment with free love was disastrous for her, personally as well as professionally, and her illegitimate daughter committed suicide.

As Shelley's women experienced first-hand, the social consequences for women of the era who were separated or divorced or otherwise "fallen" were extremely severe. Edmund is too kind-hearted to visit that fate upon his wife Mary. As well, at that time, men had default custody of the children of the marriage—the wife had no rights in law—which is why Mary Crawford Bertram was afraid of telling Edmund he had a son.

Stoke Newington, where Mrs. Butters lived, was also where James Stephen and other prominent abolitionists lived. Another neighbourhood known for abolitionists and reformers was Clapham. William Wilberforce's followers were known as "The Clapham Sect" and "Clapham Saints."

Lord Delingpole never learned why the pockets of the billiard table at Mansfield Park were stuffed with curtain rings, but readers of *Mansfield Park* will know why.

The only reference in *Mansfield Park* to Fanny's brother John is that he "was a clerk in a public office in London." When I researched "public office," I discovered that it was another term for police offices, which were a fairly new innovation for the time. So I was able to place Fanny's brother John in the maritime police office which is still in existence at the banks of the River Thames, in Wapping. The office was founded by John Harriott, who wrote his memoirs, which are available online.

Having placed John in Wapping during this time period, there was no way I could overlook the Ratcliffe Highway murders, which gripped all of England in the winter of 1811. Thomas DeQuincy wrote about the fear they caused even in far-away Lake Country. They created a moral panic, a "what-is-this-world-coming-to" reaction, as mass murders still do today. You can read more about the murders in *The Maul and the Pear Tree*, by P. D. James and Thomas A. Critchley, or watch the first episode of the mini-series, *A Very British Murder*, with historian Lucy Worsley, for more details. The initials "JP" were not immediately noticed on the murder weapon, and it is not known who found the initials. The supposed murderer was buried at a crossroads with a stake through his heart.

For information about the career, married life, and religious views of Prime Minister Spencer Perceval I am indebted to: *The Assassination of the Prime Minister: John Bellingham and the Murder of Spencer Perceval* by David C. Hanrahan, and *Why Spencer Perceval Had to Die: The Assassination of a British Prime Minister*, by Andro Linklater. The trial transcript itself is available at the Old Bailey trial website and other contemporary accounts are available through Google Books.

It's extraordinary that the assassin, John Bellingham, first took his landlady and her son to look at some paintings, and then to a lace-shop, then hastened down to Parliament and shot the prime minister. Linklater theorizes that he had an accomplice, or a financial backer, some representative of the dissatisfied merchant class, who pulled Bellingham's strings. Perhaps Bellingham retrieved his pistols at the lace shop, or perhaps, as Linklater theorizes, he received a payment. There is no proof, however, and Bellingham always insisted that he acted alone; he was thoroughly and repeatedly questioned on that point, after his arrest. On the other hand, as Linklater points out, he seemed to have an undocumented source of money during his stay in London.

The activities and movements of John Bellingham prior to his assassination of Prime Minister Perceval—with the exception of course, of his interactions with William Gibson and Fanny Price—as well as many of his speeches, are taken from the public record, and Andro Linklater's book.

Mary Bellingham, the wife of John Bellingham, was a milliner. (I wished to avoid confusion with the other Mary of this book, so I changed her name to Eliza.) She didn't move to London in the months preceding her husband's assassination of Perceval although she was greatly alarmed by his mental state and begged him to stop trying to petition the government. Her millinery business failed after the assassination, not before. She had a business partner, Miss Mary Stevens, who did go to London and met with Bellingham there and reported his doings to Mary back in Liverpool. It appears that Mrs. Bellingham was much more considerate of Miss Stevens than my fictional Eliza Bellingham was to Fanny Price.

Lord Brougham's speech in the House of Commons is adapted from a speech he gave on June 16, 1812. He and James Stephen were both in the Commons on the afternoon Prime Minister Perceval walked from Downing Street and was ambushed by Bellingham in the lobby.

Journalists could be imprisoned for libel and sedition in Regency times. Lord Delingpole warns William Gibson with the example of Peter Finnerty, an Irish journalist imprisoned for libelling Lord Castlereagh. Shelley (him again!) wrote an anti-war poem, titled "Poetical Essay on the Existing State of Things," as a fundraiser for Finnerty. This poem was thought to be lost, until one copy surfaced in a private collection in 2005. http://poeticalessay.bodleian.ox.ac.uk/

Fanny received a settlement from Henry Crawford in the amount of three thousand pounds. Invested at five percent, this would give her an annual income of 150 pounds—barely enough to be married on and maintain the life of a gentlewoman. The Society for Bettering the Condition and Increasing the Comforts of the Poor probably pays her about twenty pounds a year, but pays three times that much to Mr. Edifice, for much less work! She and Mr. Gibson would want at least four to five hundred pounds a year, before being able to live simply but comfortably on the outskirts of London, and couldn't afford a carriage or more than a few servants.

The legacy of chattel slavery in North America is currently a very fraught topic. A wider historical perspective reminds us that slavery was not exclusively practised by Europeans and Americans upon black Africans, it occurred everywhere for millennia and was thought to be a natural condition of mankind, until it was opposed by a small group of British evangelicals and politicians. For information about the sacrifices made by the men of the West African Squadron, I relied upon: *Opposing the Slavers: The Royal Navy's Campaign against the Atlantic Slave Trade*. By Peter Grindal. Mr. Grindal writes, "[P]osterity should conclude that there have been few episodes in the illustrious history of the Royal Navy which have been more deserving of true glory."

Life in Sierra Leone and the hardships of the West African Squadron are also vividly recounted in *Sweet Water & Bitter*, by Siân Rees. Rees tells how the officers of the British Navy struggled with lack of resources and a deadly climate while patrolling vast areas of the African coast to rescue captured Africans from slavery.

I took some of the details of the battle for the Portuguese slave ship, *Volcano*, and the death of Midshipman Castle, from Rees' history. Sadly, in real-life, the Portuguese crew succeeded in re-capturing the ship, and they killed the English prize crew, an incident which occurred in October 1819.

Commodore Edward Columbine, Captain Frederick Irby, Lieutenant Lumley, and the vice-admiral's daughter are all real people, and the exploits of the crews of the HMS *Crocodile*, *Kangaroo* and *Protector* mostly occurred as depicted. There was no Lieutenant William Price aboard, of course. The marital tragedies of Commodore Columbine and the *Kangaroo*'s captain are also taken from the historical record, except that both of Columbine's wives were named Anne, so to avoid confusion, I changed the name of his second wife to Jane. I have surmised how Edward Columbine felt about his first and second marriages and their outcome.

In an earlier edition of this book I promoted William Price from lieutenant to captain; I subsequently learned that there is an intermediate rank, that of commander, so I amended the story accordingly. As a commander, William would be put in charge of smaller vessels.

Andrew and Rachel Knowles's *RegencyHistory.net* was a vital source of information about the streets and parks of Regency London, as was Louise Allen's *Walks Through Regency London* and a map of London placed online by David Hale at http://mapco.net/darton1817/darton02b.htm.

Mr. Edifice, Mr. Nathaniel Meriwether, Mrs. Butters, Lord and Lady Delingpole and their son James, Viscount Lynnon, are invented characters. Mrs. Butters' relatives and the writer William Gibson are also the products of my imagination. Fanny's old employers, the Smallridges near Bristol, later attempted to hire Miss Jane Fairfax, in *Emma*. Admiral and Mrs. Croft, who encounter William Price in Gibraltar, are characters from Jane Austen's novel, *Persuasion*.

Edmund Bertram quotes from William Cowper's poem *The Task*—Jane Austen surely had that portion of the poem in mind when she wrote the Wilderness scenes in *Mansfield Park*. Fanny Price quotes from the poem as well in *Mansfield Park* and William Gibson quotes from it in *A Contrary Wind*. *The Task* was a favourite poem of Jane Austen's.

Mr. Frederick Edifice courts Fanny with a quote from a poem by Thomas Wilkinson written in memory of a devout and learned young lady, Miss Elizabeth Smith (1776-1806). He reads to the young pupils of the sewing academy from the *Elegant Extracts*. His address of welcome to Mrs. Perceval is adapted from several dedications in 18th century books. The contributors to the address of welcome are Eliza Kirkham Matthews (1802), John Stevenson, (1815), Thomas Gibbons (1750).

The reference to the sea as being the "bounding Main" predates the song, "The Walloping Window Blind." It appears in a poem dated from 1763:

Fam'd Albion's Sons, whose Rock encircling Coast,
Emblem of Virtues in your noble Race,

Repels each boisterous Billow of the Deep,
And stands triumphant o'er the bounding Main.

Vitamin C was not discovered until the 1930s. William Price might have intuited, but didn't know, that the rose hip tea he drank every day while in Africa helped preserved his health and bring him back home alive to marry Julia. And of course, it was not unhealthy vapours which were striking down Europeans in Africa, it was mosquito-borne viruses, but this would not be established for another ninety years.

The pay clerk who gives William Price the money to rush to Northamptonshire is John Dickens, Charles Dickens' father.

A note about vocabulary and spelling: I have sometimes chosen to use the modern term instead of the historically accurate one, to avoid confusion. During the time period in which this novel is set, the word "fiancé" was not in use, and people referred to their relatives by marriage, that is, a sister or brother or daughter-in-law as their sister or brother or daughter, without the 'in-law.' I resisted the urge to spell "clues" as "clews." Kru, the African tribesmen who assisted William Price and the abolitionists, were also called "Kroo." The visitors' gallery at the Houses of Parliament was referred to as the strangers' gallery. I have tried to adhere to British spelling and idioms.

DRAMATIS PERSONAE

Persons in bold face are real persons. Persons in italics are characters originally created by Jane Austen. The rest are fictional characters created for this variation.

At Thornton Lacey
Edmund Bertram, a clergyman and second son of Sir Thomas Bertram
Julia Bertram, his sister
Mrs. Peckover, the housekeeper

At Mansfield Village
David, Lord Delingpole, peer of the realm and influential Tory
Imogen, Lady Delingpole, a leading Tory hostess
James, Viscount Lynnon, their son and heir
Baddeley, the butler at Mansfield Park
Mrs. Norris, aunt to the Bertrams
Dr. Grant, clergyman
Mrs. Grant, his wife, half-sister to Mary Crawford Bertram

At Stoke Newington
Fanny Price, cousin to the Bertrams, now living with,
Mrs. Harriet Butters, a brusque but kindly widow and philanthropist
Madame Orly, her lady's maid
Mrs. McIntosh, her housekeeper
Mr. Donald McIntosh, her coachman
Mr. George Butters, her son, a solicitor
Cecilia Butters, her daughter-in-law, an ardent horsewoman
Ethelinda, Rosamunde and Isabella, their three young daughters

Mr. James Stephen, member of parliament, lawyer and abolitionist and neighbour

At Camden Town

Mrs. Blodgett, sister-in-law to Mrs. Butters, manager of the Sewing Academy

Mr. Blodgett and Master Horace Blodgett, her husband and son

Mr. Frederick Edifice, a curate

Young students of the sewing academy

Eliza (Mary) Bellingham, a milliner with mysterious family problems

At London

John Price, Fanny's younger brother, a clerk at the Thames River Police Station in Wapping

Mr. William Gibson, writer and admirer of Fanny Price

Mary Crawford Bertram, estranged wife of Edmund Bertram

Janet Fraser, a fashionable lady and friend to Mary Bertram

Margaret Fraser, her unwanted step-daughter

Mr. Nathaniel Meriwether, a very eligible widower

John Bellingham, a businessman with a grudge

Spencer Perceval, the prime minister

Mrs. Jane Perceval, his wife and the mother of his 12 children

John Harriott, founder and magistrate of the Thames River Police Office

Mr. Norton, police officer of the Thames River Police Office

Henry Laing, head judicial clerk of the Thames River Police Office

Lord Elsham, an admirer of Mary Crawford Bertram

George Gordon, Lord Byron, poet and member of the House of Lords

Lord Brougham, politician

In Africa and Gibraltar

William Price, brother to Fanny Price, admirer of Julia Bertram

Captain Columbine, his commanding officer

Jane (Mary) Columbine, wife to Captain Columbine

Captain Frederick Irby, another commanding officer

Ruth, a devout and respectable Negress

Admiral and Mrs. Croft

At Portsmouth

Mr. Price, a disabled lieutenant of marines

Mrs. Frances Price, his wife, sister to Mrs. Norris and Lady Bertram

Susan and Betsey Price, their daughters

Charles Price, their youngest son still at home

Mr. Dickens, clerk at the Naval Pay Office

At Everingham, in Norfolk

Sir Thomas Bertram, baronet, who, owing to a severe financial setback, is currently living with his daughter,

Mrs. Maria Crawford, widow of Henry Crawford, daughter to Sir Thomas and

Lady Maria Bertram, wife of Sir Thomas

Henry Crawford (Junior) Maria's young son

As well—mentioned in the book

Mr. Rivers, Sir Thomas Bertram's steward

Mrs. Renfrew, Matron at the Sewing Academy

Richard Owen, a curate, and his three accomplished sisters, one a beauty

Mrs. Owen, their mother

Sam and Tom Price, additional Price sons

Lucy Gregory and her sisters, flirtatious girls of Portsmouth

Mrs. Priscilla Wakefield, noted philanthropist and author

Mr. Wilbraham Bootle, MP and abolitionist

Percy Bysshe Shelley, a poet and idealist

The victims of the Ratcliffe Highway murders
John Williams, the accused killer
Lord Castlereagh, a Tory politician
Lord Mulgrave, First Lord of the Admiralty
George, the Prince Regent
Peter Finerty, a journalist imprisoned for libel (criticising the government)
Sarah Wilberforce, second wife of James Stephen
Sailors, freed slaves and Kru tribesmen
Magistrates, police officers, clerks of the Wapping area
Various servants, charitable ladies, friends, etc.

AFTERWORD: THE MERITS OF
MANSFIELD PARK

THERE ONCE LIVED, in the small village of Steventon, a lively and precocious girl, the daughter of an intelligent and well-educated clergyman. She was one of a large family, mostly boys, and she grew up in a household where reading and discussing books was an everyday activity. Just about everyone in the family enjoyed writing—they wrote letters, charades (what we would think of as riddles), poetry, editorials, plays, and stories, and they enjoyed sharing what they had written with one another.

Young Jane loved reading novels, but she laughed at their excessive sentimentality and their improbable plot contrivances; the unrestrained villainy of the villains, and the impossibly virtuous heroes and heroines. When she finished laughing at these things, she said to herself, "I can do better than this." And she was right.

At first, she wrote satiric little pieces to entertain herself and her family; as she grew older she wrote several full-length novels, but did not seriously attempt to put them out into the world until she was in her thirties. *Sense & Sensibility* (1811) and *Pride & Prejudice* (1813) were well-received, but there were other authors, even female authors, who out-sold and out-earned her by a considerable margin, and one of these was Hannah More.

More's 1809 novel, *Coelebs in Search of a Wife*, was a best-seller. It tells the story of Charles, a young man looking for a good, well-educated, and pious wife.

There is very little plot or action; most of the novel consists of long conversations dominated by wise, pious Mr. Stanley, (the father of the girl who will marry Charles) and he is preoccupied with the virtues and vices of his neighbours, his acquaintances, and his daughters, and how everyone ought to live their lives and raise their children.

So, just imagine: you are Jane Austen, your books have sold well, but not spectacularly, and you have read *Coelebs*, because your sister Cassandra recommended it, and you know it sold like hotcakes, and you think, between snorts of derision and eye-rolling, "I can do better than this!"

Professor Mary Waldron and other scholars have argued that *Mansfield Park* is the answer to *Coelebs in Search of a Wife* and other conduct novels. Understanding the genre of the "conduct book" and the "conduct novel," helps us to understand *Mansfield Park*, and understand why Austen's third published novel is significantly different from her other works.

It was once a truth universally acknowledged that parents had a moral duty to raise their children to be industrious, virtuous, charitable, and pious, and that doing so would prepare their offspring for a happy and useful life on earth and salvation thereafter.

Parents were expected to examine and develop the character and personality traits of their children. For example, Austen's parents said of their daughters: 'Cassandra had the merit of having her temper always under command, but that Jane had the happiness of a temper that never required to be commanded.'"

Or we may recall Mrs. Morland in *Northanger Abbey*, afraid that her daughter Catherine has "been spoilt for home by great acquaintance," because of her time in Bath. She hurries upstairs to find an improving essay in *The Mirror*, "anxious to lose no time in attacking so dreadful a malady." Parents like Mrs. Morland would often turn to written essays with which to exhort their children.

A conduct book, such as Fordyce's *Sermons to Young Women*, with which Mr. Collins bores Lydia in *Pride & Prejudice*, was typically a book of essays, sometimes written in letter form, giving advice on how to conduct one's life. The topics included good manners, education, forming friendships, courtship and so on.

Other examples of popular conduct books for young ladies are: *Essays on Various Subjects Principally Designed for Young Ladies*, by Hannah More, and *A Father's Legacy to his Daughters*, by Dr. John Gregory. These books were best-sellers.

No doubt they were often purchased by older relations and godparents for the young girls in their lives. Perhaps they were gifted more often than they were actually read, but at any rate, Hannah More died a wealthy woman!

While we are don't read these conduct books today, young ladies of the long eighteenth century, such as Jane Austen, were quite familiar with them. She pokes fun at their serious tone with Mary Bennet in *Pride & Prejudice*:

> *"Pride," observed Mary, who piqued herself upon the solidity of her reflections, "is a very common failing, I believe. By all that I have ever read, I am convinced that it is very common indeed; that human nature is particularly prone to it, and that there are very few of us who do not cherish a feeling of self-complacency on the score of some quality or other, real or imaginary. Vanity and pride are different things, though the words are often used synonymously. A person may be proud without being vain. Pride relates more to our opinion of ourselves, vanity to what we would have others think of us."*

We know that when Mary is speaking, her sisters—Kitty and Lydia at least—are rolling their eyes.

Mary might have gotten her ideas from *Letters on the Improvement of the Mind, Addressed to a Young Lady* by Hester Chapone, which explains that "pride is a high opinion of oneself," while vanity is to be anxious for "the admiration of others."

A conduct novel like *Coelebs* takes the moral lessons of the conduct book and places them into the mouths of characters in a novel, who embody various virtues, vices and sins. *Coelebs* marries Dr. Stanley's virtuous daughter at the end of the novel.

In another conduct novel, *The Two Cousins*, by Elizabeth Pinchard (1798), a spoilt young city cousin comes to live with her intelligent, good-hearted and virtuous country cousin, and is reformed.

Unlike *Coelebs* or *Two Cousins*, *Mansfield Park* is a conduct novel which tells its moral lessons in a realistic setting with exquisite prose and compelling dialogue. And, unlike the conduct novels in which the characters are little more than animated points of view, a device with which to address the reader, *Mansfield*

Park's characters are unique and well-rounded. Lady Bertram neglects the upbringing of her children and Mrs. Norris is an avaricious, judgmental, busybody. Maria Bertram marries a man she doesn't love. Henry Crawford tries to reform himself and win Fanny's love, but falls back in to his old seductive ways. Edmund Bertram, for a time, is beguiled by the witty but superficial Mary Crawford.

There are some passages in Austen which echo some of the popular conduct novels. In *The Two Cousins*, there is a scene where the virtuous mother and her young daughter talk over the rude language of a spoilt little girl at a dinner party. *"Oh indeed yes, Mama,"* exclaims little Constantia. *"I was quite astonished to hear Miss Selwyn use such an expression!"*

After a dinner party at *Mansfield Park*, Edmund and Fanny discuss Mary Crawford:

"But was there nothing in her conversation that struck you, Fanny, as not quite right?"

"Oh yes! she ought not to have spoken of her uncle as she did. I was quite astonished."

Elsewhere, the loving mother of *The Two Cousins* advises her niece: "Own your conviction, my dear Alicia, and you will have gained a great victory over your *pride and prejudice*, [emphasis added] for which you are not so blameable as your education and companions."

An abiding preoccupation in conduct novels was the proper education of girls. In *Coelebs*, the topic is canvassed several times; the speakers lament the superficial education being given to young girls in England at that time, with its emphasis upon "accomplishments" instead of solid education or even practical home economics, to say nothing of a good moral education.

Conduct novels generally have very little humour or wit, but in this wry passage in *Mansfield Park*, Jane Austen shows, rather than tells us, that the young Bertram girls are receiving much information, but very little self-awareness, in their education:

"...[M]y cousin cannot put the map of Europe together— or my cousin cannot tell the principal rivers in Russia—or, she never heard of Asia Minor—or she does not know the difference between water-colours and crayons!—How strange!—Did you ever hear anything so stupid?"

"My dear," their considerate aunt would reply, "it is very bad, but you must not expect everybody to be as forward and quick at learning as yourself."

"But, aunt, she is really so very ignorant... How long ago it is, aunt, since we used to repeat the chronological order of the kings of England, with the dates of their accession, and most of the principal events of their reigns!"

"Yes," added the other; "and of the Roman emperors as low as Severus; besides a great deal of the heathen mythology, and all the metals, semi-metals, planets, and distinguished philosophers."

"Very true indeed, my dears, but you are blessed with wonderful memories, and your poor cousin has probably none at all. There is a vast deal of difference in memories, as well as in everything else, and therefore you must make allowance for your cousin, and pity her deficiency. And remember that, if you are ever so forward and clever yourselves, you should always be modest; for, much as you know already, there is a great deal more for you to learn."

"Yes, I know there is, till I am seventeen..."

In *An Enquiry into the Duties of the Female Sex* (1797), Thomas Gisborne strongly discouraged young ladies from participating in amateur theatricals; it encouraged vanity, and "unrestrained familiarity with the other sex." Jane Austen makes masterful use of the "dangerous intimacy" of the amateur theatricals at *Mansfield Park*.

Or here is Hannah More, moralizing about household management and small-minded women:

Economy, such as I would inculcate, and which every woman, in every station of life, is called upon to practise, is not merely the petty detail of small daily expenses, the shabby curtailments and stinted parsimony of a little mind, operating on little things; but it is the exercise of sound judgment... the narrow minded vulgar economist is... perpetually bespeaking your pity for her labours and your praise for her exertions; she is afraid you will not see how much she is harassed. Little wants and trivial operations engross her whole soul.

At the beginning of that paragraph, we have Mrs. Norris. At the end, we have her sister, Mrs. Price. Jane Austen illustrates these faults through her characters, showing rather than telling.

Hester Chapone warned against forming friendships with those who are not devout: "The woman who thinks lightly of sacred things, or is ever heard to speak of them with levity or indifference, cannot reasonably be expected to pay a more serious regard to the laws of friendship…"

Austen brings this woman to life in Mary Crawford, who Austen describes as "careless as a woman and as a friend," laughing and joking in the chapel at Sotherton.

In the concluding chapters of *Mansfield Park*, Sir Thomas Bertram comes to realize that he has failed in his moral duty as a parent:

> *He feared that principle, active principle, had been wanting; that [his daughters Maria and Julia] had never been properly taught to govern their inclinations and tempers by that sense of duty which can alone suffice. They had been instructed theoretically in their religion, but never required to bring it into daily practice. To be distinguished for elegance and accomplishments, the authorised object of their youth, could have had no useful influence that way, no moral effect on the mind. He had meant them to be good, but his cares had been directed to the understanding and manners, not the disposition; and of the necessity of self-denial and humility, he feared they had never heard from any lips that could profit them.*

> *Bitterly did he deplore a deficiency which now he could scarcely comprehend to have been possible. Wretchedly did he feel, that with all the cost and care of an anxious and expensive education, he had brought up his daughters without their understanding their first duties, or his being acquainted with their character and temper.*

(For many modern readers, the fact that Sir Thomas is a slave-owner annihilates any virtues he may have as a husband and father—but Austen doesn't devote any time in her book to castigating Sir Thomas for owning slaves; he is examined and found wanting as a parent.)

Mansfield Park contains contradictions and tensions and subtleties that you won't find in a conduct novel. Conduct books feature at least one wise, benevolent, loving adult to dispense advice: Marmee in *Little Women* is an example, in *Coelebs* it's Dr. Stanley. The person in *Mansfield Park* who thinks of herself as being all-knowing, wise and benevolent is Mrs. Norris!

And then there is Edmund Bertram. He comes the closest to being the moral arbiter in the novel; he makes the most moral pronouncements about the behaviour of others. He is to be a clergyman, and elevate his parishioners through precept and example.

But, unlike the all-wise, all-seeing Dr. Stanley, Edmund deceives himself through the entire novel: he is blind to Fanny's love for him, and he makes excuses for Mary Crawford because he is attracted to her.

Fanny Price is surely intended to be the embodiment of what a young lady should be, according to the conduct books.

Lucilla Stanley, the heroine of *Coelebs*, is modest, retiring, hides her intelligence and her education, is demure in company, fastidious, charitable, and devout. The hero says of her, "of repartee she has little, and dislikes it in others." (Mary Crawford wouldn't be welcome in the Stanley household!) Like Fanny, she blushes if anyone so much as looks at her. Like Fanny, she is tender-hearted.

Yet, when Edmund urges Fanny to "be the perfect model of a woman which I have always believed you born for," and accept Henry Crawford's marriage proposal, she refuses: "Oh! never, never, never! he never will succeed with me." She is answering to a higher principle by refusing to marry a man she can neither love nor respect.

Another startling difference between *Mansfield Park* and *Coelebs* and *Two Cousins*, is that in the conduct novels, someone (a neglectful husband and a spoilt girl, respectively) is saved from their dissolute ways by the steadfast Christian example of a virtuous person. But as Professor Mary Waldron pointed out, "*Mansfield Park* deliberately rejects this stereotype; good example fails to avert a shipwreck." Henry Crawford explicitly asks Fanny for advice and guidance when he visits her in Portsmouth, and she refuses him:

"I advise! You know very well what is right," (says Fanny.)
"Yes. When you give me your opinion, I always know what is right. Your judgment is my rule of right."
"Oh, no! do not say so. We have all a better guide in ourselves, if we would attend to it, than any other person can be. Good-bye; I wish you a pleasant journey to-morrow."

That short exchange, Professor Waldron writes, is "the pivot upon which the novel finally hums towards its calamitous conclusion."

Henry goes to London and starts flirting again with Maria, rather than going to his estate and sorting out his corrupt manager; leading to, says Waldron, the "almost unmitigated disaster of the ending," with severe consequences for Maria Bertram Rushworth, and Edmund and Fanny marry, and a great many readers of Mansfield Park left unsatisfied and unconvinced.

Perhaps Jane Austen rejected the idea of Fanny 'saving' Henry Crawford as unrealistic. Perhaps she thought Henry Crawford was responsible for saving himself.

In conclusion, some familiarity with conduct books and conduct novels helps us understand the context in which *Mansfield Park* was written. I think the evidence is strong that Austen intended to write a new type of conduct novel; one with real, believable characters struggling with moral dilemmas and with an actual plot, rather than a series of parables or anecdotes.

In *Mansfield Park*, Austen knew she had written something important, something different, something rich and complex, and she was disappointed with the lack of response to it. Certainly *Mansfield Park* didn't challenge the sales of the conduct novels. No newspapers or journals reviewed it, unlike her previous novels.

But today, even as the least-popular of her novels, *Mansfield Park* has acquired a fame and immortality greater than all of the conduct novels of her day, put together.

More Reading:

Waldron, Mary. "The Frailties of Fanny: Mansfield Park and the Evangelical Movement," in *Eighteenth-Century Fiction* 6 (1994): 259–81

A Synopsis of *Mansfield Park*

A brief synopsis of Mansfield Park *is provided here for anyone who hasn't read this great novel.* A Contrary Wind *and* A Marriage of Attachment *can be read without having read* Mansfield Park, *but I recommend that you read Austen's powerful, subtle, and beautifully written novel. My novels frequently reference scenes and dialogue in the original novel, so knowledge of the original will enhance the enjoyment of my variations.*

Sir Thomas Bertram is a wealthy baronet with four handsome children, two girls and two boys. His estate, Mansfield Park, is in Northamptonshire, north of London. His wife was one of three sisters—she made a brilliant marriage when she snagged the baronet; her older sister, Mrs. Norris, married the neighbourhood clergyman. The third sister, Mrs. Price, married beneath her; she wed a lieutenant of marines and lives in squalor in Portsmouth with her husband, now disabled for active duty, and a large brood of children.

Mrs. Norris proposes to Sir Thomas that he take in one of the poor Price children to help that struggling family (this is so she may have the credit of being benevolent without any of the expense); he agrees, and awkward, timid little Fanny Price, aged ten, comes to live in the great mansion. She is overawed by everything and everyone, and only her cousin Edmund, the younger of the two Bertram boys, pays any attention to her or shows her kindness.

Lady Bertram is remarkable for her indolence and inactivity, so by default, the management of her household and the raising of her children has been taken up by Mrs. Norris, childless and widowed, who is a judgmental, self-important, miserly busybody. Fanny is particularly bullied by Aunt Norris. The novel shows us numerous scenes in which Fanny is established as the Cinderella of the household. Fanny is shy, humble and passive, but she is also very morally upright. Thanks to Edmund, she learns to love poetry and reading, and becomes an enthusiast for the sublimity of Nature. She grows up to be totally devoted to him and secretly in love. (This was at a time when first cousins could marry each other).

Sir Thomas must leave Mansfield Park to attend to his "plantations" in Antigua (that is, he is a slave-owner who owns sugar plantations, a very considerable source of wealth for England at this time) and he is away for almost two years. During his absence, his oldest daughter, Maria, becomes engaged to the wealthy but dim-witted Mr. Rushworth, who owns a large estate known as Sotherton. Then two new characters appear—pretty, witty and charming Mary Crawford, and her flirtatious brother Henry. They are the half-brother and half-sister of Mrs. Grant, wife to the local clergyman.

Mary Crawford first thinks that Tom Bertram, the older son and heir to the Bertram estate, might be worthy of her hand in marriage but finds herself, unaccountably, falling for the quieter and more serious Edmund. When she learns that Edmund is going to become a clergyman, she tries to forget about him, as she—an heiress who used to the glamor of London society—has no interest in being a clergyman's wife in some quiet country village. Meanwhile, Maria and Julia both fall under the spell of the captivating Henry Crawford. Fanny observes this dangerous situation, but worse, also has the heartache of watching Edmund fall in love with Mary.

Mr. Yates, a friend of Tom Bertram's, comes for a visit. He has just come from another stately home where a scheme to put on a play was disrupted by the death of a relative of one of the amateur players. His enthusiasm for play-acting inspires Tom, his sisters, and the Crawfords, who decide they will entertain themselves by putting on a play.

This strikes Edmund and Fanny as disrespectful to Sir Thomas, especially considering that the play chosen, *Lovers' Vows* (a real play available to read on the internet) is about a woman who is seduced and has an illegitimate child, and it contains a rather saucy soubrette. Sir Thomas would not want his virginal daughters portraying women like this. (This was at a time when professional actresses were socially at the level of courtesans.)

The others disregard Edmund's warnings, and set about casting the parts of the play. The play has two storylines—one melodramatic and one comic. Both Maria and Julia want to play the dramatic part of Agatha, but there can only be one; Maria is chosen—she will play scenes with Henry Crawford (who is playing the part of her son, not her lover) and jealous Julia vows she will have nothing to do with the play. Mr. Yates will play the sadder but wiser Baron who regrets having seduced Agatha in his youth; plodding Mr. Rushworth is miscast as Count Cassel, an over-the-top Don Juan who boasts of his conquests; Tom Bertram will play the Butler, a comic relief character who comments on the action of the play in rhyming verse, and petite, sprightly Mary Crawford is well cast as the saucy Amelia in the comic storyline.

Edmund at first resists Mary's urgings to take the role of her lover in the play, but he soon succumbs, to Fanny's dismay. The rehearsals commence, and Henry and Maria are brought in to a "dangerous intimacy" which even the thick-headed Rushworth eventually notices. But the unexpected early return of Sir Thomas from Antigua puts an end to the play. Maria expects and hopes Henry Crawford will declare himself but to her anger, he leaves Mansfield and she realizes he's been toying with her affections. She goes ahead and marries Rushworth to get out of her stifling family home and to show Henry Crawford that he has not wounded her.

Henry returns to Mansfield later that year, but Mansfield Park is very different with both Maria and Julia gone (Julia has accompanied Maria—it was then a common practice for brides to bring a female companion along on the honeymoon). Crawford decides to pass the time by "making a small hole" in Fanny Price's heart. He tells Mary of his schemes and she only half-heartedly protests against toying with the impressionable girl's affections. But when he starts really paying attention to Fanny, he recognizes her virtues and he falls in love with her!

To help win her love, he asks his uncle the Admiral to wrangle a promotion to lieutenant for Fanny's brother William. Fanny is overjoyed by the news but shocked by Henry's subsequent marriage proposal. At first, she thinks he is playing a cruel joke.

When Henry applies to Sir Thomas for his blessing, Sir Thomas is astonished to hear from Fanny that she refused the proposal. She tries to explain that Henry and she are incompatible, but she refrains from explaining just how improperly Maria and Julia behaved with Henry Crawford. Sir Thomas decides that Fanny is being foolish to turn down such an eligible young man and to punish her, he sends to her visit her family in Portsmouth, so she can see for herself what poverty is like.

Meanwhile, Edmund has become a clergyman and he dithers over whether to propose to Mary Crawford, fearing she will refuse him.

Fanny's stay in Portsmouth is described in some of Austen's most powerful and evocative language. Henry Crawford visits her there to continue his courtship of her. But when he leaves, instead of going to his estates and sorting out his corrupt land steward, he goes back to London, meets up with Maria (now Mrs. Rushworth) and is stung by her coldness toward him. He can't resist the challenge of making her fall in love with him again.

He and Maria are caught in a compromising position by a family servant and they elope together. This shocking news reaches Fanny in Portsmouth, as well as word that her cousin Tom is gravely ill. Edmund comes to fetch her home to Mansfield.

Fanny learns from Edmund that he met with Mary in London to discuss Maria and Henry's disgrace and was utterly shocked and repulsed by Mary's sophisticated and casual attitude toward their behaviour. "No harsher name than folly given!" He realizes that Mary is not the woman he thought she was, and he rejects her, to her surprise and chagrin.

Austen wraps up the story by telling us that Fanny's younger sister Susan comes to be Lady Bertram's new companion in Mansfield Park, Tom recovers from his illness and becomes a more sensible young man, Rushworth divorces Maria, Maria leaves Henry Crawford, who has refused to marry her, and is banished to live out her days in a remote cottage with Aunt Norris, Mary Crawford continues her gay life in London but carries a torch for Edmund, and Edmund falls in love with Fanny and marries her.

Fanny, once the neglected Cinderella, becomes the emotional and moral centre of the Bertram family, the upholder of virtue, stability, and moral courage.

DISCUSSION QUESTIONS

QUESTIONS FOR
MANSFIELD PARK

Mansfield Park and Slavery

Sir Thomas Bertram, the patriarch of Mansfield Park, owns slave plantations in Antigua. (At the time the book was written, the slave trade had been outlawed but English people still owned slaves). Here is the one and only direct reference to slavery in the book:

> "Your uncle is disposed to be pleased with you [Fanny] in every respect; [says Edmund] and I only wish you would talk to him more. You are one of those who are too silent in the evening circle."
>
> "But I do talk to him more than I used. I am sure I do. Did not you hear me ask him about the slave-trade last night?" [answers Fanny]
>
> "I did—and was in hopes the question would be followed up by others. It would have pleased your uncle to be inquired of farther."
>
> "And I longed to do it—but there was such a dead silence! And while my cousins were sitting by without speaking a word, or seeming at all interested in the subject, I did not like—I thought it would appear as if I wanted to set myself off at their expense, by shewing a curiosity and pleasure in his information which he must wish his own daughters to feel."

Some people have contended that *Mansfield Park* is an anti-slave tract in disguise; that the name Mansfield is a reference to Lord Mansfield, [a justice whose ruling outlawed slavery in the British Isles] and Norris is the name of a notoriously cruel slave-owner. No commentary from Austen herself survives to confirm or deny this supposition.

Do you think that Austen intended a message about slavery? Do you think it's a minor reference in passing, or is there an important, but hidden, message in the novel?

What information could Fanny have taken "pleasure" in? The news that slavery would die out? Or that slavery was continuing despite the ban?

Do you think Jane Austen was the sort of author who planted hidden messages in her novels, or are modern critics finding what they want to see (messages about slavery, women's emancipation, class warfare, etc.)?

For some people, the fact that Sir Thomas is a slave-owner means that he cannot be viewed as anything but an absolute villain. Is this a modern revisiting of history or did Jane Austen also intend for him to be seen as a villain? Does he play the role of a villain in the book? How does Jane Austen portray him in the book? What are his flaws? Does he have strengths and good qualities?

Fanny Price: heroine or wimp?

Fanny Price is a much-debated topic among Jane Austen devotees. She is unarguably the least popular Austen heroine. Why is that?

Fanny Price is often described as a sort of little Miss Goody Two-Shoes. Does she always behave impeccably? What about her jealousy of Mary Crawford, her refusal to return Mary Crawford's friendship? What about when she refuses to give Henry Crawford advice as to whether he should go back to Everingham and help his poor tenants?

CS Lewis, the noted British writer and critic, felt that Fanny Price did not work as a heroine. She is "insipid." He says this of her in his 1954 essay, "A Note on Jane Austen":

One of the most dangerous of literary ventures is the little, shy, unimportant heroine whom none of the other characters value. The danger is that your readers may agree with the other characters. Something must be put into the heroine to make us feel that the other characters are wrong, that she contains depths they never dreamed of.... In Anne [Elliot of Persuasion*], Jane Austen did succeed. Her passion (for it is not less), her insight, her maturity, her prolonged fortitude, all attract us. But into Fanny, Jane Austen, to counterbalance her apparent*

325

insignificance, has put really nothing except rectitude of mind; neither passion, nor physical courage, nor wit, nor resource.

What is your reaction to her? Is there some element that CS Lewis lists above, that you would want to add to her character? Or is she past saving? Given the high esteem with which Jane Austen is held as a skilled writer, do you regard *Mansfield Park* as an experiment which didn't quite work out, or is it an under-appreciated masterpiece?

Mrs. Norris

Mrs. Norris was described by Austen scholar Tony Tanner as "the most plausibly odious" villain in fiction, in other words, she is a believable villain, not a cartoon villain. Do you agree? What makes her plausible, or is anything she does or says "over-the-top"? What is your understanding of Mrs. Norris's motives? What makes her tick, in other words? Why is she so miserable to Fanny?

What were the consequences of the combination of Lady Bertram's lethargy and Mrs. Norris busy-body attitude, to the household in *Mansfield Park*?

The Bertrams

Maria and Julia Bertram have grown up in the isolation of the countryside. They have been to Northampton, but not to London. They are considered to be the belles of their small social circle. How does this circumstance affect the way they view themselves, their own goals and wishes, and how does it affect their reaction to the arrival of Henry Crawford in their midst?

The tone of *Mansfield Park*

Although *Mansfield Park* has comedic moments, it is the most dramatic and darkest of Austen's completed novels. Does this darker tone come as a surprise from the author of *Pride & Prejudice* and *Northanger Abbey*?

Compare the outcomes for the villains in *Pride & Prejudice* or *Sense & Sensibility* or even *Persuasion*, with the fates of Maria Rushworth, Mrs. Norris and Henry Crawford in *Mansfield Park*. Their bad deeds have serious consequences, whereas Wickham seduces Lydia in *Pride & Prejudice* and is bribed into marrying her. In *Sense & Sensibility*, Lucy Steele marries a wealthy man.

Does *Mansfield Park* have a moral? Do other Austen novels have a moral lesson?

The Crawfords

In Henry and Mary Crawford, Austen created two witty, charismatic, attractive characters who are much livelier than Fanny Price and Edmund Bertram. Some have compared Mary Crawford to Elizabeth Bennet. Some people feel that Mary Crawford should be the heroine of *Mansfield Park*, not Fanny. How are we supposed to feel about her, and the world that she represents?

Dramatically speaking, was it an error for Austen to have created such attractive counterparts to the hero and heroine?

Austen writes that if Henry Crawford had "persevered" in his courtship of Fanny and reformed his character, "Fanny must have been his reward, and a reward very voluntarily bestowed, within a reasonable period from Edmund's marrying Mary." In other words, if he had behaved himself, he would have won Fanny's hand in marriage.

Do you believe Fanny could ever have married Henry Crawford? Do you believe that he sincerely loved Fanny? Could she have reformed him? Would he have stayed faithful to her and would they have had a happy marriage?

Changing Social Mores

A group of young people, passing the rainy weeks of autumn together in "a dull country house," decide to entertain themselves by staging a play. So what's so wrong about that, as the critic Lionel Trilling asks rhetorically in his 1954 essay? Is this aspect of the novel difficult for modern readers to understand; is it difficult to pick up on the "dangerous intimacy" that the play creates? What might be a modern equivalent, that would shock the sensibilities of a today's reader?

What about the things that Mary Crawford does—speak wittily but disrespectfully of her uncle, make fun of the Church— would they shock somebody at a dinner party today? Would she be considered to be morally deficient? Is there anything she says that you find genuinely shocking or distasteful?

Also, what would be the social outcome today for a woman who left her husband and ran off with another man within a year of her marriage?

QUESTIONS FOR
A CONTRARY WIND

Fanny Price, an intelligent but timid girl from a poor family, lives at Mansfield Park with her wealthy cousins. But the cruelty of her Aunt Norris, together with a broken heart, compel Fanny to run away and take a job as a governess. Far away from everything she ever knew and the man she secretly loves, will Fanny grow in strength and confidence? Will a new suitor help her to forget her past? Or will a reckless decision ruin her life and the lives of those she holds most dear?

This variation of Jane Austen's novel includes all the familiar characters from Jane Austen's Mansfield Park, and some new acquaintances as well. There are some mature scenes and situations not suitable for all readers.

The actions of Maria Bertram

Given the emphasis placed upon chastity before marriage for unmarried girls from good families, and given the way young ladies were closely supervised, do you think that seductions and elopements were next-to-impossible, or do you think that people are people, capable of being swept away by passion, back then, just as they are today?

The maturation of Fanny Price

Fanny Price's upbringing was even more isolated than her cousins, because she was not invited to go on outings or to balls. Given her extreme isolation, is it any wonder that she is socially naïve? What are the tendencies of her character before she runs away? How does she change in personality after she runs away from Mansfield Park? What does she observe and what does she learn?

Also, she is only eighteen years old when she runs away. Are most people fully-formed and realized adults at this stage? Do people take longer to grow up nowadays, as opposed to the past?

Fanny's relationship with Edmund

Edmund Bertram is described in Mansfield Park as having shaped Fanny's mind. His influence over her is profound. Is there a bad aspect to this? Apart from the cousin-marrying-cousin thing, is there anything objectionable in their relationship? Or are they two truly compatible people who are destined to come together?

If you have read both *Mansfield Park* and *A Contrary Wind*...

Which characters change the least, between the two novels? Which characters change the most?

For Janeites

How many passages of Jane Austen did you spot embedded in the text? What references or allusions to *Mansfield Park* or other Austen novels did you notice?

QUESTIONS FOR
A MARRIAGE OF ATTACHMENT

Faults and virtues

Before Jane Austen, most novelists (for example Samuel Richardson), created heroines who were pictures of perfection and virtue. Jane Austen laughed at this as being unrealistic. "Pictures of perfection... make me sick and wicked," she famously said. She created heroines with faults. Emma and Elizabeth Bennet misjudge people. Marianne is too emotional and sentimental.

Describe Fanny or Julia as they appear in *A Marriage of Attachment*. Do they have faults? What are they? Do they grow and change during the novel or are they essentially the same people throughout the novel?

Marriage tips

A lot of characters demonstrate different attitudes towards love and marriage in *A Marriage of Attachment*. What is Janet Fraser's attitude? Lady Delingpole's? William Price's? Whose opinion is the closest to your own? Is there some comment you particularly agree or disagree with? What advice would you give to a couple thinking about getting married today?

The risks of marriage

Married women had few legal protections. Their children belonged to their husband, as did their wages. It is estimated that the mortality rate during childbirth was about 7.5 out of 1000. Three of Jane Austen's sisters-in-law died in childbirth. On the other hand, staying unmarried meant a lifetime of looking after your relatives, as Cassandra and Jane Austen did, and probably being poor as well. If you were a woman of those times, which life would you prefer?

The risks of "free love"

Why were the social consequences so dire for "fallen" women in Regency times? What has changed for women since that time, and why? Why is there still a double standard as regards male and female promiscuity?

The rituals of mourning

We no longer have many of the rituals of mourning, such as wearing black for a certain number of months after the loss of a relative. What are the advantages to these rituals? Why do we not observe them any more today?

Fanny's future

Fanny, unlike most genteel ladies of her day, has worked as a governess and as a sewing instructor, and she has discovered that she likes earning her own money. Do you think she would go on wanting to earn her own money, or will she be content to be a housewife, if she gets married?

Do you think Fanny will be happy married to William Gibson? Or do you wish she could end up with Edmund? Or with someone else? Or stay single?

For Janeites

How many passages of Jane Austen did you spot embedded in the text? What references or allusions to *Mansfield Park* or other Austen novels did you notice?

BONUS EXCERPT:
A GIRL CALLED FOOTE

If you enjoyed *A Marriage of Attachment*, allow me to introduce another writer I hope you'll enjoy. A.E. Walnofer's tale of a servant girl and her unconventional employer, both struggling with the constraints imposed upon them by society, has freshness, energy, and engaging historical detail.

Here is the beginning of her historical romance, *A Girl Called Foote*, which is available on Amazon:

1: Frightening a Maid

~ Jonathan, age 8
Whitehall

It was not an unusual occurrence for Jonathan Clyde to urinate into one of his home's many fireplaces. Nor was it unusual for one of the servants to walk into a room, sniff the air unhappily and decide that the baronet's son had urinated into the fireplace. What *was* unusual was for Jonathan to be caught in the distasteful act, and that is precisely what nearly happened one morning in late June at Whitehall.

On this particular day, he had been sitting on the library floor, drawing a picture inside of a difficultly-obtained copy of Sir Walter Scott's *Castle Dangerous*. The title had caught his eye as he had pulled various books from their places on the shelf and he thought he would do well to improve the volume through his own efforts.

Everyone knows that all the best books have pictures, he told himself, and besides, I'm the best artist in the family.

As his drawing of a soldier lighting a cannon developed, so did his need to empty his bladder. At times, if an appropriate vessel was available, Jonathan would relieve himself into it and leave it for Ploughman, the aging parlor maid, to empty when she made her rounds. Not seeing a suitable receptacle on hand on this day, Jonathan made his way to the fireplace and proceeded to urinate, drenching the dark, sooty cavity.

I'm wary not to hit the rug, he rationalized, *and the rest burns off when the fire's lit.*

At this moment, Ploughman entered the room. Had she not been bungling with an awkward and overloaded bucket of cleaning supplies, she likely would have seen Jonathan standing before the fireplace hurriedly fumbling with the front of his trousers. However, she was busy bumping into the doorjamb and keeping the tin of black from falling onto the floor. After settling her burden upon a table and straightening her cap, the slightly podgy woman selected a cloth and shuffled over to the bookshelves.

Is she going to climb the ladder? Jonathan wondered, peeking out from behind an upholstered chair. She'll snap any rung she steps on!

To his delight, he watched as the maid positioned the ill-fortuned ladder and ascended it, grunting as she climbed. Her left hand clutched the ladder's side as she started wiping down the top bookshelf with her right hand.

Jonathan felt a familiar rumbling in his lower gut and was struck with what most boys would consider an ingenious idea. Hoping Ploughman was thoroughly engrossed in her task, he quietly climbed onto the settee and positioned himself as if he was napping there. To increase the delicious absurdity of the situation, he stuck his thumb in his mouth as if he was sucking it. He watched Ploughman through barely opened eyes and waited until he felt assured of maximum output. Then, as loudly as he could, he expelled a prodigious amount of gas.

The result was fantastic.

Ploughman let out a cry and gripped the ladder as if her life depended on it. She whipped her head around, frantically looking over both shoulders. Her wild eyes settled on Jonathan who bit his thumb furiously, stifling his laughter.

Just as the fit passed, Jonathan sat up, yawning loudly as if newly awakened, looking as bright eyed and refreshed as he could.

"Why hullo, Ploughman," he said, stretching dramatically and rising from the settee.

"Master Jonathan." She nodded, dislodging her mob-cap from atop her head.

Ploughman resumed her dusting with as much dignity as a frightened woman atop a rickety ladder could as Jonathan casually sauntered out of the library, reining in the peals of laughter which threatened to escape.

Her face! Too bad Will didn't see it, he thought, though he would have likely laughed and ruined it.

2: Impressing Grown Men

~ *Lydia, age 7*
Hawthorne House

Ugh. He's telling that horrible story again.

Lydia tried not to glare at her father as she nibbled the sweet biscuit Mr. Farington had given her.

"She kicked me again, and me down there with my face near her backside. I reached out and swiped at her legs. She fell—BOOM!" John Smythe clapped his meaty hands together. "Just like that!"

"Fell a cow with one swipe, did you, Smythe?" Mr. Farington laughed wheezily. He was a very thin man who, Lydia had noticed, had difficulty opening heavy doors.

"How big was the cow, Father?" asked Lydia.

The broad man looked down at his daughter, the remnants of a prideful smile still on his face.

"What's that, Liddy?"

"Was it a full grown cow?" she asked.

Her father's face shifted uncertainly. "Uh, perhaps not…"

Lydia scrunched up her little nose affectedly and asked, "Wasn't that the calf that the knacker took away because you broke two of its legs?"

Both men looked at the girl who sat at the table, calmly examining the crumbling biscuit in her hand.

The face of the large, rough man broke into an embarrassed grin. He pulled on the scratchy collar of his shirt. "Lydia, you're blowing all the glory out of farming."

You oughtn't be telling stories of poor little broken-legged calves, Lydia countered silently.

"Ah, she's an intelligent young girl, Smythe. You can't inflate your stories with her around." Mr. Farington laughed and pushed the plate of biscuits closer to the farmer and his daughter.

"Sharp indeed, she is. You ought to hear her read," Farmer Smythe said, clapping his hand on Lydia's shoulder.

"Ah, you know your letters now, do you?" Mr. Farington asked, peering at Lydia through his spectacles, a kind smile on his face.

"Oh no, Farington! She's known letters since she was three. This one's reading words as long as your arm." He stuck out his own long, bulky appendage.

"Really?" The older man asked and stood up from the table. "I have some things from my teaching days. Let me go get one of them."

Farmer Smythe winked at his daughter who set down the biscuit.

She suppressed a smile, thinking, I shall surprise him as I do everyone.

A moment later Farington returned with a paddle shaped piece of wood and handed it to Lydia.

A thin layer of horn was tacked onto the paddle and words had been carefully scratched into its surface. Hiding her disappointment at the simplicity of the poem before her, Lydia determined to read with fluency and animation. She began:

"For want of a nail the shoe was lost.
For want of a shoe the horse was..."

"No, Farington, none of those silly hornbooks!" interrupted Farmer Smythe. "That book there. Hand that to her." He pointed at a thick brown volume resting on the far-end of the table.

"Wordsworth? Really, Smythe?" Mr. Farington smiled and lifted his eyebrows at Lydia. "Would you like to try to read some Wordsworth, Child?"

Lydia nodded, delicately brushing crumbs from her fingertips, thankful for once for her father's brashness.

"Very well." Farington cracked open the book. "Let's try the first stanza of *The Daffodils*. That's from here to here."

He held the book open before her, pointing out the first six lines with his crooked, aged index finger.

The book thunked to the table and Lydia pinned the pages down with her small hands, breathing in their distinctive wooden smell.

Even this looks rather easy, she thought.

Clearing her throat, she read:

"I wander'd lonely as a cloud
That floats on high o'er vales and hills,
When all at once I saw a crowd,
A host of golden daffodils;

Beside the lake, beneath the trees,
Fluttering and dancing in the breeze..."

Stanza after stanza she read, pausing only once at the word 'jocund' in the third stanza. She pronounced it with an 's' sound for the 'c'. Mr. Farington corrected her quietly as she internally vowed to never mispronounce it again.

"Excellent!" Mr. Farington cried, clapping his hands at the poem's conclusion.

"Thank you, sir," Lydia murmured as she began to flip through the pages. Settling on *The Thorn* she began to read silently.

"How old did you say she was, Smythe?"

"Only seven!"

"Truly, Smythe, for decades I was a schoolmaster, and very rarely did I hear a child of seven read with such ease and fluidity. Child?"

Lydia looked up from the book to see a pair of eyes glowing appreciatively at her.

"To such a reader as yourself, I open my library of books. Any book you want to borrow, you may. Just promise you will keep it safe as I love nothing as I love my books."

"Thank you, sir." Lydia smiled genuinely. She turned her eyes back to the open book before her as the conversation between the two men began anew.

3: Counting Windows

~ *Jonathan, age 9*
Whitehall

"12 and 13 for the blue parlor
14 and 15 for Papa's study
Just 16 for the drawing room as it only has one window…"

There was a slight chill in the air as the dazzling sunlight pained Jonathan's eyes. He sat in the crook of his favorite cherry tree, counting the windows of the building he called home. Having visited a few other stately homes, he knew Whitehall was impressive, not as large perhaps, but very grand.

Papa would often give tours to visitors though Mama insisted this should be done by the housekeeper as was done at other great homes.

"But no one knows the place as I do," Sir William would respond, a pleased glint in his eyes. "I know every inch of it and now that I've restored every rotunda and hidey-hole, I want to be the one to show it! Do you honestly think Old Smithy-Pot would be able to answer anyone's questions?"

At this, Lady Clyde would shake her head, though a little smile played on her lips.

Jonathan watched this slightly playful exchange between his parents quietly. It was a rare occurrence and made him feel pleasantly warm.

Old Smithy-Pot, he chuckled to himself, thinking of the dour housekeeper who frowned at him whenever she saw him sliding down the bannister.

He accompanied his father many times on these tours of the estate, silently anticipating when people would ask about this paneling or marvel at that chandelier. Always, the tour's climax was when Papa gathered the group at a specific spot in one of the upstairs hallways and surprised them all by moving a small writing desk. Doing so unblocked a small door in the wall. Once the group had ducked their heads and filed through it, they ascended a narrow staircase to emerge on Whitehall's roof within a belvedere. From there, one could see for miles to the northern rolling hills. The "Lake", which was really a large pond on the

Clyde's property, glinted in the sun. On the southern edge, past the forests and fields, the tallest buildings of Wexhall sprouted up toward the skies. Little villages dotted the landscape.

The guests would exclaim at the beauty of the expanse, squinting in the breeze which sometimes grew into an unpleasant gale, causing their eyes to tear.

Once as Jonathan stood alone in the hallway eyeing the desk, Sir William had come along. Kneeling down, Papa had firmly gripped Jonathan's arm and stared into his eyes. Speaking in a voice Jonathan had never heard before, Papa asked, "Remember how high the roof is, Jonathan? You would die if you fell from there. That's why I block the door with the desk. If you ever move it, I'll have Glaser beat you with a riding crop until the blood runs down your back."

As his father's fingers bit into Jonathan's arm, the little boy knew that he would never disobey the order. His stomach lurched at the idea that he had the power to open the small door and ascend the steep staircase up to the roof. He could do it, but he never would, especially since the notion of it transformed his father into a threatening stranger. After that, he always felt a sense of relief once the tour group was inside the house again, and his father was moving the small desk back in front of the narrow door.

"22 and 23 as I believe that is my room
24 and 25 for Sophia's room…"

The uppermost story was more difficult to determine. It contained a row of smaller windows, just under the roofline. He thought that was where the servants slept.

One of those tiny windows must belong to Old Smithy-Pot herself and one to Cook and one to Ploughman. But which ones? And who looks out of those biggest ones at night?

Built symmetrically, the two final windows at either end of the row were larger than the rest. Jutting past where the others were situated, they were quite prominent.

I'm going to find out. Why should the servants know when I don't? Maybe Will will go with me. He bit his lip thoughtfully. No, I'll tell him when I'm done.

Dropping from the tree, he headed toward the house. Careful to shut the front door quietly behind him, he stepped across the entryway. Displeased at the loudness of his steps, he slipped off his shoes and proceeded down the hall to the dining room.

"Jonathan?" came a voice from behind him.

Whipping around, he saw his little sister, a puzzled look on her face.

"Why are you…" Sophia began.

"Shhh!" he urged, glancing around.

She ran on slippered feet to his side.

"What are you doing?" she whispered, her blue eyes wide.

"I'll tell you afterward," he murmured back, starting again toward a door at the end of the dining room. It was a swinging door with no handle. At every meal, the servants would emerge from it, their hands full of serving platters and bowls. Then it would swing back into place behind them.

"But you can't go in there!" Sophia insisted, reaching for his sleeve, her voice trembling in its rough whisper. "Who knows what they'll do to you?"

His heart beat quickened at her words, but the boy pushed his sister's hand away and brought his finger forcefully back up to his lips. "Shhh…"

Pushing the door open just enough to see what lay beyond, Jonathan was relieved that none of the servants was there. Letting himself through, he crept down the hallway, past a room with a large table and paused in the doorway of the kitchen itself.

The broad backside of a woman faced him from the stove.

Cook, he thought, that beastly, contrary woman.

She was stirring something in a large steaming pot.

Jonathan looked around, taking in the row of gleaming copper pots dangling from a rafter and the many shelves crammed with boxes and bottles.

Is this the right way? How do they get up there at night?

There were three doors on the far walls. One, Jonathan saw, led outside. Another was shut, remaining mysterious. The third was slightly open. Jonathan positioned himself to see beyond it.

Stairs. That must be it.

Hoping it wouldn't creak, Jonathan crept toward the door and prepared to ease himself through, making himself as narrow as possible. He had to push it open another few inches, but the oblivious woman simply reached for a bottle on the shelf overhead.

Up the confining staircase he went, carefully, slowly, his heart beating in his throat.

Will won't believe I did this. In fact, how can I prove to him that I did? He paused, thinking.

I know!

He felt around in his trouser pocket and pulled out a top that Will had given him earlier that week. He ran his fingers over the marred wooden surface, noting how the paint was chipping off.

It's broken anyway. I'll leave it in the window and then he'll see it and know I'm telling the truth.

Up, up he stepped, expecting at any second to be hit over the head by a dripping ladle from behind. At the stairs' end was a hallway. Creeping down it, he quietly pushed open the few doors and peeked inside the rooms, his pulse wild until he saw that even the last door concealed nothing more than a bed and a few pieces of shoddy furniture.

He climbed atop the bed in the last room to peer out the window.

This must be one of the little ones, he thought, gazing down at the cherry trees. But where are the large windows? One must be just on the other side of this wall.

Stepping back into the hallway, he saw that it had ended. There was nowhere to go but back from where he had come.

But where are the largest windows? Where will I place the top? Ugh…now Will won't believe me.

He ran his hand over the wall, wondering if there was a hidden door. His search was fruitless.

Disappointment and frustration turned his wary stepping to a careless tread as he headed back down the hall and staircase. Taking two steps at a time, Jonathan descended the stairs and burst into the kitchen to see Cook, her eyes wide with surprise, her ugly mouth a little 'o'.

"Well, there's certainly no hidden treasure up there," he announced peevishly and ran out of the kitchen. Rushing through the swinging door, he left it swinging in his wake, back and forth, and ran past where Sophia waited, her little hands clasped over her chest.

"You're alive!" she cried.

Where's Will? he wondered, careening past her. He probably won't believe me.

Will did believe him, but he was no more impressed than usual.

"That's just where the servants sleep, you idiot," he said, sorting through his new set of toy soldiers on the front lawn. He shoved a heavily decorated figurine into Jonathan's hand.

"Here, you be Spain, and I get all the horses this time."

*   *   *   *   *   *   *

Days later, as they were in the drive climbing into the carriage, Jonathan looked up and remembered the windows.

"Papa? Whose windows are those?" he asked, pointing at the top story.

Holding back the curtain to peer out of the carriage, Sir William answered proudly, "Those are my windows."

"Well, of course, just as Speed's stable is yours and Cook's oven is yours, but who looks out of those large windows on the end there? Who sleeps in those rooms?"

"What, the two largest of the top row?" Papa asked, rumpling Jonathan's hair. "Those are blind dormers."

"What do you mean?"

"There is no usable space behind them. They were put there simply because it makes the house look nicer."

"You mean no one can look through them?" Jonathan asked, baffled, as the carriage jolted into motion.

"The last person to stick his nose up against that glass was the glazer who installed it, nearly 150 years ago, tapping it into place where it would serve no purpose other than glorious pretense."

"What?" Jonathan asked with such incredulity that his father laughed aloud.

Windows with no purpose but to make the house look more grand?

"Are you going to score a few runs with that new cricket bat today?" Sir William asked.

Jonathan nodded his head absent-mindedly, still contemplating.

Windows that are only for show? How perfectly stupid!

4: The Picking Up of Pebbles

~ Lydia, age 11
Hillcrest Farm

Upon entering the kitchen, Lydia saw her mother peering through the window out at the graveled yard.

"What is it?" Lydia asked, setting the egg basket down on the table.

"Your father's having Jack pick up pebbles again," her mother replied, her mouth arching into a little smile. "Most farmers sweeten their deals with a sip of brandy, but your father prefers to use Jack's spittle."

Walking to where her mother stood, Lydia looked out to see Jack, bending over, a long strand of saliva dangling from his lips. The men on either side of him watched as he suspended it lower and lower until it touched the ground. Its end rested there for a second before he slurped the whole thing back up again.

Here's his favorite part, thought Lydia, knowing there was a gleam in her brother's eyes.

Jack smiled smugly at the men, then opened his mouth and stuck out his tongue. Though she couldn't see it from the distance, Lydia knew that on its tip a tiny pebble was perched.

"There's a boy!" Smythe's voice carried across the yard as he roughly pounded his son's bony back.

"Ha ha!" laughed Farmer Midwinter. "He's got the trickiest spit in the county! Do it again!"

"Sally!" Smythe turned to holler toward the house as Jack spat out the pebble. Pert, the dog, bounded about them excitedly. "Bring out a bottle of me best!"

Sally shot Lydia a look. "It sounds as if they reached an agreement on the cow. It's to be spittle and brandy."

As her mother hurried off, Lydia turned her attention back to the scene outside where Jack, his hands on his knees, was again the men's focus. She smiled lightly and reached for the egg basket.

5: Vomiting Cherries

~ *Jonathan, age 12*
Whitehall

Once again, Jonathan sat in the crook of a cherry tree though his lanky body made this less comfortable than in years past. Every spring, he would heft himself up into the burgeoning branches and feast upon their bountiful fruit.

He belched as his stomach reminded him of its limitations.

Just one more, he thought, reaching for a dangling ruby fruit. A bee buzzed around his sun-warmed head.

He spat out the stone and the bee flew off to different territories.

Maybe just one more, he thought and reached over his head again.

Just as his eye settled on what would possibly be his final mouthful, he heard a shout in the distance, and another. He looked around, seeing no one in the yard or orchard. Then the horizon erupted with screams and anguished cries.

In spite of his painfully full belly, Jonathan dropped from the tree and began to run in the direction of all the noise.

It's down by the lake, he thought, tearing westerly through the trees. He flew over the gravel drive and splashed through the lakeside muck.

There he saw Glaser and Hardy out in the small rowboat. Glaser was standing and had a long pole that he kept pushing down into the water and then pulling up again. The other man used the oars to try to direct and steady the boat. A large lump like a soggy blanket was between them. Various servants stood on the far bank. Ploughman was stumbling from the direction of the house, slowed by her age and lack of coordination.

"No! More toward this side!" someone shouted from the lakeshore north of where Jonathan stood.

Hardy rowed this way and that as Glaser used his pole. Ploughman, now at the shore, began to talk with the others and then wailed aloud, her hands at her face.

What are they doing? Jonathan wondered, walking towards the people on the shore.

"There! My God! There!" Glaser pointed down into the water and Hardy rowed the boat nearer to the spot. Glaser cried out for Hardy to help him so he stood and the boat began to rock violently. They bent their legs to settle it and pulled up on the pole.

The people on the shore screamed and gasped as something like a humongous fish broke the water's surface. It was caught on a hook at the end of Glaser's pole.

"Too late, dammit!" Glaser shouted. "Too late!"

Muddle-headed servants. What did they drop in the lake? mused Jonathan approaching the group on the shore, peering intently at the mysterious lump. They're always losing their heads over someth...

The lump had a purplish sleeve and at its end was a hand. A large, pale hand. Realization hit him.

Father!

At the same instant, the sight of a dark-haired head lolling atop the soggy thing in the boat became clear.

Will!

A scream unlike any sound Jonathan had ever made ripped out of him and all the eyes that had been staring at the boat turned to him. Ploughman began to run at him at a speed that no woman with her physique could possibly reach.

"Don't look!" she screamed. "Don't look, Master Jonathan!" And then she was there, tackling him with her doughy form, blocking out the terrifying sight.

Standing, she dragged him to his feet, and began pulling him toward the house. He wailed the whole way there, weak-kneed and stumbling, but did not resist her determined grip. Up the steps they climbed, both of them shaking.

Once through the door and in the entryway, Jonathan stiffened and pushed Ploughman's hands away. Leaning over, he clutched his stomach and heaved an enormous amount of dark red vomit onto the black and white checkered floor.

He stood, staring down into the foul muck of too many half-chewed cherries, remembering the stillness of the sodden lump in the boat and the soggy mass at the pole's end.

Will and Father...

His stomach emptied itself again.

347

One week later, Jonathan sat on a bench beside Sophia at the grotto. His swollen eyelids felt heavy and his nose was rubbed raw.

Gone, he thought, the emptiness of the word pinging around in his hollow core.

Gone.

Before this week, he had never cried in front of Sophia, but now he did so shamelessly and sometimes noisily. Her own tears fell silently, slipping down her cheeks unchecked, falling onto the front of her black velvet bodice.

They had returned from the churchyard hours ago and the sun was setting over the horrible lake. The sinking sun reminded him of the coffins being lowered into the freshly dug pit.

He raked the arm of his jacket over his nose, the sleeve rough with dried mucus.

"Sir Jonathan," said a voice behind him.

Jonathan turned to see Pryor, clad in his black servant's wear, standing a few feet away.

"Sir Jonathan, Lady Clyde wants to see you in the blue drawing room."

Instinctively Jonathan grabbed Sophia's hand and the two children silently rose from the bench, turning toward Whitehall.

"I wonder why me and not both of us," mumbled Jonathan.

Sophia shrugged one shoulder, tightening her grip on his hand.

Their steps echoed loudly across the entry hall and down the passageway to their mother's favorite room. When they entered, Sophia stayed by the door.

"Come here, my boy," Lady Clyde said from her settee, extending her arms to Jonathan. Her eyes were swollen and red and her head seemed dwarfed by the largeness of her pregnant belly.

Jonathan felt new tears well in his eyes as he crossed the room to her.

"This has been a terrible time for us. And for you to see…what you saw. I'll never forgive the servants for allowing that." She pulled him down next to her and put her arm around him.

He felt stiff and awkward.

"Did you like the monument?" she asked. It took a moment for Jonathan to realize she meant the granite angel that had been erected at the graves. He shrugged, thinking her question odd.

"We can go there and see their gravestone and think..." she paused, her voice gruff, "...of the goodness we had in them." She patted his knee with one hand and stroked his head with the other. He relaxed a little, leaning his shoulder into her.

"Will you go..." he hiccupped as he tried to stop the tears. "Will you go with us tomorrow morning?"

"Yes, darling," she crooned. "We'll go together tomorrow morning. We'll go whenever you'd like."

Jonathan couldn't remember ever crying in his mother's arms before. Once when he was very small, he had fallen on the gravel getting out of the carriage and skinned his knee. She had been right there so he had reached for her.

"Nurse?" she had said. "Oh, blood. Mind my satin, Jonathan. Nurse!"

His nurse had swooped in and lifted him, clucking like a hen.

Now, here he was, her warm arm tight around him, and she was promising to visit the graveyard with him in the morning.

"Can we walk there?" he asked, a little calmer.

"Why ever would we do that?" She laughed lightly. "We'll take the carriage, of course." Then she sighed heavily.

"Darling," she said slowly and sighed again. "You are growing older and I believe I need to familiarize you a bit more with the ways of this world.

"It is good for your sister to hear this as well, I suppose," she continued, though she didn't invite Sophia to join them on the settee. Suddenly, the child within her lurched, pushing against Jonathan's arm.

"Did you feel that?" she asked, laughing and clutching her belly.

Jonathan nodded, his lashes still wet.

"As I was saying," she put her arm back around him and continued, "darling, have you ever wondered how it is that you came to live in such a great house and that you are so well known in and beyond the county?"

Jonathan shook his head slightly, wanting to talk more of Will and Papa.

"Please understand, this is not something we talk about with others, but your father and I made what most would call an 'advantageous marriage'. We both benefited vastly from our union. You see, your father was born with a prestigious lineage but over the last century, the wealth that formerly accompanied his estate dwindled. I, however, was born into the Fanshawes, a rather unknown family that, over the past century, acquired a large fortune through commerce and trade. When my father died, I inherited it all.

"Now that your father and elder brother…have passed from this world…you have inherited the baronetcy." She paused. "Therefore, when you come of age, you shall have wealth and a title."

Jonathan sighed, picking at the cuff on his jacket.

"Did you know, darling, that your brother was William Walter Clyde the Fifth and your father was William Walter Clyde the Fourth?"

Was…he thought and nodded his head. His little sibling bumped against his arm again.

"Yes, of course you did. And you know that your grandfather was William Walter Clyde the Third and so on all the way back to the year 1640 when William Walter Clyde the First was born." She paused. "It is a very old name, dearest."

"Yes, it is," he mumbled, absent-mindedly.

"…and it would be a great shame if it ended now as there has been a Sir William Walter Clyde living at Whitehall since 1697." She paused again and took a deep breath. "Therefore, I have decided that you, darling, will carry it on."

She smiled into his face as if she had just promised him a new horse.

"What do you mean?" he asked, suddenly listening.

"From now on, we shall…everyone shall refer to you as William Walter Clyde the Fifth."

He stiffened and leaned back from her. "But that is…was Will's name."

"It is a family name and a very important one," she explained.

"But…I'm Jonathan and he was William," he said, with equal patience.

"Don't think of it so much as a name as a title. He carried it for a while and now you shall carry it." The smile had completely faded from her face. Little lines around her mouth grew deeper as her lips settled into a tense pursing. There was a note of annoyance in her voice as she added, "This is all very important."

"Important to whom?" Jonathan asked, suddenly wanting her arm completely off of him. Springing up from the settee, he firmly planted his feet in a wide stance and nearly shouted in her face, "He was William and I am Jonathan!"

"I just lost a son and a husband. This is a very difficult time for me!" his mother said. "Don't make it more so by being obstinate. You shall be known as William henceforth and that is final. I trust that as you mature, you will understand the importance of all of this."

Jonathan stared at his mother, her face set as hard as the stone angel's. It was a familiar look, very different to how she appeared just a moment ago.

Jonathan felt something inside him flip.

No, he thought. No.

He took a deep breath and declared, "I will never answer to that name. It is my dead brother's name, which you seem to have forgotten."

She suddenly looked tired, her face loosened into slack blotchiness. "I only want what's best," she said quietly. With a slight wave of her hand she turned her face to gaze out of the window.

Drawing himself up to his full height, he turned his back to her and marched to the door, grabbing Sophia's hand as he passed, pulling her out of the room with him.

Once the door had swung shut behind them with a click, Sophia murmured, "Well done, Jonathan."

6: Saying the Definitely Wrong Thing

~ Ploughman

Ohhh, Ploughman groaned inwardly. She paused in her mopping of the marble entryway to rub her aching calves.

I musta mopped this floor eighteen times in the past month. Don't the Lady know people are comin' to see the new li'l baby, not the entryway…and with the draining of the lake there's a lotta new muck to be tracked in when people go traipsing about.

She pushed a knuckle deep into the meatiest part of her left calf, kneading the ache unsatisfactorily.

Better not let anyone see me doing this. I might be hauled off by the knacker.

Just then, the front door swung open. The young heir entered, his trousers and shoes splattered with mud.

A lifetime of servitude had taught Ploughman to mask the emotions she felt daily, hiding frustration, anger, even happiness from the people she served, but the sight of those dirty shoes about to needlessly defile the floor she had just mopped weakened her will to do so. The fact that it was this boy didn't help, either. Yes, she had done what she could to keep him from the indelible horror of seeing his father and brother dead, but she would have done that for anyone. Any decent person would have. The boy before her was mischievous, perhaps not maliciously so, but carelessly.

She leaned on her mop and woefully cast a fleeting look at the boy's feet, the pain in her calves intensifying.

The boy glanced at the mop in Ploughman's hand as he shut the door and then looked down at his feet where her eyes rested. He stood for an instant, contemplatively. Then quietly, he knelt to undo his laces and removed the shoes. Placing them against the wall, he started across the floor, his stockinged feet silent on the hard surface.

Startled by the unexpected display of thoughtfulness by the boy, Ploughman's face brightened and she burst into grateful exclamations. "Oh, thank you Sir Jona…"

Oh, when will I learn? She shook her graying head. She said we all must call him 'William'.

"Uh, that is…thank you, Sir William. Thank you."

Again the boy halted, but this time the gaze he turned toward her was stony and cold. It bore into the woman, frightening her with its intensity.

Stalking back to the door, he plunged his feet into the muddy shoes. Stomping, he began to circle the woman, the noise of it filling the room.

He spiraled inward, covering more and more flooring with dirty footprint after dirty footprint.

Around and around he marched, drawing closer to her with each heavy step. The thudding cadence was the only sound in Ploughman's ears. She clung to her mop, paralyzed by fear and wonder, her aching calves forgotten.

The eerie ritual ceased when the shoes no longer left a mark. As the boy leaned in to within inches of the maid, she could feel the heat from his breath on her forehead.

In a steady, low voice, he proclaimed, "I am Jonathan."

Riveted, the woman studied his face, recalling the sinewy sensation of his elongated body against hers when she had seized him by the lakeside. With wide eyes, she noted the newly darkened hairs upon his upper lip, the cheeks now leaner due to the incessant upward growth of his young body.

Then, he was sprinting up the stairs, gone with only the abundantly gritty floor to remind the woman of the strange and frightening spectacle she had just witnessed.

Ploughman let out a shaky breath and stood for a moment, uneasy in the solitude. She walked toward the bucket to dip the mop, filth crunching under her feet with every step.

The dirt was everywhere, each footprint a testimony of her grievous error. She lifted the dripping mop from the bucket and sloshed it onto the floor, swirling away what she could of the incident.

Well, I won't be calling him that again, no matter what the Lady says.